Praise for IRON COUNCIL

"*Council* is a masterwork . . . with a story that pops with creativity."
—*New York Post*

"Prodigiously inventive—Miéville dreams up and throws away more astonishing ideas in a paragraph than most writers manage in a lifetime."
—*Kirkus Reviews*

"Miéville's first mission is to entertain—and in that he succeeds brilliantly. [But] *Iron Council* challenges, and in some very uncomfortable ways, comments on this reality we'd all occasionally like to escape. Miéville allows this, but never lets us forget that the most terrifying world to be stirred into this mad mix is our own."
—*The Village Voice*

"Full of warped and memorable characters, this violent and intensely political novel smoothly combines elements of fantasy, science fiction, horror, even the western. Miéville represents much of what is new and good in contemporary dark fantasy, and his work is must reading for devotees of that genre."
—*Publishers Weekly* (starred review)

"Equally reminiscent of Charles Dickens and H.P. Lovecraft, the third novel of Miéville's 'antitrilogy' is . . . subversive, smart, and free of sap."
—*Details*

"A powerful, intelligent novel."
—*Daily Telegraph*

"Miéville is, as before, formidably brilliant. *Iron Council* completes the most powerful ideological and imaginative manifesto in the recent history of SF and fantasy. . . . A superb fantasy of social injustice and deliverance."
—*Locus*

CHINA MIÉVILLE

IRON COUNCIL

A NOVEL

BALLANTINE BOOKS
NEW YORK

2005 Del Rey Books Trade Paperback Edition

Copyright © 2004 by China Miéville

Published in the United States by Del Rey Books, an imprint of The Random House Publishing Group, a division of Random House, Inc., New York.

DEL REY is a registered trademark and the Del Rey colophon is a trademark of Random House, Inc.

Originally published in hardcover in the United States by Del Rey Books, an imprint of The Random House Publishing Group, a division of Random House, Inc., in 2004.

Library of Congress Cataloging-in-Publication Data
Miéville, China.
Iron council / China Miéville.
p. cm.
ISBN 0-345-45842-7
I. Title.
PR6063.I265I76 2004
823'.914—dc22   2004049394

Printed in the United States of America

www.delreybooks.com

4 6 8 9 7 5

Text design by Susan Turner

To Jemima, my sister

ACKNOWLEDGMENTS

For all their help with this book, I owe my deepest gratitude to Emma Bircham, Mark Bould, Andrew Butler, Mic Cheetham, Deanna Hoak, Simon Kavanagh, Peter Lavery, Claudia Lightfoot, Farah Mendelsohn, Jemima Miéville, Gillian Redfearn, Max Schaefer, Chris Schluep, and Jesse Soodalter. Huge thanks also to Nick Mamatas and Mehitobel Wilson, and to everyone at Macmillan and Del Rey for all their work.

Though as always I am indebted to countless writers, for this book I must especially thank William Durbin, John Ehle, Jane Gaskell, Zane Grey, Sembène Ousmane, Tim Powers, T. F. Powys, and Frank Spearman.

Erect portable moving monuments on the platforms of trains.
—VELIMIR KHLEBNIKOV, *Proposals*

In years gone, women and men are cutting a line across the dirtland and dragging history with them. They are still, with fight-shouts setting their mouths. They are in rough and trenches of rock, in forests, in scrub, brick shadows. They are always coming.

And in years long gone someone stands on a knuckle of granite, a clenched-up mountain fist. Trees cover the peak as if a spume of forest has settled. He is above a green world while feathered and tough-skinned fauna speck the air below him and pay no mind.

Up past pillars of batholith is the path he has made, and abutting it tarpaulin bivouacs. There are men and fire, little neutered cousin to the conflagrations that fertilize woodlands.

The man apart is in wind that frosts this old moment in place forever while breath cold-congeals on his beard. He consults mercury sluggish in its glass, a barometer and inch-marked cord. He locates himself and the men with him above the belly of the world and in a mountain autumn.

They have ascended. Columns of men have faltered against gravity, tight-knotted dangling in the lee of silicate walls and corners. Servants of their equipment, they have carried the brass, wood and glass oddments like dumb nabobs across the world.

The man apart breathes in the moment long gone, listens to the coughs of mountain animals, the beat of jostling trees. Where ravines are he has plumbed lines to bring them to order and know them, has marked them and annotated his drawings, and learning the parameters of the peneplain or open-sided corries, the tributary canyons, creeks, rivers and fern-scruffed pampas, he has made them beautiful.

Where pines or ash are tethered and he notes the radius of a curve, the land humbles him.

Cold takes six of his men and leaves them white and hard in make-do graves. Githwings rinse the party with blood, and bears and tenebrae leave them depleted and men broken and crying unfound in darkness and mules fall and excavations fail and there are drownings and indigens who trustlessly murder but those are all other moments. In this long-gone time there is only a man above the trees. West, mountains block his way, but in this moment they are miles yet.

Only wind speaks to him, but he knows his name is raised in abuse and respect. His wake is disputation. In the built hilltops of his city his endeavours split families. Some say they speak for gods and that he is proud. He is an insult on the world's face and his plans and route are an abomination.

The man watches night colonise. (It is a long time since this moment.) He watches the spits of shadows, and before he hears the tin clatter of his men at supper or smells the cooked rock vermin he will eat with them, there is only he and the mountain and the night and his books with renderings of everything he has seen and measurements of these disinterested heights and his want.

He smiles not cunning nor sated nor secure, but in joy because he knows his plans are holy.

part one

TRAPPINGS

CHAPTER ONE

A MAN RUNS. PUSHES THROUGH THIN BARK-AND-LEAF WALLS, through the purposeless rooms of Rudewood. The trees crowd him.

This far in the forest there are aboriginal noises. The canopy rocks. The man is heavy-burdened, and sweated by the unseen sun. He is trying to follow a trail.

Just before dark he found his place. Dim hotchi paths led him to a basin ringed by roots and stone-packed soil. Trees gave out. The earth was tramped down and stained with scorching and blood. The man spread out his pack and blanket, a few books and clothes. He laid down something well-wrapped and heavy among loam and centipedes.

Rudewood was cold. The man built a fire, and with it so close the darkness shut him quite out, but he stared into it as if he might see something emergent. Things came close. There were constant bits of sound like the bronchial call of a nightbird or the breath and shucking of some unseen predator. The man was wary. He had pistol and rifle, and one at least was always in his hand.

By flamelight he saw hours pass. Sleep took him and led him away again in little gusts. Each time he woke he breathed as if coming out of water. He was stricken. Sadness and anger went across his face.

"I'll come find you," he said.

He did not notice the moment of dawn, only that time skidded again and he could see the edges of the clearing. He moved like he was made of twigs, as if he had stored up the night's damp cold. Chewing on dry meat, he listened to the forest's shuffling and paced the dirt depression.

When finally he heard voices he flattened against the bank and looked out between the trunks. Three people approached on the paths of leaf-mould and forest debris. The man watched them, his rifle steadied. When they trudged into thicker shanks of light, he saw them clearly and let his rifle fall.

"Here," he shouted. They dropped foolishly and looked for him. He raised his hand above the earth rise.

They were a woman and two men, dressed in clothes more ill-suited to Rudewood than his own. They stood before him in the arena and smiled. "Cutter." They gripped arms and slapped his back.

"I heard you for yards. What if you was followed? Who else is coming?"

They did not know. "We got your message," the smaller man said. He spoke fast and looked about him. "I went and seen. We were arguing. The others were saying, you know, we should stay. You know what they said."

"Yeah, Drey. Said I'm mad."

"Not *you.*"

They did not look at him. The woman sat, her skirt filling with air. She was breathing fast with anxiety. She bit her nails.

"Thank you. For coming." They nodded or shook Cutter's gratitude off: it sounded strange to him, and he was sure to them too. He tried not to make it sound like his sardonic norm. "It means a lot."

* * *

They waited in the sunken ground, scratched motifs in the earth or carved figures from dead wood. There was too much to say.

"So they told you not to come?"

The woman, Elsie, told him no, not so much, not in those words, but the Caucus had been dismissive of Cutter's call. She looked up at him and down quickly as she spoke. He nodded, and did not criticise.

"Are you sure about this?" he said, and would not accept their desultory nods. "Godsdammit are you sure? Turn your back on the Caucus? You ready to do that? For him? It's a long way we've got to go."

"We already come miles in Rudewood," said Pomeroy.

"There's hundreds more. *Hundreds.* It'll be bastard hard. A long time. I can't swear we'll come back."

I can't swear we'll come back.

Pomeroy said, "Only tell me again your message was true. Tell me again he's gone, and where he's gone and what for. Tell me that's true." The big man glowered and waited, and at Cutter's brief nod and closed eyes, he said, "Well then."

Others arrived then. First another woman, Ihona; and then as they welcomed her they heard stick-litter being destroyed in heavy leaps, and a vodyanoi came through the brush. He squatted in the frog-gish way of his race and raised webbed hands. When he jumped from the bank, his body—head and trunk all one fat sac—rippled with impact. Fejhechrillen was besmirched and tired, his motion ill-suited to woodland.

They were anxious, not knowing how long they should wait, if any others would come. Cutter kept asking how they had heard his message. He made them unhappy. They did not want to consider their decision to join him: they knew there were many who would think it a betrayal.

"He'll be grateful," Cutter said. "He's a funny bugger and might be he'll not show it, but this'll mean a lot, to me and to him."

After silence Elsie said: "You don't know that. He didn't ask us, Cutter. He just got some message, you said. He might be angry that we've come."

Cutter could not tell her she was wrong. Instead he said: "I don't see you leaving, though. We're here for us, maybe, as well as for him."

He began to tell them what might be ahead, emphasising dangers. It seemed as if he wanted to dissuade them though they knew he did not. Drey argued with him in a rapid and nervy voice. He assured Cutter they understood. Cutter saw him persuading himself, and was silent. Drey said repeatedly that his mind was made up.

"We best move," said Elsie, when noon went. "We can't wait forever. Anyone else is coming, they've obviously got lost. They'll have to go back to the Caucus, do what's needed in the city." Someone gave a little cry and the company turned.

At the hollow's edge a hotchi rider was watching them, astride his gallus. The big war-cockerel plumped its breastfeathers and raised one spurred claw-foot in curious pose. The hotchi, squat and tough hedgehog man, stroked his mount's red comb.

"Militia coming." His accent was strong and snarling. "Two men militia coming, a minute, two." He sat forward in the ornate saddle and turned his bird around. With very little sound, with no metal to jangle on wood-and-leather straps and stirrups, it picked away high-clawed and belligerent, and was hidden by the forest.

"Was that—?" "What—?" "Did you fucking—?"

But Cutter and his companions were shushed by the sound of approach. They looked in unsaid panic, too late to hide.

Two men came stepping over fungused stumps into view. They were masked and uniformed in the militia's dark grey. Each had a mirrored shield and ungainly pepperpot revolver slack at his side. As they came into the clearing they faltered and were still, taking in the men and women waiting for them.

There was a dragged-out second when no one moved, when be-fuddled and silent conference was held—*are you, are they, what, should we, should we*—?—till someone shot. Then there were a spate of sounds, screams and the percussion of shots. People fell. Cutter could not follow who was where and was gut-terrified that he had been hit and not yet felt it. When the guns' heinous synco-pation stopped, he unclenched his jaw.

Someone was calling *Oh gods oh fucking gods.* It was a militia-man, sitting bleeding from a belly-wound beside his dead friend and trying to hold his heavy pistol up. Cutter heard the curt torn-cloth sound of archery and the militia man lay back with an arrow in him and stopped his noise.

Again a beat of silence then "Jabber—" "Are you, is everyone—?" "Drey? Pomeroy?"

First Cutter thought none of his own were hit. Then he saw how Drey was white and held his shoulder, and that blood dyed his pal-sying hands.

"Sweet Jabber, man." Cutter made Drey sit (*Is it all right?* the lit-tle man kept saying.) Bullet had taken muscle. Cutter tore strips from Drey's shirt, and wound those cleanest around the hole. The pain made Drey fight, and Pomeroy and Fejh had to hold him. They gave him a thumb-thick branch to bite while they bandaged him.

"They must've fucking *followed you*, you halfwit bastards." Cut-ter was raging while he worked. "I told you to be fucking careful—"

"We *were*," Pomeroy shouted, jabbing his finger at Cutter.

"Didn't follow them." The hotchi reappeared, its rooster pick-ing. "Them patrol the pits. You been here long time, a day nearly." It dismounted and walked the rim of the arena. "You been too long."

It showed the teeth in its snout in some opaque expression. Lower than Cutter's chest but rotundly muscular, it strutted like a bigger man. By the militia it stopped and sniffed. It sat up the one killed by its arrow and began to push the missile through the body.

"When them don't come back, them send more," it said. "Them come after you. Maybe now." It steered the arrow past bones through the dead chest. It gripped the shaft when it came out the corpse's back, and pulled the fletch through with a wet sound. The hotchi tucked it bloody into his belt, picked the revolving pistol from the militiaman's stiffening fingers and fired it against the hole.

Birds rose up again at the shot. The hotchi snarled with the unfamiliar recoil and shook its hand. The arrow's fingerthick burrow had become a cavity.

Pomeroy said: "Godspit . . . who in hell are you?"

"Hotchi man. Cock-fighting man. Alectryomach. Help you."

"Your tribe . . ." said Cutter. "They're with us? On our side? Some of the hotchi are with the Caucus," he said to the others. "That's why this place's all right. Or was supposed to be. This lad's clan got no time for the militia. Give us passage. But . . . can't risk a real fight with the city, so they've to make it look like it was us killed the officers, not their arrows." He understood as he said it.

Pomeroy and the hotchi rifled the killed men together. Pomeroy threw one of the pepperpot revolvers to Elsie, one to Cutter. It was modernistic and expensive and Cutter had never held one before. It was heavy, with its six barrels arranged in a fat rotating cylinder.

"They ain't reliable," said Pomeroy, harvesting bullets. "Fast, though."

"Jabber . . . we better fucking go." Drey's voice went up and down with pain. "Fucking *guns* going off going to call them for miles . . ."

"Not so many nearby," said the hotchi. "Maybe none to hear. But you should gone, yes. What you for? Why leave city? You looking for him come by on the clay man?"

Cutter looked to the others and they watched him carefully, letting him speak.

He said: "You seen him?" He stepped toward the busy hotchi. "You seen him?"

"I not seen him, but I know them as has. Some days, week or

more gone. Man come through the wood on a grey giant. Running through. The militia come after."

The light of afternoon came down to them all and the forest animals began to make their noises again. Cutter was locked in by miles of trees. He opened his mouth more than once before he spoke.

Cutter said: "Militia followed him?"

"On Remade horses. I heard."

On Remade horses with hammered metal hoofs, or with tiger's claws or with a tail prehensile and coated in poison glands. With steam-pistons giving their legs ridiculous strength or with stamina from a boiler-excrescence behind the saddle. Made carnivorous and long-tusked. Wolf-horses or boar-horses, construct-horses.

"I didn't see," said the hotchi. He mounted his cockerel. "Them went after the clay-man rider, south in Rudewood. You best go. Fast now." He turned his fight-bird and pointed a smoke-brown finger. "Stay careful. This is Rudewood. Go now."

He spurred his gallus into the undergrowth and dense trunks. "Go," he shouted, already invisible.

"Damn," said Cutter. "Come on." They gathered their little camp. Pomeroy took Drey's pack as well as his own, and the six of them went up out of the cock-fighting pit and into the forest.

They went southwest by Cutter's compass, along the path the hotchi had taken. "He showed us the way," Cutter said. His comrades waited for him to guide them. They drove between rootmasses and blockages of flora, changing whatever they passed. Quickly Cutter's tiredness was so profound it was an astonishing, alien sensation.

When they noticed darkness they fell where they were, in a pause between trees. They spoke in puny voices, affected by the undertones of the wood. It was too late to hunt: they could only pull biltong and bread from their packs and make weak jokes about what good food it was.

By their little fire Cutter could see that Fejh was drying. They did not know where there was any freshwater, and Fejh poured only a little of what they had on himself though his big tongue rolled for it. He was panting. "I'll be all right, Cutter," he said, and the man patted his cheek.

Drey was paper-white and whispering to himself. Seeing how blood had stiffened his sling, Cutter could not imagine how he had kept going. Cutter murmured his fears to Pomeroy, but they could not turn back and Drey could not make the return on his own. He stained the ground below him.

While Drey slept, the others pulled around the fire and told quiet stories of the man they were following. Each of them had reasons for answering Cutter's call.

For Ihona the man they sought had been the first person in the Caucus who had seemed distracted, who reminded her of herself. His unworldliness, the quality that some mistrusted, made her feel there was room for imperfection in the movement: that she could be part of it. She smiled beautifully to remember it. Fejh, in turn, had taught him as part of some investigation of vodyanoi shamanism, and had been moved by his fascination. Cutter knew they loved the man they followed. Of the hundreds of the Caucus, it was no surprise that six loved him.

Pomeroy said it aloud: "I love him. It ain't why I'm here, though." He spoke in terse little bursts. "Times are too big for that. I'm here because of where he's going, Cutter, because of what he's after. And what's coming after that. That's why I'm here. Because of what was in your message. Not because he's gone—because of where he's gone, and why. That's worth everything."

No one asked Cutter why he was there. When it came to his turn, they looked down and said nothing while he studied the fire.

A war-bird woke them, wattle rippling, blaring a cock's crow. They were stunned by their uncivil wakening. A hotchi on his mount watched them, threw them a dead forest fowl as they rose. He pointed eastward through the trees and disappeared in the green light.

They stumbled in the direction indicated through underbrush and the morning forest. Sunlight flecked them. It was warm spring, and Rudewood became dank and heated. Cutter's clothes were sweat-heavy. He watched Fejh and Drey.

Fejh was stolid as he moved by kicks of his hind legs, by lurches. Drey kept pace, though it seemed impossible. He leaked through his leather and did not scatter the flies that came to taste him. Blooded and white, Drey looked like an old meat-cut. Cutter waited for him to show pain or fear, but Drey only murmured to himself, and Cutter was humbled.

The simplicity of the forest stupefied them. "Where we going?" someone said to Cutter. *Don't ask me that.*

In the evening they followed a lovely sound and found a burn overhung by ivy. They hallooed and drank from it like happy animals.

Fejh sat in it and it rilled where it hit him. When he swam, his lubberly motion became suddenly graceful. He brought up handfuls and moulded with vodyanoi watercræft: like dough the water kept the shapes he gave it, coarse figurines shaped like dogs. He put them on the grass, where over an hour they sagged like candles and ran into the earth.

The next morning Drey's hurt was going bad. They waited when his fever made him pause, but they had to move. The treelife changed, was mongrel. They went by darkwood and oak, under banyan hirsute with ropy plaits that dangled and became roots.

Rudewood teemed. Birds and ape-things in the canopy spent the morning screaming. In a zone of dead, bleached trees, an ursine thing, unclear and engorged with changing shapes and colours, reeled out of the brush toward them. They screamed, except Pomeroy who fired into the creature's chest. With a soft explosion it burst into scores of birds and hundreds of bottleglass flies, which circled them in the air and recongealed beyond them as the beast. It shuffled from them. Now they could see the feathers and wing cases that made up its pelt.

"I been in these woods before," said Pomeroy. "I know what a throng-bear looks like."

"We must be far enough now," said Cutter, and they bore westward while twilight came and left them behind. They walked behind a hooded lantern hammered by moths. The barkscape swallowed the light.

After midnight, they passed through low shinnery and out of the forest.

And for three days they were in the Mendican Foothills, rock tors and drumlins flecked with trees. They walked the routes of long-gone glaciers. The city was only tens of miles away. Its canals almost reached them. Sometimes through saddles in the landscape they saw real mountains far west and north, of which these hills were only dregs.

They drank and cleaned in tarns. They were slowing, pulling Drey. He could not move his arm and he looked bled out. He would not complain. It was the first time Cutter had ever seen him brave.

There were insinuations of paths, and they followed them south through grass and flowers. Pomeroy and Elsie shot rock rabbits and roasted them, stuffed with herb-weeds.

"How we going to find him?" Fejh said. "Whole continent to search."

"I know his route."

"But Cutter, it's a whole *continent* . . ."

"He'll leave signs. Wherever he goes. He'll leave a trail. You can't not."

No one spoke a while.

"How'd he know to leave?"

"He got a message. Some old contact is all I know."

Cutter saw fences reclaimed by weather, where farms had once been. The foundations of homesteads in angles of stone. Rudewood was east, weald broken with outcrops of dolomite. Once, protruding from the leaves, there were the remnants of ancient industry, smokestacks or pistons.

On the sixth day, Fishday, the 17th of Chet 1805, they reached a village.

In Rudewood there was a muttering of displaced air below the owl and monkey calls. It was not loud but the animals in its path looked up with the panic of prey. The empty way between trees, by overhangs of clay, was laced by the moon. The tree-limbs did not move.

Through the night shadows came a man. He wore a black-blue suit. His hands were in his pockets. Stems of moonlight touched his polished shoes, which moved at head-height above the roots. The man passed, his body poised, standing upright in the air. As he came hanging by arcane suspension between the canopy and the dark forest floor the sound came with him, as if space were moaning at his violation.

He was expressionless. Something scuttled across him, in and out of the shadow, in the folds of his clothes. A monkey, clinging to him as if he were its mother. It was disfigured by something on its chest, a growth that twitched and tensed.

In the weak shine the man and his passenger entered the bowl where the hotchi came to fight. They hung over the arena. They looked at the militiamen dead, mottled with rot.

The little ape dangled from the man's shoes, dropped to the corpses. Its adroit little fingers examined. It leapt back to the dangling legs and chittered.

They were as silent for a while as the rest of the night, the man knuckling his lips thoughtfully, turning in a sedate pirouette, the monkey on his shoulder looking into the dead-black forest. Then they were in motion again, between the trees with the fraught sound of their passing, through bracken torn days before. After they had gone, the animals of Rudewood came out again. But they were anxious, and remained so the rest of that night.

CHAPTER TWO

THE VILLAGE HAD NO NAME. THE FARMERS SEEMED TO CUTTER MEAN as well as poor. They took money for food with a bad grace. If they had healers they denied it. Cutter could do nothing but let Drey sleep.

"We have to get to Myrshock," Cutter said. The villagers stared in ignorance, and he set his teeth. "It's not the fucking moon," he said.

"I can take you to the pig-town," said one man at last. "We need butter and pork. Four days' drive south."

"Still gives us, what, four hundred miles to Myrshock, for Jabber's sake," said Ihona.

"We've no choice. And this pig place must be bigger, maybe they can get us farther. Why ain't you got pigs here?"

The villagers glanced at each other.

"Raiders," said one. "That's how you can help," said another. "Protect the cart with them guns. You can get us to pig-town. It's a market. Traders from all over. They've airships, can help you."

"Raiders?"

"Aye. Bandits. FReemade."

Two scrawny horses pulled a wagon, whipped on by village men. Cutter and his companions sat in the cart, among thin vegetables and trinkets. Drey lay and sweated. His arm smelt very bad. The others held their weapons visible, uneasy and ostentatious.

The rig jarred along vague paths as the Mendicans gave way to grassland. For two days they went through sage and greenery, between boulders overhanging like canalside warehouses. Rock took sunset like a red tattoo.

They watched for air-corsairs. Fejh took brief visits to the waterways they passed.

"Too slow." Cutter spoke to himself, but the others heard him. "Too slow, too slow, too godsdamn slow."

"Show your guns," said a driver suddenly. "Someone's watching." He indicated the low rises, copses on the stone. "If they come, shoot. Don't wait. They'll skin us if you leave them alive."

Even Drey was awake. He held a repeating pistol in his good hand.

"Your gun shoots widest, Pomeroy," said Cutter. "Be ready."

And as he spoke both the drivers began to shout. "Now! Now! There!"

Cutter swung his pistol with dangerous imprecision, Pomeroy levelled his blunderbuss. A crossbow quarrel sang over their heads. A figure emerged from behind lichened buhrstone and Elsie shot him.

He was fReemade—a criminal Remade, reconfigured in the city's punishment factories, escaped to the plains and Rohagi hills.

"You *fuckers*," he shouted in pain. "Godsdammit, you *fuckers*." They could see his Remaking—he had too many eyes. He slithered on the dust, leaving it bloody. "You *fuckers*."

A new voice. "Fire again and you die." Figures stood all around them, raised bows and a few old rifles. "Who are you? You ain't locals." The speaker stepped forward on a table of stone. "Come on, you two. You know the rules. The toll. I'll charge you a wagonload of—what is that stuff? A wagonload of crappy vegetables."

The fReemade were ragged and variegated, their Remakings of steam-spitting iron and stolen animal flesh twitching like arcane tumours. Men and women with tusks or metal limbs, with tails, with gutta-percha pipework intestines dangling oil-black in the cave of bloodless open bellies.

Their boss walked with a laggard pace. At first Cutter thought him mounted on some eyeless mutant beast but then he saw that the man's torso was stitched to a horse's body, where the head would be. But, with the caprice and cruelty of the state's bio-thaumaturges, the human trunk faced the horse's tail, as if he sat upon a mount backward. His four horse's legs picked their way in careful reverse, his tail switching.

"This is new," he said. "You brought guns. This we ain't had. I seen mercs. You ain't mercs."

"You won't see anything ever again, you don't piss off," said Pomeroy. He aimed his big musket with amazing calm. "You could take us, but how many of you'll go too?" All the party, even Drey, had a fReemade in their sights.

"What are you?" said the chief. "Who *are* you lot? What you doing?"

Pomeroy began to answer, some bluster, some fighting pomp, but something abrupt happened to Cutter. He heard a whispering. Utterly intimate, like lips breathing right into his ear, unnatural and compelling. With the words came cold. He shuddered. The voice said: *"Tell the truth."*

Words came out of Cutter in a loud involuntary chant. "Ihona's a loom worker. Drey's a machinist. Elsie's out of work. Big Pomeroy's a clerk. Fejh is a docker. I'm a shop-man. We're with the Caucus. We're looking for my friend. And we're looking for the Iron Council."

His companions stared. "What in hell, man?" said Fejh, and Ihona: "What in *Jabber's name* . . . ?"

Cutter unclenched his teeth and shook his head. "I didn't mean to," he tried to tell them. "I heard something . . ."

"Well, well," the bandit chief was saying. "You've a long way to go. Even if you come past us—" And then he broke off. He worked his jaw, then spoke rhythmically in a different, declamatory voice. "They can go. Let them pass. The Caucus is no enemy of ours."

His troops stared at him. "Let them pass," he said again. He waved at his fReemade, looking quite enraged. His men and women shouted in anger and disbelief, and for seconds looked as if they might ignore his order, but then they backed away and shouldered their weapons, cursing.

The fReemade chief watched the travellers as they continued, and they watched him back until their route took him out of sight. They did not see him move.

Cutter told his comrades of the whispered compulsion that had taken him. "Thaumaturgy," said Elsie. "He must've hexed you, the boss-thief, gods know why." Cutter shook his head.

"Didn't you see how he looked?" he said. "When he let us go? That's how I felt. He was glamoured too."

When they came to the market town they found tinkers and traders and travelling entertainers. Between dry earth buildings were battered and half-flaccid gas balloons.

On Dustday, as they ascended over the steppes of grass, stones and flowers, Drey died. He had seemed to be mending, had been awake in the town, had even haggled with the air-merchant. But in the night his arm poisoned him, and though he had been alive when they went up, he was dead not long after.

The nomad tradesman tended the gondola's droning motor, embarrassed by his passengers' misery. Elsie held Drey's cooling body. At last with the sun high, she extemporised a service and they kissed their dead friend and entrusted Drey to gods with the faint unease of freethinkers.

Elsie remembered the air-burials she had heard of among northern tribes. Women and men of the tundra, who let their dead rest in open coffins under balloons, sent them skyward through the cold air and clouds, to drift in airstreams way above the depredations of insects or birds or rot itself, so the stratosphere over their hunt-lands was a catacomb, where explorers by dirigible encountered none but the aimless, frost-mummified dead.

They gave Drey an air-burial of another kind, of necessity, hauling him with tenderness to the edge of the carriage, bracing him between the ropes and letting him go.

It was as if he flew. He soared below them and his arms seemed to spread. Air pummelled him so he moved as if dancing or fighting, and he spun as he dwindled. He passed birds. His friends watched his flight with awe and a surprise elation, and turned away while he was seconds from the ground.

They went over swale and grass that grew drier as they went south. Rudewood receded. The wind was with them. Cutter heard Elsie whispering to Pomeroy, crying over Drey.

"We can't stop now," Pomeroy murmured to her. "I know, I know . . . but we can't now."

Three times they saw other balloons, miles away. Each time their pilot would look through his telescope and say whose ship it was. There were not so many of the aeronautic peddlers. They knew each other's routes.

The man had demanded a lot of their money to take them to Myrshock, but when they had heard that the militia had come past Pigtown not long before, a hussar unit on altered mounts, they could not turn him down. "We're coming the right way." And travelling now not quickly but with a relentless pace, for the first time they felt something like hope.

"Hard to believe," said Cutter, "that there's a fucking war on." No one answered. He knew his bile tired them. He watched patchworked land.

On the third morning in the air, while he was rubbing water into Fejh's wind-chapped skin, Cutter bellowed and pointed to where, miles ahead, he saw the sea, and before it in a depression of wheat-brown grass, the dirigible moorings and minarets of Myrshock.

It was an ugly port. They were wary. This was not their territory.

The architecture looked thrown together, chance materials aggregated and surprised to find themselves a town. Old but without history. Where it was designed, its aesthetic was unsure—churches with cement facades mimicking antique curlicues, banks using slate in uncommon colours, achieving only vulgarity.

Myrshock was mixed. Human women and men lived beside cactacae, the thorned and brawny vegetable race, and garuda, bird-people freebooters from the Cymek over the water, who dappled the air as well as the streets. Vodyanoi in a canal ghetto.

The travellers ate street food by the seawall. There were ranks of foreign craft and Myrshock ships, steamers with factory towers, cogs, merchant ships with great bridles for their seawyrms. Unlike the river docks of their home this was a brine harbour, so there were no vodyanoi stevedores. Lounging against walls were the mounte-banks and freelance scum of any port.

"We have to be careful," Cutter said. "We need a Shankell-bound ship, and mostly that means cactus crew. You know what we have to do. We can't face cactacae. We need a small ship, and small people."

"There'll be tramp steamers," said Ihona. "Pirates, most of them . . ." She looked vaguely around her.

Cutter spasmed and was quite still. Someone spoke to him. That voice again, up close whispering into his ear. He was iced in place.

The voice said: "*The* Akif. *Steaming south.*"

The voice said: "*Routine run, small crew. Useful damn cargo—*

sable antelopes, broken for riders. Your deposits are paid. You sail at ten tonight."

Cutter stared at each passerby, each sailor, each waterfront thug. He saw no one mouthing words. His friends watched him, alarmed at his face.

"You know what to do. Go up the Dradscale. That's the way the militia went. I checked.

"Cutter you know I could make *you do this—you remember what happened in the Mendicans—but I want you to listen and do it because you* should *do it. We want the same thing, Cutter. I'll see you on the other shore."*

The cold dissipated, and the voice was gone.

"What in hell's wrong?" said Pomeroy. "What's going on?"

When Cutter told them, they argued until they began to attract attention.

"Someone is *playing* with us," said Pomeroy. "We don't make it easier for them. We don't get on that godsdamned boat, Cutter." He clenched and unclenched his bulky fist. Elsie touched him nervously, tried to calm him.

"I don't know what to tell you, man," Cutter said. The close-up voice had exhausted him. "Whoever it is, it ain't militia. Someone from the Caucus? I don't see how, or why. Some free agent? It was them who held off the fReemade: that backward horse-man got whispered, like I did. *I don't know what's going on.* You want to take another boat, I ain't going to argue. But we best find one soon. And seems to me we might as well find this one, just to know."

The *Akif* was a rusted thing, little more than a barge, with a single low deck and a captain pathetically grateful for their passage. He looked uncertain at Fejh, but smiled again when they mentioned the price—yes, already half-paid, he said, with the letter they had left for him.

It was perfect, and it decided them. Though Pomeroy raged against the decision, Cutter knew he would not desert them.

Someone's watching us, thought Cutter. *Someone who whispers. Someone who says they're my friend.*

The sea, then the desert, then miles of unmapped land. *Can I do this?*

Only a small sea. The man they searched for left trails, left people affected. Cutter could see his friends' anxieties and did not blame them—their undertaking was enormous. But he believed they would find the man they followed.

He went with his friends to search for rumours of a clay-rider or militia hunters, before they sailed. They went to send a letter back to the city, to their Caucus contacts, saying they were en route, that they had found tracks.

The drifting man passed through arcane geography, between fulgurites and over alkaline pools. He stood still while he drifted, folding and unfolding his arms. He picked up speed, gliding full of wrongness.

A bird was his companion but it did not fly, only clung to his head. It opened its wings and let the air spread its feathers. There was a growth on it, something that mangled its outlines.

The man passed villages. What animals were there to see him howled.

At the stub-end of the hills, in a drying landscape, the drifting man neared an interruption. Something embedded in the dirt, a star of rust-red and ragged brown-black cloth. A dead man. Come from very high and ironed down into the land. A little blood had soaked into the ground and blackened. The meat was tendered and flattened into outlines.

The man who drifted above the earth and the bird who rode him paused above the dead. They looked down at him, and they looked up with unnatural perfect timing into the sky.

CHAPTER THREE

Oᴺ ᴛʜᴇ ꜱᴇᴄᴏɴᴅ ᴅᴀʏ ᴏᴜᴛ, ɪɴ ᴛʜᴇ ɢʀᴇʏ ᴡᴀᴠᴇꜱ ᴏꜰ ᴛʜᴇ Mᴇᴀɢʀᴇ Sea, Cutter's party hijacked the *Akif*. Pomeroy held a pistol at the captain's head. The crew stared in disbelief. Elsie and Ihona raised their guns. Cutter watched Elsie's hand shake. Fejh reared out of his water-barrel with a bow. The captain began to cry.

"We're taking a diversion," Cutter said. "It's going to take you a few extra days to get to Shankell. We're going southwest first. Along the coast. Up the Dradscale River. You'll make Shankell a few days late, is all. And minus a bit of stock."

The crew of six men sulked and surrendered their weapons. They were all casuals on a daily rate: they had no solidarity with each other or their captain. They looked at Fejhechrillen hatefully, out of some prejudice.

Cutter tied the captain to the wheel, by the dehorned sables the *Akif* carried, and the travellers took turns to menace him while the mounts watched. His blubbering was embarrassing. The sun grew harsher. Their wake widened as if they unbuckled the water. Cutter watched Fejh suffer in the hot salt air.

They saw the north shores of the Cymek on the third day. Merciless baked-clay hills, dust and sandtraps. There were scraps of plantlife: dust-coloured marram, trees of hard and alien nature, spicate foliage. The *Akif* churned past brine marshes.

"He always said this would be the only way to get to Iron Council," Cutter said.

The minerals of the Dradscale estuary made lustre on the water. The brackish slough was full of weed, and Cutter gave a city-dweller's gape to see a clan of manatees surface and graze.

"Is no safe," said the helmsman. "Is with—" He gave some obscenity or disgust-noise, and pointed at Fejh. "Up farther. Full of riverpig."

Cutter tensed at the word. "On," he said, and pointed his gun. The pilot moved back.

"We no do," he said. Abruptly he tilted backward over the rail and into the water. Everyone moved and shouted.

"There." Pomeroy pointed with his revolver. The pilot had surfaced and was heading for one of the islands. Pomeroy tracked him but never fired.

"Godsdammit," he said as the man reached the little shore. "Only reason the others haven't gone after him is they can't swim." He nodded at the cheering crew.

"They'll fight back with their fucking hands if we push this," Ihona said. "Look at them. And you know we won't shoot them. You know what we have to do."

So in ridiculous inversion, the hijackers ferried the crew to the island. Pomeroy waved his gun as if carrying out necessary punishment. But they let the sailors off, and even gave them provisions. The captain watched plaintively. They would not let him go.

Cutter was disgusted. "Too fucking soft," he raged at his friends. "You shouldn't have come if you're so soft."

"What do you suggest, Cutter?" Ihona shouted. "You make them stay if you can. You ain't going to kill them. No, maybe we *shouldn't* have come, it's already cost us." Pomeroy glowered. Elsie and Fejh would not look at Cutter. He was suddenly fearful.

"Come on," Cutter said. He tried not to sound wheedling or scornful. "Come on. We're getting there. We'll find him. This bloody journey'll end."

"For someone so known not to give a damn," Ihona said, "you're risking a lot for this. You want to be careful, people might think you ain't what you like to think."

The Dradscale was wide. Ditches and sikes joined it, channelling in dirty water. It was unbending for miles ahead.

On the east bank, dry hills rose behind the mangroves, wind-cut arids. It was a desert of cooked mud, and way beyond it was Shankell, the cactus city. On the west the land was altogether harsher. Above the fringe of tidal trees was a comb of rock teeth. A zone of vicious karst, an unbelievable thicket of edged stone. By Cutter's imprecise documents, it stretched a hundred miles. His maps were scribbled with explorers' exhortations. *Devils' nails* said one, and another *Three dead. Turned back.*

There were birds, high-shouldered storks that walked like villains. They flew with languid wingstrokes as if always exhausted. Cutter had never suffered in so brute a sun. He gaped in its light. All of them were pained by it, but Fejh of course most of all, submerging again and again in his stinking barrel. When eventually the water around them was saltless he dived with relief and refilled his container. He did not swim long: he did not know this river.

The man they followed must have been a vector of change. Cutter watched the riverbanks for signs that he had passed.

They steamed through the night, announcing themselves with soot and juddering. In the hard red light of dawn the leaves and vines dandled in the current seemed to deliquesce, to be runoff streams of dye, matter adrip into meltwater.

While the sun was still low the Dradscale widened and bled into a pocosin. The marsh-lake was met by the end of the karst, uncanny fingerbones of stone. The *Akif* slowed. For minutes, its motor was the only sound.

"Where now, Cutter?" someone said at last.

Something moved below the water. Fejh leaned up half out of his barrel.

"Dammit, it's—" he said but was interrupted.

Things were surfacing ahead of the *Akif,* broad-mouthed heads. Vodyanoi bravos waving spears.

The captain came upright and shrieked. He shoved down on his throttle, and the water-bandits scattered and dived. Fejh upset his barrel, spilling dirty water. He leaned out and yelled in Lubbock at the vodyanoi below, but they did not answer.

They came up again, burst out of the water and for a moment were poised as if they stood upon it. They threw spears before they fell. Spumes of water arced from below their outflung arms so that their shafts became harpoons, riding it. Cutter had never seen such watercræft. He fired into the water.

The captain was still accelerating. He was going to drive the *Akif* onto the shore, Cutter realised. There was no time to moor.

"*Brace!*" he shouted. With a huge grinding the boat rode the shallow bank. Cutter pitched over the prow and landed hard. "Come on!" he said, rising.

The *Akif* jutted like a ramp. The antelopes' pen had broken and, tethered to one another, they were hauling off in a dangerous mass of hooves and hornstubs. Fejh vaulted the listing rail. Elsie had hit her head, and Pomeroy helped her down.

Ihona was cutting the captain's bonds. Cutter fired twice at oncoming swells. "Come *on!*" he shouted again.

A spire of water rose by the broken boat. For an instant he thought it some freakish wave, or watercræft of an astonishing kind, but it was more than twenty feet high, a pillar of utterly clear water, and from its top jutted a vodyanoi. He was a shaman, riding his undine.

Cutter could see the vessel distorted through the water elemental's body. Its thousands of gallons pushed down on the boat with strange motion, and bucked it, and Ihona and the captain fell down the sloping deck toward it. They tried to rise but the water of the undine flowed up and lapped at their feet then broke, a wave, and engulfed them. Cutter shouted as his comrade and her prisoner were buffeted into the undine's belly. They kicked and clawed, trying to swim out but which way was out? The undine gave its innards currents that kept them in its core.

Pomeroy bellowed. He fired, and Cutter fired, and Fejh let an arrow go. And all three missiles hit the elemental with splashes like dropped stones, and were swallowed up. The arrow was visible, vortexing in the liquid thing, coiling down to be voided like shit. Again Cutter fired, this time at the shaman atop the monstrous water, but his shot was wide. With idiot bravery Pomeroy was pummelling the undine, trying to tear it apart to get at his friend, but it ignored him, and his blows raised only spray.

Ihona and the captain were drowning. The undine poured itself into the cargo hold, and the shaman kicked down into its bowels. Cutter screamed to see Ihona's still-moving body carried in the matter of the undine belowdecks and out of sight.

The vodyanoi were all over the *Akif*. They began to throw spears again.

Water poured up out of the boat, the undine geysering from the hold, and it carried within it engine parts—iron buoyed on its strange tides. And rolling like motes were the bodies of its victims. They moved now only with the water that bore them. Ihona's eyes and mouth were open. Cutter saw her only a moment before the elemental came down in a great arch into the lake, water in water, carrying its loot and dead.

All the travellers could do was curse and cry. They cursed many times, they howled, and moved at last into the grasslands, away from the boat, away from the rapacious water.

* * *

At night they sat exhausted in a motte of trees beside their sables and watched Elsie. The moon and its daughters, the satellites circling it like tossed coins, were high. Elsie, cross-legged, looked at them, and Cutter was surprised to see her calm. She moved her mouth. A shirt was tied around her neck. Her eyes unfocused.

Cutter looked beyond her through the canebrake at the veldt. In the night light the tambotie trees and ironthorns were silhouetted like assassins. Baobabs stood thickset with their splintered crowns.

When Elsie stopped she looked defensive. She untied their quarry's shirt from her neck.

"I don't know," she said. "It weren't clear. I think maybe something that way." She gestured at a distant rise. Cutter said nothing. She was pointing north-northeast, the way they knew they had to go. He had been relieved that Elsie had come, but he had always known she had only hedge-charms, no mirific strength. He did not know if she was sensing true emanations, and neither did she.

"We've got to go this way, anyway," said Cutter. He meant it kindly—nothing's lost even if you're wrong—but Elsie would not look at him.

Days they rode through landscape that punished them with heat and plants like barbed wire. They were inexpert with the muscular mounts but made a pace they could not have done on foot. Their guns dipped in exhaustion. Fejh languished in a barrelful of the lake tethered between two sables. It was stagnant; it made him ill.

They were made to panic by gibbering from above. A brood of things came at them out of the sky, snapping and laughing. Cutter knew them from pictures: the glucliche, hyaena hunching under bone and leather batwings.

Pomeroy shot one and its sisters and brothers began to eat it before it reached the ground. The flock came together ravenous and cannibal, and the party got clear.

"Where's your damn whisperer, Cutter?"

"Fuck you, Pomeroy. I find out, I'll be sure to tell you."

"Two already. Two comrades dead, Cutter. What are we *doing*?" Cutter did not answer.

"How does *he* know where to go?" Elsie said. She was talking about their quarry.

"He always knew where it was, or thereabouts, he told me," Cutter said. "He hinted he got *messages* from it. Said he heard from a contact in the city that they're looking for the Council. He had to go, get there first." Cutter had not brought the note, had been so hurt by its terse vagueness. "Showed me on a map once where he thought it was. I told you. That's where we go." As if it were just like that.

They reached the base of a steep rise at twilight, found a rivulet and drank from it with vast relief. Fejh wallowed. The humans left him to sleep in the water, and climbed the shelf in their way. At its ragged cliff-edge they saw across miles of flattened land, and there were lights the way they were heading. Three sets: the farthest a barely visible glinting, the closest perhaps two hours away.

"Elsie, Elsie," Cutter said. "You did, you did feel something."

Pomeroy was too heavy to take the steep routes down, and Elsie had not the strength. Only Cutter could descend. The others told him to wait, that they would find a way together the next day, but even knowing it was foolish to walk these hostile plains alone, at night, he could not hold back.

"Go on," he said. "Look after Fejh. I'll see you later."

He was astonished by how glad he was to be alone. Time was stilled. Cutter walked through a ghostworld, the earth's dream of its own grasslands.

There were no nightbirds calling, no glucliches, nothing but the dark vista like a painted background. Cutter was alone on a stage. He thought of dead Ihona. When at last the lights were close he could see a kraal of heavy houses. He walked into the village as brazen as if he were welcome.

It was empty. The windows were only holes. The big doorways gaped into silent interiors. Each of them was stripped.

The lights were clustered at junctions: head-sized globes of some gently burning lava, cool, and no brighter than a covered lamp. They hung without motion, dead still in the air. They muttered and their surfaces moiled: arcs of cold pyrosis flared inches from them. Tame night-suns. Nothing moved.

In the empty alleys he spoke to the man he followed. "Where are you then?" His voice was very careful.

When he went back to the cliff, Cutter saw a light on its edge, a lantern, that moved slowly. He knew it was not his companions'.

Elsie wanted to see the empty village, but Cutter was firm that they had no time, they had to see the other lights, to see if there was a trail. "You picked up something," he reminded her. "We better see. We need some fucking guidance."

Fejh was better, his water renewed, but he was still afraid. "Vodyanoi ain't supposed to be here," he said. "I'm going to die here, Cutter."

Midmorning, Cutter looked back, pointed into the brightness. Someone, some speck figure, sat on horseback on the shelf they had reached the previous night. A woman or man in a wide-brimmed hat.

"We're being followed. It's got to be the whisperer." Cutter waited for a mutter in his ear, but there was nothing. Throughout the day and in the early night the rider tracked them, coming no closer. It angered them, but they could do nothing.

The second village was like the first, Cutter thought, but he was wrong. The sables wheezed and slowed through deserted squares and under the sputtering light-globes and found a long wall all bullet-scarred, its mortar punctured and stained with sap. The travellers dismounted, stood in the cold remains of violence. In the township's outlands Cutter saw tilled land; and then he felt the moment still, realised it was not a field but was disturbed in another way, turned over and charred. It was the topsoil on a grave. It was a mass grave.

Breaking the soil like the first shoots of a grotesque harvest were bones. They were abrupt and blacked by fire, fibrous like dense wood. The bones of cactus-people.

Cutter stood among the dead, above their moulding vegetable-flesh. Time came back. He felt it shudder.

Planted scarecrow in the middle was a degraded corpse. A human man. He was naked, slumped, upheld by spikes that pinned him to a tree. Javelins pierced him. One emerged point-first from his sternum. It had been forced up his anus and through him. His scrotum was torn off. There was a scab of blood on his throat. He was leathered by sun and insects worked on him.

The travellers stared like worshippers at their totem. When after many seconds Pomeroy moved he still looked carefully, as if it would be a disrespect to break the dead man's gaze.

"Look," he said. He swallowed. "All cactacae." He poked at the earth, turned up bits of the dead. "And then there's him. What in Jabber's name happened here? The war ain't reached here . . ."

Cutter looked at the corpse. It was not very bloody. Even between its legs there was only a little gore.

"He was already gone," Cutter whispered. He was awed by the brutal tableau. "They done this to a dead man. After they buried the others." Below the corpse's chin was not a clot but blooded metal. Cutter looked away while he worked it from the dead man's neck.

It was a tiny escutcheon. It was a badge of the New Crobuzon Militia.

The dangling man crossed the water. His hair and clothes gusted in his motion. The Meagre Sea chopped scant feet beneath him, and spume spattered his trousers.

A body like a bolt breached abruptly, a swordfish arcing up beside him, reaching high enough for him to touch at the keystone of its leap then curving down to stab back under with its body-spear. It kept up with him. It kept pace with his uncanny motion.

When it came up, when it vaulted into the sun, it caught the dangling man's eye with its big sideways stare. Something dark clutched its dorsal fin. Something that shifted and dug under its fish's skin.

CHAPTER FOUR

T HEY WENT OFF-MAP, TOWARD THE THIRD SET OF LIGHTS. BEYOND them was a wall of stone like spinal scales, through which they must find a way.

Cutter held the blood-rusted badge. He felt sick, knowing the militia were ahead of them. *We could be too late.*

There were sinkholes full of water, though it was dirty stuff. Fejh replenished his barrel, but his skin was scarring. They shot little jackrabbits and slow birds. They passed antelopes, went cautiously by coveys of tusked hogs the size of horses.

Cutter felt as if the path they left was an infection in the land. At dawn on their third day out from the cruciform militiaman, they approached the last village. And as they came nearer the sun crested and they were washed in roseate light and something moved, that they had thought a rock spur or a thinning tree.

They cried out. Their mounts stumbled.

A giant came at them, a cactus figure far greater than they had seen before. Cactacae stood seven, eight feet tall, but this one was more than double that. It was like an elemental, something base and made of the land, the grassland walking.

It jerked on twisted hips, its vast legs and toeless stump-feet ricketed. It swayed as if it would fall. Its green skin was split and healed many times. Its spines were finger-long.

The massive cactus staggered at them, fast for all its palsied gait. It held a cudgel, a slab of tree. It raised it as it came, and from a face that hardly moved, it began to shout. It called words they did not understand, some variant of Sunglari, as it lurched murderously toward them.

"Wait, wait!" Everyone was shouting. Elsie pointed, her eyes bloodshot, and Cutter knew she was trying to reach its mind with her feeble charms.

The cactus came in unstable strides. Fejh fired an arrow that hit it with a moist drum-sound and remained dripping and painless in its side.

"*Kill you,*" the cactus crooned in its feeble voice, in an ugly Ragamoll. "*Murder.*" It heaved its enormous weapon.

"*It weren't us!*" shouted Cutter. He threw the militia insignia in the cactus-giant's path, and fired his repeater at the badge, making it dance and ring until all six barrels were empty. The cactus was still, its shillelagh paused. Cutter spat at the badge until his mouth was dry. "It weren't us."

He was something they had never seen. Cutter thought he must be Torqued, cancered by the bad energy of a cacotopic zone, but that was not right. In the last empty village, the vast cactus-man told them of himself. He was *ge'ain*—between them they rendered it "tardy."

By arcane husbandry, cactacae of the veldt kept a few of their bulbs nurtured in a coma for months after they should have been born. While their siblings crawled squalling from the earth, the *ge'ain,* the tardy, slept on below in their chorions, growing. Their bodies distended as occult techniques kept them unborn. When finally they woke and emerged they were mooncalf. They grew prodigal.

Their aberrance afflicted them. Their woody bones were bowed, their skins corticate and boiling with excrescence. Their augmented senses hurt. They were the wards, the fighters and lookouts for their homesteads. They were tabooed. Shunned and worshipped. They had no names.

The fingers of the tardy's left hand were fused. He moved slowly with arthritic pain.

"We not Tesh," he said. "Not our war, not our business. But them come anywise. Militia."

They had come from the river, a mounted platoon with rive-bows and motorguns. The cactacae had long heard stories from the north, where militia and Tesh legions skirmished. Exiles had told them of monstrous acts at militia hands, and the cactus villagers fled the snatch-squad.

The militia reached one village before it was emptied. Those cactacae had sheltered northern refugees full of carnage stories, and they had determined to fight first. They met the militia in a fearful band, with their clubs and flint machetes. There had been butchery. One militiaman body was left behind, to be punished by the ge'ain amid the ripped-up cactus dead.

"Two weeks gone they came. They hunt us after that," the tardy said. "They bring Tesh war here now?" Cutter shook his head.

"It's a fucking mess," he said. "The militia we're following— they ain't after these poor bastards, they're after our man. These cactacae've panicked because of what they've heard, and made themselves targets.

"Listen to me," he said to the leviathan green man. "They who done this to your village, they're looking for someone. They want to stop him before he can give a message." He looked up into the big face. "More of them'll come."

"Tesh come too. To fight them. Fight us on both sides."

"Yes," said Cutter. His voice was flat. He waited a long time. "But if he's to win . . . if he can get away, then the militia . . . maybe they'll have other things to think on than this war. So maybe you want to help us. We have to stop them, before they stop him."

With misshaped hands to his mouth the tardy gave a cry as base as animal pain. His lament rumbled over the grass. The animals of the hot night paused, and in the still there was an answer. Another cry, from miles off, that Cutter felt in his guts.

Again and again the tardy sounded, announcing himself, and over the hours of that night a little corps of the *ge'ain* came to him on huge and painful steps. There were five, and they were various: some more than twenty feet tall, some barely half that, limbs broken and reset, unshapely. A company of the lame, the crippled strong.

The travellers were cowed. The tardy mourned together in their own language. "If you might help us," Cutter told them humbly, "maybe we can stop the militia for good. And either way, it'll mean a reckoning, and that can mean revenge."

The tardy spent hours in a circle, talking with brooding sounds, reaching out to each other. Their motions were careful under the weight of their limbs. *Poor lost soldiers,* thought Cutter, though his awe remained.

At last the convenor of the parley said to him: "Them gone, one militia band. They gone north. Hunting. We know where."

"That's them," said Cutter. "They're looking for our man. They're the ones we have to reach."

The tardy plucked handfuls of their spines and lifted Cutter and his comrades. They carried them, easily. The deserted sables watched them go. The cactacae took mammoth strides, swayed across terrains, stepping over trees. Cutter felt close to the sun. He saw birds, even garuda.

The *ge'ain* spoke to them. The feathered figures circled when they passed, with a sound like billowing. They jabbered in severe avian voices. The *ge'ain* listened and crooned in reply.

"Militia ahead," said Cutter's mount.

They staggered, resting rarely, their legs locked in the cactus-manner. Once they stopped when the moon and its daughters were low. At the very edge of the savannah, west, there was light. A torch, a lantern moving.

"Who is he?" said Cutter's tardy. "Man on horse. Follows you?"

"He's there? Jabber . . . get to him! Quick. I need to know his game."

The *ge'ain* careened in drunken speed, eating distance, and the light went out. "Gone," the tardy said. A whisper sounded in Cutter's ear, making him start.

"Don't be a damn fool," the voice said. *"The cactus won't find me. You're wasting time. I'll join you by and by."*

When they continued the way they had been going, the light came back, kept pace with them to the west.

After two nights, breaking only for brief rests or to sluice Fejh with what water they found, the *ge'ain* stopped. They pointed at a track of pulped greenery and ploughed-up landscape.

Over miles of dried grass, before greener hills, a haze was rising, what Cutter thought was dust-smoke, then saw was mixed with darker grey. As if someone had smudged an oily finger on a window.

"Them," said Cutter's *ge'ain*. "Militia. Is them."

The tardy did not plan. They uprooted knotted trees of the prairie and made them bludgeons, then continued toward the murderers of their kin.

"Listen!" Cutter and Pomeroy and Elsie shouted, to persuade them of the sense in a strategy. "Listen, listen, listen."

"Keep one alive," said Cutter. "For Jabber's sake let us talk to one," but the tardy gave no sign that they heard or cared.

The veldt buckled; heat reverberated between stones like houses. Animals scattered at the *ge'ain* oncoming, loud as the fall of trees. The tardy stamped up a fold of land and became still. Cutter looked down over the militia.

There were more than a score, tiny figures in grey, and they had dogs, and something expressing the smoke: an ironclad tower as tall as the tardy pulled by Remade horses. Its summit was corbelled, and two men looked out from between battlements. It tore up the bushes and left ruined land and oil.

Very slowly the tardy put their passengers down. Cutter and his comrades checked their weapons.

"This is idiocy," said Pomeroy. Some dusty bird of prey went over, sounding excitement. "Look at their firepower."

"What do they care?" Cutter nodded at the tardy. "They only want revenge. It's us who want more. I ain't going to stand in the way of this lot getting what's theirs. As if I could." The tardy lumbered down the slope toward the militia. "We best get going."

The companions spread out. They did not need to hide. The militia had seen the tardy, and could see nothing else. Cutter ran in the dust that the cactus-giants left.

A motorgun fired. Bullets purged from the rotating barrels. The militia were running their horses in panic. They had left the cactacae regions and thought themselves safe. Their bullets pattered like gravel against the tardy, with little bursts of sap, not even slowing them.

One *ge'ain* hurled her weapon like a trebuchet. It was a club in her hand, but as it spun it was visible again for what it was: a tree. It hit the minaret and bent its plating. Cutter lay on his belly and fired his repeater into the milling militia.

They fired; they showed impressive and stupid bravery, standing their ground so that a tardy could lift his leg high and stamp them down, crushing them and their mounts in a brutal two-step. The cactus-man swept his huge sapper, cracked a man's neck with the fringe of its roots.

The militia with rifles fell back behind those carrying rivebows and tanks of pyrotic gas. The tardy raised their hands. The fire-throwers made them dance back, their skins black and spitting.

The smallest *ge'ain* staggered as rivebow chakris of sharpened metal spun into his vegetable muscle and severed his arm. He held his left hand against the stump, kicked at the dismounted men and sent two dead or broken-boned; but his pain took him to his knees, and a marksman killed him with a chakri to his face.

Fejh's arrows and the growl of Pomeroy's blunderbuss uncovered them. The tower's guns fingered at the copse where Fejh hid. Cutter shouted as the motorgun spun, its chains and gears loud as hammers, and a storm of bullets tattered the vegetation.

There were four tardy now in an ecstasy of murder, stamping and grabbing. The tower pitched and moved. Its motorgun took another *ge'ain*, a line of bullets perforating her hip to breast, so she staggered then hinged in gross unnatural movement along her new seam.

Pomeroy was standing. He was shouting and Cutter knew he was shouting Fejhechrillen's name. Pomeroy rammed shot down and fired repeatedly. The dogs were frantic, snapping pointlessly with misshapen jaws.

From a long way off, there was a shot. Again, and a man fell from the top of the iron tower.

That voice spoke up close in Cutter's ear. *"Down. You're seen."* Cutter dropped, and watched through gaps in the wiry grass and heard another of those far-off shots. A militiaman fell from his horse.

Cutter saw a captain-thaumaturge, watched veins and tendons score his skin while dark sparks dissipated from him. Cutter fired and missed, and it was the last bullet.

The thaumaturge shouted and his clothes smouldered, and a

lance of milky energy spurted from the ground below the largest *ge'ain*'s feet and punctured her right through, soared skyward and was gone. She flailed as her sap poured. Black flame immolated her. The thaumaturge stood bleeding from his eyes but triumphant, and he was shot down by the unseen marksman. The last two *ge'ain* were treading the militiamen to death.

One hugged the gun-spiked tower, wrestling it, twisting it violently. While his sibling crushed the last men and horses and mutant dogs, he shoved and grappled the column. It reared, grinding, overbalanced, panicking the horses that dragged it. It fell slowly, smashed and split, spilt men living and dead.

They ran, those who could, and the two tardy ran after them, stamping very much like grotesque children. A horseman was visible beyond the battleground, galloping toward them. Cutter heard his whisper again—*"Keep the dogs alive, don't let them kill the dogs for Jabber's sake"*—but it was not a command, he ignored it and was running, as his friends were, for the rough where Fejh had been. They found him spread across the green.

He went and went, the dangling man, he flew, and his stance was stiff and he sped through the air. Through the byways of the swampy estuary, between stubbish islands, past mangroves and through the arches of their vines, over banks of mulch and mud into karst, rock splints, a serrated landscape.

His companion was a bird, a hare, a jag-wasp the size of a dove, a rockling a fox a cactus-child, always with its tumour of mottlesome flesh moving upon it as it clung to the dangling man or kept pace with him, impossibly pushing whatever its body was from spire to spire of stone. The dangling man emerged into grassland. For a time the beast below him was an antelope that ran like none of its kind had ever run.

They went and went, they tore through the scorching scrubland in sped-up time. They went north through little trees and the burnt villages and onward north and their pace was up and whatever the animal was that followed the man or held to him or flew above him their speed increased and they hunted, watching signs in the earth and air that only they could see, narrowing in, following, coming after.

CHAPTER FIVE

They gathered Fejh to bury. The strange dogs surrounded
the militia bodies and howled for their masters.

The two tardy remaining stood with their legs locked, in slumber. Not all the militia were dead. There was a thin screaming, and
fast breathing from those too broken to crawl away. There were no
more than four or five, dying slowly but with all their energy.

As Cutter dug, the horseman came through the frantic dogs. The
companions turned their backs on their dead friend, to face him.

He nodded at them, touching the front of his brimmed hat. He
was the colour of the dust. His jerkin sun-bleached, his trousers of
buck leather and the chaps smoking with dirt. He had a rifle below
his shabrack. On each hip he wore a pepperpot revolver.

The man looked at them. He stared at Cutter, held his right
hand cupped by his lips and muttered. Cutter heard him, close-up,
as if the mouth was by his ear.

"Best hurry. And we'd best get one of the dogs."

"Who are you?" Cutter said. The man looked to Pomeroy, Elsie,

Cutter again, mouthing. When it was his turn Cutter heard: *"Dro-gon."*

"A susurrator," Pomeroy said with distrust, and Drogon turned to him and whispered something across the air. "Oh aye," Pomeroy answered. "You can be damn sure of that."

"What you doing here?" said Cutter. "You come to help us bury—" He had to stop and could only gesture. "Why you been fol-lowing us?"

"Like I told you," Drogon whispered. *"We want the same thing. You're exiles now, and so am I. We're looking for the same thing. I been looking for the Iron Council for damn years. I wasn't sure of you, you know. And maybe I still ain't. We're not the only ones looking for the Council, you know that. You know why these fuckers are here."* He pointed at a militiaman supine and bloody. *"Why'd you think I fol-lowed? I needed to know who you-all are looking out for."*

"What's he saying?" said Elsie, but Cutter waved her quiet.

"I still don't know I trust you, but I been watching you and I know the best chance I got's with you. And I showed you your best chance is with me. I'd have gone with your man if I'd been able, after I heard he'd gone."

"How do you know . . . ?" Cutter said.

"You ain't the only one with your ear to the ground, who knows what he is. But listen, we ain't got time: it ain't just him who's being followed. This lot were after your man—they don't know any more than we do already—and there's others are after you. Been tracking you since Rudewood. And they're gaining. And they ain't just militia, either."

"What? What's coming?" And what Cutter heard he repeated in terror.

"Handlingers," he said.

More frightened of dying alone than of the anger of their enemies, those militia still alive began to call out. They were without plan or intrigue—they cajoled not to any end but only eager to be spoken to as they lay in the heat.

"Hey, hey, hey mate, hey mate." "Come on. Come on, then, come on." "Jabber, my arm's gone man, Jabber, *Jabber* it's gone."

They were mostly men in their thirties with expressions of pride and resignation that seemed scoured-on; they did not expect or even want quarter, only to be acknowledged before they died.

The dogs still screamed and circled. Drogon corralled three of the weird-skulled things, herding them with his big horse. He calmed the frantic animals with inaudible commands.

"Why's he helping?" Elsie said. "What does he want?"

Pomeroy was for killing him, or at least constraining him and leaving him behind.

"Dammit, I don't know," said Cutter. "Says he heard what was happening. That he's out for the Council, too. I don't *know*. But look what he's done—he could've killed us by now. He saved my life—took out the man who'd sighted me. You saw how he used them guns. And you said yourself, Pom, he's a thaumaturge."

"He's a susurrator," said Pomeroy with scorn. "He's just a whispersmith."

"I been whispered to by him, brother. Remember? This ain't a little susurrus to make a dog lie down. He sounded across *miles*, put me and that fReemade highwayman in thrall."

It was a petty field, subvocalurgy: the science of furtive suggestions, a rude footpad technique. But this man had made it something more.

The dogs were Remade. The olfactory centres of their brains had been hugely enlarged. Their crania were doughy and distended, as if their unshaped brains bubbled over. Their eyes were tiny, and at the end of their jaws their nostrils were dilated and set in flared and mobile flesh like pigs'. Their wrinkled snouts wore wires and they carried batteries, making thaumaturgic circuits. Each had a rag in its collar.

"Oh Jabber, those are his damn clothes," said Cutter.

"These'll track across continents," whispered Drogon. *"That's how they were following him."*

They did not kill the militia left alive, nor spit in their faces nor give them water, only left them stone ignored. Drogon concentrated on the dogs. He was whispering, and they were calming. They were eager to trust him.

"Them dogs is ours," Pomeroy said. Drogon shrugged and held out the leash, and the distorted animal looked at Pomeroy and showed its teeth. "What's your story?" Pomeroy said.

Drogon pointed at Elsie, whispered, and she walked toward him. He took her hands and put them on his forehead, and she went into her hexing state. He kept speaking, enunciating something only she could hear.

When he was done she opened her eyes. "He told me to read him. He told me to verity-gauge. And he said, 'I want what you want, I want to find the Council.' He said he's from the city, but he sure isn't bloody Parliament, and he isn't militia. Says he's a vaquero, a horseman. Lived nomad for twenty years.

"He says there are too many stories for the Council not to be real. And it's precious to wilderness-men. Iron Council. Like a promised place. So when he got word what was happening—when he heard who'd gone to protect it—he had to come after him to help. To find it. He followed us. Till he was sure he could trust us."

"You ain't a truesayer," Pomeroy said. "This don't mean shit."

"No I ain't, but I've got something." Elsie glowered. "I can feel. I was verity-gauging."

The whispersmith replaced his hat and turned back to the dogs, subvocalising till they skittered for his affection among the bodies of their handlers.

"She ain't got the puissance to be sure, Cutter," Pomeroy said.

Why am I supposed to fucking decide? thought Cutter.

Drogon held the cloths to the dogs' absurd noses, and the animals slobbered and wheeled north. "*We have to go.*" Drogon spoke to Cutter. "*We're still being followed. We're close, now, we're close.*"

Elsie tried to thank the tardy, with no reaction. "You have to go," she shouted. "Handlingers are coming." But the *ge'ain* did not answer. They stood among their revenge and waited for nothing. The humans could only shout their thanks and leave the plant-giants in stupor. Cutter saluted Fejh's grave.

The dogs fanned on their leads ahead of Drogon, sniffing urgently. Sometimes he let them career through the hard vegetation, their outsized heads swinging. While Cutter and the others continued their trudging, he would ride out.

He whispered to the travellers each in turn, from miles ahead. He let the dogs run, their leads trailing behind them, and when they went too far he would whisper commands and they would come back.

"*Keep walking,*" he told Cutter. "*Handlinger's behind you.*"

Handlingers. The malefic hands of history. Five-fingered parasites, come out now to the light.

Up through a col in the hills. Cutter thought of Fejh slowly baking in the earth. He looked at the mark they had left, the dead and nearly dead, the two tardy standing like trees, the ruins of the skirmish like a soot stain.

The land before them was more wooded, the ground become peaked, slopes of scree gripped in the roots of olives. Drogon's dust scattered into a low cloud. He was ahead, his path visible like a seam. There was sage, and dog-rose. Each of Cutter's steps dispersed a gathering of cicadas.

It was not the only moment of the journey when time clotted, and Cutter was stuck fast. A day was only an instant drawn out. Motion itself—the putter of insects, the appearance-disappearance of a tiny rodent—was an endless repetition of the same.

They did not sleep long that night for the sounding of the bloodhounds and Drogon's whispers from his camp ahead. They were weighed down by weapons they had taken from the militia, and they left a trail of boot-knives and heavy rifles.

Once they saw a garuda way above them, stretched out like someone on a cross. They saw her dip, lurch earthward, veer toward Drogon, then break and ascend.

"He tried to whisper her," Cutter said. "But she got out of it." He was pleased.

Their rhythms were not the day's: they slept for minutes while the sun was up, as well as at dusk and night. If the whispersmith slept it was in the saddle. On the sierra they passed smudged pebblebeasts, something between giraffes and gorillas, knuckle-walking and eating low leaves.

"*You have to speed,*" the whispersmith told Cutter. "*The hand-linger's coming.*"

By moonlight they followed Drogon and their quarry toward a hill-line topped by plateau. They saw dark, a corridor through the butte. They would reach it in daylight, and Cutter could imagine the relief it would be, the punishing hot sky just a band seething above lichened rock walls and stone stiles.

Elsie said: "Something's coming." She looked gaunt. She looked horrified. "Something's coming from the south." There was a disturbance behind many waves of landscape, beyond sight. Cutter knew that Elsie was a weak witch, but she felt something.

The east was weakly shining, and in the first light Cutter saw the dust of Drogon's horse below the mesa. The whispersmith was almost at the entrance to the chine.

"*Follow the way through,*" Drogon said to Cutter. "*Quick. The handlinger's closing, but you can make it here if you keep on. The dogs're howling. They can smell our man, he's close, through here. Make it here, maybe we can . . . maybe we can face the handlinger, an ambush.*" A weak plan.

Drogon must have turned then and hauled behind the pack as they bayed and ran into the split rock path. Cutter thought of the overhangs they would pass and saw with clarity what he had seen in the room of his runaway friend, that had sent him here. Cutter saw the tripwire and the men dead and stoved in, lying under anthropoid outlines in random materials.

"Godsdammit. *Get back! Get back!*"

He shouted as loud as he ever had. Pomeroy and Elsie staggered; they had been sleeping as they walked. Cutter made his hands a trumpet and roared again.

"*Stop! Stop!*" He fired his repeater into the air.

Drogon was in his ear. "*What you doing? The handlinger'll hear you . . .*" But Cutter was speaking, and lurching on exhausted legs. "Stop stop stop!" he shouted. "Don't go in, don't go in. It's a trap."

Dust came toward him and reconfigured as if moulded by the growing heat, and became a man on a horse. Drogon was riding back. Cutter shouted.

"You can't go in," he said. "It's a trap. It's a golem trap."

Drogon rode around them as if they were steers, and when they buckled he would whisper to them, to their underbrains, and they could only obey. "*Run,*" he whispered, and they were helpless not to.

By the raised plain were slippy scree paths, so they held onto boscage while they climbed toward the dark. Drogon took his horse at speed along a route that looked impossible. The dogs, tied by the crack's entrance, pulled, imbecilic with their porcine eyes and bared teeth. They were in agony to enter, to reach what they could smell.

"He knows," Cutter said. He leaned against his knees to cough up the stuff of the path. "He knows they're coming for him."

"*Handlinger,*" said Drogon. A fleck at the edge of the plain. "*We have to go.*"

Cutter said: "He *knows* they're coming and he's not tried to hide his scent. He thinks it's the militia after him, and he's *funnelled them here*. It's a trap. We can't go in there. We have to go over. He'll be on the other side, waiting."

They did not debate long, with the handlinger curdling the air as it approached. The dogs bayed and Drogon shot them dead inside the tunnel. The others followed him up a steep root-ladder to the rocktop plateau. Drogon whispered to them *"Climb,"* even suspended as he was himself, and they found their footing and their grip.

Drogon led them by the edge of the crack. They saw his horse and the carnage of dog-flesh below them. He whispered to the horse, and it snorted and turned as if to go through the conduit.

"What you doing?" said Cutter. "If you don't keep it still I'll shoot it, I swear. We can't risk it triggering anything." There was an instant when it seemed the whispersmith might fight, but he turned and ran again, and the horse was still.

Cutter looked back and cried out. What followed them, dangling, had the shape of a man. It carried a burden. It was scant miles off, arrowing with grim unnatural motion toward the wall and the shaft.

On the other side they looked down across sierras, a slowly rising landscape. In the full sun of dawn Cutter saw runt trees.

"We have to wait until that bastard thing's gone," said Pomeroy.

"We can't," Drogon said to Cutter and Pomeroy in turn. *"It's not tracking your friend, it's tracking us. By our mind-spoor. We have to get beyond. Turn and fight it."*

"Fight it?" Pomeroy said. "It's a *handlinger*."

"It'll be all right," Cutter said. He felt a great and sudden conviction. "It'll be taken care of."

It was he, not Drogon, who found a way down. One by one they descended, the whispersmith last. *"Damn handlinger's so* close," he said to Cutter. *"He's by the entrance, he's seen the dogs, he's going in."*

Cutter looked around them. *Come see*, he thought. *Come look at your trap.* He ran toward the tunnel exit. "What you *doing*?" his comrades shouted. "Cutter get back!"

"*Stop*," the whispersmith said, and Cutter had to stop. He screamed in anger.

"Let me *go.* I have to *check* something," he said. His feet were rooted. "Godsdammit, let me fucking *go.*"

The whispersmith set him free. He stumbled up to the breach. With terror and care he came closer to the opening strewn with stone debris, the trash of boulders. He leaned in. He said, "Come help me. Help me find it."

There was a sound. He could hear air moving. An exhalation from the stone.

"*It's coming,*" the whispersmith said. Drogon did not move, nor did Pomeroy or Elsie; they only watched Cutter as if they had forsaken any idea of escape.

"Come *help* me," Cutter said, and peered into the dim. The crooning of what approached buckled him.

He saw a glistening of light. A wire taut across the threshold, extending into piled-up rocks at either side, tethered to batteries and engines Cutter knew were hidden within.

"I found it," he shouted.

Cutter looked up and heard the dismal howling. Leaves and shreds of moss were pushed through the cleft. The noise of the handlinger was very bad. In the fissure Cutter saw swirls of leaf-mould gust. He could hear staccato, a snaredrum beating and a horse's exhalations. He slid back to his companions. "Be ready to run," he said. "Be ready to fucking run."

It came. Loud. A horse galloped for them. Its legs moved with such mutant rapidity that they sounded like a company. Drogon's mount. It tore itself faster than any horse had ever run, over jags and unstable ground that turned its ankles and splintered its hoofs but it ran on through these injuries, and sweat and blood from its abrasions streaked its body. Something clamped to it. A mottlesome thing grasping its neck, a stub-tail growing maggotlike and nosing into horse-flesh.

Behind it a man emerged. A man. He stood in the air, his arms folded; he guttered toward them at dreadful speed. He saw them. He angled down, his body motionless. They began to fire, and the man came at them so the tips of his toes bumped on the rock.

Cutter stood and fired and fell backward and slid on shale. They were all firing. The whispersmith had his feet apart and sent off rounds like an expert, a gun in each hand, Pomeroy and Elsie shot wildly, and their lead hit; they saw blood burst from the horse and the impassive man, but nothing slowed them.

The dangling man opened his mouth and spat fire. The searing breath licked the wire and made it glow, so there was an instant, a fragment of a second when the handlingers saw the metal, and their momentum took them toward it and man's mouth and horse's opened in alarm but they could not stop. They breached it, and came into the sun.

Rocks unfolded. The rocks turned to them. Coils unwound and sent thaumaturgic current through circuits, a stutter of valves, and a mass of pent-up energy released and did what it had been hair-trigger-primed to do, which was to make a golem.

It made with what was around it. The substance of the gap. All the matter in that puissant field was charged instantly into motion. The rocks unfolded and seemed always to have been shaped vaguely like a human, recumbent, twenty feet high, these slopes of stone-shard an arm and these brittle dried-up bushes another, and these great boulders a paunch with rock legs below and a head of baked earth.

The golem was crude and instructed with murderous sim-plicity. Moving with assassin speed it reached arms that weighed many tons and held the handlingers. They tried to face it. It took only minute beats of time for the golem to drive stone into the animal and break its neck, crushing the handlinger, the hand-parasite squirming in the horse's mane.

The man was quicker. He spat fire that billowed without effect over the golem's face. With impossible strength the man wrenched at the arm of coagulated stone and dislocated it, so the golem moved clumsily. But its grip held. Even with its arm falling off in grots, the golem pulled the dangling man down, gripped his legs with one pebbled hand and his head with another and twisted him apart.

As the host was killed, while the flung-apart corpse was still in the air, the golem ceased, its task done. Its rocks and dust fell. They cracked and rumbled in a bloodied pile, half buried the dead horse.

The host's ruined parts rolled into bracken and sent blood down the stones. Something was spasming beneath the suit.

"Get away," Cutter said. "It wants another host."

Drogon began to fire at it while the corpse still descended. The thing had just come to rest when something many-legged the purple of a bruise scuttled from its clothes. It came with arachnid gait.

They scattered. Pomeroy's gun boomed but the thing did not let up, and it was only feet from Elsie screaming when Drogon's repeated shots stopped it. The whispersmith walked toward it firing as he went, three bullets sent precisely to the thing hidden in grass. He kicked it, hauled it up ragged and bloody.

It was a hand. A mottled right hand. From its wrist a short tail grew. It swung deadweight and dripping.

"*Dextrier*," the whispersmith said to Cutter. "*Warrior caste.*"

There was another commotion, like some big animal was shifting through trees. Cutter turned and tried to bring unloaded guns to bear.

The noise again, and something shifted in a grove a half mile off. Something came out into the sun. A giant, an immense grey man. They watched without knowing what to do or say as it walked toward them. Cutter cried out and began to run. He picked up speed as the clay man approached and he saw someone waving to him from its back: a man who leapt down and came toward him with his arms wide, shouting something no one could hear, every one of his steps, and Cutter's, sending up pollen and sticky insects that stained them.

Cutter ran up; the man ran down. Cutter called out; he called the man by name. Cutter was crying. "We found you," he said. "We found you."

part two

RETURNS

CHAPTER SIX

A WINDOW BURST OPEN HIGH ABOVE THE MARKET. WINDOWS everywhere opened above markets. A city of markets, a city of windows.

New Crobuzon again. Unceasing, unstintingly itself. Warm that spring, gamy: the rivers were stinking. Noisy. Uninterrupted New Crobuzon.

What circled around and over the city's upreached fingers? Birdlife, aerial vermin, wyrmen (laughing, monkey-footed things), and airships of cool colours, and smoke and clouds. The natural inclines of the land were all forgotten by New Crobuzon, which rose or fell according to quite other whims: it was mazed in three dimensions. Tons of brick and wood, concrete, marble and iron, earth, water, straw and daub, made roofs and walls.

In the days the sun burned away the colours of those walls, burned the raggedy ends of posters that covered them like feathers, making them all slowly a tea-yellow. Oddments of ink told of old entertainments, while concrete desiccated. There was the famous

stencil-painting of the Iron Councillor, repeated in incompetent series by some dissident graffitist. There were skyrails, strung between jags of architecture like the broken-off pillars of some godly
vault. The wires sliced air and made sound, so wind played New
Crobuzon as an instrument.

Night brought new light, elyctro-barometric tubes of glowing
gas, glass in convolutes, made to spell out names and words or
sketch pictures in outline. A decade gone they had not existed or
had been very long forgotten: now the streets after dark were all
dappled by their distinct and vivid glare, washing out the gaslamps.

There was such noise. It came without remorse. There were always people everywhere. New Crobuzon.

". . . and then the *othe*r op-er-at-or told the *form*al in-stee-gay-tor
that his *suit* could not be heard the very *thought* was quite absurd . . ."

On stage chanteuse Adeleine Gladner, under her singing name
Adely Gladly (pronounced to rhyme, *Aderly Gladerly*), yelled and
crooned through her number "Formal Instigation" to applause and
catcalls drunken but loud and totally heartfelt. She minced, kicking
under her skirts (her costume a long-dated exaggeration of a streetwalker's flounces, so she looked more coy than libertine). She shook
her lace trimmings at the punters and smiled, scooping up the flowers they threw without breaking her song.

Her celebrated voice was everything it was held to be, raucous
and very beautiful. The audience were hers completely. Ori Ciuraz,
at the rear of the hall, was sardonic but by no means immune. He
did not know the others at his table well, only to tip his glass to.
They watched Adely while he watched them.

Fallybeggar's Hall was huge, clogged with smoke and drug
smells. In the boxes and raised circle were the big men and their
hangers-on, and sometimes the big women too. Francine 2 the
khepri queenpin came here. Ori could not see well over the fringe

of plaster drakows and obscene spirits, but he knew that the figure he saw moving in that box was a player in the militia, and that that one was one of the Fishbone Brothers, and that in that one was a captain of industry.

Up close to the orchestra by the stage it was a cramped clot of men and women, polyglot and many-raced, gazing at Adely's ankles. Ori tracked tribal boundaries.

A slick of vagabonds, petty thieves and their bosses, discharged foreign soldiers, discharged jailbirds, dissolute rich and tinkers, beggars, pimps and their charges, chancers, knife-grinders, poets and police agents. Humans, here and there cactus-heads poking over the crowd (allowed in only if their thorns were plucked), the scarab-heads of khepri. Cigarillos hung from mouths, and people banged their glasses or cutlery in time while waiters went between them on the sawdusted floor. At the room's edges small groups coagulated, and one like Ori—well-used to Fallybeggar's—could see where they overlapped and where they separated, and make out their composition.

There must be militia in the hall, but none wore uniforms. At the back the tall and muscled man, Derisov, was an agent— everyone knew it but did not know how high or how connected he was, so would not risk killing him. Near him a group of artists, debating their schools and movements with sectarian passion.

Closer to Ori and watching him, a table of well-turned-out young men, New Quillers, dry-spitting ostentatiously when any xenian came too close. They would hate Ori more than khepri or cactus, as he was race-renegade; and emboldened suddenly by the environs, by cosmopolitan and raucous Fallybeggar's, Ori raised his head to meet their gazes and put his arm around the old she-vodyanoi beside him. She turned in surprise but, seeing the Quillers, gave a grunt of approval and leaned into Ori, making exaggerated eyes at him and them in turn.

"Good lad," she said, but with his heart fast Ori would only stare at the four men who watched him. One spoke angrily to his companions but was hushed, and the one who quieted him raised his eyebrows to Ori and tapped his watch and mouthed *later*.

Ori was not afraid. His own tribe were near. He almost nodded at the Quiller in sarky challenge, but such complicity revolted him and he turned away. He could see his friends and comrades at their arguments, disagreeing more fiercely than the painters, but they would come together to fight with him if needed. And there were several of them. The Quillers could not face the insurrectionists.

The crowd were raving for Adely by now, singing along with her show-opener and making delighted pitter-patter motions with their fingers as she concluded—"once a*gain*, in the *raaaaain*"—and then becoming delirious with applause. The Quillers, artists, and all the other grouplets joined in with no restraint.

"Oh now thank you all, oh you're my darlings, oh you are," she said into the cheers and, professional as she was, they could hear her. She said: "I came out here to say good evening and ask you all to show a bit of willing to them who's come up here tonight, give 'em a good welcome, let 'em know you love 'em. It's their first time, some of 'em, and we all know what the first time's like, don't we? Bit of a disappointment, ain't it, girls?" They broke up with laughter at that, and in anticipation because it was so obvious a lead-in to her song "Are You Done?" And yes, there was the familiar comedy hoboy quacking like a duck, the opening bars, and Adely drew in a big breath, paused, then shouted "Later!" and ran offstage, to light-hearted boos and shouts of *tease!*

The first act came into the lights. A singing family, two children done up as dolls and their mother playing a pianospiel. Most of the audience ignored them.

Cow, thought Ori. She came on, Adely, and seemed so generous ushering in the beginners. But the crowd were there for her, so her little surprise opener could only weigh heavy on those who had to follow. She'd made them disappointments, no matter how good they were. Hard enough to come before a big name without sabotage like that, however sweetly done. Everyone would be limping through their acts, the audience eager to get back to Adely.

The harmony threesome gave way to a dancer. He was aging but agile, and Ori out of politeness paid attention, but he was one of only a few. Then a singing comedian, a poor hack who would have been jeered with or without Adely's intervention.

All the entertainers were pure, unRemade human stock. It concerned Ori—he did not know if it was coincidence that with these Quillers looking on there were no xenian performers. Was the New Quill Party pulling strings at Fallybeggar's? The suspicion was hateful.

At last the useless comedian was done. It was time for the final warm-up. THE FLEXIBLE PUPPET THEATRE, it said on the handbills. PERFORMING THE SAD AND INSTRUCTIONAL TALE OF JACK HALF-A-PRAYER. It was them Ori had come to see. He was not there for Adely Gladly.

There were minutes of preparations behind the curtain, while the audience chatted about the main event, the Dog Fenn Songbird. Ori knew what the Flexible Puppet Theatre were getting ready, and he smiled.

When the velvet finally parted it did so without brass or percussion, and the performers waited, so for seconds there was no notice, until a couple of little gasps as the tobacco smoke seemed to clear and show the stage-within-a-stage. There were oaths. Ori saw one of the Quillers stand.

There was the usual—the cart-sized puppet theatre with its little carved figures in garish clothes stock-still on their stage—but the miniature wings and proscenium arch had been torn off, and the puppeteers stood in plain view dressed too-nearly like militia officers in dark grey. And the stage was littered with other things, strange debris. A sheet was stretched and hammered taut and on it some magic lantern was projecting newspaper print. There were people onstage whose roles were unclear, a gang of actors, and musicians, the Flexibles disdaining the house orchestra for an unkempt trio who wore pipes and flutes and held drumsticks by pieces of sheet steel.

Ori flashed his upturned thumb at the stage. His friends were standing dead still and silent until the mutters grew intrusive and slightly threatening, and from the back came a shout of *piss off*. And then with a massive, painful sound, someone pounded the metal. Instantly and underneath that still-reverberating noise another music-man struck a lovely, lively tune half-modelled on street-chants, and his companion played the steel gently like a snare. An actor stepped forward—he was immaculate in a suit, waxed moustaches—bowed slightly, tipped his hat to the ladies in the front row, and bellowed an obscenity just-hidden from the censor by a consonant inserted at its beginning, an unconvincing nonsense-word.

And there was outrage again. But these Flexibles were consummate—arrogant pranksters yes but serious—and they played their audience with skill, so that after every such imposition was quick and funny dialogue, or jaunty music, and it was hard to sustain anger. But it was an extraordinary challenge or series of challenges and the crowd vacillated between bewilderment and discontent. Ori realised it was a question of how much of the play they could get done before it was unsafe to perform.

No one was sure what it was they were seeing, this structureless thing of shouts and broken-up lines and noises, and cavalcades of intricate incomprehensible costumes. The puppets were elegantly manoeuvred, but they should have been—were designed to be—wooden players in traditionalist moral tales, not these little pro-vocateurs whose puppeteers had them speak back tartly to the narrator, contradict him (always in the puppets' traditional register, a cod-childish language of compound nouns and onomatopoeia), and dance to the noise and mum lewdness as far as their joints and strings would allow.

Images, even animations—pictures in such quick cycles that they jumped and ran or fired their guns—came in stuttering succession onto the screen. The narrator harangued the audience and argued with the puppets and the other actors, and over growing dissent from the stalls the story of Jack Half-a-Prayer emerged in chaotic form. This stilled the angry crowd somewhat—it was a popular story, and they wanted to see what this anarchic Nuevist crew would do with it.

The barebones introduction was familiar. "No one of us'll forget, I'm sure," the narrator said and he was right, no one could, it was only twenty years ago. The puppets sketched it out. Some obscure betrayal and Jack Half-a-Prayer, the legendary Jack, the fRee-made boss, was caught. They cut his great mantis claw from his right hand—they'd given it to him in the punishment factories, but he'd used it against them, so they took it away. The puppets made this a scene gruesome with red-ribbon blood.

Of course the militia always said he was a bandit and a murderer, and he did kill, no one doubted that. But like most versions of the story, this one showed him as he was remembered: champion-rogue, hero. Jack got caught and it was a sad story, and the censors let the people have it so.

It wasn't quite a public hanging they gave him—that wasn't in the constitution—but they found a way to show him off. They'd tethered him on a giant stocks in BilSantum Plaza outside Perdido Street Station for days, and the overseer had used his whip at the slightest wriggle, deeming it resistance. They paid people to jeer, it was mostly agreed. Plenty of Crobuzoners came and didn't cheer at all. There were those who said it was not the real Jack—*he's no claw, they've found some poor bugger and lopped off his hand, is all*—but their tone was more despairing than convinced.

The puppets came and went in front of the little plywood whipping post to which the wooden Jack was strapped.

And then *da-da-da-da-da* went the metal drum. All of the actors on the stage began to shout and gesture at the militia-puppets, and the screen came up with the word EVERYONE! and even the sceptical audience played along and began to shout *over here, over here*. That was how it had been—a diversion from some in the crowd, orchestrated or chance was debated, though Ori had his own thoughts. As the militia dangled across the little puppet-stage, Ori remembered.

It was a young memory, a child's memory—he did not know why he had been in the plaza or with whom. It was the first time for years the militia had been seen like that in their uniforms, had been a forerunner of their turn from covert policing, and in a grey wedge they had targeted the shouting segment of crowd. The overseer had drawn a flintlock and dropped his whip and joined them, and left the tethered figure.

Ori did not remember seeing the rough man who had ascended toward Jack Half-a-Prayer until he was near the top. He had a vivid image of him, but he did not know if that was his six-year-old's memory or one constructed from all the reports he had later heard. The man—here came his puppet now, look, on the stage, while the militia's backs were turned—had been distinctive. Hairless, viciously scarred, pocked as if by decades of ferocious acne, his eyes sunken and wide, dressed in rags, a scarf pulled over his mouth and nose to hide him.

The puppet that skulked exaggeratedly up the steps called out to Jack Half-a-Prayer with a harsh voice, a twenty-year-old echo of the real man's loud and piercing call. He called Jack's name, as he had that day. And neared him and pulled out a pistol and a knife (the puppet's little tinfoil constructions glinted). *Remember me, Jack?* he had shouted, and his puppet shouted. *I owe you this.* A voice like triumph.

For years after the murder of Jack Half-a-Prayer the plays had followed the first conventional understanding. The pockmarked man—brother, father or lover to one of the murdering Man'Tis's victims—was too moved by rage to wait, overcome and righteous and straining to kill. And though it was understandable and no one could blame him, the law did not work that way; and when they heard and saw him it was the militia's sad duty to warn him off, and when that didn't work to fire at him, putting an end to his plans, and killing the Half-a-Prayer with stray bullets. And it was regrettable, as the legal process had not yet been completed, but it could hardly have been in any doubt that the outcome would soon have been the same.

That was the story for years, and the actors and puppeteers played Jack as the pantomime baddie, but noticed that the crowds still cheered him.

In the second decade after the events, new interpretations had emerged, in response to the question, *Why had Half-a-Prayer shouted in what sounded like delight when the man came for him?* Witnesses recalled the torn-skinned man raising his pistol, and thought that they had perhaps seen Jack strain as if to meet him and then *of course* a *mercy* killing. One of Jack's gang, risking his own life to bring the humiliations of his boss to an end. And maybe he had succeeded—could anyone be sure it was a militia bullet that had ended the Remade captive? Maybe that first shot was a friend saving a friend.

The audiences liked that much more. Now Jack Half-a-Prayer was back as he had been in graffiti for decades—champion. The story became a grand and vaguely instructional tragedy of hopes noble-but-doomed, and though Jack and his nameless companion were now the heroes, the city's censors allowed it, to the surprise of many. In some productions the newcomer took Jack's life then ended his own, in others was shot dead as he fired. The death scenes of both men had become more and more protracted. The truth, as Ori understood it—that though Jack had been left dead and lolling in his harness the pock-faced man had disappeared, his fate uncertain—was not mentioned.

Up the little stairs ran the scarred-man puppet, his weapons outstretched, scooping up the overseer's dropped whip (a complicated arrangement of pins and threads facilitating the movement), as tradition said he had done. But *what was this*? "What is this?" the narrator shouted. Ori smiled—he had seen the script. He was clenching his fists.

"Why pick up the whip?" the narrator said. Having been caught in the rude charm of the Nuevist production, the Quillers were definitely standing now, shouting again *shame, shame*. "Iber gotter gun," said the scarred-man puppet directly to the audience over their rising cries. "Iber gotter knifey. Whybe gonner pick anubber?"

"I've an idea, pock-boy," said the narrator.

"Ibey idear already too, see?" the puppet said back. "One an *dese*," holding out the gun and the whip, "tain't fer me, see?" An elegant little mechanism spun the pistol in his wooden hand so that suddenly he held it out butt-first, a *gift* for his tethered friend, and he took his knife to Jack Half-a-Prayer's bonds.

A heavy glass trailed beer as it arced over the crowd to burst wetly. *Treason!* came the calls, but there were others now, people standing and shouting *yes, yes, tell it like it is!* Dogged, only dancing over the skittering glass, the Flexible Puppet Theatre continued with their new version of the classic, where the two little figures were not doomed or cursed with visions too pure to sustain or beaten by a world that did not deserve them, but were still fighting, still trying to win.

They were inaudible over the shouting. Food pelted the stage. A disturbance, and the master of ceremonies came on, his suit rumpled. He was hurried, almost pushed on by a thin young man— a clerk from the Office of Censorship who listened backstage through all registered performances. His job had abruptly stopped being routine.

"Enough, you have to stop," shouted the MC and tried to pull the puppets away. "I've been informed, this performance is *over*."

He was shocked out of his pompous patter. Thrown scraps hit him, so he cowered even more than he already was. The supporters of the Flexibles were few but loud, and they were demanding the show continue, but seeing Fallybeggar's man lose control the young censor himself stepped up and spoke to the audience.

"This performance is cancelled. This troupe is guilty of Rudeness to New Crobuzon in the Second Degree, and is hereby disbanded pending an enquiry." *Fuck you, shame, get off, show must go on. What rudeness? What rudeness?* The young censor was quite unintimidated, and was damned if he'd put this dissidence into words. "The militia have been called, and on their arrival, all still here will be deemed complicit with the performance. Please leave the premises immediately." The mood was too mean for dispersal.

There was more glass in the air and the screams that told it had landed. Quillers were targeting the stage, Ori saw, heading to beat the performers, and he pushed himself up and indicated to nearby friends and they headed off to intercept the knuckle-cracking Quillers, and the riot blossomed.

Adely Gladly ran out, already in her risqué costume, and shouted for peace. Ori saw her, just before he split his fist on the back of some Quill-scum head, then looked back at the matter in hand. On the stage the Flexible Puppet Theatre were scooping all their props out of the way. Over the noise of beating and shouts and percussions of glass the wonderful voice of the Dog Fenn Songbird begged for the fighting to stop, and no one paid her any notice.

CHAPTER SEVEN

THE PLAY WAS DEFUNCT AND DONE, AND THE MILITIA WHEN THEY came were more concerned with clearing the building than with making arrests. Ori blocked the Quillers long enough for the puppeteers to clear their pieces, and with the Flexibles he ducked backstage past brawls that were now mostly drunken, without political hatreds to refine them.

They came out into an alley, bloodied but laughing, a mass of theatre people stuffing costumes into carpet bags, and one or two like Ori, observers. It had rained a little moments before, but the night was warm, so the film of water seemed like the city's sweat.

Petron Carrickos, who had been the narrator, pulled his moustache off, leaving its ghost in spirit gum above his lip, and stuck it on the alley's lone poster, giving the revivalist whose sermons it advertised thick eyebrows. Ori went west with him and several others to Cadmium Street. They would double back and head for Salacus Fields Station without passing Fallybeggar's entrance.

Late but not so late, the streets where Salacus met Howl Barrow were full. There were militia on corners. Ori jostled through late

window-shoppers and theatre-goers, the music-lovers at voxiterator booths, a few golems like giant marionettes, wearing their
owners' sashes. There were markings on walls. Illicit galleries and
theatres, artists' squats, signposted by graffiti for those who could
read it. Salacus Fields itself was becoming colonised by the weekend
bohemians. There had always been moneyed slummers, bad-boy
younger children seeking tawdry redemption or dissolution, but
now their visits were temporary and their transformations tourist.
Ori felt contempt. Artists and musicians were moving out as agents
and merchants moved in and rents rose, even while industry floun-
dered. So to Howl Barrow.

The streets sputtered under the bilious elyctro-barometric
shopsigns. Ori nodded at the faces he knew from meetings or
performances—a woman by the silversmith's door, a thickset
cactus-man handing out flyers. Brickwork buckled and held on,
and leaned house on house, repaired in a patchwork of metal and
cement, paint in anarchic styles, and spirals and obscenities; and
coming out and over into the sky were temple spires and lookout
pitches for the militia, and towerblocks. The crowds were thinning
as the evening went toward deep night.

By raised train through the roofs to Sly Station, changing platforms and bidding friends goodnight, till even Petron had gone for
Mog Hill, and Ori was alone among late-night travellers sprawled
on seats and smelling of gin. He stepped past some in overalls from
late shifts, who turned to not look at the drunkards. Ori sat next to
an older woman, and followed her gaze through dirt-stained glass
into the miles of city, a fen of buildings thick with glints. The train
crossed the river. The woman was staring at nothing in particular,
Ori realised, and it caught his attention too—just a juddering of
lights at some intersection, a kink of city.

The windows of Ori's street in Syriac were mostly uncurtained, and
when he woke he looked out and in gaslamp-light saw large still figures standing in their houses, sleeping. It was a street colonised by

cactacae. He rented from a kind, gruff she-cactus who had effortlessly hefted his bags in one greenling hand when he had moved in.

The small-hours' trains passed the top windows shining dimly.
They went to The Downs southerly or on north up to their huge
terminus, that synapse of troublesome architecture between the
city's rivers, Perdido Street Station.

The business of night continued. The air was warm and wet,
and it unstuck glue and ate at brickwork's pointing. From the oldest parts of the city, tough hut-work, ivy-swaddled ruins in Sobek
Croix. Families slept rough in warehouses at the edges of Bonetown. Brock Marsh was crossed by cats, then by a badger waddling
home under cluttered shop facades. Sedate and baleful aerostats
waited below clouds.

Two rivers ran, and met, and became one big old thing, the
Gross Tar, guttersome and groaning as it passed out of city limits
through the stubs of a bridge, through shantytowns in New Crobuzon's orbit, looking for the sea. The city's illicit inhabitants came
out briefly and hid again. There was midnight industry. Someone
was always awake, countless someones, in towerblocks or elegant
houses or the redstones of Chnum or in the xenian ghettos, in the
Glasshouse or the terraces of Kinken and Creekside, configured by
the khepri grubs, reshaped with brittled insect spit. Everything continued.

There was nothing of the riot in any news-sheets the following day,
or the next. It did not stop people hearing something had happened.

Ori made it known to the right people that he had been there.
Passing the shops and pubs of Syriac he saw that he was seen, and
knew that some who glanced at him—the woman here, the vodyanoi, the man or cactus-man, even the Remade there—were with
the Caucus. Not showing his excitement, Ori might pat his chest
gently with a fist in surreptitious greeting, which they might ignore

or might thump back at him. Between themselves the Caucusers flashed complicated finger-shapes, messages in downtown hand-slang Ori could not decipher. He told himself they were perhaps about him.

The Caucus, in its closed and hidden session, talking about him. He knew it wasn't so, but it delighted him to think it. Yes, his friends were Nuevists, but not decadent or wastrel nor satisfied only to shock. He thought of the Caucus, delegates from all the factions, breaking off from consideration of strategy and rebellion, breaking off from evasion of the militia and their informers, to commend Ori Ciuraz and his friends for a fine provocation. It wouldn't happen, but he liked it.

In Gross Coil, Ori took what day-work came his way. He hauled and delivered for food and poor pay. Gun-grey components of some military machine that must be heading around the coast and through the Meagre Sea and the straits and on to the distant war. He worked at whatever siding or yard, whatever wreckers would take him, unloading barges by Mandrake Bridge, and when the days were done he drank with workmates become temporary friends.

He was young, so the foremen bullied him, but nervously. They were edged with unease. There were all the troubles. Tense times for the factories of Gross Coil, for Kelltree and Echomire. Past the foundry on Tuthen Way, Ori saw scars from fires on the ground, where in recent weeks pickets had been. The walls were marked with sigils of dissidence. *Toro; The Man'Tis lives!;* the stencilled councillor. Bullet holes marked walls at the Tricorn Fork, where less than a year before the militia had faced down hundreds of marchers.

It had started at the Paradox Concerns, in unorganised complaint at some dismissals, and then had been on the streets with great speed, and shop floors in the surrounds were fractured as others joined the demonstrators, whose slogans had veered from reinstatement of friends to increased wages, then were suddenly denunciations of the Mayor and of the suffrage lottery, were demands for votes. Bottles were thrown, and caustic phlogiston; there were shots—the militia shot back or started it—and sixteen people were dead. Chalked homages appeared regularly at the junction and were cleaned away. Ori touched his fist gently to his chest as he passed the site of the Paradox Massacre.

On Chainday he went to The Grocer's Sweetheart. A bit before eight, two men left the taproom and did not come back. Others followed, in casual and random order. Ori drank the last of his beer and went as if for the privy, but seeing he was not followed he turned down a damp-mottled corridor, lifted a trapdoor down into the basement. Those assembled in the dark looked and did not greet him, almost as much suspicion as welcome on their faces.

"Chaverim," he said to them. A category stolen from an old language. "Chaver," they said back—comrade, equal, conspirator.

One Remade man, and it was the first time he had come. His arms were crossed at the wrists and were fused, and when he clenched and unclenched his fingers it was as if he imitated a bird.

There were two women from a sweatshop under the Skulkford railway arches, knit-machine workers, by a docker and a machinist, and a vodyanoi clerk in light-cloth mimicry of a human suit that he could wear in the water, complete with stitched-on tie. A cactus-man stood. The barrels of cheap beer and wine served as tables for dissident publications: a crumpled *Shout*, *The Forge*, and several copies of the best-known seditionist sheet, *Runagate Rampant*.

"Chaverim, I want to thank you for coming." A middle-aged man spoke with calm authority. "I want to welcome our new friend Jack." He nodded at the Remade. "War with Tesh. Militia infiltration. Free trade unions. The strike at Purrill's Bakery. I've word on each of those. But I want to take a few minutes to talk about my approach—our approach, *Double-R*'s approach—to the question of race." He glanced at the vodyanoi, at the cactus-man, and began to speak.

It was these introductions, these discussions, that had first brought Ori close to the *Runagate Rampant* circles. He had bought a copy every fortnight for three months from a fruit-seller in Murkside, and eventually the man had asked him whether he was interested in talking through the issues covered, had directed Ori to these hidden meetings. Ori had been a regular, raising more points and objections, engaging with more enthusiasm—and eventually less—until after one meeting, while they were alone, with affecting trust the convenor had told Ori his real name, Curdin. Ori had responded, though like everyone they still went by Jack to each other within the meetings.

"Yes, yes," Curdin was saying, "I think that's right, Jack, but the question is *why*?"

Ori unfolded his *Runagate Rampant,* read it in snippets. Exhortations for unity in action that he had seen before, angry and illuminating analyses, columns and columns of strikes. Each workplace, each two or three people who had put their tools down, won or lost, a gathering of twenty or a hundred, a half-hour walkout, the disappearance of every guildsmember or suspected unioner. A catalogue of every dispute, murderous or paltry. It bored him.

There were stories missing. Ori's frustrations with the meetings was growing. Nothing was happening here. It was elsewhere, though, fleetingly. As in Fallybeggar's.

He tapped his *Runagate Rampant.* "Where's Toro?" he said. "Toro took another one. I heard it. In Chnum. Him and his crew took out the guards, shot the magister that lived there. Why's that not in here?"

"Jack . . . it's clear what we say about Toro," Curdin said. "We had the column last-but-one issue. We don't . . . it ain't the way we'd do things . . ."

"I know, Jack, I know. You criticise. Carp at him."

The convenor said nothing.

"Toro's out there and he's *doing* something, yeah? He's fight-ing, and he's not *waiting* like you keep waiting. And you sit and *wait,* and tell him he's getting ahead of himself?"

"It's not like that. I won't snip at anyone fighting the magisters, or the militia, or the Mayor, but Toro can't change things on his own, or with his little crew, Jack . . ."

"Yeah but he's changing something."

"Not enough."

"But he's changing *something.*"

Ori respected Curdin, had learnt so much from him and his pamphlets, he did not want to alienate him. But the complacency of his convenor had begun to infuriate him. The man was more than twice his age—was he just old? They sat and glowered at each other wordlessly while the others looked back and forth between them.

Afterward Ori apologised for his bad temper. "It's nothing to me," said Curdin. "Be as rude as you want. But I tell you the truth, Jack"—they were alone and he corrected himself—"I tell you the truth, Ori. I'm worried. Seems to me you're going down a certain road. All your plays and puppets . . ." He shook his head and sighed. "I ain't against it, I swear to you, I heard what happened at Fally-beggar's and, you know, good on you, on your friends. But shock and shooting ain't enough. Let me ask you something. Your friends the Flexible Puppeteers—why'd they choose that name?"

"You know why."

"No I don't. I know it's a homage, and I'm glad for that, but why *him,* why not Seshech or Billy le Ginsen, why not Poppy Lutkin?"

"Because we'd get arrested if we tried that."

"Don't play stupid, lad. You know what I mean—there's scores of names you could've chose to send a message, to piss in the Mayor's bath, but you honoured *him.* The founding editor of *Runa-gate Rampant*—not *The Forge* or *Toilers' War* or *The Bodkin.* Why him?" Curdin tapped his paper against his thigh. "I'll tell you why, lad—whether you know it or not, he's the one scares the powers. Because he was *right*. About factions, about war, about the plurality. And Bill and Poppy and Neckling Verdant, and them others—Toro, Ori, Toro and his band and all, even Jack Half-a-Prayer—good people, *chaverim*, but on stuff like this their strategy's for shit. Ben was right, and Toro's wrong."

Ori heard arrogance, or commitment, or fervour, or analysis in Curdin's voice. Angry as he was, he did not care to disentangle them.

"You going to sneer at Half-a-Prayer now?"

"I didn't mean that, I ain't saying that . . ."

"Godspit, who you think you are? Toro's *doing* things, Curdin. He's making things happen. You—you're *talking, Double-R*'s just talking. And Benjamin Flex is *dead*. Been dead for a long time."

"You ain't being fair," he heard Curdin say. "You ain't hardly got fluff on your chin, and you're telling *me* about Benjamin Flex, for Jabber's sake." And his voice was not unkind. He meant it lightly, but Ori was outraged.

"At least I *done* something!" he shouted. "At least I'm doing *something*."

CHAPTER EIGHT

NO ONE SEEMED TO KNOW WHAT HAD STARTED THE WAR WITH Tesh. The Runagaters had their theories, and there were official stories and the unseen machinations behind them, but among Ori's circle no one knew quite what had started it, or even exactly when it had begun.

As the long recession had bitten, years before, merchant ships from New Crobuzon had started returning to dock reporting piratical manoeuvres against them, sudden brigandry from unknown ships. The city's exploration and its trade were under attack. History was marked by New Crobuzon's oscillations between autarky and engagement, but never, its wounded captains said, had its emergence into mercantilism been so punished, so unexpectedly.

After centuries of uncertainty and strange relations, the city had made understandings with the Witchocracy, and the passage of New Crobuzon ships through the Firewater Straits had been unhindered. So a sea-route was open to the grasslands and islands, the legendary places on the far side of the continent. Ships came back

and said they had been to Maru'ahm. They sailed for years and
brought back jewelled cakes from thousands of miles away, from
the crocodile double-city called The Brothers. And then the piracy
had begun, hard, and New Crobuzon came slowly to understand
that it was being attacked.

The arcane Tesh ships, the barquentines and dandy catboats all
raggedy with coloured cloth, whose crews wore henna and filed
their teeth, had ceased coming to New Crobuzon's docks. There was
a rumour that through long-disused channels, Tesh's secret and
hidden ambassador had told the Mayor that their two states were at
war.

Reports of Tesh depredations in the Firewater Straits became
more common and higher-profile, in the papers and government
newsposters. The Mayor had promised revenge and counterattack.
Recruitment to the New Crobuzon Navy was intensified, along, Ori
heard, with "booze recruitment"—press-ganging.

It was still distant, abstract: battles at sea thousands of miles off.
But it had escalated. It had featured more and more in the speeches
of ministers. The city's new mercantilism was unrewarded; markets
did not open for its exports; the war blocked its sources of uncommon commodities. Ships went and did not come back. New Crobuzon's boarded-up plants did not reopen, and others closed, and the
signs on their doors grew mildew that mocked their proclamations
of "temporary suspension of industry." The city was stagnant; it
slumped and slummed. Survivors began to come home.

Destroyed soldiers left to beg and preach their experiences to
crowds in Dog Fenn and Riverskin. Scarred, their bones crushed,
cut by the enemy or in frantic battlefield surgery, they also bore
stranger wounds that only Tesh's troops could have given them.

Hundreds of the returned had been made mad, and in their
mania they raved in unknown sibilant tongue, all of them across
the city speaking the same words together, in time. There were men
whose eyes were haemorrhaged blood-sacs but who still had sight,

Ori heard, who cried without ceasing as they saw the death in everything. The crowds were afraid of the veterans, as if at their own bad conscience. Once, many months ago, Ori had come past a man haranguing the horrified crowd and showing them his arms, which were bleached a dead grey.

"You know what this is!" he was shouting at them. "You know! I was at the edge of a blast, and you see? The sawbones tried to take my arms, told me they had to go, but they just *didn't want you to see* . . ." He waggled his ghastly limbs like paper cutouts, and the militia came and stifled him, took him away. But Ori had seen the onlookers' terror. Had Tesh truly remembered the lost science of colourbombs?

So many uncertainties, a spiralling-down of morale, fear in the city. New Crobuzon's government had mobilised. For two, three years now it had been the time of the Special Offensive. There was more death and more industry. Everyone knew someone who had gone to war, or disappeared from a dockside pub. The shipyards of Tarmuth, that estuary satellite town, had begun to push out iron-clads and submersibles and had spurred something of a recovery, and the mills and forges of New Crobuzon followed, war turning their gears.

Guilds and unions were outlawed capriciously, or restricted and emasculated. There were new jobs now for some of those grown used to pauperism, though competition for them was cruel. New Crobuzon was stretched out, pulled taut.

Every age had its social bandits. Jack Half-a-Prayer when Ori was a boy, Bridling in the Week of Dust, Alois and her company a century ago. Jabber himself, if one looked at it a certain way. Made strange by their context, overthrowing rules: the crowds who would spit on the Remade would have sworn themselves to Half-a-Prayer. Doubtless some were imagined by history, mean little cutpurses embellished through centuries. But some were real: Ori would swear by Jack. And now there was Toro.

* * *

Skullday, Ori ran with the Nuevists. He took his day-wages and joined them in The Two Maggots pub by Barrow Bridge, and with the beetle-spit-smeared rooftops of Kinken visible over the river they played games and argued about art. The students and exiles of the arts quarter were always happy to see Ori because he was one of a handful of real labourers in the circle. In the evening Ori and Petron and several others staged an art-incident, dressing as pantomime pigs, parading to Salacus Fields and past The Clock and Cockerel, long fallen on its honour, where the parvenus and uptown posers came to play at bohemia. The Nuevists grunted at the drinkers and shouted "Ah, nostalgia!" in porcine voices.

Dustday Ori stevedored, and drank in the evening in a workers' pub in Skulkford. Among the smoke and beer-laughter, he missed the flamboyance of The Two Maggots. A barmaid caught his eye, and he recognised her from some illicit meeting. She folded back her apron for him to see the *Runagate Rampant*s in her pinny pocket, inviting him to buy, and the resentment and frustration he had felt for Curdin came back to him hard.

He shook his head so brusquely she obviously thought she had misremembered. Her eyes widened. Poor woman, he had not meant to scare her. He persuaded her that he was safe to talk to. He called her Jack. "I'm tired of it," he whispered. "Tired of *Runagate Rampant*, forever saying what's what but never *doing* anything, tired of waiting for change which don't come." He executed a ridiculous handslang parody.

"What's the point, you saying?" she said.

"No, I know there's a point . . ." Ori poked the table in fervour. "I been reading this stuff for months now. I mean . . . but the militia are doing something. Quillers are doing something. And the only ones on *our* side doing anything are nutcases like the Excess League or bandits like Toro."

"But I mean you ain't serious, right?" Jack let her tone come down carefully. "I mean, you know the limitations . . ."

"Godspit and *shit,* Jack, don't start with 'the limits of individual action' right now. I'm just tired. Sometimes, don't you sometimes wish you *didn't care*? I mean course you want a change, we want a change, but if a change ain't godsdamn coming, then the next thing I wish is that I *didn't care.*"

Fishday evening Ori disembarked at Saltpetre Station. In the smoggy gloaming, he went through the brickwork warrens of Griss Fell, past householders scrubbing their porches of the grit of machinofacture and graffitied coils, chatting from window to window across the little streets. In an old stable, a soup kitchen doled out bowls to a line of destitutes. Nominally the charity was run from Kinken, and keeping order were a trio of khepri armed in imitation of their guard-gods, the Tough Sisters, with crossbow and flintlock, spear and hooknet, and one with the metaclockwork stingbox.

The khepri stretched their lean and vivid women's bodies. They spoke to each other without sound, moving the antennae and headlegs of their headscarabs, the iridescent two-foot beetles at the top of their necks. They vented chymical gusts. They turned to Ori—he was reflected in their compound eyes—and recognised him, waved him to one of the cauldrons. He began to dole out soup to patient tramps.

Kinken money had started the service, but it was kept running by locals. When the Mayor said the city could not provide for the needy, alternative structures arose. To shame New Crobuzon's rulers or out of despair, various groupings provided social programs. They were inadequate and oversubscribed, and one spawned another as the sects competed.

In Spit Hearth they were run by the churches: care of the old and the orphaned and poor was in the hands of hierophants, monks and nuns. With their ersatz hospitals and kitchens, apostate and zealot sects built up trust that a thousand years of preaching would not have gained them. Seeing that, the New Quill party had started its own human-only relief in Sunter, to complement its street-fighting. The insurrectionists, who would be arrested instantly they went public, could not follow.

They followed Kinken money instead—it came, they heard, from Francine 2, the khepri crime-queen. It was not unknown for the captains of illicit industry to subsidise such charities: in Bonetown Mr. Motley was reputed to keep local loyalty with his own goodwill trusts. But wherever the money came from, the Griss Fell Retreat was run by locals, and the Caucus tried carefully to be known to be involved.

With a few Caucusists from various tendencies working together alongside the unaffiliated, it could be fractious. The activists had to whisper their tea-break debates.

Ori spooned broth into bowls. He recognised the faces of many of the outcasts; he knew some of their names. Many were Remade. A woman whose eyes had been taken in punishment, her face a skin seal from nose to hairline, shuffled past holding the rag-coat of her companion. Mostly human but not all, there were other races too, on hard times. An ancient cactus-man, his spines withered and brittle. Men and women scarred. There were some whose minds were gone, who sang hymns or yammered nonsense words, or asked questions that made no sense. "Are you a doubler?" a lank-haired oldster asked everyone who passed, the ancient remains of some accent still audible. "Are you a doubler? Are you excessive? Are you proscribed? Are you a doubler, son?"

"Ori. Come for absolution?" Ladia was the full-timer on duty. She teased all the volunteers that they came only to unload guilt. She was not stupid—she knew their allegiances. When Ori took a break, she joined him and poured liquor in his tea. He knew their conversation could not be heard over the table manners of the starving.

"You're like Toro," he told her. "You're the only ones *doing* anything, making changes *here,* now."

"I knew it. I knew you was here because you felt guilty," she said. She made it light. "Doing your bit."

He finished his shift, and kept his patience. Ori muttered to those momentarily in his care. Some smiled and spoke back to him; some cussed him with alcohol or very-tea on their breath. "Are you excessive? Are you proscribed? Are you a doubler?" the insistent old man said to him. Ori took his bowl away.

"You are," the old man said. "You *are* a doubler. You're a doubler, you little terror." The man smiled like a saint and was pointing at Ori's midriff, where his shirt had fallen forward and exposed his belt, and tucked into it a folded copy of *Runagate Rampant, Double-R*.

Ori tucked his shirt back in, careful not to be furtive. He washed the bowls at the pump (the man chuckling and pulling at his beard, and saying *you are, you doubler* at Ori's back). He did another round of the room, made it slow, offering last dabs of bread, and came back to the laughing man.

"I am," he said, conversational and quiet. "I'm a doubler, but it's best you keep that down, mate. I'd rather not everyone knows, understand? Keep it secret, eh?"

"Oh yes." The man's manner changed quite suddenly. The cunning of madness came over him, and he lowered his voice. "Oh yes, we can do that, isn't it? Good people them doublers. You doublers. And them excessive, and free and proscribed."

The Excess Faction, the Free Union, the League of the Proscribed—it was not just *Runagate Rampant;* the old man was itemising groups in the Caucus.

"Good people but *blather,*" he said and snapped his hand open and shut like a talkative mouth. "All a bit blatheration." Ori smiled and nodded. "They like talking. And you know, that's all right, talking's good. Ain't always . . . blather."

"Who's the old boy?" Ori said to Ladia.

"Spiral Jacobs," she said. "Poor old mad sod. Has he found someone to talk to? Has he decided he likes you, Ori? Decided you're proscribed, or free, a doubler?" Ori stared at her, could not tell if she knew what she was saying. "Has he started on at you about arms or tongues?" She shouted, "Arms and tongues, Spiral!" and waggled her arms and stuck out her tongue, and the old man crowed and did the same. "He's for the first, against the second, as I recall," she said to Ori. "Has he chanted for you? 'Too much yammer, not enough hammer.' "

As Ori left that evening, another of the volunteers met him at the door, a kind and stupid man. "Saw you talking to Ladia about Spiral Jacobs," he said. He grinned. He whispered, "Heard what they say about him? What he used to do? He was with Jack Half-a-Prayer! Swear to Jabber. He was in Jack's crew, and he knew Scarface, and he got away."

CHAPTER NINE

THE NEXT NIGHT SPIRAL JACOBS WAS NOT AT THE SHELTER, NOR THE next. The pleasure and surprise with which Ladia greeted Ori began to change. He saw her watch him to make sure he was not dealing drugs or contraband, but he worked hard, and she could only be puzzled.

On Skullday, as Ori swept the shelter floor, he heard, "Are you proscribed? Are you a doubler?" Spiral Jacobs saw him and smiled and said, "There's the boy. There you are, ain't you, you—" and he blinked and raised one finger and winked. He leaned in and whispered "You doubler."

One try, thought Ori. He made himself sceptical. One piece of indulgence for this casualty. Only when the food was all distributed and the first homeless families were coming in from begging or thievery to doss down did Ori idle to Spiral's side.

"Buy you a drink sometime?" Ori said. "Sounds like you and me've interests in common. Could chat about stuff. About doubling. About our friend Jack."

"Our friend, yes. Jack."

The man lay down in a blanket. Ori's patience diminished. Spiral Jacobs was digging something out, a bit of paper, dirt ground into its cross of folds. He showed Ori, with a child's grin.

It was cool when Ori walked home. He traced the route of the railway, by tracks carried over the slates on loops of brick, arches like a sea-snake. Light like gaslight or candlelight spilt from a train's dirty windows and sent shadows convulsing over the angled roofscape to hide, darkness creeping out again from behind chimneys in the engine's wake.

Ori walked fast with his head down and hands in pockets when he passed militia. He felt their eyes on him. They were difficult to see, their uniforms woven through with trow yarns that ate what light there was and excreted darkness. At night the clearest thing about them was their weaponry: they were armed, it seemed, at random, and in the dim he could see their batons or stingboxes, their dirks, rotating pistols.

He remembered twelve years ago, before the slump, to the Construct War, when for the first time in a century the militia tradition of covert policing—networks of spies, informants, plainclothes officers and decentralised fear—had become inadequate, and they had gone unhidden and uniformed. Ori did not remember the roots of the crisis. A child among others, with his boisterous gang he had mounted the roofs of Petty Coil and Brock Marsh on the Tar's north shore, and watched the militia barrage the Griss Twist dumps.

With children's aggression they had joined in the purge of the city's constructs, the panicked hounding of the clockwork and steam-powered cleaners suddenly deemed enemy. Mobs cornered and destroyed the welded, soldered things. Most of the constructs could only stand patient while they were torn apart, their glass trod into dust, their cables ripped.

There were some few that fought. The reason for the war. Infected with viral consciousness, programmes that should not be, that had infected New Crobuzon's constructs, the gears of their analytical engines turning in heretic combinations to spin a cold machine sentience. Thinking motors for which self-preservation was a predicate, that raised their metal, wood and pipework limbs against their erstwhile owners. Ori never saw it.

The militia had levelled Griss Twist's jungle of trash. They shelled it, rinsing it with fire, advancing in wrecking teams through the melt and ash-scape. There had been some kind of factory there for the pernicious programmes, and it and the monstrous mind behind it were destroyed. It had been a demon or something, or a council of the aware constructs and their flesh followers.

There were still constructs and difference engines in the city, but far fewer, strictly licenced. An economy of golems had half replaced them, making a few thaumaturges rich. Griss Twist's dumps were still bone-white and blackened wreckage. They were out of bounds, and New Crobuzon's children would climb or creep in and take souvenirs, and tell each other that the dumps were haunted by the ghosts of the machines. But the most lasting result of the crisis, Ori thought, was that the militia still went unhidden. It was only months after the Construct War that the recession riots had begun, and few of the militia had ever afterward gone back to plainclothes disguise.

Ori could not decide if it was better or worse. There were those among the rebels who argued each way, that emerging was an expression of militia strength or of weakness.

The paper Spiral Jacobs had showed Ori was a heliotype, taken long ago, of two men standing on the rooftops by Perdido Street Station. A poor print, washed out by light and feathery with age, its exposure too slow, its subjects wearing motion-coronas. But recognisable. Spiral Jacobs white-bearded, looking old even then, wearing the same madman's grin. And beside him a man whose face was turning and hazed, who raised his arms to the camera, stretched the fingers of his left hand. His right arm was unfolding, was a brutal and massive mantis claw.

Early the next morning, as the tramps were ushered out of the centre, Ori was waiting.

"Spiral," he said as the man came out scratching and wrapped his blanket around him. The old man blinked in daylight.

"Doubler! You the doubler!"

It cost Ori a day's wages. He had to pay for a cab to take the weak old man to Flyside, where Ori did not know anyone. Spiral prattled to himself. Ori bought breakfast in a square below the Flyside Militia Tower, with the skyrails hundreds of feet overhead linking the tower to the Spike in the city's heart. Spiral Jacobs ate for a long time without speaking.

"Too much yammering, not enough hammering, Spiral. Ain't that the truth? Too much of this—" Ori stuck out his tongue. "—not enough of this." He clenched his fist.

"Hammer, don't yammer," the tramp said agreeably and ate a grilled tomato.

"Is that what Jack said?"

Spiral Jacobs stopped chewing and looked up slyly.

"Jack? I'll Jack you," he said. "What you want to know about Jack?" The accent, that indistinct trace of something foreign, resonated for a second more loudly.

"He hammered not yammered, didn't he, Jack did?" Ori said. "Ain't that right? Sometimes you want someone to hammer, to do something, don't you?"

"We had half a prayer with Jack," said the old man, and smiled very sadly, all the madness momentarily gone. "He was our best. I love him and his children."

His children?

"His children?"

"Them as came after. Bully for them."

"Yes."

"Bully for them, Toro."

"Toro?"

In Spiral Jacobs's eyes Ori saw real derangement, a dark sea of loneliness, cold, liquor and drugs. But thoughts still swam there, cunning as barracuda, their movements the twitchings of the tramp's face. *He's sounding me out,* thought Ori. *He's testing me for something.*

"If I'd been there a little older, I'd've been Jack's man," Ori said. "He's the boss, always was. I'd have followed him. You know, I saw him die."

"Jack don't die, son."

"I saw him."

"Aye like *that* maybe, but, you know, people like Jack they don't die."

"Where is he now, then?"

"I think Jack's looking and smiling at you doublers, but there's others, friends of ours, mates of mine, he's thinking, 'Bully for them!' " The old man clucked laughter.

"Friends of yours?"

"Aye, friends of mine. With big plans! I know all about it. Once a friend of Jack's, always, and a friend of all his kin too."

"Who are you friends with?" Ori wanted to know, but Jacobs would say nothing. "What plans? Who are your friends?" The old man finished his food, running his fingers through the residue of egg and sucking them. He did not notice or care that Ori was there; he reclined and rested, and then, without looking at his companion, he shuffled into the overcast day.

Ori tracked him. It was not furtive. He simply walked a few steps behind Spiral Jacobs, and followed him home. A languorous route. By Shadrach Street through the remnants of the market to the clamour of Aspic Hole, where a few fruiterers and butchers had stalls.

Spiral Jacobs spoke to many he passed. He was given food and a few coins.

Ori watched the society of vagabonds. Grey-faced women and men in clothes like layers of peeling skin greeted Jacobs or cursed him with the fervour of siblings. In the charred shade of a fire-gutted office, Jacobs passed bottles for more than an hour among the vagrants of Aspic Hole, while Ori tried to understand him.

Once a group of girls and boys, roughnecks every one, a vodyanoi girl kick-leaping and even a young city garuda among them, came to throw stones. Ori stepped up, but the tramps shouted and waved with almost ritualised aggression and soon the children went.

Spiral Jacobs headed back east toward the Gross Tar, toward the brick holes and the Griss Fell shelter that were as much as anything his home. Ori watched him stumble, watched him rifle through piles of rubbish at junctions. He watched what Jacobs picked out: bewildering debris. Ori considered each piece carefully, as if Spiral Jacobs was a message to him from another time, that he might with care decrypt. A text in flesh.

The wiry little figure went through New Crobuzon's traffic, past carts piled with vegetables from the farmlands and the Grain Spiral. Hummock bridges took him over canals where barges ferried anthracite, and through the afternoon crowds, children, bickering shoppers, the beggars, a handful of golems, shabby-gentile shopkeepers scrubbing graffitied helixes and radical slogans from their sidings, between damp walls that rose and seemed to crumble, their bricks to effervesce into the air.

When after a long time deep colours leeched across the sky, they had reached Trauka Station. The railway cut overhead at an angle that ignored the terraces below it. Spiral Jacobs looked at Ori again.

"How did you know him?" Ori said.

"Jack?" Jacobs swung his legs. They were on the Murkside shore, their thighs under the railings. In the river a tarred frame broke water, an unlit vodyanoi house. Jacobs spoke with a lilt, and Ori thought he must be hearing a song-story tradition from Jacobs' homeland. "Jack the Man'Tis, he was a sight for sore eyes. Come through on the night-stalkers. It was him stepped up, saved this place from the dream-sickness all them years ago, 'fore you was born. Scissored through the militia." He snip-snipped his hand, hinging it at the wrist. "I give him things he needed. I was an informationer."

By the light of the gaslamps, Ori was looking at the helio. He ran his thumb over Jack Half-a-Prayer's claw.

"What about the others?"

"I watch all Jack's children. Toro's a one with fine ideas." Jacobs smiled. "If you knew the plans."

"Tell me."

"Can't do that."

"Tell me."

"Ain't me should tell you. Toro should tell you."

Information—a place, a day—passed between them. Ori folded the picture away.

The New Crobuzon newspapers were full of stories of Toro. There were fanciful engravings of some terrible muscled bull-headed thing, descriptions of feral bovine roars over Mafaton and The Crow, the uptown houses and the offices of the government.

Toro's exploits were all named, and the journals were addicted to mentioning them. A bank's vaults had been breached and slathered with slogans, thousands of guineas taken, of which hundreds had been distributed among the children of Badside. In *The Digest* Ori read:

By great fortune, this, THE CASE OF THE BADSIDE MILLIONS, has not had so bloody an outcome as THE CASE OF THE ROLLING SECRETARY or THE CASE OF THE DROWNED DOWAGER. These earlier incidents should remind the populace that

the bandit known as TORO is a coward and a murderer
whose *panache* is all that grants him a degree of local sympathy.

Messages reached Ori through New Crobuzon's intricate and secret
conduits. He had waited three times at the corner that Spiral Jacobs
had told him, in Lichford, beneath signs to Crawfoot and Tooth
Way, by the old waxwork museum. He had leaned in the sun, back
against the plaster, and waited while street-children tried to sell him
nuts and matches in twists of coloured paper.

Each time cost him wages and his profile among the day-
recruiters of Gross Coil. He had to space them out or he would
starve, or his landlady's indulgence would dry up. He returned to
the *Runagate Rampant* reading group, to sit, a Jack among Jacks,
and talk of the city's iniquities. Curdin was pleased to see him. Ori
was much calmer in his disagreements now. He felt his secret with
pleasure. *I'm not quite with you any more* he thought, and felt himself a spy for Toro.

At the street corner he was greeted by a girl in a torn dress, no
more than ten years old. She smiled at him as he leaned against
the museum, endearing with her missing teeth. She handed him a
paper cone of nuts, and when he shook his head she told him, "The
gen'man already paid. Said they was for you."

When the packet unfolded, even greasy from the roasted nuts
the message written on it was legible. *Seen you waiting. Bring vittles
and silver from a rich man's table.* Below was a little horned circle,
the sigil of Toro.

It was easier than he had thought. He watched a house in East Gidd.
Eventually he paid a boy to break the windows in front, while he
vaulted into the shrubbery, forced the garden door, grabbed knives
and forks and chicken from the table. Dogs came, but Ori was
young and had outrun dogs before.

No one would eat the greasy mess that marinated overnight in his sack. This was an examination. The next day at the usual spot he put his bag at his feet, and when he left he did not take it. He was well excited.

Mmm good, said the next note, uncurled from more street food. *Now we needs money my frend forty nobles.*

Ori fulfilled his commissions. He did what he was told. He was not a thief, but he knew thieves. They helped him or taught him what to do. At first he did not enjoy the anarchic adventures, running down alleys at night with bags bobbing in his hands, the shrieks of well-dressed ladies behind him.

He loathed being a lumpen cutter of purses, but he knew that anything more refined risked bringing the militia. As it was when he careered down crowded streets at twilight, the street gangs filled his wake as arranged and the officers would only plunge a little way into the rookeries, swinging truncheons.

Twice he did it, and could hardly stop his trembling. He became energised, vastly excited to be committing these acts, to be doing something palpable. The third time and the times after that, he had no fear.

He never took a stiver from the money he stole. He delivered it all to his unseen correspondent. It took several deliveries. He lost track. The robberies became routine. But he must have made his forty nobles: a new commission appeared. This time it was a wax tube, scored with grooves, that he had to take to a voxiterator booth.

Over the spit of the needle he heard a voice, faded through crackles: *"All good my boy now let's get serious let's you bring us a militia crest."*

He saw Spiral Jacobs every week. They had developed a language of ellipsis and evasion. He was not categorical—he admitted to nothing—and Spiral Jacobs still spoke with erratic logic. Ori saw the old man's madness was at least in part a mime.

"They've got me doing things," Ori said, "your mates. They're not the most welcoming coves, are they?"

"No they ain't, but when they make friends with you they're friends for *life*. Been at that shelter a long time. Been there a long time, wondered if I'd find anyone to introduce them to."

Ori and Spiral Jacobs discussed politics in this careful and mediated way. Among the *Runagate Rampant* chaverim, Ori was quiet and watchful. Their numbers dwindled, rose again. Only one of the women from the Skulkford sweatshop still came. She spoke more and more often, with increasing knowledge.

He listened with a kind of nostalgia and wondered, *How am I going to do this?*

He went to Dog Fenn, where he knew the militia would be harder to find but where he could hide. It took two attempts, a lot of planning and several shekels in bribes. By night in the darkness of Barley Bridge's girdered underside. A two-man patrol lured by a breathless street-boy telling them someone had been thrown in, while a gang of his fellows shouted. A young streetwalker wailed in the black water while trains wheezed overhead. She thrashed with genuine fear (she could not swim but was kept afloat by two vodyanoi children below her who swilled water in their submerged equivalent of giggles).

The first night the militiamen only stood at the edge and shone their lanterns at the bobbing woman while the children hollered at them to save her. They shouted for her to hang on and went to find help; and Ori emerged, dragged the disgusted prostitute out and hurried everyone away.

On the second night, an officer left his jacket and boots with his companion and waded into the cool water. The vodyanoi descended, and the woman panicked very badly and began to sink. The chaos in the water was not feigned. The children milled shrieking around the remaining militiaman, clamouring for him to help, jostling him until he bellowed and swung his truncheon, but it was too late by then. They had opened the bundle of his partner's clothes, even still in his grip, rifled its contents.

Ori left the badge in an old shoe at Toro's corner. When he came back two days later, someone was there to meet him.

Old Shoulder was a cactus-man. He was thin and dwarfed for his kind, shorter than Ori. They walked through the meat-market. Ori saw that prices were still rising.

"I don't know who pointed you our way and I ain't going to ask you," Old Shoulder said. "Where you been before now? Who you been with?"

"*Double-R*," said Ori, and Old Shoulder nodded.

"Yeah, well I ain't going to moan about them, but you better make your choice, lad." He looked at Ori with a face bleached the faintest green by years of sun. He made Ori feel very young. "Things go very different with our friend." He scratched the side of his nose, extending his first and last fingers splayed into horns. "I don't give spit about what Flex or any of his lot would have said. You can kiss good-bye to philosophising. We ain't interested in the toil concept of worth, or graphs of the swag-slump tendency and whatnot. With *Double-R* it's just more and more notions.

"I don't care if they can lecture like we was at the university." They stood still among the flies and the warm smell of meat, among the cries of the sellers. "What I care about's what you *do*, mate. What can you do for us? What can you do for our friend?"

They had him as a messenger. He had to show his worth, picking up packages or messages that Old Shoulder left for him, ferrying them across the city without investigating them, delivering them to men or women who eyed him without trust and sent him away before they would open them.

He drank in The Two Maggots, keeping his friends among the Nuevists. He went to the *Runagate Rampant* discussions. Hidden histories: "Jabber: Saint or Crook?"; "Iron Councillor: The Truth

behind the Stencil." The hard young machine-knitter had become a
political authority. Ori felt as if he watched everything through a
window.

In the first week of Tathis, at a time of sudden cool, Old Shoulder had him as lookout. It was only at the last second that he was
told what his job would be, and all his excitement came back.

They were in Bonetown. They watched evening come in livid
shades through the silhouettes of the Bonetown Claws, the Ribs.
The ancient bones that gave the area its name curved more than
two hundred feet into the air, cracking, yellowed, mouldering at a
geological pace, dwarfing the houses around them.

There was to be a delivery to the kingpin Motley. Ori could not
even see where his gang would intercept it. He was exhilarated. He
watched and watched, but no militia came. He could see to the
clearing below the bones, to the city scrub where acrobats and
print-vendors were counting their takings, oblivious to the monstrous ribcage above them.

He watched nothing, frantic, wishing he had a pistol. Young
men passed in a gang and eyed him, decided not to bother. No one
approached. The whistle stayed in his tense fist. He had no idea anything had even started till Old Shoulder tapped him from behind,
jerking him violently, and said, "Home again, boy. Job's done." That
was all.

Ori could not have said when he was made a member. Old Shoulder began to introduce him to others, to muttered discussions.

In the pubs, in the tarry shacks and mazes of Lichford, Ori
talked tactics with Toro's crew. He was a probationer. He felt a
queasy guilt when his new companions mocked the Caucus—
"the people's pomp" they called it—or *Runagate Rampant*. He still
went to *Double-R*'s under-pub discussions, but unlike his many
months there, he could see the impact of his new activities immediately. They were in the papers. Ori had been lookout on what they
called the Case of the Bonetown Sting.

He was paid, with each haul. Not much, but enough to compensate for the wages he was missing, and then a little more. In The Two Maggots and Fallybeggar's, he bought generous rounds, and the Nuevists toasted him. It made him feel nostalgic.

And in Lichford, he had new companions—Old Shoulder, Ulliam, Ruby, Enoch, Kit. There was an élan to Toro's outlaw gang. Their lives were different, were richer and more tenuous, because they were being risked.

If they catch me now they won't just lock me up, Ori thought. *They'll Remake me for sure, at least. Probably I'm dead.*

There were strikes most weeks in Gross Coil now. There was trouble in Smog Bend. Quillers had attacked the khepri ghetto in Creekside. The militia went into Dog Fenn, Riverskin and Howl Barrow, took unioners and petty crooks and Nuevists away. The foremost exponent of DripDrip poetry was beaten to death in one such raid, and his funeral became a small riot. Ori went, and threw stones with the mourners.

Ori felt as if he were waking. His city was a hallucination. He could bite down on the air; he could wring tension out of it. Daily he passed pickets, chanted with them.

"It's gearing up," Old Shoulder said. He sounded gleeful. "When we get it done—when our friend can finally get through and, uh, meet up with you-know-who . . ."

The gang glanced, and Ori saw several quick looks his way. They were not sure they should be speaking in front of him. But they could not keep themselves quiet. He was careful, did not give in to his desire to ask them *Who? Who is I-know-who?*

But Old Shoulder was staring at a streetside fixing-post, its fat pillar many-skinned in ancient posters. There was one block-printed heliotype, a stark rendition of a familiar face, and Old Shoulder was looking at it as he spoke, and Ori understood what he was being told. "We'll finish it all off," the old cactus-man said. "We'll change everything when our friend meets a certain someone."

* * *

He had not seen Spiral Jacobs for days. When at last Ori tracked him down, the tramp was distracted. He had not been to the shelter in a long time. He looked exhausted, more unkempt and dirty even than usual.

Ori followed leads from other forgotten men and women to find him, at last, in The Crow. He was shuffling between the great shops of the city's central district, its statues, facades of grand marble and scrubbed white stone. Jacobs had chalk in his hand, and every few steps he would stop and murmur to himself, and draw some very faint and meaningless sign upon the wall.

"Spiral," Ori said, and the old vagrant turned, his rage at the interruption making Ori start. It was a moment before Spiral Jacobs composed himself.

They sat in BilSantum Plaza among the jugglers. In the warm colours of the evening, Perdido Street Station loomed beside them, its variegated architecture unsettling, massive and impressive, the five railway lines spreading out of its raised arch-mouths like light from a star. The Spike, the militia minaret, soared up from its western side. Perdido Street Station seemed to lean on it like a man on a staff.

Ori looked at the seven skyrails that stretched from the Spike's summit. He looked along one tugged to the southeast, over the red-light district and the salubrious Spit Hearth, over the scholars' quarter of Brock Marsh, to another tower, and on to Strack Island, to Parliament itself, surrounded by the conjoining rivers.

"It's the Mayor," said Ori, while Spiral Jacobs seemed not to listen, only to play with his chalk and think whatever he wanted to think. "Toro's crew are fed up with taking out militia corporals and what-have-you. They want to kick things off. They're going to kill the Mayor."

It might have seemed that Spiral Jacobs was too gone to care, but Ori saw his eyes. He saw that gummy mouth open and shut. Was it a surprise? What else was there for the people's bandit to do?

And though Ori might have told himself that he let Spiral know only for some kind of duty, out of some sense that the old fighter, Jack Half-a-Prayer's comrade, deserved to know, there was more than that. Spiral Jacobs was involved, had in his random way ushered Ori to this brutal and liberatory political act. A plan like this, Ori said, would take guts and strength and information and money. This was the start. Come for the soup tomorrow, said Spiral Jacobs suddenly, promise me.

Ori did. And perhaps he knew what was in the bag that Jacobs brought him. Opening it in his room much later, alone by his candle, he could not silence his gasps.

Money. In rolls and tight wraps. A huge haul of coins and notes, in scores of currencies. Shekels, nobles and guineas, yes, the newest decades old, but there were ducats too, dollars and rupees and sandnotes and arcane bawbees, square coins, little ingots from maritime provinces, from Shankell, from Perrick Nigh and from cities Ori was not sure he believed in. It was the dregs of a highwayman's life, or a pirate's.

A contribution, said the note enclosed. *To help with a Good Plan. In Jack's memory.*

part three

WINE LAND

CHAPTER TEN

THE GOLEM WATCHED THE SLEEPING TRAVELLERS. IT STOOD BY THE embers taller than a man or a cactus-man. Thickset, with arms too long that hung in front of it, vaguely simian. Its stance was buckled, its back hunched into a saddle. Its clay skin was sun-cracked.

With dawn the golem was blundered across by woken insects. It did not move. Burrs and spores blew over the sleepers in their hollow. Breezes prickled their flesh. They were north of the relentless heat.

Drogon rose first. When the others woke he was gone, scouting, and Pomeroy and Elsie went too, to leave Cutter alone with the golem's master.

Cutter said, "You shouldn't have left. Judah, you shouldn't have gone."

Judah said, "Did you get the money I left?"

"Of course I got the money, and I got your instructions too, but I fucking didn't follow them, did I? And ain't you glad? With what I brought you?" He slapped his pack. "They weren't ready when you left."

"And now one's broken." Judah smiled sadly. "One's not enough."

"Broken?" Cutter was stricken. He had dragged the equipment so far.

"You shouldn't have gone, Judah, not without me." Cutter breathed hard. "You should have waited for me."

Cutter kissed him, with the urgency that always came when he did, a desperation. Judah responded as he always did—with something like affection and something like patience.

Even now, Cutter realised with wonder, Judah Low seemed not quite focused on what was before him. It had been that way as long as Cutter had known him. A typical distracted researcher in something or other, Cutter had thought at first. Cutter's shop was in Brock Marsh, and scholars were his customers. He had been surprised when he traced the remains of some downtown accent in Judah's voice.

More than ten years ago they had met. Cutter had emerged from his back room to see Judah looking at the esoterica crammed on darkwood shelves: notebooks, metaclockwork, vegetable secrets. A tall thin man with dry, uncut hair, much Cutter's senior, his face weathered, his eyes always open wide at whatever he saw. It was shortly after the war in the dumps, after Cutter had been made to surrender his cleaning construct. He was washing his own floors, and was in a bad mood. He had been rude.

The next time Judah came, Cutter tried to apologise, and the older man just stared at him. When Judah came back a third time—stocking up on alkalids and the best, most dense clay—Cutter asked his name.

"And should I say Judah or Jude or Dr. Low?" Cutter had said, and Judah had smiled.

Cutter had never felt so connected, so understood, as at that smile. His motives were uncovered without effort or cynicism. He knew then that this was not a man distracted like so many of the scholarly, but someone beatific. Cutter had come very quickly to love him.

They were shy with each other. Not only Cutter and Judah, but Judah and Pomeroy, Judah and Elsie. He asked them again and again for the stories of Drey's death, and Ihona's and Fejh's. When they had told him who had been lost, he had been aghast. He had crumpled.

He had them tell the deaths as stories. Ihona in her column of water; Drey's cruciform fall. Fejhechrillen's dissolution under the iron barrage was harder to sanctify with narrative.

They tried to make him tell them what he had done. He shook his head as if there was nothing.

"I rode," he said to them. "On my golem. I took him south through the forest and on the ties and lines. I bought passage across the Meagre Sea. I rode him west, through the cactus villages. They helped me. I came through the cleft. I knew I was followed. I set a trap. Thank Jabber you realised, Cutter." A brief terrible look went over him.

He looked tired. Cutter did not know what Judah had had to face, what had taxed him. He was scabbed: the evidence of stories he would not tell. It did not take much from him to keep this golem alive, but it was one drain among the many of his escape.

Cutter put a hand on the creation's grey flanks. "Let it go, Judah," he said. The older man looked at him with his perpetual surprise. Smiled slowly.

"Rest," Judah said. He touched the golem on its basic face. The clay man did not move, but something left it. Some orgone. It settled imperceptibly, and dust came off it, and its cracks looked suddenly drier. It stood where it had stood, and it would not move again. It would fall slowly away, and its hollows would be homes for birds and vermin. It would be a feature of the land and then would be gone.

Cutter felt an urge to push it over and watch it break apart, to save it from being stuck like that in time, but he let it stand.

"Who's Drogon?" Judah asked. The susurrator looked lost without his horse. He was busying himself, letting them discuss him.

"He'd not be here if I'd my way," Pomeroy said. "For a whisper-smith he's got a damn lot of power. And we don't know where he's from."

"He's a drifter," said Cutter. "Ranch-hand, tracker, you know. Some horse tramp. He heard you'd gone—gods know what the rumours are now. He's attached hisself to us because he wants to find the Iron Council. Out of sentiment, I think. He's saved us more'n once."

"He's coming with us?" Judah said. They looked at him.

Carefully, Cutter said: "You know . . . you don't have to go on. We could go back." Judah looked oddly at him. "I know you think you burnt your bridges with the golem trap in your rooms, and it's true they'll be watching for you, but *dammit,* Judah, you could go underground. You know the Caucus would protect you."

Judah looked at them and one by one they broke his gaze, ashamed. "You don't think it's still there," he said. "Is that what this is? You're here for *me*?"

"No," said Pomeroy. "I always said I wasn't just here for you."

But Judah kept talking. "You think it's gone?" He spoke with calm, almost priestly certainty. "It hasn't. How can I go back, Cutter? Don't you realise what I'm here for? *They're coming for the Council.* When they find it, they'll bring it down. They came for the Teshi, but now they found it they can't let the Council be. I heard it from an old source. Told me they'd found it, and what they'll do. I've to warn them. I know the Caucus won't understand. Probably cursing me."

"We sent them a message," Cutter said. "From Myrshock. They know we're after you."

From his satchel Judah brought out papers and three wax cylinders.

"From the Council," he said. "The oldest letter's near seventeen years old. The first cylinder's older'n that. Almost twenty years. The last ones arrived three years ago, and they were only two years old when they came. I know the Council's there."

The messages had travelled by unknown routes. Fellid Forest to the sea, by boats to the Firewater Straits, Shankell and Myrshock, to Iron Bay and New Crobuzon. Or through byways in the hills, or through woods by paths hundreds of miles into the swamps below Cobsea. To Cobsea itself in the great plains. Or by air, or thaumaturgy, somehow making their ways at last to Judah Low.

And could you write back, Judah? Cutter thought. *You know they're waiting. Do they know you're coming? And how many of their messages were lost?* He saw austere gullies strewn with fragments of wax. Gusts sending scraps of encoded paper like blossom across the grassland.

He was awed to see the paper, the grooved cylinders, sound fixed in time. Artefacts from a Caucus rumour, from the stories of travellers and dissidents.

What would he know? When first he had heard of Iron Council he was a boy, and it was a folktale like Jack Half-a-Prayer, and Toro, and the Contumancy. When he grew old enough to know that his Parliament might have lied to him—that there might have been no accident in the quagmires to the south—the Iron Council some said had been born there could never be found. Even those who said they had seen it could only point west.

Why did you never show me those, Judah? he thought. Through all their discussions, through all their growing closer. Judah had taken Cutter's cynicism and tried to do something to it, tried to tell Cutter that it had clogged him. There were other ways of doubting everything that need not sullen him, Judah had said, and sometimes Cutter had tried.

A dozen years they had known each other, and Cutter had learnt many things from Judah, and taught him a few. It was Judah had brought Cutter to the fringes of the Caucus. Cutter thought of the debates in his shop and in his small rooms, in bed. And in all those political ruminations—Judah a most unworldly insurrectionist, Cutter never more than a suspicious fellow-traveller—Cutter had never seen these stocks from the Iron Council itself.

He did not feel betrayed, only bewildered. That was familiar.

"I know where the Council is," Judah said. "I can find it. It's wonderful that you came. Let's go on."

Judah spoke to the whispersmith. No one but Judah could hear Drogon's replies, of course. At last Judah nodded, and they understood that Drogon was coming with them. Pomeroy glowered, despite all the susurrator had done.

Judah the somaturge did not seek leadership, did nothing but say he would continue and that they could come, but they became his followers, as they always did. It had been the same in New Crobuzon. He never ordered them, often seemed too preoccupied to notice they were with him, but when they were they attended him carefully.

They prepared. There must be weeks of travel. Miles of land, and more land, and rocks and more trees, and perhaps water, and perhaps chasms, and then perhaps the Iron Council. They slept early, and Cutter woke to the sound of Pomeroy and Elsie's lovemaking. They could not help their little exhalations, nor the scuffing of their bodies. The noise aroused him. He listened to his friends' sex with lust and an upswelling of affection. He reached for Judah, who turned to him sleepily and responded to his tonguing kiss, but gently turned away again.

Below his blanket Cutter masturbated silently onto the ground, watching Judah's back.

CHAPTER ELEVEN

A WEEK THEY WENT NORTH AND NORTHWEST INTO GREENING. IT was exhausting. The plains buckled. Sloughs and cenotes in the landforms grew deeper, and hills flecked with chaparral and heat-stunted trees. They walked gulches. Three times the whispersmith showed them they had found their way unknowingly onto a trail, that they walked in the ghosts of footprints.

"Where do we go?"

"I know where it is," Judah said. "In what part." He checked maps, and conferred with Drogon, the plains-traveller. Judah rode with an implacable wilderness calm.

"Why are you here?" Judah said to Drogon. The susurrator answered straight into Judah's ear. "Yes," said Judah, "but that tells me nothing."

"He ain't doing it to you now," Cutter said. "He can take you over with his bloody voice. At least twice that's how he kept us alive."

Cougars and githwings eyed them from the low hills or the air, and the party sounded their weapons. Copses of waxy plants like bladed succulents menaced them, moved not by breeze.

"See there." Drogon's whisper. He hauled the accoutrements of nomadism. He was a man of these ranges, anxious without a horse. He pointed to things they would not have seen. *"A village was there,"* he said; and yes, they learnt to see it in the ground, walls and foundations sketched in regolith, a landscape's memory of architecture. *"That ain't no tree,"* he said, and they realised that it was the barrel of some ancient gun or gunlike thing, swaddled in ivy and the scabs of weather.

One night while the others slept off their gamy supper, Cutter sat up hours before dawn and saw that Judah was gone. He rifled stupidly through Judah's bedcloth as if he might find him there. The whispersmith looked up, his face soured to see Cutter needily gripping Judah's wool.

Judah was off in the direction the wind was going, in a little hillside rincon. He had taken from his pack a cast-iron apparatus, so heavy a thing Cutter was astonished he had brought it. Judah motioned Cutter to sit by the voxiterator. One of his wax cylinders was inserted, and his hand was on the crank.

He smiled. He replaced the plectrum-needle at the top of the grooves.

"You may as well," he said. "Seeing as you're here. This keeps me going." He turned the handle and in the sputter and random tuts from the trumpet, a man's voice sounded. It was bled of bass, and it sped and slowed gently as the crank's pace varied, so his inflection was hard to gauge. The wind took the voice as soon as it emerged.

". . . don't feel as if I hardly know you but they say you're family sister so I thought you should hear this from family not wrote down fact is he's dead Uzman's dead and gone I'm sorry you've to hear it like this I'm sorry you've to hear it at all truth is weren't a bad passing mind he was at peace we buried him ahead and now he's in our tracks there was those said we should put him in the cemetery but I weren't having

that I said to them you know it ain't what he wanted he told us do it
right do it like it used to be done so I made them we're mourning him
he told us not to don't mourn organise he said when we was fighting
they told me and after the stain he told us don't mourn celebrate but
sister I can't help it we're allowed to mourn you mourn sister go on you
mourn and I will too it's me it's Rahul I'll say good-bye . . ."

The needle snapped stop. Judah was crying. Cutter could not bear it. He reached out, faltered when he saw that his touch would not be welcome. Judah did not sob. The wind sniffed them both like a dog. The moon was faint. It was cool. Cutter watched Judah weeping and he hurt, he was fervent to hold onto the grey-haired man, but he could do nothing but wait.

When Judah had finished and wiped himself dry he smiled at last at Cutter, who had to look away.

Cutter spoke carefully. "You knew him, the one he's talking about. I see. Whose was that message? Whose brother was that?"

"It's for me," said Judah. "I'm the sister. I'm his sister, and he's mine."

Hills rose shallowly, pelted with flowers in regal colours. Dust stuck to Cutter's sweat, and he breathed air thickened with pollen. The travellers stumbled through strange landscape, weighed down by dirt and the sun as if they had been dipped in tar.

They tasted carbon. Somewhere above the bluffs before them the sky was discoloured by more than summer. Lines of dark smoke were drawn up and dissipating. They seemed to retreat like a rainbow as the party approached, but the next day the smell of burn was much stronger.

There were paths. They were entering inhabited lands, and approaching the fires. *"Look there!"* said the whispersmith to each of them in turn. On downs miles off there was movement. Through Drogon's telescope Cutter saw that it was people. Perhaps a hundred. Hauling carts, hurrying their meat-beasts: fat cow-sized birds,

thick and quadruped, scrawny featherless wings stumping as forelegs.

The caravan was decrepit and desperate. "What's happening
here?" Cutter said.

At noon they came somewhere the earth had split, and they
walked the bottom of arroyos much higher than houses. They saw
something dun and battered, bound, like a giant brown-paper par-
cel in string. It was a wagon. Its wheels were broken and it leaned
against the rock. It was split and burned.

There were men and women around it. Their heads were stove
in or their chests opened up and emptied by bullets, the contents
spilt down their clothes and shoes. They sat or lay in neat order
where they had been killed, like a troop waiting instructions. A
company of the dead. A child spitted on a broken sabre huddled at
their front like a mascot.

They were not soldiers. Their clothes were peasants' clothes.
Their belongings littered the chine floor—irons, pots and kettles,
all alien designs, cloth made rags.

Cutter and his companions stared with their hands at their lips.
Drogon wrapped his kerchief around mouth and nose and went
into the deads' stench through the billows of insects that ate them.
He took a wooden spoke and poked at the bodies so carefully he
looked almost respectful. They were sunbaked, their skins cured.
Cutter could see their bones in ridges.

The cart listed as Drogon leaned in. He squatted and looked
at the wounds, probing them as the others watched and gave off
sounds. When the whispersmith took gentle hold of the sabre that
protruded from the child, Cutter turned away so he would not see
the dead boy move.

"*Days gone,*" Drogon said in Cutter's ear, even as Cutter kept his
back to the investigation. "*One of your'n. This is New Crobuzon
issue. This is a militia blade.*"

It was militia bullets killed them, a militiaman or a militiawoman who ran the child through. Militia knives tore through their wagon; New Crobuzon hands had thrown their belongings down.

"I told you." Judah spoke very quietly.

Can't we get out of here? Cutter thought. *I don't want to talk in front of them.* He looked up, breathing fast, saw Pomeroy and Elsie holding each other.

"In my letter, Cutter. You remember?" Judah held his gaze. "I told you I was going because of this."

"We're near the outskirts of Tesh lands," Cutter said. "This don't mean the militia are onto the Iron Council."

"They've a base by the coast, from where they send these squads out. This . . . work . . . This is only half of what they do. They're going north. They're looking for the Council."

Beyond the dead was open country. They knew that the militia that had done this to these runaways might be close, and they moved carefully. Cutter saw those patient dead when he closed his eyes. Drogon took them on a path through the sagebrush. On the hills ahead were scraps of farmland, of a half-wild, scrubby kind, from where the smoke came.

It was a day to the depredation. The air was clogged with smouldering. They entered the first little field with their guns drawn.

Through ridges of turned-over earth into what had been a copse of olives. They trod over the spread claws of roots where the little trees had been torn down. Drying olives scattered like animal pellets. There were craters, where stumps were made carbon sculptures. There were bodies cooked down to skeletons.

There had been huts, and they were burnt. On a plain of scrub and drying creeks were mounds of black rubbish that smoked like slag. A rank, meat and sweet smell. Cutter hacked through dried summer boscage.

For seconds he could not make sense of what he saw. The mounds were heaped-up carcasses, a charnel mass—blacked remnants of snouted ungulates, tusked, big and heavy as buffalo. They were encased in ash and crisped leaves. Roots spread out in their pebbled flesh.

"Vinhogs," said Judah. "We're in *Galaggi*. We've come so far." The wind moved and hilltop dust and the burnings of olives, vines and vineleaves hurt their eyes. The dead animals rustled.

Pomeroy found a trench, where scores of men and women rotted. The decay of days had not yet disguised their crosshatched tattoos. Their pumice-colour skins were death-besmirched, stone jewels piercing them.

They were the wineherds. The clans, the Houses, nomads of this hot northern steppe, custodians of the vinhog coveys. They tracked them, protected them and, at harvest time, leapt in dangerous brilliant husbandry between the horns of the aggressive herbivores to prune the fruit that plumped on their flanks.

Cutter swallowed. They all swallowed, staring at the dead ragged with gunfire. Judah said, "Maybe this is House Predicus. Maybe it's Charium or Gneura." The vinhogs, the animal-hosts and their harvest, mouldered and burned away.

All day they walked swells of ruined land, through olive groves ground to nothing, and despoiled crop-herds, and great numbers of scorched cadavers from the winemaker tribes. A corral of the huge meat-birds gone to maggots. The soft spit of embers and the knock of dead wood surrounded them. On some corpses the specifics of murder were still clear. A woman, her skirt rucked up and stiff red; a big wineherd man, his belly flyblown, stabbed in both eyes. Rot made Cutter gag.

They found one vinhog alive, fallen in a stone basin. It shook with hunger and infection. It limped in circles and tried to paw the ground. Its skin was ridged with rootwork and a leaf-pelt from its symbiotic vines. Its lichen-grapes were wizened. Cutter shot it in pity.

"This is why the cactacae fought, down south," said Pomeroy

after a long silent time. "This is what they heard about. They saw the militia, thought this was what they'd get too."

"Why this? Why this?" said Elsie. She struggled. "Galaggi ain't Tesh land, it's wild. These ain't Tesh tribes."

"No, but it's Tesh they're hurting," Judah said. "Galaggi wine and oil goes through it. They aren't strong enough yet to hit the city, but do this and you hit Tesh in the coffers."

They were way beyond their mapped world. Tesh was there, two or three hundred miles south and west on the coastal plain. Cutter thought of it, though he did not know what it was he should picture. How should he think it? Tesh, City of the Crawling Liquid. Its moats and glass cats, and the Catoblepas Plain and merchant trawlers and tramp diplomats and the Crying Prince.

Thousands of sea miles from Iron Bay to the remote coast, to the foothold that New Crobuzon had established north of Tesh. The militia had to go past Shankell, past seas thick with piasa and pirates, through the Firewater Straits where the Witchocracy backed their Tesh neighbours. There were no land-routes across Rohagi's wild interiors, no shortcuts. It was a desperately hard war to wage. New Crobuzon had to send ships across months of hostile waters. Cutter was awed at the brute vigour.

That night they ate unripe fruit they found unspoiled on a dead vinhog and made forlorn jokes about what a good vintage it was. Their second day on the vintners' land they found wreckage of the marauders. The New Crobuzon militia had not had it all their way. It was the remains of a nashorn, a rhino ironclad and Remade into a veldt tank. Two storeys high, a raised arse-end gunnery, a piston-strengthened neck. Its horn was corkscrewed, a huge drillbit. The nashorn was burst and savaged with peasant weapons. Its gears and innards lay about it.

There were six militia dead. Cutter stared at the familiar uniforms in this unlikely place. The officers were killed with blades. There were wineherds' sickles on the ground.

The land was full of scavengers. Dead-eating fox-things dug at the earth. That night Drogon woke the travellers with a shot. "*Ghul,*" he whispered to each in turn. They did not believe him, but in the morning its corpse was there: grave-pale and simian, its toothy mouth wide, blood drying on its eyeless forehead.

There was the start of a cooling as they went north, but only the very start. In the heat, among the ghuls and the dead and the dizzying smell of rotting fruit and the smoke, in a land become a torn-up memory of itself, Cutter felt as if he were walking in the outskirts of some hell.

In days through rugged transverse rises, a haze of forested hills became just visible to the north, and Judah was elated. "We've to go through that," he said. "It's the end of the veldt; it's the far edge of Galaggi."

Behind them the earth was broken by the tracks of militia. They had passed out of that crushed zone of husbandry and feral wine, those few score of miles once worth something. This was a wetter reach of hills all summered, copper and slick. It rained warm rain—virga that did not reach the ground.

They were in places only antique sages and adventurers had been. They had heard about these strange reaches—patches of ice in deep summer, the hives of dog-sized termites, clouds that fossilised into granite. On a Dustday, new smoke and a smell reached them. They climbed slopes of scree and breccia to see the scrubland all the miles to the forest, and something burning before them. One by one they let out sounds.

A few miles off. A chelona. Its titan legs were splayed, its plastron flattened to the ground. Its sides rose vastly, and from halfway up were gnarls of carapace-matter coaxed over generations into overhangs and towers, the walls of a keratin village. The great tortoise was more than a hundred yards long, and over the centuries of its life it had accreted on its back a many-layered jag township. Brittle outgrowths of its scute had been grown and carved into blocks, ziggurats and spires, their planes and lines imperfect, cut with windows, belfries connected by rope bridges, coursed with horny streets and tunnels; everything made, paved and walled in the mottlesome tortoiseshell. The chelona was dead and on fire.

It reeked of burning hair. Smoke rose from the walls in a thionic gush. Muck and gore dripped from its cave mouth.

Milling at its base were fastnesses on wheels and tracks, mobile guns—a New Crobuzon force. Crews rode two nashorns, the captains in sunk seats behind the rhinos' heads, gripping controls sutured directly to ganglia. The militia cannon must be more powerful than they appeared to have blasted such wounds.

Militia infantry were heading in the travellers' direction. They followed a line of refugees fleeing the remains of their chelonatown.

Drogon and Judah led them on through scrub, until a sharp *coughcoughcough* sounded, and there was screaming, and the echoes of bullets. They lay where they had thrown themselves until it was obvious that they were not targets, continued, staying low, to the base of a hill where they bunkered behind a marl barricade. Above them, out of the tree-cover, was a line of broken-down families. Not all were human. Some were behind fallen trunks or in hollows; some were running. Their shouts of fear were like the sounds of scraping.

At the hilltop, a corps of militia took positions. They were just discernible. They kneeled before motorguns; there was a monsoon of noise and bullets and many of the refugees fell.

Cutter watched in rage. More bullets pressed down the earth, and the dying twitched and tried to crawl away. A chelonaman raised something to his lips, and there was a thin noise, and way above there were cries and some of the militia stumbled at some thaumaturgy in the trumpet.

Drogon was watching the hilltop through his telescope. Judah turned to him in response to a whisper, and said, "She's unpacking *what?*"

From the hilltop unfolded a shape of wire and dark leather,

taller than a man. It became in a stutter of extending metal. Like a music stand, it unfurled many times. A humming of thaumaturgy made the air thin as a militia officer made shapes on the thing, and there was crackling, and the wire-and-hide moved.

It threw back a head with glass eyes, and its skin wings beat twice and it was airborne and careering down the hill toward the Galaggiites. Its limbs were not legs or arms but knifed extensions, insectan and agleam. They slid together with the sound of sharpening.

The ugly sculpture flew toward those cowering. Judah's eyes were wide, and when he spoke he was choked with rage and contempt. "A prefab," he said. "You use a damned *ready-made*?" He stepped up and onto the shallow hill, and Cutter stayed with him and aimed.

The militia's gliding assassin passed over the wailing wounded and reached the trumpeter. He blew another thin note, but the thing had no life for him to disrupt. It rived him with its bayonets, and he screamed and bled out quickly.

Judah was growling. Cutter fired up the hill to protect him. Judah howled and stared not at the wired monstrosity but at the officer controlling it. The thing rose from the meat mess of its victim and beat its built wings. Judah puffed his chest like a pugilist.

No one fired. They watched—even the Galaggiites, astonished by this bizarre figure—while the cutting leather bird swept down on Judah, wings spread. Cutter fired and could not even tell if his bullet hit.

Judah picked up stones and dust. His growl grew louder and became a shout as the shadow rolled over him.

"On me?" His voice was splendid. "You use a golem on *me*?"

Like a child he threw his handful of charged dirt into the thing's path. There was a stunning detonation of energy. The golem dropped instantly. It fell straight out of the sky, the momentum of its flight dissipated.

Judah stood over the collapsed metal, all its little borrowed life gone. For seconds there was no sound. Rage made Judah shake. He pointed up the hill. *"You use a golem on me?"*

The motorgun swung toward him but there were rifle-shots and the gunman barked and died at Drogon's hidden hand. Suddenly there were scores of bullets in the air, from the whispersmith, Pomeroy's blunderbuss, Elsie and Cutter and the appalled militia.

Judah strode through the fusillade. He was bellowing but Cutter could no longer hear what he said, only ran to protect him. The New Crobuzon militia, yards off, were shouting and firing blindly down the hill. Judah Low reached a pile of Galaggi dead.

The somaturge shoved his hand among the cadavers and barked. There was a fermentation as the world's energy was channelled, the moment bowed and swelled and spat out strangeness. And the corpse-pile stood in a new configuration, a golem of flesh still twitching as the nerves within it died.

It was a shambles of the recent dead, gory and dripping. It walked in the base shape of a human: five, six bodies pushed together without respect for their outlines. The golem's legs were stiffening corpses, one inverted, its dead head become a foot, crushed and made more shapeless with every step; the trunk a coagulate of arms and bones; the arms more dead; the head more of the Galaggi dead; the whole aggregate stamping at terrible speed up the hill, leaving a trail of itself. Leaving screams from the vineyard workers who saw their lost lovers and children reanimated into this grotesquerie. It walked quickly with Judah behind it, energies spitting from him, connecting him to his monstrosity with an uncanny funiculus.

The militia were pinned by gunshot, and the charnel golem reached them. The thing shed matter as it crested the hill, and the New Crobuzon soldiers who emptied their rifles and motorguns into it bloodied and desecrated it further. But it lasted long enough to smother and punch them to death. It beat them down with blows from the dead men and women that made its fists.

When the hilltop was quiet and the last of the soldiers had

fallen, the flesh golem collapsed. It was carcasses again by the time it hit the ground.

The militia dead wore ragged, guerrilla versions of their uniforms, adorned with ears and teeth and obscure symbols for how many dead they had taken. They still wore their masks, every one of them.

Two were still alive. One whom the trumpet had struck down was delirious, raging with occult fever the music weapon had given him; the other had taken Pomeroy's shot through his hands, and he screamed at his fingerless red messes.

Drogon went through the corpses. It would not be long before the main force at the chelona sent scouts after this little death-squad.

Judah was tired. The golem he had made—so big, so quickly—had taken energy. He searched the dead captain-thaumaturge whose fold-up golem he had so easily deactivated. He took her accoutrements: batteries, chymical vials, and hexstones.

He would not meet Cutter's eye. *He's shamefaced,* Cutter thought. *Because of his little display.* Judah stalking up the hill like some vexed spirit, infecting the dead with a kind of life. Judah was a golemist of extraordinary puissance and expertise: since the Construct War had forced the rich to replace their steam-driven servants, his skills had made him wealthy. But Cutter had never seen Judah Low acknowledge his power or revel in it until that deadly walk behind the corpse-giant.

You use a golem on me? There had been an ease to his rage. Now Judah Low was trying to fade.

The refugees watched. There were people from the chelona, men and women with skins of varied colours and clothes of astonishing designs. There were beetles the height of a child, walking upright. They stared with iridescent eyes, and their antennae swung toward Cutter. Their dead were cracked open and smeared with their ichor.

Among the humans there were a few dressed in the natural colours of hunters. They were taller than the chelonans, their skin a stark grey.

"Wineherds," Cutter said.

"Twice refugees," Elsie said. "Must have run from the militia to the shelltown, and then run again."

A wineherd spoke, and he and the travellers and the chelona renegades went through what languages they knew and found only a few cognates. There were trails of dust in the bush as refugees made for the warm forest while Drogon searched and Judah sat. Behind them, the surviving militiamen made sobby sounds.

"We have to move," said Elsie.

They went on with the last chelonans, a few of the silent insect people, two exile wineherds. They walked into the forest. Behind them, the New Crobuzon militiaman spasmed and raved in his hexed sickness.

It was nothing like Rudewood. These selva trees were tougher, draped with vines and succulent leaves, hanging with dark foreign fruits. There were alien animal sounds.

The lost chelonans were cowed, and looked with open-eyed hopelessness at Judah. They tried to stick to the power they had seen save them. They walked, though, with a clumsiness Cutter and his companions had shed, and that now angered them.

They could not be delayed, and they left the refugees behind, simply by pacing with their lean, wood-hard muscles. Cutter knew the militia would follow them, and that those they left would not do well if they were found. He was too tired to feel much guilt.

Without ever speaking, the insect people found their own forest paths and went. When the warm night came, only the two wineherds had kept up. They moved with hunters' stamina. Finally, far enough from the exhausted chelonans they had shed, the travellers stopped. They made an odd community, the wineherds and Cutter's party staring at each other as they chewed, each grouplet count-ing the other's oddities, companionable and unspeaking.

For the first two days they heard munitions behind them. For days after that they heard nothing, though they were convinced they were still followed, and they kept their pace quick, and tried to hide their trails.

The wineherds accompanied them. They were named Behellua and Susullil. They often became melancholy, weeping half ritually, lamenting the loss of their wine-beasts. In the evenings they would talk lengthily in singsong by the fire, untroubled by their compan-ions' lack of understanding. Judah could only translate snips.

"It's something about the rain," he would say, "or thunder maybe, and . . . there's a snake and a moon and bread."

Elsie had spirits: the wineherds got drunk. They told a story in dance. At one point they performed a complex little double slap and turned to their audience with new faces—clannish thauma-turgy made them playfully monstrous, splayed their teeth like un-couth tusks. They gurned and pulled out their ears into batwings while the charm lasted.

The wineherds asked where they were going. Judah spoke in pidgin and pantomimed, told Cutter he had said they were looking for friends, for a myth, for something missing, for something they had to save, that would one day save them, for the Iron Council. The wineherds stared. Cutter did not know why they stayed. In the evenings, the wineherds and the travellers learned and taught a lit-tle of each other's languages. Cutter watched Susullil close, and saw Susullil notice him.

It rained warmly each morning, as if the jungle sweated with them. They cut through lianas and the chaparral, and batted off mosquitoes and vampiric butterflies. At night they fell where they dropped their packs, dirty and exhausted and flecked with blood. Pomeroy and Elsie would smoke, and use their cigarillos to burn off leeches.

Their elevation rose and the forest changed, cooled gently and became montane. The canopy lowered. Ibises and sunbirds watched them. The wineherds cooked tree crabs. Behellua was nearly killed by a pangolin rex that whipped at him with its poisoned tongue. Rarely, when one of them became very tired, Drogon would ask permission, which all but Pomeroy gave, and would whisper them, telling them *walk* so they had to obey.

"Do you know where we're going, Judah?"

Judah nodded to Cutter, conferred with Drogon, nodded again; but Cutter saw anxiety in him. He checked his compass and dampening maps.

Cutter felt a sudden and very great weariness, as if New Crobuzon were shackled to him and wherever he went he dragged it after him. As if every new place he saw became infected by where he had been.

Pomeroy and Elsie renewed their lovemaking. Judah slept alone. Cutter listened, and saw Behellua and Susullil listening too, and then watched astonished as they chatted quietly in their wineland language and sitting up began offhandedly to masturbate in time, touching each other. They saw him watching and paused, and then he closed his eyes hurriedly as Susullil gestured to himself like someone offering a glass of wine.

In the morning Behellua was gone. Susullil tried to explain.

"Gone to tree town," Judah said, after a long attempt. "There's a township. Where those who've been displaced by the militia go. All the remnants from a clutch of villages, chelona, nomads from the bushveld. An outcast town in the forest. Where they found a god who can tell you anything you want to know. He says . . . Behellua's gone, to tell them about . . . us."

About you, Cutter thought. *About what you done. To the militia. You're coming to be a story. Even out here.*

"So why's he staying?" said Elsie.

"Judah done inspired him, didn't he?" said Cutter quietly. "Inspires us all." He did not speak unpleasantly.

Cutter was close behind Susullil. With night they came into a clearing, and had Susullil not pushed him aside, Cutter would have trudged into the fringe of mossy bones that telltaled a wake-tree. The tree's willowy tendrils were feathered and bracken-thorned. He could not tell what animals had given their bones, but he could see that some were recent, without lichen.

A man—someone strayed from the deep forest—sat in the tree's lower branches. His body and head disappeared into thicket. His legs dangled, swinging and kicking randomly from the attentions of the tree digesting him. Susullil stepped into the reach of the tree and Cutter wailed.

The wake-tree reached down with tentacle boughs that bloomed open with motion that might, almost, be nothing but the random waving of foliage. The wineherd rolled below the grab and flicked his sickle. He somersaulted and crawled back out of the anemone shadow. The legs of the caught woodsman shuddered.

"Oh that's disgusting," Elsie said. Susullil was holding up the fruit that he had cut. It was small and browning, lumpy skinned. It took the rough shape of a human head. Of all the prey-fruit on the tree, Susullil had taken one of the humans.

Another cultural difference, Cutter thought that night as they sat around the fire and Susullil ate what he had taken. Pomeroy and Elsie, even quiet Judah, made revolted sounds. They would no more eat prey-fruit than dogshit. It turned Cutter's stomach to see Susullil swallow and lie back to dream the dregs of the dead man's mind. Susullil looked at him once, carefully, before he closed his eyes.

Pomeroy and Elsie withdrew, and Judah and Cutter talked a little more. When, finally, he lay down, Cutter caught Judah's appraising glance and was certain Judah knew what he would do. He felt a familiar mix of emotions.

He waited many minutes until everyone but he breathed steadily with sleep, and their camp was very moonlit. When he touched Susullil to wake him and kissed him deeply, he could still taste the dead man on the wineherd's tongue.

CHAPTER TWELVE

A ND THEN SUNLIGHT CAME THROUGH THE THICK AND ROPY canopy. Elsie and Pomeroy saw Cutter, lying close to Susullil. They gathered the camp without speaking or meeting Cutter's eye.

If Susullil was conscious of their embarrassment, he made no sign of it, nor did he show Cutter any affection now night was gone. While Cutter rolled the blanket that had been a pillow for him and Susullil, Judah came to him and gave a slow beatific smile. A benediction.

Cutter burned. He swallowed. He stopped to stow his kit. He leaned in close and said quietly just for the somaturge: "I don't, not now, not ever, need your fucking blessing, Judah."

It was like the times in New Crobuzon he had been taking men home and met Judah in the street. In Cypress Row, in Salom Square Casbah. Once Judah had come to Cutter's rooms early on a Shunday, and the door had been opened by the black-haired boy Cutter had woken up with. Then, as always when he saw Cutter's partners, Judah had smiled with peaceable pleasure, with approval, even when Cutter pushed the young man aside and stood before Judah, closing the door behind him.

When Cutter went looking he found himself glancing backward in case Judah was there to see him.

Cutter imagined being an artist or a musician, or a writer or libertine pamphleteer, one whose life was a scandal, a Salacus Fields man, but he was a shopkeeper. A Brock Marsh shopkeeper whose customers were scholars. Brock Marsh was a strange and quiet district; its excitements were not those of the artistic southern bank.

In Brock Marsh, renegade hexes might make doors where there should be no doors. Entities cultured in thaumaturged plasm might escape and make the streets deadly, and debates could go murderous as rival thinkers sent bleakly charged ab-ions at each other. Brock Marsh had history and a sort of glamour, but there were no places for Cutter to find men. When there were familiar Brock Marsh faces in the southside inns he would not acknowledge them nor they him.

Cutter despised the dollyboys in their petticoats and painted faces, the aesthete inverts draped in flowers in the Salacus Fields night. He would scowl and walk the canalsides of Sangwine past the she-men whores to whom he did not speak. He would not go into bawdy houses, would not rent some man's arse. Not anymore. He only rarely visited the warrens by the docks where those sailors who did not just make do at sea, but preferred it that way, would tout for men.

Instead he might perhaps once in a rare while push past crowds into certain inns with half-hidden entrances, thin rooms, thin bars and lots of smoke, older men watching each newcomer eagerly, men in groups laughing raucous as hell and others sitting alone and not looking up, and what women were there were men, dollyboys, or were Remades who had once been men and whose in-between status was a peccadillo to some.

Cutter was careful. Those he chose would never be too handsome: who knew if they were militiamen on honey-trap duty offering a stint for Gross Depravity to any who approached them, or if their squad outside might indulge in an ad hoc punishment of beating and rape.

Neither ashamed nor indulgent, Cutter would simply wait, hating the place and feeling provincial for that, until someone like him came in.

It was twelve years since Cutter had met Judah Low. He had been twenty-four, angry much of the time. Judah was fifteen years his senior. Cutter had quickly loved him.

They hardly ever touched. No more than a few times each year, Cutter had been with Judah Low, every time because of his insistence, never quite begging. More often in the early days, until Judah had become harder and harder to persuade. It seemed, Cutter thought, less a waning of whatever desire was there in Judah than something more thoughtful, to which Cutter could not give words. Each time they were together Cutter felt very strongly that from Judah it was an indulgence. He hated it.

He knew Judah went with women too, and he supposed perhaps with other men, but from what he imagined and heard it was no more often, with no more or less enthusiasm than Judah had for their own encounters. *I will make you cry out,* Cutter thought as they sweated together. He went at it with passion bordering violence. *I will make you feel this.* Not with vindictiveness but a desperation to inspire more than kindness.

Judah had taught him, put money into his business, taken Cutter to Caucus meetings for the first time. When Cutter understood that their sex would only ever be an act of patrician friendship, profane and saintly generosity, would only ever be a *gift* from Judah, he tried to bring it to a close, but could not sustain the abstinence. As he grew he left behind some of his young man's snarling, but there was anger he would not slough off. Some the Caucus directed at

Parliament. Some, beside the fervent love he felt for him, would always be raised by Judah Low.

"Cutter, chaver," Pomeroy had said to him once. "I don't mean it badly, excuse me asking, but are you . . . omipalone?" Pomeroy said the slang inexpertly. It was not a bad term and it was meant almost kindly—a playground nomenclature. Cutter wanted to correct him—*No, I'm an arsefucker Pomeroy*—but it would have been cruel and a complex affectation.

All the chaverim had known for a long time and studiously did not judge Cutter, but only, he had twice been told, because good insurrectionists did not blame victims for being distorted by a sick society. He did not bring it up but nor would he by Jabber apologise or hide.

They knew Judah lay with him, but to his anger there were no careful hesitations around the older man, even on the day they came to a meeting wearing each other's clothes.

"It's *Judah*."

When Judah did it, sex was not sex any more than anger was anger or cooking was cooking. His actions were never what they were, but were mediated always through otherworldly righteousness. Cutter was an invert but Judah was Judah Low.

Elsie and Pomeroy were shy with Cutter, now. Travel did not allow awkwardness: soon they were gripping hands with him and hauling him and being hauled down loose and rooted banks.

The encounter had little effect on Susullil. He seemed neither to regret it nor to court a repeat. Cutter was self-deprecating enough to find humour in that. Three nights on, Cutter went to him again. It was an awkward coupling. Cutter had to learn his partner's proclivities. Susullil liked to kiss, and did it with a novice's enthusiasm. But he would only use his hands. He reacted to Cutter's insistent tonguing descent with distaste. Cutter tried to present his arse, and when the nomad finally understood he laughed with sincere hilarity, waking the others, who pretended to sleep.

They became inured to strange fauna. Things like limbed fungus that made sluggish progress half-climbing half-growing on bark. Chaotic simians that Pomeroy called "Hell's monkeys," clutches of gibbon limbs exploding from conjoined cores, in varying numbers, that brachiated at insane speed.

"You know where we are, yes?" Cutter said to Judah and to Drogon.

The woodland density was lessening. Rain kept coming, and it was cooler. The air was less like steam, more like mist. *"We're still on the paths,"* Drogon said. *Do you know where we're going?* Cutter thought.

When they heard something approach they held up their guns; but there was shouting, no attempt to hide, and Susullil answered excited and accelerated. When the others reached him he was slapping hands with Behellua, and behind him were two cowed-looking men in forest camouflage who nodded careful greeting.

The returned man smiled at the travellers. The wineherds talked.

When at last Susullil turned he spoke carefully to Judah, though they all understood some now. "He's come from the forest town," Judah said. "They want help. Something's coming for them . . . wiping them out. Behellua told them about us, what we did for them. They think we've powers. They're offering something. If we help them . . ." He listened again.

"If we help them their god will help us. Will give us what we need. They say their god'll tell us the way to the Iron Council."

Hiddentown was huts in a clearing. Cutter had visioned an arboreal metropolis, with raised walkways between boughs and children spiralling down vines from the leaf sky.

At the edges of the village were attempts at stockades. Hiddentowners in forest-coloured clothes stared at the travellers. Much of the village was tents tarred or painted with gutta-percha. There were some warped wood huts, damp fires, a midden pit. Most of the inhabitants were human, but several of the child-high insects scuttled through the mud trails.

They were making quarters of their own in the corners of the town. They were chitin gardeners. They herded millions of insects, arachnids and arthropods, nurturing them through quick generations till they had colossal numbers of pinhead-sized ants, foot-long millipedes, and crawling wasps of countless species. With strange techniques they turned their flocks into walls, pressing them gently together, merging them and smoothing them, squeezing the still-living, conjoined mass of chitin-stuff into a kind of plaster. They made bungalows and burrows of their living mortar, feeding it carefully, so the tiny lives that made it did not die, but wriggled, embedded and melted with others, become architecture, a ghetto of living houses.

The human Hiddentowners spoke Galaggi in various forms, and here and there Tesh, and made a mongrel language. The chief was a thuggish man: nervous, Cutter saw, because he knew he was a mediocrity become by kink of history a ruler.

Cutter supposed those refugees who could look after themselves would not waste time with this settlement. Hiddentown was a convocation of the hopeless. No wonder they were desperate. No wonder they were such simple meat-stuff for some beast.

Jabbered at and bowed to with cursory politesse, the travellers were hustled to a long-hut with a tower of stakes, a rude minaret in split wood. It was a church, symbols cut and stained in the walls. There were tables with blades of mirror on them, papyrus. A robe of fine black wool. The chief left them.

For some seconds there was silence. "What are we fucking doing here?" Cutter said.

There were echoes; shadows moved that should not have been

there. Cutter saw Elsie shiver. They moved into a circle, back-to-back.

"There's something," Elsie whispered. "Something's here . . ."

"I am here." The voice was throaty and snarled. They dropped with bushrangers' speed. They waited.

"What are you?" Judah said.

"I'm here." It was accented, glutinous as if words were congealing in a throat. There was a movement they could not follow. "They brought you here for my blessing, I think. A minute. Yes, yes they did. And to tell you what to do. You're here to hunt for them."

Drogon pointed at the table. The woollen robe was gone.

"You speak our language," said Cutter.

"I am a little god but still a god. You are champions. That's the idea, you know. Did you reckon yourselves *champions*?" The voice seemed to bleed from the walls, seemed to be in several places.

"That's what they have in mind, yes," said Pomeroy. "What's wrong with that?" He circled slowly, a pugnacious godless man in the presence of a god. Drogon was turning his head by little increments, his lips moving.

"Nowt," the voice said. "At all. Only . . . a waste of your efforts, really. You, mmm, you, you have a little daughter, by a whore in a place called Tarmuth. You should go. This town's doomed. Save them from this, there'll be another thing to get them."

Pomeroy's mouth worked. Elsie watched him. She kept her face motionless.

"So why are you here?" said Cutter.

"Because this is my town I had them build for me. They want me. Mmm, you, you aren't sure of your Caucus, are you, shopkeeper?"

Cutter was stricken. The others looked at him. Drogon's head jerked forward. He made a motion like spitting. The disembodied voice gave a hard gasp. There was a commotion, something fell and there was puking, the substance of things jerked and then, shaking with effort, someone cowled rose from behind the table. A thin and jaundiced face, deep lines and shaven head, mouth adrip with vomit, staring in horror.

She or he stood for moments, quivering as if in ice, then retched and ran across the room to a pillar, behind it and out of sight. Cutter followed, and Pomeroy went the other way; but they came to each other and found nothing. The figure had disappeared.

The voice returned, angry and afraid.

"You *never* do that to me *again*," it said. Drogon was speaking secretly into Cutter's ear.

"Found it. Guessed where it was and whispered to it. Ordered it. 'Don't read us,' I said. 'Show yourself,' I told it."

"Wait, whispersmith," Cutter said. "Fucking god, eh?" he said to the room. "What's your name? How do you speak our tongue? What *are* you?"

There was silence for seconds. Cutter wondered if the figure had slipped out under thaumaturgic caul. When the voice come back it sounded defeated, but Cutter was sure there was relief there too.

"I speak Ragamoll because I learned to read it, for all the hidden things in your books. I'm here because . . . like everyone else who's here, I ran. I'm a refugee.

"Your militia are steering clear of Tesh, yet, but they've come up close to the Catoblepas Plain. They've attacked our towns and outposts. Tesh monasteries. I'm a monk. For the Moment of Lost Things. Moment of the Hidden."

The militia had rampaged in the shadow of Tesh. The city had closed its doors and refilled the moatlands. The monastery was beyond, in the briarpits. It should have been safe.

When they realised a New Crobuzon slave squad of Remade assassins was coming, the monks had waited for Tesh to send protection. It had been days before they had realised that no one was coming; they'd been deserted. They panicked up desultory plans.

They were a temple consecrated to the Manifold Horizon, with cadres of monks dedicated to its various Moments, and each of these Moments became a brigade.

Some fought; some went seeking holy death. The monks of Cadmer, Moment of Calculation, knew they could not win and waited in the briarpits to receive the bullets. The monks of Zaori, Moment of Magic Wine, drank themselves to visionary death before a militiaman could touch them. But the Moment of Doves sent its birds to destroy themselves in the militia's wheels and stop their engines; the Moment of Desiccation turned militia blood to ash; Pharru and Tekke Shesim, the Moments of Forgotten Snow and of Memory, came together and made ice storms.

But the militia thaumaturges were expert, the slave-officers relentless, and in the end the monastery could not hold out. And when it fell, it was only the monks of Tekke Vogu, the Moment of the Hidden and Lost, who escaped.

Their neophytes were murdered, but the monks' devotions hid them. They were lost to their attackers. They crept away—away from the burning ruins of their temple and from Tesh, City of the Crawling Liquid, which was closed to them, which had been ready to let them die. They had gone out into the land.

The monk told them everything. Was eager to, somehow, Cutter could tell. "We're hidden. We know hidden things. They're entrusted to us. We find lost things. I travel quick: I travel by hidden passages, lost ways. When I came here, I had them build this place. It's easy to be a god here. Whoever comes I tell a little secret, something hidden. So they believe in me."

"What's your name, monk?" Cutter said.

"Qurabin. Eighth-ring red monk of Tekke Vogu."

"Is that a man's name?" There was a laugh.

"Our names don't discriminate. Are you asking am I a man?" The voice was suddenly very close. "I don't know."

* * *

Every monk of Tekke Vogu was enfolded within the Moment, but it was a bargain. They would learn the hidden, and how to find the lost. But Vogu's sacrament was sold, not given. The price for the Moment's protection was something made lost, something hidden from the devotee, given to Vogu.

"I know monks who don't know their names. Who had them hidden. Who lost their eyes. Their homes, or families. Me—when I submitted to Vogu it was my sex went hidden. I remember my childhood, but not if I was a boy or a girl. When I piss I look down but it's hidden from me. My sex is lost." Qurabin spoke without rancour.

"So you want us to clear out this thing that's attacking?" Cutter said.

"Not me," said Qurabin. "*They* want you, they want champions. There's no point protecting this hovel."

The party looked at each other.

"As gods go, you ain't much by way of a protector, are you?" Elsie said.

"I didn't say I was, did I? It's them—they built the stupid town around me, and they keep *wanting* things from me. I didn't *ask* this. Where was my protector? What Tesh did to me, I can do. Let the town burn."

"That ain't what you said before," Cutter said, but Judah interrupted him.

"And who are you to say?"

He stepped forward and stared at the makeshift altar as if he could know that was where Qurabin hid. "Who are you to say?" His voice rose. "They come here, make what they can of this place, running from those who'd kill them because they live close to Tesh; they try to build something, and they make one mistake. To look for a god, and find one in you.

"They promised us help—promised us a guide. So tell us. We'll find whatever it is and help them. And you can find us what *we're* looking for."

The forest wetness drip-dripped in the makeshift church.

"Tell us where it is. I don't damn well believe you don't care. You care. You want to tell us. You want to look after them. You know it. So tell. We got your offer. They need us to kill this thing, and then you give us what you promised."

"I won't take anything out of Vogu's house for *you*—"

"I don't want to hear about your damn *piety*, when you'll take snippets out of your god's house to impress the damn natives. Tell us where the beast is, and we'll fix it, and then you tell us where the Iron Council is."

"I don't betray," said Qurabin. "I buy. Everything I learn, I lose something. And it hurts. Vogu don't give it up free. I unhid your man's whore and daughter it *stings*, and I lose something. Lost and hidden by the Moment. I'm naked in front of you. I unhide this? *Iron Council*? It'll *cost* me."

There was silence and the dripping again.

"The beast," Judah said. "Where is it?" There was long quiet.

"Wait," said the voice, and again there was relief under the resentment. *Tired of being a god,* thought Cutter. He looked at Judah, who stood trembling and splendid. Qurabin was lost, Cutter saw. Broken. Eager for something, deserted and newly eager, before righteous Judah.

"I try," said the voice, and gave a glottal retching. When Qurabin sounded again, it was with pain, in the voice of one used to pain.

"Damnfire. Damn. It's unhidden. The beast."

"What did you lose?" said Cutter.

"Someone's name." Someone who mattered, Cutter could hear.

CHAPTER THIRTEEN

IT WAS DAWN WHEN THEY REACHED THE DANK PLACE. MUD AND DAN- gerous paths, and stripped white trees. The marsh sweated. Trees rustled but barely.

They came, the New Crobuzon outcasts, Susullil and Behellua, a tiny number of brave Hiddentown men. Qurabin was with them, unseen.

Cutter was eager for sound. He wanted to sing or laugh. The landscape ignored him and he felt offended. He tried to think him- self a presence, and could only be conscious of the parings of New Crobuzon left behind him. He befouled where he was with where he had been.

Judah walked in front. An enormous golem walked with him. Eight feet tall, of wood, and what blades Hiddentown could spare. Judah had hammered it together with hinged joints, a crude swivel neck. He could have manifested something with a touch on a wood- pile, but with only thaumaturgy holding it it would have drained him quicker or fallen apart.

Judah had played the wax cylinder again. *Don't feel as if I hardly know you but they say you're family,* the voice said. *He's dead, Uzman's dead.* Cutter saw Judah's sadness at the old message, and wondered what Uzman had been to him.

"D'you know why I became a golemist, Cutter? Years before the Construct War. There was no money in it when I started. It was the arcane end of golemetry that was a draw. Not even in matter. D'you know there's such a thing as a sound golem? It's hard, but you can make one. You've never seen a shadow golem, have you? This kind of golem—" He indicated the wood. "All this is really a by-product, for me. This isn't what it's all about."

Perhaps. But still, the thing they had made was powerful and fine. It swung its head so the faint sun touched its cheap bead eyes. Rusted knives made its fingers.

"The beast's close," came Qurabin's voice. There was pain in it: he had exchanged something for the knowledge.

Cutter prodded his toe at a lump of sickly colours, cussed in shock. It was animal remains. They came unstuck with an unrolling of stench. He tripped, and Pomeroy turned and was shouting as Elsie said something.

"Here!" Elsie said again. She stood over a body. Cutter saw the sheen of decomposition. Most of the chest was gone.

"Dear Jabber," Cutter said. "We're in its godsdamned parlour."

"Quick!" said Judah. "Quick, here!" He was at the swamp's edge, reaching out toward a young man who sat flecked with leeches. The boy was hideously thin. He did not look up, kept his eyes on the greying meat he gnawed.

Cutter broke off a cry. He saw an emaciated man, camouflaged by weeds and knubs of wood. The man was chewing. Beside him was a deep-jungle tapir. Its jaws moved.

"Judah," Cutter said. "Judah, get back," and Judah turned. There were bodies all around in the water, motionless but for chewing. Men and women, a shivering dog. Each was smeared with old matter around their mouths, and seemed to trail a vine.

Gases moiled, and what Cutter had thought a coagulate of

muck began to rise. It blinked. What he had thought stones or holes were eyes. A tight studding of black eyes. It rose.

Those were not vines but the thing's sucker-studded limbs. One stretched from each scrawny figure—each adult or child, each animal, tethered by the back of their necks. What they ate was rerouted into those grotesque intestinal leashes, passing peristaltically. They were made mindless conduits for food. And suspended at the centre of the arms, and shaggy with others whipping free, was the thing that ate through them.

Corpulent as an obese man, vaguely and horribly polyp. It did not hang deadweight but buoyed full of gas or thaumaturgy. Cutter saw a crablike nub of crustacean legs unfolded below, impossibly spindly and close together. It stood very tall as if on a handful of thin stalks. It dripped. It watched. Its tentacles twitched, and it unflexed bony talons.

The thing scuttled quick and grotesquely dainty on legs that should not support it. Its tendrils stretched: it moved without disturbing its idiot feeders.

The Hiddentowners ran, pursued by ghosts of warm fog and by the creature's arms. It gripped trees with its bird claws and scobs of flesh budded from it like snails' eyes. Cutter's repeater felt tiny. He ran toward Judah. The creature's appendages seemed to fill the air. Cutter saw little eyes at one limb's end, a flexing orifice, concentric rasp-teeth like a lamprey's.

Cutter fired at the flanged body, hit and did nothing but burst a little piece with milky bleeding. A snare of arms crawled over each other for him like bickering worms.

"Kill it!" Qurabin spoke from somewhere. There were more shots.

Cutter heard Judah—"Wait, wait"—and then wood and leather and he saw the golem. It cut across the plait of tentacles, severed some right through. Others wrapped around it, ground into the golem's neck. The ropy limb twitched. It shuddered for several seconds, flexed glands, spurted enzymes into the wood. It paused as if confused.

The golem attacked in its simple way, beating down with its knives and great hexed strength. Gouts of matter and the thing's blood burst up and it staggered, and every one of its tethered creatures stopped eating. Pomeroy ran up, jabbed his muzzle into its fat. The explosion was muted by flesh, but the fist of bullets punched into innards.

Even then it did not fall, only staggered with its prim little steps and reeled, but the golem was on it again. Cutter watched Judah move. The somaturge moved his own body, a little, and the wood-and-knife golem echoed him. Handful by handful the golem took the predator apart.

The creature's victims were dead or comatose. They had long been only eating machines for the insatiable thing.

Susullil and Pomeroy were wounded. Susullil let Cutter clean his gashes. Two of the Hiddentowners had been killed. One had fallen near enough to the unnaturally famished men and women in the animal's thrall that they had reached for him weakly, and bitten.

The Hiddentowners took organic trophies, rooting in the creature's flesh for its beaks or talons. Cutter was disgusted. He wished that he had a camera. He imagined a heliotype: Susullil by Judah by Elsie by Pomeroy with his blunderbuss, and he Cutter at the end beside the golem, all of them with the set-faced pride of the hunter.

That night there was rude conviviality in a Hiddentown long-hut. Men and women who had been gatherer-hunters and the inhabitants of chelonas danced, drunk on poteen.

The room was crisscrossed with the little beetle-people. They never spoke; they did nothing to get in anyone's way. They came, silently picking up discarded food, gently fingering the cloth of clothes, sawing their antennae together.

Susullil was with Behellua. Cutter watched them and knew that night they would have the friendly encounter he could not but think of as sex, though he doubted *they* did.

Around the table, people were telling stories. To the Hiddentowners, Qurabin was a god become suddenly interventionist and earthly. The monk moved unseen among the diners, translated for them.

Through Qurabin, Susullil the wineherd told a story of the best harvest House Predicus had ever seen, of the culling of the vinhog bull prime, to let bull secundus, whose fruit was drier and better, stud. He told of the struggle it had been, the sadness he had felt at the bull's passing. When the story was done, the New Crobuzoners applauded with everyone.

It was their turn, and it fell to Cutter. The Hiddentowners chanted softly, in a drumbeat, so when he spoke it took their rhythm. He stalled, looked down and up again and—contrary and drunk, with a pleasure of bravado—he spoke.

"This is a love story," Cutter said. "That shouldn't ever have been. It lasted a night and a morning.

"Five years ago. I found a man. We was in a pub in the docks. I asked him home with me. That night we was on very-tea and shazbah, and we did what we all want to do, you know, and it was fine." There were laughs from the wineherds as Qurabin translated. Elsie and Pomeroy were looking down. "And then later while he slept I turned him over and went to the pisspot, and I saw his clothes. And coming out of his pocket was some little tiny pistol. I'd never seen nothing so clever, and though it weren't my business I pulled it out, and with it comes a little sigil.

"It's militia. He's a militiaman. I don't know what to do. What duty's he on? Is he a drugsman? Is he on Depravity watch? Either way he's got me. I even think of shooting him, but that ain't going to happen. So I'm thinking maybe I can get away early, and maybe I can plead him away on the way to the jail, and maybe this and maybe that. And in the end, I see there ain't nothing I can do. So I go back to bed. And on the way I wake him up. So we do it all over again." Again the cheers. "And then early in the morning we do it *again*." *I'm drunk,* thought Cutter. He did not mind.

"And I'm waiting, and I'll beg him, or bribe him—because I know what he likes, don't I, by now? And I get up, and I run out and think maybe I just won't stop. I'll get to the ships, I'll change my name, I ain't going to jail, I ain't going to be Remade. But then I pass a baker's, and then a greengrocer's, and I just can't up and lose everything. I can't just disappear. So instead of doing a bunk, I do some shopping. And then I come back.

"I wake him up. And we have breakfast together, over my shop in Brock Marsh . . . and then he goes. Big kiss good-bye, and gone. Never seen him again. And I'm left to wonder. Maybe he was never going to do nothing. But the way I see it, the way I like to see it, what with what I done for him that night and what with the beautiful breakfast I made—grilled fish, spiced hash and creamed fruit, with a flower in the middle of the table as if we was married—I think he fell in true love with me for a few minutes that morning. No, I mean it. I fell in love with him too. I ain't never loved nothing like I loved him when he kissed me and said good-bye. Because I'm sure, I'm sure he knew that I knew. It was his present to me, that leave-taking, that good-bye. Just like breakfast was my present to him. I ain't never loved anyone like that before or since, except one man."

When it was obvious he had finished there was barking from the wineherds, and other applause sounds from here and there among the audience. Elsie and Pomeroy clapped a bit, though Pomeroy did not look at him. Watching the big man beat his palms together Cutter felt a blossom of affection. *Gods bless,* he thought, and to crown it Elsie even gave him a quick smile.

And then he saw Judah, and the smile on the golemist's face was different—there was no effort or connection to it, it was like the smile on an idol, and through his passion for the older man Cutter burned.

* * *

Cutter was uninterested in gods. There were a few from New Cro-buzon's pantheons he felt some small affinity for, usually for heretic reasons: like Crawfoot, whose antics seemed not inept clownery but tactical subversions. *You're insurrectionist, ain't you?* he had always thought, while the priests affected patient indulgence with the fool-god on Crawfootfete E'en. But he did not worship. Such prayers as he offered were cynical or time-serving. But he could see the power of Qurabin's devotions.

The monk could find the hidden and the lost, though it cost. But in Qurabin's voice Cutter no longer heard the arrogance of that power. He could hear that something had shifted. *The monk's giving up,* Cutter thought.

"Galaggi, they say it is . . . *sobrech* or *sobrechin lulsur.* It's pun." Qurabin's voice came and went as the monk unhid the informa-tion. "*Sobresh* is 'hateful,' and *sobr'chi,* is 'captain.' In my language it has no name. In Tesh . . . we do not classify so much as you." And Cutter heard the disgust, the rage in Qurabin's voice when Tesh came up.

He was not surprised the next day, when Qurabin came to them as they rose and told them that they would not be travelling alone. That the monk would not tell them where Iron Council was but would show them.

He wants to rest, Cutter thought. *And to be alone. With us. Pluck-ing up courage. The monk'll unhide more and more, no matter what the cost. What does it matter? What does he—she—have to live for? To be loyal to?*

It rained but it was a different rain. The sun's rays were frozen in each drop like insects in amber, so it seemed to rain light. The Hiddentowners waved them gone.

Susullil smiled at Cutter and nodded. "Never did understand each other, did we, boy?" Cutter said with true humour. Qurabin's voice, the odd androgynous hooting, gusted good-bye. No one seemed distraught that their god was leaving.

Of course Cutter had no notion of what Qurabin was saying. *"You are your own people now, you have no need of gods,"* he thought. Or *"Be true to my memory or I'll come back to blind you with my rage,"* or *"I was never a god, I'm a bloke like you, got lost because of an idiot religion."*

The travellers went northwest and north. A day, and another, through the slowly cooling forest. The ground rose and the canopy fell.

Trees became more sparse. By pools creatures like spindly bears and serrated wasps the size of cats came to drink. Cutter thought he saw things; he thought they were watched.

In the unseen company of the monk, they moved very differently. It was Drogon who saw it first. *"We're travelling too fast,"* he told Cutter. He pointed down, toward where an ancient Y-shaped tree poked clear of the surrounds. *"Keep it in sight,"* he whispered.

Cutter tried to watch his feet but it disoriented him; the terrain changed uncertainly as if the path were skittish. Ahead a half mile he saw the tree by a river; he heard Qurabin move and speak loudly and Cutter ducked below a thorny branch and when he released it he walked on two more steps then stopped while Drogon whispered, *"I told you."*

The water was behind them. Cutter could see it through the growth, and there was the tree, black-barked, its boughs spread and thrusting skyward like supplicating arms. It was behind him too.

There had been no dislocation. He had only walked. His companions looked consternated, except Judah. "What does it cost you?" the golemist said to Qurabin. "To find these ways?"

"These are hidden ways, shortcuts—lost paths," said the monk. "Sometimes the Moment'll let me take them. Sometimes." The monk sounded tired. "I said I'd take you."

* * *

Why so fast, monk? Cutter thought. *You don't have to travel like this. What's this costing you, all these secrets?*

So they sped up though they walked, and shucked their packs and scrambled at the same pace they ever had. The everyday uncanny of the monk's trails took them at increasing speeds. They passed pillars of rock in the middle of trees, and rounded them to emerge in dry plateau. The woods were threadbaring; it was as if they trod through an old and thinning tapestry.

"Through . . . *here* I think," Qurabin would say, and their compass needles yawed haywire as they crossed leagues. They went faster than horses.

Qurabin's efforts, Cutter understood, were apostate. Qurabin was wrenching things from the Moment's domain of lost and hidden things. Every day Qurabin sounded lessened.

"You want to disappear." Cutter spoke it in a tiny voice. The monk was displaced, renegade, renounced by history and home. *You want to disappear. Every lost route you uncover, you lose something— something's hidden from you. You've had enough. And this is how you'll do it. To make it mean something.* Their journey was Qurabin's protracted suicide.

"You know what the monk's doing," Cutter said to Judah. "We better hope Qurabin don't be all hidden or lost before we get where we're going."

"It's close," said Judah. He smiled then, a look of such joy that Cutter could not help but smile back.

The land was deep in grasses. Kettled glacial till, sloughs and dustbeds intermitted the low slopes. There had been so many weeks of journey. They saw mesquite copses and ruins. With the wind, the wild crops moved like sea. The monk grew weaker, more hidden, but cajoled and led them past water, past animal herds, python-sized centipedes wrapped around trees.

One day they saw things leave a trail of pollen and dust and shake the grasses like whales in shallows. Borinatch, strider, the ungulate plains nomads. A family clan, young at the front, the queen behind. The striders stood much taller than a man. They careered by with their tottering gallop, their legs unbending and swinging like crutches.

One of the sows turned a friendly bestial face and saw them, waved as she thundered past. Borinatch hands worked in strange ways. It looked as if her limb appeared and disappeared.

The travellers had become a tough crew. Their muscles were bunched; they were expert shots. Pomeroy's cuts had stained inside, so he wore splendid dark scars. Elsie fastened a bandana about her wild hair. The men's beards were long, their shag tied back with leather: only Drogon defied this, shaving dry every few days. They husbanded their dwindling bullets, carried fire-hard spears. They looked, Cutter thought, like adventurers, the continent's mercenary freebooters.

We ain't though. There's a damn reason for all our travels.

"It must be nearly Sinn, ain't it?" he said. "Or is it already? I've lost track." They tried to work through the weeks on their fingers.

One night Judah made four little figures from the earth, and with muttered cantrips he had them dance while his companions clapped to give them music. When they were done he had them bow; then they fell back into earth.

He said: "I want to tell you all that I'm grateful. I want you to know that." They drank a toast in water. "I want to tell you . . . we've been going so long, it's like the journeying's what it's for. But that's not so.

"I don't even know for sure if you believe in the Iron Council." He smiled. "I think you do. But maybe for some of you it isn't even about that anymore. I think you're here because of the time in the claphouse, Elsie," he said, and she met his eyes and nodded. "I know why you're here," he said to Cutter.

"Even you, maybe, Drogon . . . A stravager like you . . . Myths and hopes are your currency, right? That's what you trade in; that's what keeps horse-tramps moving. Are you here because you think Iron Council's like the Marzipan Palace? Are you looking for a heaven?"

"It's not why *I'm* here, Judah Low," said Pomeroy. Judah smiled. "You mean the most to me, Judah, I'd die for you, but I'd not die *now*. Not with what's happening in New Crobuzon. There's too much at stake. I'm here because of what you say's coming for the Council. And because I think you can stop it. That's why I'm here."

Judah nodded, and sighed. "That's what I want to say. This is greater than any of us. Iron Council . . ." He was silent for very long. "It's tough, because that's how it's had to be. But it's the Council. It's Iron Council. And the governors of New Crobuzon—I don't know how—they've found it. My contact, my erstwhile friend, he had every reason not to tell me but he did, thank Jabber. They've found it, after all this time. Long enough that plenty of citizens aren't sure it ever existed, and thousands more think it's long gone.

"Chaverim . . . friends . . . We're going to save Iron Council."

The next day Qurabin had a long conversation with the Moment. The unfindable monk cried, supplicated, made a desolate sound.

At last Cutter spoke. "Monk," he said. "Monk, what happened? Are you there? Are you gone?"

"It's not hidden anymore," Qurabin said in a voice that was deadened. "I know where to find it. But it cost . . . I lost my own language."

Qurabin had been left only with Ragamoll, the brash infant tongue of the travellers.

"I remember my mother," Qurabin said quietly. "I remember what she whispered to me. But I don't know what it means." There was no horror in the voice. Only a passionless assent. "One thing is lost, another found. I know where to go."

They went uncanny routes. The sky's colour fluxed.

It was a Chainday when the plain fell away and they realised they had been rising a long time; the ground had angled and they walked a hackberried butte in thin air. Before them was a basin in red laterite, a canyon that widened into land too vast to be a valley, where the continent had shrugged itself apart. From behind one long stone fin, black smoke was spoiling the air.

Judah stood at the edge of the cliff and looked down at the fumes that did not come from grassfires and howled. A noise of such pure feral joy it was as if he was thrown back through history, as if no human, no sentient thing, should feel such absolute emotion. Judah bayed.

He did not slow. He descended fast and did not wait for his companions but headed off along faint foot-lines in the prairie. Cutter caught him up but did not try to speak. Thick light like syrup went across the sierra.

Someone shouted at them and they were taunted by echoes. A query, a command in several different languages, in rapid change. And then their own. Ragamoll, nearly two thousand miles from home. Cutter gasped. Three figures stood from some hide.

"Hold it, hold it," one shouted. "Speak Ragamoll?"

Cutter showed he was not holding his weapons. He nodded his head in strange delight. The young man spoke with a hybrid accent, something else shaping his phonemes beside the familiar snarl of the south city, of Dog Fenn, of backstreet New Crobuzon.

Judah was running toward the three: a woman, and a man, and a gnarled cactus. The sun was going down behind them, so they were shadowed, and Cutter could see them only as cutouts. Stumbling toward them his arms upraised, Judah must be drenched in late-day light as they saw him, awash with it, creasing his face against it, ambered. Judah was laughing and shouting.

"Yes, yes, yes, we speak Ragamoll!" he said. "Yes, we're of your party! Sisters! Sisters!" He gave that cry again and was so clearly no threat, so obviously in a delirium of warmth and relief that the human guards stepped forward and opened their arms to him, to receive him as a guest. *"Sisters!"* he said. "I'm back, I'm *home,* it's me. *Long live Iron Council!* Gods and Jabber and, and, and in Uzman's name . . ." They started at that. Judah embraced them one by one, and then he turned, his eyes streaming, and smiled without mediation, without face, a smile Cutter had never seen him wear.

"We're here," Judah said. "Long live, long live. We're here."

anamnesis

———◆———

THE PERPETUAL

TRAIN

W ITH EACH STEP WATER AND THE ROOTS OF WATERWEEDS SNAG him. It is years ago and Judah Low is young and in the wetlands.

—Again, he says. That is all. There is no *please* and no need for it. This language is deep-structured with courtesy. To be rude takes effortful and irregular declensions.

—Again, he says and the stiltspear child shows him what it has made. Its eyebrows flex in what he knows to be a smile and it opens its hand and a stiltspear toy made of mud and waterlilies stands between its fingers. The child pinches it to shape and sings to it in a tiny wordless trilling, and makes it move. The figurine has only one motion, flexing and unflexing its stem legs. It does it several times before bursting.

They stand at the edges of wide space edged with gnarly treelife and intricately fronded byways, random canals. Boughs hide passages, and vegetation is so thick and so heavy, so saturated with the water of the swamp it is glutinous, it is like a viscid liquid dripping from the branches and briefly coagulates in the shape of leaves.

The swamp mimics all landscapes. It opens into meadows and it can be forest. There are places where mud solidifies enough to pile into swamp-mountains. Tunnels below the rootstuff, floored in water, pitch and labyrinth. There are dead places where bleached trees jut from rank water. Tribes of mosquito and blackfly come to Judah and bleed him terribly.

To Judah the fen air is not oppressive. It is like a caul. In the months he has lived there Judah has learnt to feel cosseted by it. For all his bites gone septic and his diarrhoea, he loves the swamp. He looks up through clouds thin as watered milk, to a late sun. He feels himself greened, mildewed and inhabited by infusoria, a host, a landscape as well as a life.

The child dips its hand with the grace of its species. Its fingers are radial from its little palm, a star. It clenches in its way: hinges its tapered digits like the petals of a closing flower, into a point. Nails concatenate, its hand become a spearhead.

The stiltspear young walks quadruped from Judah Low. It turns its head on a neck that is all sinews and wordlessly queries whether he will come, and he does, with the slushing clumsiness that the stiltspear indulge as if he is neonate.

When the child walks, its limbs precisely pierce the water. Judah Low seems to drag the swamp with him and scar it with a wide wake. He is lucky the dams and sires of this stiltspear piglet let him go with it, as every moment he walks he attracts attentions it would be better to avoid. The black caiman and constrictors must hear his passage as the thrashes of something wounded.

The stiltspear commune have tolerated and even welcomed him because of the time he saved two youngsters from some rearing glade predator. It came for him, he still believes, but veered for the little duo who when it rose hissing and slick with bog had frozen and whose camouflage glands had secreted thaumaturgons such that they might have been tree-stumps not silent children, but the creature had been too close to be dissuaded.

But Judah had shouted and banged together his specimen pot

and cudgel, shockingly alien in the dim quiet of the bayou. He could not have frightened the thing—a towering amalgam of sea lion and jaguar and salamander with finned flanges that could have broken his skull—but he confused it. It had burrowed below the water-weed.

Since then, since the pair he saved had run home and sang the story in a quickly constructed cavatina to stress its truth, Judah has been tolerated.

The stiltspear do not often speak. Days can pass.

Their commune has no name. Its hutlets rise from the reeds and water and are conjoined with walkways and slung with hammocks, and other rooms are sunk in pits in the sodden ground. Insects the size of Judah's fist amble through the air, purring like big stupid cats. The stiltspear will skewer and eat them.

Stiltspears' coats of oily down bead with swamp muck. They move like wading birds. They are like birds, and like scrawny cats, with unmoving, near-unfeatured faces.

Sires sing worshipful lays if they are red sires and build tools and reed-houses and tend the mangrove farms if they are tan sires. The dams hunt, one leg at a time raising so slow they have dried by the time the spread-out claws emerge, so no drips trouble the surface as the asterisk of fingers come together into a stiletto that poises over its reflection. Until some fat fish or frog passes and everything is still and the hand lances back into the water and is instantly withdrawn, the fingers opened, the game spiked on the stiltspear's wrist, a prey bracelet dripping blood.

Between houses, stiltspear young play with mud-made golems as children in New Crobuzon play marbles and shove-stiver. Judah makes notes, takes heliotypes. He is no xenologist. He does not know how to decide what is important. All these charms—the stiltspears' instinct camouflage, their golems, their herbalist physic, their unsticking of moments—he wants to investigate.

He does not know the names of any or even if they have names, but there are those according to some faint specificity of physique he christens: Red-eyes and Oldster and The Horse. Judah asks Oldster about the mud figures. Toys, his informant says, or games: something like that. —So you'd no longer make them? Judah asks, and the stiltspear snorts and looks skyward in embarrassment. Judah no longer blushes at his gaffes. So far as he can tell it is a question of propriety not ability: it would be as inappropriate for an adult stiltspear to make the little figures as for a New Crobuzon adult to demand the lavatory like a toddler.

Judah accompanies the dams. They seem glazed with the daylight. They catch armfuls of shelled waterspider larger than Judah's spread hands. They milk their silk, weaving webs between roots and submerged boughs, turning rivulets into fish-traps.

Judah sees something uncanny. A lithe musclefish jackknifes, lapis scales vivid. And then Judah hears a moment of song, a two- or three-layered stripped-down breath of rhythm, *buh buh buh buh* in quick intricate time, several dams together, and the musclefish is still. It is set in its coil, unmoving, frosted in place in the water, and a hunter spears it with her jag-hand and at the instant she stabs for it she and her companions cease singing and the musclefish twitches again but too late. Judah sees it happen again, days later, a little near-silent choir, a muttered hum that for a moment keeps prey still.

Freshwater dolphin pass in deeper channels. They are ugly, inbred-looking things. The snorts of a sarcosuchus spook them. The stiltspear young try to teach Judah to make a mud-figure of his own. They have decided he is a child like them. His models are desperately crude and make them breathe the sighs that are their laughs.

When they sing to their statuettes he tries good-humouredly to copy them, knowing he can only be a clown and, performing with good grace, —Shallaballoo, he says. —Callam callay cazah! And of course nothing happens, of course all the stiltspear children

set their mud walking and his own folds sticky on itself and col-
lapses.

It is the end of summer and the paludal air is stretched thin. Shots
sound. With the distant percussion of the rifle every stiltspear
freezes in camouflage and for seconds Judah is alone in a copse of
sudden trees. With silence the swamplanders slowly return to their
appearance. Every one of them looks at Judah.

THERE ARE HUNTERS, DRAPED IN THE LITTLE CORPSES OF SWAMP mammals. They are exploring and collecting in the bogland.

Judah passes one within ten yards, but he has become local, so the man does not hear or see him, only hefts his rifle and looks stupidly past Judah to the watercourses. Another man is sharper. He aims directly at Judah's chest in expert motion.

—Godsdamn blast, he says. —Came near to killing you. There is a cautious look to him as he makes out Judah's clothes and his swamp-pallor. He thumbs a way north. —They out that way, 'nother three four miles, be there by sundown, he says.

The bayou animals are quiet. There is not the chittering and faint scuttle and splash. Judah slows. This is a hinge moment and though there is none to blame for getting him here save himself, he must close his eyes and think on what will be and what has been. He will not let the moment finish: by ornery bastard will he hangs onto it, like a dog worrying a man, till time drags itself away bleeding and Judah is back and sadder.

—Oh now, he says. He is some misbegot thing in time. There is
a shudder.

There is a lip of earth, a jetty. There is a clearing at the edge of a big
muskeg, flat and detritus-studded acres of gently moving liquid.
There is a new trail through dripping trees, to a huddle of tents and
wagons, sod huts roofed in moss on the tamed ground. There are
shots.

Judah carries a present in his pack and a posy of swampflowers.
He sees a party of men in besmirched white shirts and thick
trousers. They investigate charts and are squinting at obscure in-
struments. They boil kettles of food over fires that roll off oily
smoke like squid-ink billows. They half-greet Judah. He must look
like some mud-and-slurry spirit. The Remade pack-animals tread
uneasily as he approaches.

The leader stands. An older man, still scrawny and tough as
a dog. Judah looks only at him, follows him into his tarpaulined
room.

Light grubs dimly through the canvas. There is simple darkwood furniture, a cabinet that will fold out to a bed, in the tight
confines.

The old man smells the battered bouquet. Judah becomes
confused—he has forgotten his city manners. Should he be giving flowers to this aging man? But the man responds with grace,
smelling the still-beautiful blooms and putting them in water.

He is poised. His hair is white and gathered in a precise pigtail.
He has very vivid blue eyes. Judah rummages in his bag (the bodyguards stiffen and raise pistols) and brings out a figurine.

—This is for you, he says. —From the stiltspear.

The man receives it with what seems very genuine pleasure.

—It's a god, Judah says. —They don't do so much by way of art
or carvings. Only little simple things.

It is a rope-swathed ancestor spirit. This one Judah made himself. The man looks into its swaddled face.

—I want to ask you something, Judah says. —I didn't know you'd be here yourself . . .

—Always, when we break new ground. This is holy work, son.

Judah nods as if he has been told something precious.

—There are people in the swamp, sir, he says. —I'm here for them, I guess.

—Do you think I don't know that, son? Think I don't know why you're here? That's why I'm telling you this is holy work we're doing. I'm trying to save you sorrow.

—They aren't as you'd think from Shac's bestiary sir . . .

—Son I respect the *Potentially Wise* more than most but you don't need to tell me. It's a long time since I've thought it, ah, accurate shall we say. That's not at issue.

—But sir. I need to know, what I want to know is how . . . is exactly where you think you might go because there are, these people, these stiltspear, they, they . . . I don't know as they could face what you might bring here . . .

—I wouldn't mean no harm but I by gods and by Jabber will not turn away now. There is nothing harsh to his voice but the fervour makes Judah cold. —Understand, son, what's coming. I have no plans for yon stiltspear, but if their way intersects with mine then yes, my way will crush them down.

—Do you know what you see here? he says. —Every one of us here, and every one coming, the dustiest navvy, each clerk, each camp whore, each cook and horseman and each Remade, every one of us is a missionary of a new church and there is nothing that will stop holy work. I mean you no unkindness. Is that all you have to say to me?

Judah stares at him in terrible sadness. He works to speak.

—How long? he says at last. —What are the plans?

—I think you know the plans, son. The old man is calm. —And

how long? You need to ask the downs. And then you need to ask the gods and spirits of yon fen how much good clean grit they can eat up.

He smiles. He touches Judah's knee.

—You sure there's nothing else you'd like to tell me? I had hope of hearing other things from you, but you'd have spoken them by now. I want to thank you for the god you gave me, and I'll be obliged if you'll go to your stiltspear people and tell them that they have my deepest most respectful gratitude. You know I'll be seeing them soon, don't you?

He points to the wall, to a map that shows all the land from New Crobuzon to Rudewood, to the swamps and on to the port of Myr-shock, and some hundreds of miles into the continent, into the west. Details are vague: this is debated land. But Judah can see the crosshatched levelling in the heart of the swamp.

—I know what I see, the old man says and there is real kindness in his voice. —I have in my time seen enough men go native. It's an affectation, son, whatever you think now. But I won't lecture you. There's no recrimination. I will only tell you that history is coming, and your new tribe best move from its path.

—But dammit, says Judah. —This isn't empty land!

The old man looks bewildered. —What they have, what they've had lying there for centuries in that marsh, whatever it is, it's welcome to face the history I bring, if it can.

Back in deep waterland among the stiltspear, Judah does not know what to say. The fronds gather behind him, a closure he knows is a lie.

The children try to make him learn their golems again. He has never affected the smallest glamour before, has thought himself without talent. A stiltspear elder approaches while he strains, and touches Judah's chest. Judah opens his eyes, feels things move in him. Whether it is the touch, the air of the swamp, or the raw things

he has been eating, he feels a facility he never has, and in astonishment he sees that just faintly he can make his mud model move.
The stiltspear children give little hums of acclaim.

—There are some coming, he says at night. The stiltspear only
stare politely. —There are men coming and they will fill your
swamp. They will split your wetlands, and diminish them.

Judah recalls the map. A neat trisection. Ink that will come to be
a changed land, millions of tons of displaced scree and a devasta-
tion of the trees.

—They will not stop for you. They will not move for you. You
must go. You must go south to where the other clans hunt, deeper,
farther away.

There is nothing for a long time. Then the monosyllables of
stiltspear gently.

—It is where the other clans hunt. They do not want us.

—But you must. If you do not go you will see what the men will
bring. The clans must come together and hide.

—We hide. When the men come we shall be trees.

—It will not be enough. The men will make the land dry. They
will cover your village.

The stiltspear look at him.

—You must go.

They will not.

In the next days Judah chews his fingernails. He eats with the stiltspear and watches them and heliotypes their activities and notes
them, but with a waxing sickness he feels now that it is for their re-
membrance.

—There have been fights, they tell him when he demands to
know of their wars. —We fought another clan three years ago and
many of us were killed.

Judah asks how many and the stiltspear holds up its hands—
this one has seven fingers on each—opens and closes them and
holds up one more finger. Fifteen.

Judah shakes his head. —Very many, very very many more
will be killed if you do not go, he says, and the stiltspear shakes
its head too—it has learnt the motion from him and uses it with
pride.

—We will be trees, it says.

Judah can make his mudling dance. Each day he is stronger at it.
Now he makes foot-tall figures from the clay and peat. He does not
know what it is he makes happen or how the stiltspear children
have taught him or what the adult put in him, but his new capabilities delight him. His little model can beat others now, at the golem
circus they play.

It is his only pleasure, and he hates that it feels like an evasion.
Once or twice more he begs the stiltspear to come with him to the
deeper swamp. It degrades him that he cannot find the words to
move them. It is their culture, he says to himself, it is their way, it is
their nature. They—not he—are to blame. But he does not believe
his own thought.

He feels pinioned by history. He can wriggle like a stuck butterfly but can go nowhere.

There are more reverberations and the explosions from
hunters' guns are audible throughout the days. Judah understands
something. He watches the stiltspear corner a calf-thick amphibian,
and together sing-breathe the *uh uh uh uh uh* rhythm and for half a
second the newt-thing petrifies midflick, held in time made thick,
and Judah realises the rhythm they have sung is an echo of the
children's mud-golem song. The same, made vastly more complex,
given several parts.

He is obsessed with the chant. He wants to preserve the moments of its utterance, congeal the sounds, strip them down. He can
only time them as closely as he can and write them to work out
their relations.

Judah works fast. He feels a knot tying in him. His near-friend
Red-eyes helps him. —We make shapes that move. All of us: young

one way, hunters another. And Judah sees that the children's chants are only mimicry; it is their hands that make their golems. The rhythm of the hunters does the work of the children's pinching fingers. Both intercessions are of a kind.

There is a noise of industry, far off. A growled rhythm.

The first stiltspear to die is a young too confused to control its camouflage. It is shot by a hunter frightened by the rapid flickering between states of a four-footed animal thing and what seems a rotting tree. He does not know what he has killed and it is only chance and neophobia that he does not eat the child. The clan find the little body.

They've reached the lake, Judah thinks. He imagines uncountable wagonloads of nothing, of soil, stone and dirt bloating the swamp.

The time is now. To make his new clan go deep and disappear. There is no other time for this. He has been beaten down. Though every night he says again what he has said—you must go, it is not safe, more will die—he has given up. He is disengaging. An observer again.

The stiltspear debate quietly. Their food grows scarce. The fish and the food-animals are fleeing or being choked. There is venom in the swamp, the runoff of a thousand men and women, the slurry from latrines and cleaning crystals, from black powder, from make-do graves.

There is another death, a lone dam surprised. The roar of industry is always audible.

A party of stiltspear hunters return and try to say what they have seen. A drained core, something approaching. By now there are steam shovels, Judah knows, ever-growing gangs.

—One tried to hurt us, a stiltspear says, and it shows the company the gun it has taken. It is stained with human blood. They have killed, and Judah knows then it is over and done. The time is finished. They do not see it. The sun is dead for them. There is nothing left. He is frantic to learn, to preserve these people in his notes, to salute them.

After that kill the stiltspear become prey.

The red sires unwrap their coddled god and recarve him as a murder spirit. They revive a death-cult. Chosen dams and tan sires dip their spear-hands in poisons that will kill with a tiny cut and will seep through their skins over a day and a night and kill them too, so they have no choice but to be suicide berserkers, against the incoming company.

Judah sees the corpses of New Crobuzon men punctured by stiltspear hands, bloated with toxin, bobbing in cul-de-sacs of greenery. If he is found with the stiltspear he will be a race-traitor, a city-traitor, and will be put to a slow, unsanctioned but approved death. Stiltspear braves ambush the men of the roadway.

They kill humans and some cactacae in threes and fours. There is a reward on each pair of stiltspear hands. Within days there are newcomers in the swamp, bloodprice hunters. They dress in apoc-alypse rags in defiance of all societies, renegades of a hundred cultures. Judah sees them through the trees.

Bounty scum from Cobsea, and from Khadoh, and pirate cactacae from Dreer Samher. There are vodyanoi, the dregs of Gharcheltist and New Crobuzon. A woman seven feet tall fights with two flails and hauls off many stiltspear dead. There are ru-mours of a gessin in his armour. A witch from the Firewater Straits snares many pairs of hands, makes a grotesque bouquet of them, sleeping a hunt-sleep to conjure dreamdevils that prey upon the camp.

—Go deep, Judah says again, and those still alive in the town-ship are listening.

They head south. Red-eyes tells Judah they will find shelter among the new mongrel tribe of runaways from all the stiltspear nations.

—I will go soon, Judah tells him. Red-eyes nods, another learned gesture.

There are no children left in the township to challenge with little golems. There are only adults whose grace is now martial, who count kills and set traps. The grinding of stone and gears is unending as the works approach.

ONE DAY JUDAH RISES AND GATHERS ALL HE HAS—NOTES, SPECI-mens, heliotypes and drawings—and walks out of the village, through water maze to the new industrial zone. He is unstuck. The moment has passed him.

There is a foreman at the edge of a new clearing, shouting at his crews. Judah stares. They are crude and small and hubristic, but they are reshaping the land.

The foreman nods at Judah as he passes, and tells him, —This ain't no fuckin' godsdamned fuckin' lake this piece of shit is a devil. He gobs into the black water. —Eats and eats every godspitting ton of shite we put in it. It don't have no bottom.

Axemen and flagmen, chainmen, hunters, engineers cutting trenches; cactus-people, vodyanoi, men and Remade. They work with spades and saws, picks, barrows. The swamp is thinning.

Man after man, Remade, cactus, comes with cart full of gypsum and gravelled earth and tips it from the new quay. A steam shovel spastically drops its loads. Ballast is swallowed. Waterweed and the pelage of leaves and dust is gone, the muskeg's camouflage is defeated, its water uncovered in a spreading ring. Barrow after barrow is sucked down with a throat noise.

—See? See? the foreman says. —This godsdamned thing's deeper than a whore's cunt.

This was quagmire once, where mud would wrestle you in as vigorous as the constrictors. Stone hauled from the foothills rises in blocks, lapped by the thick water. They are bulwarks that hold in gravel and earth. Dry land is cut out. A road of matter has been excised, a swath of tamaracks, mangroves, runt grasses and the debris of spatterdock. It is a ribbon of flattened earth a score of yards wide and endlessly long, sweeping backward through wet thickets, purged of trees, tended by haulers and hewers as far as Judah can see.

There is a stretched-out tent-town. Carts are carried by mules Remade to swamp things, amphibian. Judah walks the raised road. Stumps stubble the ground, and beyond them the fingers of the swamp move. Pumps howl and drain the waterways, make them mudflats, and then these mudflats become beds for new stones. There are gangs of cactus-people, their muscles moving hugely beneath spined skins.

And there are many Remade. They do not look at the whole men, free workers, the aristocracy of this labour.

The Remade are always various. All Judah's life. Their bodies made impossible. On the roadbed there is a man whose front pullulates with scrawny arms, each from a corpse or an amputation. Chained to him a taller man, his face stoic, a fox stitched embedded in his chest from where it snarls and bites at him in permanent terror.

Here a crawling man spiral-shelled in iron and venting smoke. Here a woman working, because there are women among the Remade, a woman become a guttered pillar, her organic parts like afterthoughts. A man—or is it a woman?—whose flesh moves with

tides, with eructations like an octopus. People with their faces relo-
cated, bodies made of iron and rubber cables, and steam-engine
arms, and animal arms, and arms that are body-length pistons on
which the Remade walk, their legs replaced with monkey's paws so
they reach out from below their own waists.

The Remade haul, their overseers watching and sometimes
whipping. The roadbed goes back forever through the trees.

—My stiltspear friend, the old man says. He welcomes Judah.

—My stiltspear friend, it's good to see you. Are you come back
to us? Judah nods. —I'm glad, son. It's best. How are your clan?

Judah looks up coldly but he sees no crowing. The question is
not a provocation. —Gone, Judah says. He feels his failure.

The man nods and purses his lips. —And will you show us their
homestead? he says. —I want to take it down. It'll be unacceptable
if there's a place for them to come back to. There'll be a town here,
you know. Yes there will. We sit on the subsoil of Junctiontown or
Forktown or Palus Trifork, I've not yet decided. And I could make
the stiltspear village a museum, so a half-day's hike from the Plaza
di Vapor visitors could go to see it. But I'm of a mind to raze it. So
will you show me where it is?

If it is left there will be stiltspear who will want to return; children will try to find their old playgrounds.

—I'll show you.

—Good lad. I understand and I admire you. You've come
through something and I respect that. Did you find what you
wanted? I remember when first we spoke. When I hired you, you
remember. I wanted something from you but I always thought
you wanted something from the swamp, or the stiltspear. Did you
find it?

—Yes. I did.

The old man smiles and holds out his hand, and Judah gives
him the sheafs of maps, of notations, of fen-lore. The old man does

not say how late the information is. He flicks through it but does not say how poor it is, how inadequately Judah has kept his part of the wage-bargain. Another man comes in and speaks rapidly about a dispute, a failing deadline. The old man nods.

—We have so many problems, he says. —The foremen are angry with the city's magisters. They have no sense of what we're doing; they send us Remade with no capabilities. Our pilings are breaking. Our retaining walls buckle, our trestles collapse. He smiles. —None of this surprises me.

—Welcome back, he says. —Now, are you on my payroll? Will you go back to New Crobuzon? Or stay? We'll speak. I have to go. We've been so long here, with the flat behind us, the rust-eaters have caught us up. They've reached the trees.

Yes, there they are. Only a short time along the roadbed, which is flatter and more finished the farther back Judah goes. It has a beauty, this trained land. An oddity, this road at which the swamp claws.

A corner and a new workforce is there. Cosseted by diminished trees, like the crew that flattens the fenland but moving with unique rhythm, a syncopation of construction.

A crowd unfolds toward him. There is a rapid thudding as sleepers are dropped and then a sound like something being sliced as girders unroll from a flatcar, crews Remade and whole picking them up with tongs, a baffling dainty motion, letting them down as sledge-wielding brawnies step in and timed as perfectly as an orchestra hammer the ties and rails. Behind them all something huge and noisy vents and watches their efforts, and edges constantly forward. A train, deep among the mangroves.

IT WAS MONTHS EARLIER THAT HE FIRST MET THE OLD MAN. WEATHER Wrightby. Crazyweather, Iron Wright. In the offices of TRT, at the recruitment meetings, with all the other young men in starch and braces.

University boys, clerks' sons, the adventurous rich and aspirational young men like Judah, Dog Fenn and Chimer apprentices bored by their work, fired by children's stories and travelogues.

—I have wanted this for decades, Wrightby said. He was compelling. The recruits were respectful of this man nearly three times their age. His money did not diminish him. —Twice I went west finding routes. Twice, sadly, I had to come home. There's a crossing that's still to be done. That's the big task. This that we do now is only a start. A little tinkering southerly.

A thousand miles of track. Through rottenstone, forests and bog. Judah was cowed by Wrightby's fervour. This undertaking is so vast it could bankrupt even such a wealth as his.

Wrightby had felt him, sounded his chest like a doctor. Handed out commissions, put teams together. —You can report to us from the swamps, boy. It'll be tough terrain. We need to know what to expect.

That is how Judah got here.

THE FIRST JOURNEY FROM NEW CROBUZON. A TEAM: ENGINEERS, gendarmes, scholars and rugged scouts who had looked at long-haired Judah with friendly condescension. They started two, three miles west of New Crobuzon, under heavy guard. A flatbed town carved out of the land, a range of buffers, a fan of rails.

Warehouses big enough to hold ships, mountains of gravel, planks from stripcutting Rudewood. A mob of humans and cactacae; khepri, their scarab heads fidgetsome; vodyanoi in the canals that linked to the city, crewing open-bottomed barges; rarer races. A garden of different limbs. Cheap deals, contracts, assignations. The Remade were corralled, shovelled like meat animals onto barred trucks. And on into the empty land, skirting the edges of the forest through cuts blasted with blackpowder, went the railroad.

It was late spring. Dirigibles puttered overhead, sweep-surveying the landscape, tracking the iron way. At the train window Judah watched the wilderness.

The train was full with recruits: labourers on wood benches, the prison-trucks of the Remade. Judah sat with other surveyors. He listened to the pistons. The squat, simple trains within New Crobuzon were always accelerating or slowing, only ever jerking between stations. There was no time for them to pick up pace, to maintain it and create this new sound, this utterly new beat of a speeding train.

They passed a village: an odd and ugly sight. Sidings slid toward it, and Judah could see the original wattle-and-daub dwellings alongside rapidly thrown-up wood houses. It must have trebled in size within a year.

—Frenzy, said one man. —Can't last. They'll be crying within two years. Every piece-of-shit town we pass gives the railroad money, or some syndicate from New Crobuzon comes down, takes it over, pays Wrightby's railroad so's they get the damn rails. They can't all make it. Some towns are going to die.

—Or be killed, another said, and they laughed. —Before we even broke ground they started building. There's a township to the west, Salve, built by men from Wrightby's own Transcontinental Railroad Trust, if you please. They drew up the plans for this Myrshock-Cobsea route with Iron Wright hisself, got their town ready for him. From nothing. A halfway place before the swamp junction.

—Only there was some shenanigans, Jabber knows what, and Iron Wright isn't talking to them. So now we'll be skirting away and no iron road's coming to Salve. The men laughed. —Still there. Still modern. Cold-dead empty. The youngest ghost-town in Rohagi.

Judah imagined music halls, a bathhouse, visited only by dust, eaten by creepers.

They stopped at a newly bloated township, and hawkers rushed for the train. They held up cheap food, cheap clothes, hand-printed gazetteers promising a bestiary and maps of the newly opening lands. They sold rail-end papers—Judah bought one, a roughly inked sheet *The Wheelhouse*, thick with errors in spelling and grammar. It was full of workers' complaints, contumely about the failings of the Remade, scatology and hand-drawn pornography.

The rails angled southwest by churned mud and rubbish where a temporary town had been dismantled, on to rocks and grasslands. Once the train scaled a ravine on a new trestled bridge that swayed under them.

They switchbacked up inclines where they had to but mostly the train went straight—deviations were failures. Where stone reared it was split, become scree-edged furrows stained by smoke. To the west, mountains overlooked them. The Bezhek Peaks, girdled in shadow. When the train began to slow again, it was for the end of the line.

There were people in those wilds. Many women, in hill-dirted petticoats. Some carried children. Suddenly they were hundreds, in a tent city close to the bright rails. Streetwalkers bizarrely displaced to the desolate landscape.

The sun lowered and there were fires. Judah thought of the people left behind, the dead, diseased and killed, the children abandoned or smothered, buried by the line. They slowed past a herd of cattle, mongrel, stringy and subtly Remade, a grex breed. The *box capra* chew and live on what poor food there is, their cross-slit eyes betraying goat affinities. At last, ahead of the whoretown and the cattle, was the perpetual train.

Judah had walked its length, skirting the crews. It was a rolling-stock town, an industrial citylet that crawled. At the end of a no-man's-land of empty rails, he saw the work. New Crobuzon reaching so far. The leviathan unfolding of metal, the greatest city in Bas-Lag rolling out its new iron tongue, licking at the cities across the plains.

Then there were days of trekking beyond the edge of iron. Judah's party passed the carts of the tie-layers. Crews cut down copses, treated and shaped the slabs, piled them in mounds and hauled them. Beyond the ties, the roadbed was bare rock-shards. Walking the sleepers it had seemed a ladder across the earth: now it was a road. It furrowed through high land and rose above low. They were a long way behind the graders.

For five days they were alone but for birds. It was an uncanny, rangy interior of slopes and little rivers. The rocks that reared like stelae were wind-carved into unplanned bas-reliefs. The roadbed tracked like a huge ruin, like the remnants of a city wall. They heard noise, approached a mouth in rock.

Tunnel-cutters had ploughed a path through the talus. There was a camp of men by the hole, and more men emerged from stone's innards, hauling carts of the hill's litter. They were too far from New Crobuzon for any steam-excavators to reach them. And the rock was probably too hard, though it gave Judah pleasure to imagine one of the drill-nosed things, big as a carriage, emerging from the ground. The tunnellers were alone in the wilds with picks and blackpowder, digging routes for rails that would not reach them for months.

The Remade, with limbs become pistons and jackhammers, were deafened by their own labours. One was a man whose arms were replaced with the outsized splayed claws of a mole: there was no way he could scrape through this stone but the crews had made him a mascot, and he sat in the tunnel's core and sang encouragement. TRT gendarmes guarded.

—Where you heading? said the superintendent.

—South. Cobsea, the plains.

—The swamps, said Judah's survey partner.

—The swamps, the supervisor said. —Be a bloody laugh when the rails get there. What the bloody hell, eh?

Judah smiled. His partner laughed. Seven weeks after that he would succumb to a wasting quag disease and leave Judah alone. Judah had thought of the heliotypes and etchings he had seen of the wetlands, the creatures emerging from the groves, the sodden plants, imagined them all set in mud made concrete, paralysed in place.

* * *

Their road ran out. They came to the graders, who dug where the land reared up, and took its excess, and poured it in where the land dipped down.

They cut a hill into receding shelves of industry. The landmass became steps, acrawl with roustabouts and pack animals. Loess dust gusted. Over the hours of work, the steps sank to the grade. There would be a ravine where the hill had been.

There are crews strung out like worry beads, Judah thought, *across the downland.*

NOW JUDAH HAS COME BACK. THE PERPETUAL TRAIN HAS CAUGHT him. It has breached the marshland.

The darker of the swamps spreads like a slick, but now it is intruded. There is a line drawn into its interior, buttressed with stone. The rails shine on it. Judah sees a split in the trees, and the black smoke of the train.

Supply trains come, weighed with sleepers and salted beef, with black iron rails. Judah could ride home to New Crobuzon. But a calm has settled him. Things are unfinished. He does not want to go back.

The saturated ground has stalled production, and the gangs have caught each other up: the graders, tie-men and the spikers before the perpetual train itself. Wyrmen scavenge. The camp followers have conjoined. A tent town has come behind the perpetual train. Beerhall tents, dancehall tents, cathouse tents, prefabricated buildings in cheap wood, circuses for the workers' breaks.

—I was in there, Judah says to himself, looking into the fen. He

says to himself, —I should go home, but, but . . . It is difficult for
him to say why he does not. He is drawn to the grandeur of this intervention.

He goes back to the deserted stiltspear encampment. It is being
eaten by itself, giving in to mud. A part of him wants to go deep and
find the stiltspear in the middle of their shrinking wetland. But he
is human, and the stiltspear kill humans now. He effects some inadequate communion. He feels hollowed out.

Judah watches the graders' progress. He is like a seagull, a carrion-
eater in the train's slow slow wake. It and its tracks might progress
only a few score yards each day in this merciless swamp. Autumn is
speeding up.

The tent-town and its shanties at the boundary of the fens are
a hub of commerce and crude industry. They are full of country
runaways, workers not working, prospectors, the pistolled horse-
wanderers who are growing in numbers across the plains opened by
the iron road. Cactacae, vodyanoi, llorgiss, khepri, and races more
arcane: crustaceans walking on two legs and cowled like monks, figures with too many eyes. Mercenary glory-hunters; canaille of scores
of cultures.

—How can I just go *back*, Judah says to one as they throw bone
dice, —with that thing, that train, there? How can I?

He is a tramp wandering the steam-and-piston town of the
rails. There are thousands of men and women, many without work.
A pitiable reserve army trudges behind the perpetual train. They
beg when the gendarmes are not watching.

Judah makes golems from the trodden-down mud of the track-
end. He cannot leave the tracks.

The villages they pass become rich and murderously violent—
decadent, liquor-swilling, whore-filled and lawless—for the few days
or weeks of the railroad, and then die. The towns live mayfly lives.

Sex is as much part of the iron-road industry as spiking, grading, herding and paperwork. A tent city of prostitute refugees from New Crobuzon's red-light districts follows the rails and the men that set them down. The men call it Fucktown.

The train comes and changes everything. For centuries there have been communities by the scrags of forests. Wars between subsistence farmers and hunters, hermits and trappers; trade and treaties between the natives and settlers from dissident sects hiding from New Crobuzon. The city's runaway Remade have taken to these steppes and become fReemade. Now this native economy is cut open, and New Crobuzon hears its rumours.

There are small exoduses of prospectors from the metropolis trekking from the line to where they say rockmilk or jewels or the puissant charged bones of monstrosities can be mined. Criminals have new places to run, and bounty hunters new ways to follow them. All of these newcomers, explorers and the city's dregs and the curious from across the continent, track into the new landscape. Like tributaries, like the thread-roots of ivy, their routes spread out from and to the railroad. Judah's is one of them.

ROAMING MILES OF TRACK, JUDAH KNOWS HE IS IN SOME LOW-level shock. Each night he dreams of stiltspear. He hears their staccato utterance, the chronopausal breath. In his dream they return to him bloodied and stripped of their hands.

Judah walks days, crosses a trestle bridge aswarm with workers and Remade brachiating from extending simian arms. At the end of a siding, a loop of track into a chert-rimmed dustbowl, is the town Such. It is renamed with pioneer verve: they call it Haggletown, Cardtown, the Old-Eye-In-The-Hole, and Hucksterville.

In the casinos track-laying men throw their money down alongside dandies with silver flintlocks and black silk hats: gamblers, cardsmen, aleatori. From New Crobuzon, Myrshock and Cobsea at the end of the proposed routes, and some from farther. The cactus-man from Shankell; a nameless vodyanoi said to come from Neovadan; Corosh, a shaman from the Wormseye Scrub who supplements his traditional turtle-shelled coat with slacks and spats.

Judah watches them greet each other and play.

—BarkNeck, Corosh says in unflawed Ragamoll. —Not seen you since Myrshock. Judah sees him unclip a Wormseye weapon from his belt, a gris-gris mace studded with whispersome cowries.

There are scores of styles of dice and cards. Dice with six, eight, twelve sides, lopsided dice with differing likelihoods of settling on various faces. Cards with seven suits, suits of wheels flames locks and black stars, decks of picture cards without suits at all.

There are women among the chancers: Frey with her tough and beautiful smile; the Rosa in the prettiest blood-coloured dresses, cooling herself with what is supposed to be a razored metal fan. In his second week in Such, Judah sees a Remade—no, with that bearing he is *fReemade,* an outlaw—acrawl on a lower body like a den of fighting snakes, pass the gendarmes, who pretend they do not see him. —Jaknest, the name is spoken quietly, —Jaknest the Free Stakesman. Jaknest leaves a trail into a back room, where there must be some high-roller game where anyone's money is good, law be fucked.

Judah does not want to play. Instead he tries to steal. He makes a golem of sticks, has the little made man scurry beneath the table with the night's biggest pot. It clambers up a chair's crossbars to sit below Place How, a gambling man in black and silver who is amassing chips and promissory notes. The casino is full and loud, and no one sees the figurine save Judah.

It moves to his commands, trying to unpick Place How's bag. There is a rushing, a red sulphur gash in the air, and the golem is smouldering carbon. A clot of smoke and dim flame crawls fast as a rat back up How's coat, to circle his neck and disappear. Everyone rises but How pats the air to calm them.

Judah blinks. Of course a man of How's wealth and profession goes protected. He does not rely on the casinos' vodun to sniff out illicit augury. He has his own ward dæmon. When he has won all he wants How stands at the bar and buys drinks and tells stories of his games and the places he has been, and how the new railroad has brought him back to New Crobuzon. *He is unwinding the road,* Judah thinks. *He's counting it backward, telling its miles like he counts cards.*

—Sir I'd like to come with you. And Place How laughs not unkind at this sullen bruised young man half his age. He does not take so much convincing: the thought of a butler appeals to his pretensions. He dresses Judah for the part, and teaches him to ride the mule he buys him. —Now you in hock to me a while, How says.

They go between trail-towns through sage and heather, sometimes overlooking the railroad and its crews. The landscape changes by the tracks: the animals are wary, the trees thin.

Judah does not golem except when he is alone. Between towns Place is loquacious and charming to him: when they reach a place where he can play he puts on a master's face and has Judah wait behind him, bring him bonbons and kerchiefs. Judah is part of How's uniform, as much as his velveteen jacket.

The same players recur, and Judah learns their styles. BarkNeck the cactus-man is surly and disliked, tolerated because he is not the cardsman he thinks. The Rosa is a delight to watch, to hear. And there is Jaqar Kazaan, and O'Kinghersdt, and the vodyanoi Shechester, and others, all with their preferred plays. How has his dæmon, and the others have their own protections: hexes, familiars, tamed air elementals gusting through their hair. Judah sees cheats and bad losers shot and harpooned.

Place How loses more money than Judah has ever owned, one night, and makes it up again, with more, two days later. Judah sees him play for shacks, for weapons, for embalmed oddities, for knowledge, and above all for money. Judah bleeds off a few coins when he can. He is sure that is expected.

In the wilds, Judah's duties include the sexual. He does not mind: he feels no less or more than when he is with a woman. There is a nugget of compassion in him, and he feels it growing. He feels something inchoate, some beneficence.

A day's ride from the railroad, they hear that Maru'ahm gamblers are coming. Everyone is excited.

—I ever was a gambling man, Place How says that night. —Ain't a style or a way of play I ain't come up against: I play the naturals, the numerologicians, and the graduates of academies made them gnostics of stake-raising. Won more'n I lost or I'd not be here. But Maru'ahm, oh. I been once years gone and I tell you if I'm good and say my prayers that's where I go when I die.

Maru'ahm, the casino parliament.

—Sure it's mostly for them as like roulette and half-a-hole snapjack and dice, but it's not just the ally-ate-ors, they do for cardsmen too. Ten year gone, now, 1770. I was playing like La Dama Fortuna was wet for me. Staked my horse, my weapons, my life, and kept winning. And then there were stakes as they only have in Maru'ahm: I'm winning law after law, playing grandbridge and black sevens, till an all-night session of quincehand and I stake a big property law against one of the Queen's cardsharp senators and I *lose,* but I seen him pull hidden cards from his sleeves to win the whole pot of legislation and I call him out, and I ain't such a fighter but dammit I was sore, and there was a duel—*ten paces and turn*—hundreds of townsfolk watching and most of them cheering me, my law would be better for them. To this day I think it was one of them killed him, not me. I never was much with a gun. He smiles.

No one plays like the Maru'ahmers, and they bring their house rules with them. Gamblers congregate. In a little town where basin rivers meet, the iron road a day's ride, the pilgrims converge. The townspeople are astonished at the rakes in their streets, well-dressed men and women carrying ornamented wicked weapons, filling taverns, bringing foreign wines, selling them to the landlords and buying them back, prostituting the local young.

Winter is in. There is snow. Judah hears that the track builders have stopped, are hunkered down, punished by the weather. He feels something eating at him. The road is a sentence written on the ground and he must parse it, and he is failing.

Something extraordinary comes out of the ice-flat sky. The Maru'ahm gamblers arrive in an outlandish biokiteship, a spindly, feathered, beetle-nacred thing. It lands and blinks its headlamp eyes, disgorges the gamblers. They wear jade- and opal-coated jumpsuits; they carry cards; their leader is a princess. In accented Ragamoll and with outrageous theatre, she raises her hand and shouts, —Let's play!

The locals attempt country dances, a banausic and inappropriate entertainment. There are the rat-tats of dice, of shatarang discs. A syncopation like the clatter of wheels on rails. The softer shuffle of cards.

Place How faces one steadfast rebis, an androgyne cardsharp from Maru'ahm who wins unhurriedly at baccarat, at tooth bezique, at poker. How clicks his fingers for Judah to bring hot sherbert, but the swagger is merely vulgar. The he-she smiles.

They play a game Judah does not know with a deck of heptagonal cards. They turn them, discard some, concatenate others in an overlapping pattern on the tabletop. Other players come and go, raise bets by some opaque system, lose, while the pot grows, and only How and the hermaphrodite remain.

Each bet now causes How some physical pain. A crowd has gathered. With the turn of a card the Maru'ahm gambler wins the life of How's ward dæmon, and the little presence manifests as a flaming marmoset that screams and clutches How's lapels and makes them smoulder, but bursts and is gone in a fart of soot. How is afraid. He rallies and wins a handful of clockwork gems, but in the next round the he-she turns a triple-trick and Place How can only moan. He looks insubstantial. He is growing hard to make out as he loses.

How bets aggressively. He shouts his stake, —For my horse, a year of my thought, for my man yonder. He waves at Judah, who blinks and shakes his head—*I ain't no godsdamned stake*—but it is too late, that is just what he is, and How has played and lost and Judah is forfeit. So Judah runs.

H E HEADS BACK FOR THE RAILROAD ON HIS HARRIED MULE, CROSS-
ing trappers' and hunters' trails. He has money he has stolen.

Judah passes through emptied shells of towns that were tracks'-
end carnivals months before. He follows freshets swollen with
snowmelt. In the coils of hills he watches the railroad, the cavalier
onrush of the trains, their flared stacks bellowing blackly, full of
chancers for the halfway towns.

Within three days Judah discovers that the rebis who won him
is on his trail. Rumours cross the distance. So south, close to the
swamp again where the workforce crawl frozen on, Judah finds
a gulch-town of gunmen. The plains are suddenly full of them,
scapegrace bushrangers. The permanent dacoits of the region have
been joined by newcomers made bandit by the iron road. It exerts.

In a tavern Judah buys the service of gun-layer Oil Bill, whose
right hand had been a tool for the servicing of motors and is reconfigured by a gunsmith in brass with splayed barrel for a peppering
of shot. He refuses to let Judah run, earns his protection money by

letting the androgyne gambler catch them. There is a showdown in the freezing winter dust. As the townspeople of the punk village get out of range the gambler releases a brace of daggerpigeons that gust bladily at Oil Bill, but with a rate of fire Judah has never seen before (clockwork and coil mechanisms refilling his cannon-hand) the fReemade shreds them and fires through their feathers to send the Maru'ahmer sprawling wet and dead.

Judah runs with Oil Bill. He has neglected his golems, his stilt-spear memories and the railroad itself. He sees in the brigand a hunger for the rails that reminds him of his own. The fReemade's passion is less complex, and Judah wonders if it is a purer thing. Deep in himself, below the calm that has settled on him, he knows he must come to understand the rails.

They pay in some taverns, extort in others. Oil Bill sings songs of wandering renegades. Judah performs for him, makes golems—it is his only trick—out of the food they eat and has them dance across the table. He tries to breathe in time, to mimic the stilt-spear.

Each dwelling makes its own rules and enforces them if it can. New Crobuzon does not claim the plains. It does not yet want them; it does not despatch militia here: it cedes the rights to policing and its spoils to the TRT, to Weather Wrightby and his monopoly railroad. The TRT gendarmes are the law here, but they are mercilessly liberal: their gunners guard only some mines and barter-towns.

Bill's reputation means it is some time before anyone opposes him and Judah sees him kill again. When he does it is an act against someone foul, a snarling drunkard who threatens everyone he sees with his moving hexed tattoos, but still it is disproportionate. Judah stares at the corpse, stripped by the town's gutterchildren.

The thing he has felt born within him, a creature of his congealed concern, flicks its tail. He does not like his companion.

Still he stays with Oil Bill, becomes a gunsman himself, in his duster, swaps his mule for a stolen horse. Because Oil Bill cannot leave the railroad alone. They tramp the winter hills. Bill brings them back to the rails endlessly.

—Look now, that there with them old trailers like that, them's the work train's supplies, goin' all the way into the swamp. And them others we seen is for the sightseers from New Crobuzon come to see wild country, and that other'n with the guntowers 'hind its engine . . . that's the wages train. He smiles.

Judah is curious. There have been tries to rob the railroad before. Vivid and daring raids from horse riders and carriages and from fReemade shaped for speed with bevies of stolen legs, who keep up with the speeding engines and harass their firemen, boarding the train and disappearing again with snatched money.

Oil Bill's plan might work. It is base, utterly without finesse, and it might work because Oil Bill is neither cowed nor awed by the iron road. Others have tried to shear off sections of a bridge to halt a train for ambush: Bill wants to blow the bridge while the train is on it. He wants to commit an act of war. Judah is so astonished by the plan's imbecility that it is almost admiration.

—The trellis at Silvergut Gap, Oil Bill says, drawing in the dirt. —Fuckin' bridge is hundreds of yards long. We wait below, light fuses and scarper when the fuckin' train hits the bridge. That shoddy piece of shite can't take that. It's coming down.

And then the plan is that the iron train will unfold in air and shatter on the frozen flint a hundred feet below, and though yes there will be huge wastage as fire takes boxes of money, and carriages are sealed shut by crushed metal, and the blood of dead trainmen and passengers stains the notes, some ingots are bound to fall free. Some guineas are sure to gust out in the wind of the cut, and Oil Bill will simply pick spoils from the ground and the air.

Oil Bill's genius is the limits of his ambition. A greater thief would insist on taking every stiver from the coffers, could not support this idly conceived carnage. Oil Bill though does not care if the bulk is left to ruin in the broken train, so long as he can reach *some money,* and in its blithe and vast violence his plan might work.

The grub in Judah, not conscience but some nebulous virtue, moves. He feels disassociate from it, but it gnaws him. He will not follow Bill's plan, but he cannot outfight Oil Bill so he must pretend insouciance, even as they steal powder and ride back along the Silvergut Pass by winter cactuses and weathered black rock, to where the cat's cradle of wood arcs overhead, to pack the explosive—Bill with lack of care that makes Judah blench—to struts in the cold-hard earth. It is only after that, while they wait for a train and Bill sleeps, that Judah can move against him.

He leaves his horse and climbs the steep rocks, cresting with fingers so insensate with cold he is afraid he will lose them. He runs for near a day until he comes to a railside hut, a siding and a mail-drop, and a TRT signalman.

—The gendarmes, Judah says, waving his empty hands. —I need to get them a message.

JUDAH RETURNS WITHIN A DAY AND A NIGHT, ON A NEW ANIMAL A MILE behind the TRT rangers. When he reaches the roots of the trestle two gendarmes are dead, Bill's blackpowder scattered.

Bill is gone. The gendarmes station a guard. Judah watches them with contempt. They are motley; they do not have the presence of the New Crobuzon Militia. These are recruits hardly distinguished from drifters and chancers, given guns and sashes in the colours of the TRT. They have little idea of how to pursue Oil Bill, and less inclination. They put a price on him.

Judah is in danger while Oil Bill is free. He joins the bloodprice hunter.

First Judah thinks the bounty man is human, but he accepts his commission with a guttural alien chuckle, flexes his neck and closes his eyes in ways that mark him as abnatural. He rides something that is not a horse but a vague equine semblance, the impression of a horse, a horse burr under the skin of the real. He shoots with a matchlock pistol that spits and mutters and is sometimes a rifle and sometimes a crossbow. He will not tell Judah his name.

They run together on their horse and their horse-bruise through the plainlands in the ripples of the rails, lands not colonised but infected, as life once infected rockpools. Four days of tracking with ideograms of hexed dust and the bounty-man finds Oil Bill, confronts him in a quarry. The white stone is marked, crosshatched with chisel lines, which make a grid behind the bandit's head.

—You, he shouts at Judah with the rage of the stupid betrayed, and the bondsman kills him and his weapons eat the corpse.

Perhaps I will be this, Judah thinks, and rides with the hunter. They go town to town on the trail of those the gendarmerie will not take. They stop at TRT trackside stations and sift through the WANTED notices. The bounty hunter does not ask Judah to stay nor make him leave. He speaks in a sibilant whisper so quiet that Judah cannot tell if he speaks Ragamoll well or hardly at all.

He injures or kills his quarries with the spines from his weapons or with his living nets or with sudden throat-sounds, and drags the bodies back to the way stations for bounty, and asks nothing of Judah, nor provides him anything. The count of sheep-stealers and rapists and murderers goes up, money comes in. Those the unman kills are scum, but the presence in Judah is not at ease.

Three days' ride across pale stone ways. Clots of rock like aggregates of grey air that burst into nothing under horseshoes. A stripmined hole, the bodies of sappers and gendarmes, and the entrances to tunnels where the marrow of some epochs-dead godbeast has become ore and in which a little tribe of trow live.

The Arrowhead Concerns will take what they can of the boneload. The troglodytes have beaten off miners and made a stand, and the gendarmes want them gone. This is the commission.

Judah watches while his companion unpacks chymicals. He tries to feel equanimity. Nothing moves, not bird nor dust nor cloud. It is as if time is waiting. Judah turns and feels it start again sluggishly as the bounty hunter prepares a huge pot with distillates and oils and hoods it, over a fire, trails a leather tube to the entrance of the cave, anchors it in place with rubber and skin sealing off the air inside. It is the end of night. The fire and the brass cauldron cover them in moving tan light. The bounty-man mixes poisons.

In the mountain's belly the trow must be waiting. They must be watching, Judah thinks. They must know that something is coming. He thinks, he cannot do otherwise, of the stiltspear and their hopeless unkenning resistance. He is cold, but inside him the worm of uncertainty, the oddity that is not a conscience but an *awareness* of wrong, a *goodness,* is uncoiling. He sighs. —Lie down, he tells it. —Lie down. But the oddity will not lie down.

It moves in him and secretes disgust and anger he is sure are not *his,* but that stain him, and whether they are his or not he feels them. They well up in him. He thinks of the stiltspear cubs, and the trow in the little mountain.

The chymicals are mixing and boiling, and the bounty hunter adds compounds till the red muddish mixture burps gas and a caustic oily smoke begins suddenly to pour from it and is funnelled into the mine. The hunter waits. Poison howls into the tunnels, the liquid boiling at enormous speed.

Judah's rage takes him. He hesitates more seconds and will always be aware of the cubic yards of murderous gas he lets free in that time, then walks to the cauldron, staying upwind, and puts his left hand below the hood, above the rim, into the smoke. The bounty hunter is horrified and uncomprehending.

The gas is acid and hot and Judah screams as his skin splits, but he does not withdraw his hand, and he makes his scream into a chant, and he forces all the energies he has learnt and all the techniques he has stolen up from his innards and focuses them with the glass-pure nugget of hate and revenge he finds in him and channels and lets go with a cathexis purer and stronger than he has ever felt before, and thaumaturgic energies pour from him and make a golem.

A smoke golem, a gas golem, a golem of particles and poisoned air.

Judah falls back holding his ravaged hand. The smoke still spews from the pot but it does not vent into the tunnels, it collects and rolls in a bolus of pollution over the lip, and retreats back out of the hood and the pipe. The smoke crawls from the pot with evanescent limbs like monkeys' or lions' that retract again and emerge, and the cloud stands as a two- three- four- one- none-footed hulk of moiling and it steps or rolls or flies against the wind at the bounty hunter, following Judah's agonised direction.

He has never created anything this size before. It is unwieldy and unstable, and the wind tugs grots of it away so it shrinks as it advances but not fast enough to be gone by the time it reaches the hunter, who is firing at it and uselessly through it, sending thin coils of it out with the paths of bullets like brief spines, not seeing Judah beyond, not seeing how he moves his hands and puppeteers the golem. The thing twitches a gas tail. It hugs the bounty hunter in a mindless surround so he cannot but breathe the golem's substance, and his inhuman skin and the delicate membranes within him pustulate and break apart and he drowns on his liquescent lungs.

When the unman is dead, Judah has the diminishing golem leap high, and he releases it to the wind and it spasms and is gone. He bandages his hand and robs the bounty hunter's corpse. It smells just very faintly of the gas.

Judah does not know how much of the trow town the smoke has envenomed. He knows this is only one day. He knows the Arrowhead Concerns will have the TRT send another bounty hunter to this boneyard and will find the detritus of this failed poisoning, this dead. Judah knows the trow will be eradicated and their homes lost to history, but he will not be party to it, and he has tried to stand in its way.

The trow will die. If he could leave something behind for them. If he could give these rocks a guardian shape and make it wait, to wake when it is needed. The bounty hunter's unhorse runs from him and into rock, leaving an animal-shaped bruise of lichen.

I'm done here, thinks Judah. His hand trembles; he trembles. *I've done in a man or something that looks like a man.* He is exhausted with the effort of his somaturgy, of sustaining the thing's shape, of killing. He shakes with fear and awe at what he has done, that he could do such a thing, that he could make a golem not from clay but from heavy air. *I'm done out here in these wilding lands. They're wilding because we're here.* He cannot believe what he has been able to do.

Judah scatters the pots and the guttering fire. He turns back for the iron road.

IN SOMETHING LIKE A FUGUE HE IS TAKEN BY THE WAKE OF THE TRAINS.
He meets the roadbed in some utterly lonely place. His horse is
tired. It shivers in snow-dust. Judah goes to the hills, to a village
overlooking the track labourers.

Though the men are provided for, though even so far from
tracks'-end there is a tribe of prostitutes in their tent brothels,
men from the grading teams and the rock-crushers come up sometimes to the tiny village of goatherds where Judah sits and watches.
The local girls go with the New Crobuzon men, though their
families impotently disapprove and fight and get beaten down.
The villagers tend their wounded and weather these intrusions.
—What can we do? they say. They are blighted by forbearance, by
restraint.

A new calm has embedded in Judah since the line was cut into
his swamps. He looks at the world through glass.

He becomes some kind of storyteller of the city to his goatherd
hosts. They let him live in the wickiup encampments. They are

grateful that he is not as brutish as the men of the perpetual train.
They ask him questions in their barbarous Ragamoll.

—Is true the road make milk sour?

—Is true it kill young in the womb?

—Is true it make fish in river bad?

—What's name of the road?

—I was at its end, Judah says. *What is the name of the road?* The
question startles him.

He has found a young woman from the hillside peasants who
lies with him. Her name is Ann-Hari. She is several years younger
than he, farouche and pretty. He thinks of her as a girl though her
enthusiasms and her stare sometimes seem to him more adult and
calculating than ingenue.

Judah wants her with him. Ann-Hari is lost to her family and
her village. There are several like her, some boys but mostly young
women, utterly charged by the arrival of these tough roustabouts
and the breathing pistons of the trains. Their families lament while
they let their flocks run, or sell them for meat to railroaders for
scrimshawed trinkets from the tool-rooms. The goatkeep young
men join the grading teams and fill the rivers. The young women
find other outlets.

Ann-Hari is not Judah's; he cannot keep her. He first finds her
when she is flushed by the road, and she takes him and discards
her virginity with eagerness he knows has little to do with him. For
the few days that she is only his he tries to make it as much as he
can; he tries to give the arc of a life's love. It is not an affectation but
a role; he gives himself over. She is looking over his shoulder while
she straddles him, for something else—not even something better,
but else, more. She makes friends. She comes to him in the village
smelling of other men's sex.

Her clipped Downs Ragamoll is changing. She uses city slang,
steals it from the hammermen. Judah can see the calm and ruthless intelligence under her giddiness, her voracious acquisition. He
shows her the golems he can make, that still grow in strength and

size. She is entertained but no more than by a thousand other things.

There is bad blood among the camp followers. The whores who have dutifully followed these men, splitting from the perpetual train to work with these mountain diggers, are affronted by their new rural rivals, these farmgirls who expect no pay. Some of the workers themselves are threatened by these newly voracious young women who do not sell or even give sex but take it. They know no rules. They have yet to learn taboos: some even try to go with the camp's prisoners, the shackled Remade. The Remade are terrified by this, and go to their overseers.

One cold night Ann-Hari comes to Judah terrified, blackened, bloodied and welted. There has been a fight. A gang of prostitutes has gone from tent to tent. They have pulled apart any lovers they find, overwhelming the outraged men by numbers, holding them, checking the face and voice of each woman. Those that are locals taking no pay, they have hauled outside and decorated with engine oil and feathers. The gendarmes have sympathies with the working girls, and they let them carry on.

Ann-Hari was rutting a man at the edges of camp when the raucous whores' justice caught her. She fought back. She punched with all her peasant strength. She knocked three of them down, jabbed out with a little gimlet that punctured an older woman's stomach. Ann-Hari ran from her whitening victim.

Judah has never seen her so meek. He knows that this is only a small thing. No one has died, and likely will not—the blade is tiny. Now the locals know the rules, and no one will remember Ann-Hari who fought back. But the fear this sudden violence has left in her does not fade, and a part of Judah is glad, because now she is afraid to stay he can persuade her to come with him. He wants out of the wilderness; he wants to buckle the iron road closed behind him, go home; and he wants another's eyes through which to see.

They go two days' walk to a dying station, to the trains. They have third-class seats. Judah watches Ann-Hari watching the receding grass and buttes, the river they flank, the gashes, the darkness of tunnels. Hours in silence but for the complex rhythm of wheels, to the city he has not seen for many months, and that she has never seen.

H E IS BACK, AND BLINKING LIKE A COUNTRYMAN AT NEW CROBU-
zon. Ann-Hari and he squat in a tent on a rooftop in Badside. They
overlook the carcass of Grand Calibre Bridge, its pivoting section
jammed, rusted immobile as it has long been, become only a break-
water.

All Ann-Hari's fear went away with the miles, and there is nothing that will stop her learning New Crobuzon. Each day she comes
back to him and tells him with excitement about the city.

She has never seen khepri before. —There are women here
who've heads like bugs, she tells him. She visits the Ribs. —They're
bigger'n the biggest trees ever grew. They're old and harder than
stone, bones way up over the roofs, something dead and the whole
city's its grave.

Ann-Hari takes New Crobuzon's trains, the five rails and their
offshoots, from Abrogate Green in the east to Terminus, to Chimer's
End, to Fell Stop and the Downs. —There's a shanty all falling down
below a hill and the forest comes right up to it and the rails go on
into the wood but the trains won't go there.

There is a station in Rudewood on the useless tracks. It has long been deserted. Judah knows of it, but has never seen it. Ann-Hari goes to the dangerous ghetto of Spatters, where the city's few garuda live above the lowest of its subcitizens, and walks blithely through its stink and middened streets into the forest, and the overgrown remnants of the station, and comes back, taking the train to Dog Fenn to tell Judah. She is teaching him about New Crobuzon.

She tells him about the Fuchsia House, about BilSantum Plaza and the Gargoyle Park, the domed cactus ghetto, the zoological gardens, and many of these things he last visited in his youth if ever. She tells him all the races that she sees. She loves the markets.

Judah makes enough to eat, entertaining crowds with his hedge-magic golemetry. One day he makes a more sturdy figure from wood, with loose chain joints. He attaches strings to her limbs and now while his thaumaturgy makes her dance, he waggles a frame as if he is manipulating her. Judah makes noticeably more when punters think him a puppeteer than when they think he is animating matter.

In rooms by the Kelltree Docks, they are woken each morning by the sirens of factories and the slow stampede of the workforce. Ann-Hari meets dealers. She comes home with wide eyes and the acid smell of shazbah on her. She stays away some nights. When she is with Judah she sleeps with him and takes money from him.

She likes to walk. Judah walks miles with her, between onlooking houses, in the shadows of all the crossbred architecture. She asks him why things are built as they are, and he does not know the answers. Once he is with her as a khepri couple pass, their sashes plaited together, their headlegs rippling and sprays of bitter air emitted around them, their chymical whisperings. Judah feels Ann-Hari tense, and for the first time in his life he sees the strangeness of the khepri, hears the scissor-sounds their gnathic movements make. He sees the strangeness of everything.

It is boomtime. There is money, and there is competition for pavement change. Judah dances his puppets beside singers and instrumentalists, tumblers and artists in chalk.

It is winter but the city is freakishly warm. It is a languid season. In the red of tinted flares Judah's golem performs for the students in Ludmead. The undergraduates are overwhelmingly young men, well-dressed uptown boys and a few studious clerks' sons, but there are women among them, and even a few xenians. They walk by Judah's high-stepping wooden dancer. He is only a little older than most of them.

Some give him stivers, marks and shekels: most give him nothing. One young man attuned to the figure's movements and the flows of thaumaturgons stops and sees that the marionette is a fake.

—This is what *I* do, he says. —This is what we do here. I'm in the damned somaturgy programme. You got the face to come here and palm off your jury-rigged hexes?

—Match me then, Judah says.

Which is how the stiltspear sport of golem wrestling comes to New Crobuzon.

The little crowd of students watch while the arrogant boy squints over his glasses at Judah, who is all ruddy and sinewed-muscled scrawn, dressed in third- and fourth-hand rags. Though they bray support for their classmate Judah senses their ambivalence, and realises these moneyed sons would almost rather their fellow, a middling boy from a journeyman family, lose to him the utter outsider. Sheer class sympathy almost makes him walk away, but money is being counted and his own odds are good: he bets on himself.

He whispers to his golem, stutter-hisses at it like the stiltspear, and it takes the undergraduate's earth-man apart. It is not a hard win.

Judah counts his money. The loser swallows several times and approaches him. He has grace and intelligence. —Good win, he says. He even smiles. —You've some techniques, and some power to you. I never seen anyone conjure a golem like that.

—I didn't learn here.

—I see that.

—Try again? Another match?

—Yes! Yes! Again! It is one of the other students. —Come back tomorrow, puppetman, and we'll do it again, and we'll find a better damn 'turge than Pennyhaugh to take you on.

Neither Judah nor Pennyhaugh look at the interrupter. They only look at each other, and they smile together.

It will never challenge the glad' circuses, the illegal blood-halls of Cadnebar's and its imitators, where enthusiasts of real brawl sports can watch knife bouts, two-on-cactus hack matches and bite fights. But Pennyhaugh and Judah become partners and systematise the games, and their league gains attention, and golem wrestling becomes a fashion.

At first it is mostly students in the plasmic sciences come to the meets, then some of their professors. Then as word gets out autodidact somaturges and gutter hexers from the falling-down parts of town arrive. The sport is not particularly illegal but nor is it sanctioned, and like most such activities it is always on the point of being banned. It becomes a business very fast, and there are militia informers to pay off, and porters and university officials to keep happy. Pennyhaugh takes care of this.

They are unlikely heroes, the enthusiasts: intense, nervous and studious. They meet in venues of increasing size. They specialise, stud their creations in blades or slabs of tin armour, or give them bodkin legs and serrated dorsal ridges. These are golemachs, fighting constructions, matched against each other weight for weight.

Judah tops the rankings. He does not find it hard to win. His spare and coarse stiltspear techniques work. He loses a handful of times, but in that unforgiving laboratory he is quick to improve.

—You've a rare talent, Judah, says Pennyhaugh.

Pennyhaugh cannot beat Judah, but he can train him. He does not understand the alien stiltspear, but he can test them, and marry them to what he does know. He straps Judah to a thaumatograph, tests his cathexis, that concentrate furrowing of mind.

—You're strong, he says to Judah.

Twice Ann-Hari comes to watch the bouts. She cheers for Judah and smiles when he wins, but the sport does not interest her. She is more for engines. She goes to the termini of the railway lines, to watch trains slow. She goes to those factories that will let her in and wanders among the workers, watching their machines.

Judah likes winning. His skill excites him. For a while he and Pennyhaugh try the most antiquated sting, pretending to lose until his odds rise, but Judah is notorious fast.

He is a star, Swamp-Taught Low. Another is Lothaniel Durayne, a professor of somaturgy who fights his feline tar-golems as Loth the Catman. They relish these stage names. There is the Dandler, a quiet woman Pennyhaugh says is likely a militia scientist. She gives her golemachs whipping chain tails. This troika exchange the top rank between them, but Judah keeps it most.

The stronger the somaturge, the greater the mass they can control. Soon they are setting upper limits to weight. Nothing heavier than a large dog can fight. Judah wonders how much he could control if he chose.

As organisers, bookie and top golemachist, Pennyhaugh and Judah amass good money. Golem wrestling is noticed by New Crobuzon's press, and there are many newcomers. Judah is growing bored. He only fights Loth and the Dandler now. He watches how they animate their constructions. He listens to their hexes. He fights enough to make money, but mostly he fights to learn.

Every time his golems move, Judah feels his connection to the stiltspear. —I want to know everything about this, Judah says. Pennyhaugh brings him to the university library, and shows him relevant texts. He reads the titles: *Theories of Somaturgy, The Limits of Plasmic Range, Beyond the Abvital Debate.* —I want to know everything, he says.

Ɪᴛ ɪs ᴀ sᴡᴇᴇᴛ ᴡɪɴᴛᴇʀ. Jᴜᴅᴀʜ ᴛᴀᴋᴇs Aɴɴ-Hᴀʀɪ ɪᴄᴇ-sᴋᴀᴛɪɴɢ. Sʜᴇ likes the way he is recognised by some they pass. —Swamp-Taught! one says. It makes Judah less happy.

They walk in the frost-glazed shopping streets of The Crow, which are strung with ropes of lights and winter flowers. They drink hot chocolate mulled with rum. Ann-Hari is not looking at him. Her eyes pass over his and she smiles, and it is a real smile, but she is not looking at him.

Good-bye, Judah thinks, and smiles back.

When snow comes, for a few hours it effaces all the edges of architecture: the tight-coiled cornices of old churches, dark stone buttresses and all the countless poured and moulded concrete and brick terraces, and workers' cottages too mean or crude to have any style at all. They become undulations below snow; then they are themselves again, as they sweat off sleet.

Judah dresses in the exaggerated clobber of a street-success. When he walks, the Dog Fenn children run after him, with a few skinny cactus youths and leaping vodyanoi, and beg him to make golemachs for them. Sometimes he animates a squeezed-together handful of coins and lets it totter toward them, for them to watch and pick apart.

Ann-Hari has no interest in learning to read, but when she discovers that he plumbs the newspapers for the progress of the Transcontinental Railroad Trust, she demands Judah read to her every day she is with him (there are more and more days that she does not come home).

—. . . a brutal winter, he reads from *The Quarrel*. —Those men still in the swamp spend much of their time acurse at the cold, but they have at least the advantage that the stiltspear, perfidious wetland savages, have retreated and no longer harry them. Messages from the south suggest construction crews from Myrshock are, despite less punitive weather, making poor progress . . .

—What is Myrshock? Ann-Hari says. Judah stares. She knows nothing of the railroad's shape, or its future.

He makes her a map. —Three branches, he says, drawing the upside down and slanting Y. —New Crobuzon. Myrshock on the coast of the Meagre Sea. Cobsea in the plains. A track out from each, meeting in the swamps. Five hundred miles down from New Crobuzon, half as much again to each of the others.

Judah disguises his own fascination with the rails as indulging Ann-Hari's. He thinks of the men all the time; he thinks of what he's seen, that community of hammer-swingers, intervening in the land.

The road has not yet forked. Reports tell of brief and costly strikes. Some writers argue that the TRT gendarmerie is defunct, unable to control its workforce or subdue the little principalities it comes to. The Mayor must end the subleasing of authority, they say. It is time for New Crobuzon's militia to police the tracks. No one thinks this will happen. The government is against it.

—The strikers complain of the weather, Judah reads. —They strike against the chill. What would they have the TRT do? Does not the whole of the workforce, the overseers, the Remade, Wrightby himself, feel the same cold?

—No, says Ann-Hari.

Judah looks at her. She is eating a sugared plum.

She shrugs. —No, they don't.

Judah studies. With Pennyhaugh to guide him, he not only grows his capacities but begins to understand what he is doing. His approach remains gut and intuitive, but the laborious and esoteric texts make a kind of sense to him, and better his ability.

— . . . what we do is an intervention, Pennyhaugh lectures Judah from his notes, —a reorganisation. The living cannot be made a golem—because with the vitality of orgone, flesh and vegetable is matter interacting with its own mechanisms. The unalive, though, is inert because it *happens to lie just so.* We make it meaningful. We do not order it but point out the order that inheres unseen, always already there. This act of pointing is at least as much assertion and persuasion as observation. We see structure, and in pointing it out we see mechanisms and grasp them, and we twist. Because patterns are asserted not in stasis but in change. Golemetry is an *interruption.* It is a subordinating of the static IS to the active AM.

Judah thinks of the stiltspear, and of the railroad. He still breathes his stiltspear whisper when he makes his golems move. Increasingly he understands this science. It obsesses him.

They fail to pay the right officer, and the golem-wrestling hall is raided. It is not hard for the masked militia to find among the crowd shazbah and very-tea, and even, they say, dreamshit. The organisers give money where they have to, and while Pennyhaugh keeps them in business, Judah thinks of other things.

Golemetry is interruption. Golemetry is matter made to view itself anew, given a command that organises it, a task. How to make the field in his absence? How to prepare and make it wait?

He buys batteries, switches and wires, he buys timers, he tries to think. The journals are reporting accounting wrongs at the TRT. Someone is insinuating scandal.

Iᴛ ɪs ᴅᴀʏs sɪɴᴄᴇ Jᴜᴅᴀʜ ʜᴀs sᴇᴇɴ Aɴɴ-Hᴀʀɪ. Hᴇ ʀᴇᴀʟɪsᴇs sᴜᴅᴅᴇɴʟʏ that she has not merely found someone else to be with for some days but has gone. He knows where.

She has liked New Crobuzon, has looked on it with passion and interest, but for her all its mass and history—its accreted stones and struggle—could only ever be an adjunct to the iron road. It is the rails that are Ann-Hari's home.

Ann-Hari has gone home to the rails and the perpetual train. She knows no prostitute militia will punish her. The X on Judah's mirror in her lipstick is a kiss good-bye. She helped him see the city again and he is grateful for that. He discovers that she took a deal of money from him.

The golem fights bore him. Pennyhaugh is gone more and more, liaising with bureaucrats in Parliament, which protrudes like a verdigrised nail from the meeting of the rivers. And the fights slow, and stop, and Pennyhaugh is more distracted, and has more money, and one night he takes Judah to a restaurant more sumptuous than any he has ever entered before, a sedate place in Ludmead where Judah in his street-finery feels absurd, and Pennyhaugh says to him, —There's another way, you know, there's another, ah, market for your golem skills.

Judah knows his moment has gone, and that Pennyhaugh is a government man now. Judah is without work, without the library. He is quickly forgotten.

FOR SOME WEEKS PENNYHAUGH SENDS HIM LETTERS SUGGESTING THEY meet. Judah declines in his ugly hand, just often enough not to be rude.

In the markets full of old and stolen books he asks for volumes on golems. He spends many shekels on useless crap and some on great works with which he struggles.

What is it I've done? he thinks. He does not understand his own skills at all. *I made a golem from gas. Can I make a golem from even less solid things? Golemetry's an argument, an intervention, so will I intervene and make a golem in darkness or in death, in elyctricity, in sound, in friction, in ideas or hopes?*

Judah takes a few commissions. For the eccentric rich who disdain the clanking of constructs, he makes beautifully realised men and women in wire and sand-filled leather. He charges a great deal: they tire him.

He walks the city at the behest of the grub, the oddity in him that will not be still. He is tugged by it; he feels it seeing through him. *It's a strong goodness in me,* he thinks without arrogance, *but it's an intruder. I don't feel it as my own. Does that make me good? Does that make me better? Does it make me wicked?*

Judah thinks of Ann-Hari and reads that progress at tracks'-end is picking up again. There are questions in Parliament. The TRT and Weather Wrightby are censured for strange dealings. Workers have died in some accident, a gradient has been levelled in a way the inspectors cannot explain, and the heat-ripples and the lifeless zone for yards to either side raise questions the TRT will not answer. No one will say *sacrifice,* no one will say *dæmon,* but there is a growing sense that Weather Wrightby is a visionary of money and engineering who will not let geography or climate or politics block him. His plans are embedded in his company's name, and they are bigger by far than this road.

Judah, Judah, Judah. He thinks his name. Something will happen.

Products are created or remembered from the Full Years. In the arts there is a languid flux. New Crobuzon is full of building, its docks with ships. Shops carry novel commodities. Beside the poster-kiosks booths appear like wildflowers, in a spate of marketing, die-stamped signs of a man holding his hand to his mouth and shouting.

—What are these? Judah asks and enters. There is a chair, an engine, a range of lettered and numbered buttons, a tube and earpiece. He reads instructions, puts his coin into the slot. There is a list of titles.

THE MAYOR'S NEW YEAR SPEECH.
THE PITY IT'S A DITTY
TREBUSCHAND SYMPHONETTE

And others. He summons a music-hall song, "Rather the Poorhouse," puts his ear to the trumpet and listens quite rapt to something that has been held back snapping into place, a potential energy unlocked, the unwrapping of sound with a thudding; and then he starts as a noise emerges and it is the song, some unknown chorus girl, the nuances of her voice imprisoned behind crackling but unmistakably a voice and unquestionably singing. Judah can hear all the words.

—*And if it means the poorhouse dear that's right the poorhouse do you hear that's what I'll do to stick with you to keep you near my deary dear.* Judah can hear all of them trapped.

It is wax that makes sound physical. He is absolutely fevered by this. The wax can make sound wait and recur.

A new technology, the taming of time. They are using it for the endless, endless recursion of street songs. Judah wants it for another reason. He looks at the notes he made in the swamp. He is all breathless energy, and he feels New Crobuzon ebbing from him.

How many times have I missed the moment power spoke? He thinks of those who have died because he has seen a moment coming, has known that the bounty hunters or the militia or the rails or the gas will come, and has frozen before ineluctability. *I am frightened of time.*

But time's heartbeat has been stopped by these entertainers. *They have pickled these pasts.* His parasite goodness stirs, his saintly innard thing.

Suddenly it is easy to kick New Crobuzon off; his months there become memories effortlessly.

He writes to his few clients. He writes to Pennyhaugh, thanking him for his efforts, wishing him luck, telling him they will see each other again when Judah returns, which he does not believe.

There is one more technique he is eager to achieve. In Kinken he talks to khepri in the workshops, spoken questions and their handwritten answers, has them tell him what they will of their metaclockwork. He buys thaumaturgic batteries and charges them exhaustingly from his own veins.

It takes him a few tries. He sets up a tripwire by the falling-down house where the street-children who love him live. The sky is just changing when the first of them wakes and goes to steal breakfast. Her dirty feet break the filament and with a hum and snap the circuit connects, and then, oh, from the rocks by the door a little figure comes dancing. The girl is quite still and watchful.

The little golem is the size of her hand, and it dances as Judah instructed it to dance when he set his hex, stored his energies, ready for the trigger. It dances toward her. It is made of money. It staggers and falls down and falls apart into coins and the little girl comes forward and picks the money up.

Judah watches her from a doorway. He has stored up a golem and its orders. Has made it wait, for the little snare. He does not know if anyone has done this before.

ND HE IS IN THE SWAMPS AGAIN. THERE IS ICE, AND THE RAGS OF vine from the canopies are hardened, and the animals are sleeping and the swamp is quiet. Miles off is the work camp, and the work train.

The tracks have taken him past towns become corpses. Into lands not tamed but misshapen by the work and the workers, and on at last into the trees on constructed islands, isthmuses of displaced stone, into the fens. Judah goes deep, looking for those who were once his tribe.

He is laden: his new voxiterator and its cylinders, his camera, his guns. He is careful not to sound like a hunter, is careful to make noises as he walks. He sings the songs he has learnt from his stilt-spear. He sings the song of the breakfast, the song of hello, the song of a good day. He walks with his hands showing.

When they come for him they are of tribes he does not know, and he sings the song of good neighbours and the song of may I come in? They surround him as trees and stiltspear in flickering and they display their teeth and their weapon-hands, and when he still does not run they hit him and when still he does not run they take him to their hidden village. Their clans and kith-groups have broken down: these are the last of their people.

Children come to stare at him. He looks at them and sees a final generation.

His goodness moves, but Judah knows they are a dead people and nothing will change that. They take him hunting—dams and sires together, no time for traditional divisions—and he hears their *uh uh uh,* their counterpointed breaths and patted rhythms. The water eddies then ceases to eddy.

He thrusts out the listening trumpet and captures their sound on wax. He listens to it; he winds his handle and hears their rhythm. Judah can *see* it. He can see its shape. He looks through a lens and is a geographer on the wax continent of the song, tracking chasms, the coiled valley, its peaks and arêtes. He winds slowly, hears the song in sluggish time.

To his shame Judah feels drab among the doomed people. He works as best he can in the horrible wet cold, noting all the layers of the stiltspear songs, every faint and ill-performed bark, but the environs oppress him. No bower in the woods, no green den, but a frosted huddle of mulch and constant war parties, stiltspear out to fight, haunted by the ghosts they will certainly become.

Judah will not watch them. His interior thing jackknifes. He has their soul in his wax. He leaves them, for the second time.

BACK TO THE TRAIN. IT HAS MOVED. HE SEES A THOUSAND FACES HE has never seen before. The rails have forked. A town is growing. What a wonderful thing.

Tracks slick and train-polished. They coil into half-built sheds and empty sidings, into yards, past the warping wood of this half-built town they bifurcate. One line juts into the darkest part of the wetland and stops abruptly, hemmed by trees.

Another disappears westward. Men come out of their clearing and they carry dripping hammers, and they carry nails, and they are as stained and sweating as if they have been at war. With each breath they wear and shed momentary scarves of vapour.

As he enters the clearing where Junctiontown grows, Judah's good thing kicks happy like a baby and he knows he will stay here, that he is back and will be part of what he sees, not a parasite in its trail. He came for the interventions, of which the song is one. And this, this buckling down of rails, is another.

He is a veteran of the railroads, but he has never worked them before. The thing in him cajoles him. It wants him to join this great effort.

Judah follows the rails out of wet trees into hills, and the iron is implacable. The yellow roadbed rises. There are people everywhere. Lines of horses, the smell of fires—grass, wood, lignite. Judah comes through tents, sees them pitched on the roofs of the perpetual train. Remade and cactacae drag ploughs of chain to flatten the ground. Gendarmes walk in crews.

The perpetual train creeps forward with tiny turns of its wheels. Pushed and pulled by four hulks, diamond-stacks splaying and venting from yards up. Vastly bigger than the engines that ride New Crobuzon's elevated railways. These wilderness versions wear cowcatchers, their headlamps burn vividly, and insects touch like fingertips against the glass. Their bells are like churchbells.

There comes an armoured car with a swaying guntower. An office on wheels, closed wagons for supplies, what seems a parlour, one at least that is blood-fouled, a rolling abattoir, and beyond that a very tall and windowed wagon painted with pinchbeck gilt, slathered with symbols of the gods and Jabber. A church. Four, five enormous carts with tiny doors and rows of little windows, triple-decked bunkrooms thronged with men. Under their own great weight the sleep-coaches sag in the middle as if they have sows' bellies. There are flat cars, open and covered. And beyond them the crews. The music of hammers.

They are on a flat through the brush. The track-layers are speeding, closing the gap with the graders.

Judah is only one man walking beside the train. There is nothing to mark him except the sense that he is waiting. Judah is lifted. But there is sourness. He sees men and cactus-men muttering and the fear of the Remade tethered near their stockades. The foremen go armed. They did not used to.

MANY MILES AHEAD SURVEYORS MAP OUT THE LAND ACCORDING to charts drawn a score of years before by Weather Wrightby and his crews, when the old man was a scout himself. Behind them, in the unland between the train and the explorers, graders make their fat raised line. And behind them the bridge-monkeys push trestles across impassable land, and the tunnellers keep cutting through their rocks.

All this is ahead. Judah carries ties.

This is how the laying goes. Early morning the hundreds of men wake to bells and breakfast in the dining car on coffee and meat from bowls nailed to tables, or eat in vague congregations along the tracks. First are the whole: the hard human labourers; cactus-men from New Crobuzon's Glasshouse, a few renegades from Shankell.

Behind them, cuffed to their meal by guards, the Remade eat what is left. There are a few women among them, Remade with steam-driven integuments, iron-and-rubber or animal bulk. Those prisoners with boilers hexed to them are issued enough culm and low-grade coke to work.

The trains hang back. Horses or pterabirds or Remade bullocks drag carts from huge piles of rails along the line, to the last of the track, and back. The crews move for each other, industrial dancing. They quickstep in and down, and the hammering, and more rails come, and the carts refill and rejoin the extending road. Ten feet, hundreds of pounds of iron at a time, the road continues.

Jabber, what are we bringing? Judah thinks to see the work of all those many hundreds. *What are we doing?* He is awed by its raucous and casual splendour.

He sings songs to himself as he works, and invisibly he makes each cold rectangle of wood a limbless golem that for the tiny interval of its ablife strives to cross from the horse-hauled carriage of sleepers to the dust of the bed. Judah feels the thoughtless tugging from each piece, and it helps him. He carries more than he should. When the waterboys come from the train out of sight behind them there is a scramble to drink first, before dust and spit fouls the water. The many Remade wait.

Judah's tent-mates like him. They listen to his stories of the swamps and tell him of labour troubles.

—Fuckin' Remade been causin' trouble too. Over food and that. And the whores' prices goin' up and up. Somebody said the money's dryin' back home. You know anything about that? Somebody told me prices are fallin', money's runnin' out.

Behind the sleeper-men are the rail-layers and spikers, and behind them the intricate bulk of the train comes swaying snarling closer, tended like some steam-animal god.

Judah sees Remade chastised with whips, and the presence inside him spasms each time so he nearly falls. Once there is a fight between free workers and a Remade man with the pugnacity of the newly changed. The other Remade pull him away very quickly and only huddle under the whole men's blows. Remade women bring the sleeper-men chow. Judah smiles at them, but they react like stone.

On paydays or thereabout a train comes like a miracle through the thawing swamp. Mostly the free men give over their money in Fucktown and in the stills and hooch-tents. Judah does not go out those nights. He lies in his tent and listens to the echoes of gunshots, fighting, the gendarmes, screams. He takes out his voxiterator and plays the breathy stiltspear songs. He annotates his notebooks.

End o'the Line is a newspaper printed on the work train. It is illspelt and salacious, and vulgarly partisan for the TRT who sanction it. All the men read it and argue about its worst points. Twice Judah sees people reading other journals surreptitiously.

He drifts back toward the train. He takes his turn hauling rails.

Judah draws the line. The metal is mercilessly heavy. In the flat light of the sky he feels himself watched by rocks. Each rail almost a quarter of a ton, four hundred rails to the mile. He lives by numbers.

Crews work in cadres, all convict Remade or all freemen, no mixing. With tongs or their own metal limbs they slide the rails out, five men or three cactus or big Remade to each, and lay them down with midwife gentleness. Gaugemen space the irons out, and they in turn are gone, and the spikers move in.

Judah makes each rail momentarily an absurdly shaped golem. No others on his team feel the faint fishlike flutters of the metal as it tries to help him. He lays down angles in the random land. He grows strong. Once he sleeps on the roof of the train to know what it is like. Men have tethered goats up there and even make carefully corralled fires.

A tinker-showman works the length of the road, performing. Judah watches him make his own tiny dancing dirt figures, but they are not golems. They are only matter tugged as if by hand at a little distance, direct manipulations. They have no bounded reality, no ablife, no mindless mind to follow instruction, any more than puppets do.

Slogans are written on the train and the rocks. Each morning they appear, some nothing but crudities to shock the earth, some personal, some polemical, SCREW YOU WRIGHTBY. Twice when the bell brings Judah out of sleep into the dark morning posters are slathered to the train and to trees.

Some are very simple: FAIR PAY, UNIONS, FREEDOM FOR THE RE-MADE, and below a little doubled R. Others are a mass of tiny writing. Judah tries to read them while the foremen tear them down.

RUNAGATE RAMPANT.
TRACKS'-END SUPPLEMENT 3.

The death toll on the TRT Railroad continues to rise, as safety is spurned in the rush for money. The rails go down on the bones of workers, free and Remade . . .

—What in Jabber's name these fuckers on about? one man says. —Who ain't for fair pay? And if there are them as wants guilds I ain't got no problem, but free Remade? They're fucking criminals, or don't these dozy fuckers know that?

Judah is beguiled by the bravery of the dissidents. They creep at night when the gendarmes patrol. If they were caught they would not walk away. They would be made part of the landscape.

*Runagate Rampant*s are left under tables, on rocks. It is poor distribution, but it is all they have. Judah takes copies, and reads when he is alone.

He is only just aware of the dramas of the line. He works, hardly looking up at a rain-patter of shots down the rail. Later he hears that a joint war party of fReemade and striders, a long way east of their supposed territory, attacked the crews in the rear. They were driven off, but the gendarmes are concerned that so proud a race as striders are allying with the punk fReemade against the trains.

With the weeks and the miles and tons comes spring and the slow lengthening of days. The land around the iron road becomes sparse. Judah huddles with his crew behind an overturned cart while a strider family hurls indistinct missiles. The guntower of the perpetual train swivels and lays down craters like flowers.

Judah reads *Runagate Rampant*.

The borinatch, striders, have reason to hate the TRT. Their land is being stolen by the businesses of New Crobuzon, and the state and militia will not be far behind. Who has not heard the stories of Nova Esperium and the carnage of the natives? Each dead railworker is a tragedy, but the blame lies not with the borinatch, whose revenge is misplaced but whose fears are real. The blame lies with Weather Wrightby, and the Mayor, and the moneyed classes of New Crobuzon suckling at the teat of corruption. *We say: For a people's railway, and peace with the natives!*

Fucktown is close. Judah is not a customer there, preferring his own right hand or the guilty shut-eyed clutching of men on men in the hollows each Chainday night to the boredom of the whores.

Each week in the stockades where the Remade are kept there is a concession to conviviality, drunken parties where Remade women are given to Remade men and cheap drink is given to all under the aegis of the overseers. Judah watches the Remade women in the aftermath being bathed in the cold river, screaming at the temperature and drinking purgative to stop pregnancies. One guard oversees this. He is gentle with them. He dresses their bite marks and bruises, and punishes the Remade men who hurt too much or often. —It ain't right how some of them women is used, he says.

It is common for the wages train to be delayed. A day or two and there are only grumbles, but sometimes as long as a week goes without money. Three times when this happens there is a strike. By some chaos of democracy the track-layers put down their tools and block the train until they have their shekels in their pockets. They are nonplussed by their own mass, by their numbers. Hundreds of muscled men, the tall green brawn of cactacae emerging from them. The prostitutes, the surgeons, clerks, scholars, off scouts, and hunters come to watch them.

Judah stands among them, ashudder with excitement. He is unlocked by this, and is briefly at one with the thing inside him. *An intervention,* he thinks. He is never among the first wave to put his tools down—like Thick Shanks the cactus spiker who Judah thinks is a Runagater, like Shaun Sullervan the pugnacious alltradesman—but he is always among the second.

In response to the picketing, the Remade are worked hard. The foremen assure the strikers once that every effort is being made to expedite the money, and then they turn to the Remade, who are made to make up for the strike. The chained and altered men rock from blows, from the hexes of thaumaturge-guards; they drip under the weight of their own limbs as well as the loads they carry.

—Fucking *useless,* one overseer screams and beats a fallen man who wears many delicate eyes on his hands. —What fucking point is there making more Remades if they're peacocks like *you*? I tell 'em every godsdamned week we need Remade built for industry, not for their sodding whims. Get up and fucking haul.

The free men and cactus workers watch the punitive work, and cannot stop the road unrolling. They wince and watch.

—Stupid scab bastards, a cactus-man says.

They pity the Remade, but cannot forgive them breaking the strikes. The pay train always arrives in the end.

An absurd orgy of speculation, the financiers swimming like grease-whales in a slick of stolen and invented cash, prices for land and the stocks of the TRT soaring. It will not last. As returns slow, as the stench of TRT corruption and government collusion grows overpowering, the weakness at the base will show. When the rich grow afraid, they get nasty. *We say: A government for need not greed!*

The Remade draw a line. One of them is beaten by the guards and dies, and though he is not the first he was old enough and liked enough that many Remade refuse to work the next day, and carry the corpse in a raucous funeral. The unprecedented situation is digested; messages are expedited back and forth along the track.

The intransigent Remade are ranged alongside the train. The gendarmes take up positions. The guntower on the perpetual train turns.

Oh my gods, Judah thinks.

—Anyone willing to return to work now, raise your hand, a captain says. The Remade are confused. He does not wait more than five seconds before turning his back. He signals someone and the tower fires.

A shell arcs into the mid of the Remade. Later, Judah will realise its load must have been reduced, not to send burning shrapnel into the train itself. Now all he hears and sees is the fire and explosion, the circle of bloody clearance in the Remade.

A STRONG ACCOMPLISHED MAN DRIVES A SPIKE DOWN IN THREE strikes. Many men take four swings: cactacae and the most augmented steam-strong Remade two. There are three prodigious and respected cactus-men who can push a spike home in one blow. There is one Remade woman who can do this, too, but in her the ability is judged grotesque.

Judah is a free spiker. No one on the TRT line is higher. He makes each spike a golem, tasked to hide in the earth, so that with each blow it strives to embed itself.

He hears the metal slaps of his maul as the breaths of a stilt-spear. *Ah ah* ah. *Ah ah* ah. It sends him back to his voxiterator, listening and teasing apart the elements of the sounds, the overlapping beats. Judah sees Thick Shanks talking to someone without looking at them, standing with his back to the Remade stockade, a refigured man behind the chains lounging as if by chance but Judah knows he is listening.

It is in the company of Thick Shanks that Judah finds Ann-Hari again.

Judah courts the friendship of the militant cactus-man. They talk of the railroad and the uncanny dust-rock landscape and the dry cold of this late winter, and of the rumours that creep down the tracks to them like boxcars. Myrshock's crews striking again, Cobsea's government falling again with its meaningless regularity.

They smoke and share drugs around the Fucktown fires, and some of the women join them. It is in the shaking fireside shadows that Judah sees Ann-Hari. She is dressed in the functional provocation of a whore; she sees him as he sees her, but where he stands and cries out and runs to her, she only smiles.

She lets Judah accompany her. Ann-Hari the prostitute has become a nurse, an organiser, a grassroots madame. She has become a counsellor, her strangeness—knowing and credulous in some pastoral combination—meaning the younger and newer girls speak to her for help. Ann-Hari speaks to Shaun and to Thick Shanks. Ann-Hari organises and intervenes.

Judah watches her at the chain stockade. She comes at night to a place where the guards are not watching, and does as Thick Shanks has done, her back to the fence, a Remade man behind her, pretending to be there by chance.

Another man is there, a boy, less than twenty years old. He is propelled to Ann-Hari by the panic that sometimes overtakes Remade. Judah comes forward. In these shocks of psychotic self-revulsion they can hurt themselves or others, and the boy could reach Ann-Hari through the chain. But he hears what they are saying to each other, and he slows.

—I'll die I'll die, I can't go on, I'm cold, look at me, the boy says. He scrabbles at the outsize insect arms that radiate from his neck like a ruff, that clutch and scratch at him. —I'll run away.

—Where will you run? Ann-Hari says.

—I'll follow the rails home.

Ann-Hari's contact is watching. He has an integument of pipes and pistons emerging from his flesh, a steam-powered skeleton inside and outside.

—You'll follow the rails.

—I'll go home. I'll join the fReemade.

—Go home to New Crobuzon? A Remade. You want to go there? Or you go fReemade? Scrabble like a bandit. They miles from here, they don't come so close. You be killed by gendarmes within twenty mile.

The boy is quiet for a minute. —I go south. I go north. West.

—South is the sea. Hundreds of miles away. You know how to fish? North into an empty plain and to the mountains? West? Boy, west is the cacotopic zone. You choose that?

—No . . .

—No.

—But if I stay I die . . .

—Maybe. Ann-Hari turns and looks at the boy, and Judah can see her seeing him, and the thing in Judah uncoils. —Plenty of us going to die on this road. Maybe you die, be buried like a freeman under the iron. Maybe not. She reaches out and holds the chain so she is all but touching him. His insect neck-legs quiver. —You alive now. Stay alive for me.

Judah cannot speak. He does not think she has ever seen the boy before.

Ann-Hari does not lie with him, though she will kiss him, for long breathless moments, which she does not do with anyone else. But when he wants more she charges with a principled resolution that disturbs him.

—I ain't a client, he tells her. She shrugs. He can see it is not venality that motivates her.

Spring again, and there is a strong smell of burning metal by the points. It has been slow going in the cold, but now as men shed clothes the pace improves and the railmen get closer to the graders.

They are in the great vegas that surround Cobsea. The perpetual train comes with the growing heat into a merciless flat region of alkali dust that sets in eyes and mouths like rheum, that stinks like embalming fluid. It seems to hold warmth so the crews go from winter cold and are pitched into a dry heat. The train-town is bedraggled. The herds of beef-animals develop sores. Their meat is foul. There is a constant caravan of water carts going miles to siphon off the streams and rivers they find.

The land is alive. It hollows beneath them, reveals the craw and feeders of huge dust-sucking predators. The land bucks. There is an earthstorm, disks of rock careering skyward, buffeting the train. —We're in the badlands now. Everyone is saying it.

Research crews return from the desert of skin-soft dust, whipping their camel into spitty terror, and in their cart lies a man stiff with the muck that coats them all, no, he is a statue, no, he is covered with accretions, tumours of stone. They embed him, a man-shape whose lips are trembling.

—It came out of the ground . . .

—We thought it was mist . . .

—We thought it was smoke from a fire . . .

It is smokestone that has vented up and quickly set. They have to chisel him free. Flesh comes with the carapace.

Days later, the perpetual train comes to the residue of that drift. There are languid striae of smoke, utterly still. Stone in impossible spindly shapes, wafting, insinuate billows, coil and smog recoil. Harder than basalt, rock fumes.

It has drifted across the roadbed, and the biggest men take their mallets to the new formations. They grip fossilized moments of wind, and it looks as if they clamber the sides of a cloud. The smokestone comes away in tiny shards, and over the hours they clear a path just wide enough for the tracks. They split a passage through fog.

They are harried by fReemade who raid with what seems rampaging petulance. THE fREEMADE ARE NOT THE ENEMY! says a new spate of handwritten posters, but it is hard for the workers to hear that as they see the aftermaths of the attacks.

Judah cannot understand what the fReemade want. They die in the raids, too. Judah does not see it, but he hears that a litter of fReemade bodies and their nearly dead are laid across the line for the perpetual train to dismember. They steal odds of iron, machinery, a few cattle. Can it be worth it?

The ground kinks toward higher rocks and trees. The grading crews are nearby, slowed by the sudden gnarlings in the way; they have met tunnellers who have been rasping out a hollow in granite for two years, and who have not yet come through.

A tide approaches, a rill of brown. It is a forestful of insects fleeing the graders and the cutters.

Men swear and try to cover themselves. The insects buffet the crews, millions of tough bodies: their chitin cuts. They are big as cactus thumbs. Mindlessly they fight the train. They immolate themselves in the gears and beneath the wheels, and the tracks become slippery with oily carnage. Pipes vent sand for traction.

From behind the perpetual train comes a welling-up of shrieks as the insects reach the whores and few beggars who have come this far, the cattle, the economy stretched back on the rails.

THROUGH THE UNHOMELY LITTLE FOREST. THE GRADERS ARE ENsnarled with these skeletal trees. The earth has fought them and they have slowed. The graders meet the tunnellers and the bridgemen, the train and track-layers meet the graders, the whore and mendicant followers meet the train, and everything stops.

Land wrinkles into a lip of stone two hundred feet high, too steep for rails. The roadbed pushes into a gaping, almost-finished tunnel. Judah climbs the rise. On the other side it is sheer, edging a ravine. He can see the nearly finished bridge, girders emerging two hundred feet below him, marking where the tunnel will break through. There are men suspended in baskets, tamping charges into the holes they drill, hauled away as fuses spit.

There are Remade everywhere on the bridge. The scaffold reaches down to the crevasse bottom. The bridgemen wave up at the newcomers above. There is a great convivial joining.

Crews have worked months in the bone-coloured trees. They are like men made of the dust. The rust-eaters and the stokers on the huge engine are pied with the dirt of travel. Clerks and scientists lean from their cabs as the train stops; the wyrmen above wheel. The train's semiferal cats highstep.

There is a huge celebration that night, the tunnellers and bridgemen delirious with new company. Judah drinks. He dances to the drone of the hurdy-gurdy with Ann-Hari, and she with him, and then with Shaun Sullervan, and with Thick Shanks. They smoke; they drink. Men are speechless from the cheap drugs and hexed moonshine they have concocted in stills.

There are differences in the crews. Judah sees how the tunnellers and the bridgemen who have been trapped so long in the badland that they have become part of it do not differentiate as his workmates do. That though the Remade here are billeted separately, and there is some effort made to segregate them, the punitive landscape here does not support divisions so strongly as among his own. It is as if the iron link to New Crobuzon conducts its prejudices. The iron-road Remade watch the local Remade. Judah sees them see, sees the gendarmes and the overseers see.

Judah and his team lay tracks into the tunnel, up to its clawed end. They move very slowly. The men who have lived like worms step aside into wax-smeared alcoves. They see by fires and lux hexes in the stone. Judah's friends are cowed. They blink under the pale wide eyes of the diggers. The slap of their hammers is horrible and loud in that darkness.

There is nothing else for them to do. They clean the train, uselessly, scout the land a few miles, widen a well. But they cannot join the tunnellers, and they cannot build the bridge, and they can only wait, play cards, fuck and fight.

The graders can work. They can continue cutting beyond the ravine, toward Cobsea, still more than a hundred miles of hard wilderness away. But before they go, they want to be paid, and once again there is no money.

* * *

Very quickly, everyone knows there has been another clogging in the cash-pipes. The tunnellers are enraged. They have been working on promises, are owed months of backpay they thought the train would bring. The graders refuse to continue. It has been weeks since any trains from home have reached tracks'-end.

What is it? It is not a slowdown or confrontation; nothing is happening except an accretion of anger, looks held too long. The tunnel-headers gouge while the newcomers cut down dirty trees to make poor ties.

A tunnel-man is injured—an everyday terror in this black-powder land, but he responds with an outrage as if it is the first time such a thing has happened. —Lookit, he says holding up his blooded hand. The red on the white dust that coats him is vivid. —They letting us fucking die here.

That night Judah goes to the hollow where the men who fuck men gather, and when he comes back Thick Shanks is waiting. —Meeting going on, he says. —Not us, them. He indicates the lights in the perpetual train's guntower. —We got to think. They sending riders back along the line, telling Wrightby to send money now.

There is a fight the next day with sledgehammers, between two cactus-men so massive the overseers can only watch the vegetable men crush each other's wood-fibre bones. —Something's happening, says Ann-Hari to Judah. They sit on a blackened half-rock split by fire and cold water and the strikes of the biggest Remade man. —The girls are frightened.

A scattered few handwritten *Runagate Rampant*s are left at the mouth of the hill. Each day and night another fight or some petty act of anger, a headlight of the perpetual train shattered, obscenities carved into the paint.

Daily the graders gather and refuse to cross the ravine. Their foremen find other work for them. The graders are not striking, but are refusing to do what they are supposed to. They will sweep away the detritus of the tunnel, and carry tools, but if they cross that cut they will be in perhaps the last part of their digging; they will be dragging the roadbed the last hundred-some miles to Cobsea. And they will not, not yet, not now while the iron road withholds their money. That would be a surrender.

AND THEN THERE IS A NIGHT. THE LENGTH OF THE TRAIN AND AT the black of the tunnel there are fires. The roamstars are bright, crawling by their sedentary cousins. Judah has made a golem from thistles.

—What's that?

Judah looks up. People are staring, heading up the rock hill. They seem pulled; they move in little stuttering steps.

—What is it? Judah says, but the man he asks only shouts and points up the hill. —Look look! he says. —Come, it's there.

There is a noise along the ridgeback of the slope as if the stones and the very bushes are resonant, are singing an aberrant hymn. People on the incline shout and begin to scramble back again, in a river of scree. Falling men careen into their friends. Judah grips roots and keeps his feet.

The tremulous song, the sound of the wilderness anxious, is loud. There is a spider above him. No no that is not, that is not a spider that great shape that cannot be, it is the size of a tree, a fat tree with branches splayed in perfect symmetry that cannot be but that is what it is, it is a spider, so much bigger than the biggest man.

—Weaver.

—Weaver.

They say it. Their voices are beyond fear, quite stripped by awe.

Weaver. The spiders that are not gods but are nearly, that are something so other, so much farther than men or xenian, than dæmon, than archon, that they are unthinkable, their power, their motives, their meanings as opaque as iron. Creatures who fight murder die and reconfigure everything for beauty, for the intricacy of the web that is the world they see, a concatenation of threads in impossible spiral symmetry.

Songs about Weavers fill Judah's head. Nonsense-fears for children—*He promised me her hand in mine, / then smothered her in all his twine, / the Weaver swine*—absurdities and pantomime foolery. Looking up at this thing glowing unlight or is it light over the rock edge he knows the songs for the atoms, the infinitely tiny specks of stupidity they are.

The Weaver hangs in complex stillness. Body tarry black, a teardrop globe, a glintless head. Four long legs angled down to end in dagger-feet, four shorter up, as if in the centre of a web, hanging in the air. Ten, twelve feet long, and now, what, what is it, turning slowly, slightly, as if suspended, and the world seems snagged. Judah feels a tug as if the world is tethered by silks the Weaver is gathering as it turns.

Judah makes a debased throat sound. It is dragged out of him by this Weaver's unseen threads. It is a kind of unbidden worship.

All along the slope the men and women of the railway stand seared by what they see, and some try to get away and some stupid few crawl closer as if to an altar but most, like Judah, only stand still and watch.

—Don't touch it, don't fucking go near it, it's a godsdamned Weaver, someone is saying, someone a long way below. The spider-thing turns. The rocks continue to sing, and now the Weaver joins them.

Its voice comes out from under stones. Its voice is a shudder in dust.

. . . ONE AND ONE AND ONE AND TWO AND RED RED-BLACK RED-BLUE BLACK THROUGH HILLCUT WIRETRAWL AGASH AGASP AGAPE LEGATE AND CONSTRUCT MY TIES MY EYES CHILDER KINDER WHAT STONECUT AND DUSTDRUM YOU SOUND A SLOW ATRAP TRAPPING A RHYTHM IN TOOL AND STONE . . .

Its voice becomes a bark in time, a beating that makes the little rocklets dance on the slope.

. . . EAT MUSIC EAT SOUND PUSH THE PULSE PULSILOGUM THE MAGIC . . .

Thoughts and the textures of things are snared and pulled in to the Weaver.

. . . GRIND AND GROUND CARE AND UNCRUSH WHAT IS BEFORE UNCRUSH UNCRUSH YOUR NAME IS RAKAMADEVA ROCK MY DEVIL YOU FLINCH INCH ATWARD OF WHAT WILL BE YOU BUILD . . .

And the Weaver pulls in all its arms and drops lightly unreeled from its turning point in the air still sucking in what light there is and bloating on it as if it is the only real thing and Judah and the ground he stands upon and the threadbare trees he clutches are all old images, sun-bleached, on which a vivid spider walks.

The Weaver picks up its legs one by knifepoint one and treads at the edge of the ravine and it dances along it as the uncoloured women and men edge behind it and it turns its head in sly playful slide to stare at them with a constellation of eyes like black eggs. Each time it does the people who follow it freeze and haul back until it turns again and moves on and they follow it as if bound to.

It slips over the rim of the cliff and they run to see the arachnid thing pick dainty as a high-shoed girl down the sheer. It runs, it begins to run, until its huge absurd shape careers downward and it is by the roots to the bridge, the girders that spit out from the rock halfway to earth, and the Weaver leaps out and without passing through intervening space is on the half-done stump of construction, and small in the distance it begins to spin, to turn cartwheel, becomes a rimless wheel and skitters the girders where in the day the Remade bridge-monkeys hang and build.

. . . AND BREAK AND BREAK . . . The Weaver's voice comes as loud as if it were next to Judah . . . PUSH BRUSH THEY AWAIT WITH BREATH-BAIT AND ADRIP FOR YOUR INTERVENTION DEVILS OF THE MOTION ELA-TION CITATION CITE THE SITE TOWER SIGH NIGH VEER STAR AND CLEAR YOU ARE YOU ARE FINE IN TIME YON OF THE PLAINS STEAM-MAN . . . And the Weaver is gone and the weak night light bleeds back into Judah's eyes. The Weaver is gone and it takes many seconds of staring at the spider-shaped absence on the bridge until the men and women of the railroad turn away. Someone begins to cry.

The next day a handful of men are dead. They stare up at their canvas or at the sky with eyes quite washed of all colour and with smiles as if of quiet pleasure.

There is an old man long gone mad who has come quietly with the railroad for miles, sitting while the hammermen swing and the whores sell relief, a man become a mascot, become a piece of luck. After the Weaver he stands above the tunnel mouth and declaims in glossolalia and then in words. He says he is a prophet of the spider, and though they do not obey the commands he gives them the workers of the iron road watch him with hesitant respect.

He walks among the forced idleness of the track-layers. He shouts at the tunnellers to put down their picks and go nude and run away north into the unknown places of the continent. He shouts at them to copulate with the spiders in the dust. They are all draped in threads from the Weaver's spinnerets. They are knotted in a new configuration.

—We saw a Weaver, Judah says. —Most people never see that. We saw a Weaver.

* * *

The next day the women strike.

—No, they say to the men who come to their tents, and who stare at them uncomprehending. The women stand together in a militia, holding what weapons they have. A picket of rags and petticoats.

There are scores of them, determined and surprised by themselves. They turn away the hammermen, tunnel-men, gendarmes. The rebuffed gather. A counterdemonstration of surly lustful men. They mutter. Some go to masturbate behind rocks; some simply go. Many stay.

The dust of the two gatherings rises as they face each other. The gendarmes come—they do not quite know what to do; the women are doing nothing but refusing, the men are only waiting. —No pay, Ann-Hari says, —no lay. No pay no lay no pay no lay.

—We'll not do it no more for promises, she says to Judah. —Since we come here and there ain't no money, they been doing and doing it on credit. Our men, our gendarmes, now the new lads. And they ain't had women here for a long time; they hurt us, Judah. They come and say put it on my tab girl and you can't say no and you know they ain't going to pay.

—Cyra lost her eye, she said. —Some tunnel-man comes, put it on my tab, she tells him no and he knocks her so hard it splits her eye. Belladona had her arm broke. No pay no lay, Judah. Money first from now.

The women defend Fucktown. They have patrols with sticks and stilettos; there is a frontline. They take turns to watch the children. There must be those among them who are not happy with the confrontation, but they are quietened into solidarity. Ann-Hari and the others swish their skirts and laugh while the men watch. Judah is not the only man who is a friend to these infuriated whores. He, Shaun Sullervan, Thick Shanks, a clutch of others watch together.

—Come on girls what's this then, says a foreman. —What's the story? What are you after? We need you, beauties. He smiles.

—Won't be beat down anymore, John, Ann-Hari says. —Won't take promises. You pay; until then no lay.

—We ain't got the money Ann you know that sweetheart . . .

—Ain't my problem. Have your man Wrightby pay his men, then . . . She jigs her hips.

That night a group of men try with something between light-heartedness and anger to push their way past the picket, but the women block them and beat them hard and the men retreat holding split heads and screaming in astonishment as much as pain. —Stupid fuckpig *bitch,* one man screams. —You stupid *bitch,* you smashed my fucking *head,* bitch.

They do not let the men touch them the next day and there is no longer novelty or near-humour to the situation. A man takes out his cock, shakes it at them. —Want payment? he shouts. —I'll give you payment. Eat this you fucking dirty moneygrab sluts. There are those in the crowd of men who have enough affection for the women they have travelled with that they do not like that, and they hush him, but there are others who applaud.

—Get money, and come in, the women shout. —Don't blame us, horny bastards.

There is another attempt on their camp. This time it is led by the tunnellers. It is a rape squad intent on punishment. But there is an alarm, a panic from Remade women sent to clean clothes near the Fucktown tents. They see the men creeping and yell, and the men are on them quickly and attacking to silence them. A squad of the prostitutes come running.

Men are stabbed, a woman's face is broken, and when the prostitutes have overcome the intruders one of the Remade women is found concussed and leaking from her head. The whole women hesitate briefly before they carry her in to tend her.

In the morning the tunnel-men strike. They gather at the tunnel mouth. The foremen run to negotiate. The tunnellers have their spokesman: a thin man, a weak geothaumaturge, his hands stained basalt black by the stone he makes into slurry.

He says, —We go back in when them girls let us back in, too, and his men laugh. —We've got needs, he says.

The prostitutes and tunnellers have made demands. The graders will not work. The track-layers cannot, and only sit in the sun and play dice or fight. It is becoming violent like a prairie town. The perpetual train sits. The gendarmes and foremen confer. There is rain, but it is hot and unrefreshing.

—Mate with the spiders, the old man says. —It's time to change.

Everything is still. Only the bridge is being built, and now in the evenings when the bridge crews come off their work, some cross the ravine to their sister encampment, because they want to see the trouble. They come—hotchi in spines, apes trained and constrained by Remaking, Remade men given simian bodies. They come to see the strikes. They tour from one to another.

The newspapermen on the perpetual train, who have been despatching their stories when there are messengers, suddenly have something new to cover. One takes a heliotype of the picket of women.

—I don't know what I'll say, he says to Judah. —They don't want me talking about tarts in *The Quarrel.*

—Take all the plates you can, says Judah. —This is something you should remember. This is important, he says, and it is his oddity, his beatific innard that speaks. His breath leaves him a moment at the thought that he can hear its words.

—We are all spiders' children, says the mad old man.

There are handwritten *Runagate Rampant*s on the rocks.

This is not three strikes, or two strikes and a half. This is one strike, against one enemy, with one goal. The women are not our opponents. The women are not to be blamed. No pay no lay they tell us, and that can be our slogan too. We will not lay another tie, another rail, until the money promised is ours. They say it, and we say it too. *We say: No pay no lay!*

When the overseers and gendarmes realise that the disparate groups are not tiring of the strike, will not exhaust themselves with re-crimination, there is a change. Judah feels it when he rises and sees the foremen moving with new purpose.

It is already hot, he is already sweating, when unbreakfasted he goes to the tunnel mouth with others from the idle workforce. The tunnellers are arranged like a fighting unit, and they carry their picks. The foremen and gendarmes are before them, with a corps of tethered Remade.

—Come on now, says an overseer. Judah knows him. He is the man they bring in to do unpopular things. There is a delegation from the prostitutes, twelve women walking close together, headed by Ann-Hari. The tunnellers begin derisive calls. The women only watch. Behind them all the train wheezes like a bull.

The overseer stands before the Remade. He turns his back on the strikers and looks at the motley Remade in their integuments of foreign flesh and metal. Judah sees Ann-Hari whisper to Thick Shanks and another man, sees them nod without turning. They are staring at the Remade who have been gathered. One of them, a man with pipes that emerge from his body and enter it again, stares back at Thick Shanks and moves his head. He stands by a much younger man with chitined legs emerging from his neck.

—Pick up the picks, the foreman says to the Remade. —Go into the tunnel. Cut the rock. We'll instruct you.

And there is a silence and no motion. The gendarmes have interposed between the strikers and the Remade.

—Take the picks. Go into the tunnel. Follow it to the end. Cut it.

There is silence again a while. The men of the perpetual train know how the Remade are being used, and some begin to shout *scab, scab* preemptively. But the shouts die because none of the Re-made are moving.

—Take the picks.

When there is no movement still, the overseer strikes with his whip. It lands loudly and with the blossoming of a scream. A Re-made drops, hands to his opened face. There are fear noises, and some of the Remade start and begin to move but one of them makes a low command and they shudder and hold, except one who breaks and runs for the tunnel and shouts, —I didn't want to and I won't, you can't make me, it's a stupid plan, it's a stupid plan.

The others do not look at him and he goes into the dark. The young man with the insect-leg tumours is shaking. He is looking hard at the ground. Behind him, the piped man is saying some-thing.

—Take the picks. The overseer moves closer to the Remade.

Something rises in Judah. There is muttering and an anger around him.

—Take the picks or I'll have to intervene to stop troublemakers. Take the picks and go in or—

People are beginning to shout now but the overseer speaks over them.

—or I will have to take action against . . . He looks slow and os-tentatious over the terrified Remade, one by one, pauses while he looks at the piped man, the only one who even momentarily meets his eyes, then grabs the trembling boy, who cries and stumbles. —Or I will have to take action against *this* ringleader, the overseer says.

There is a moment without speech or sound, and he motions two of the gendarmes, and as they move in the crowd begins to shout again, and the gendarmes beat the young man down.

And as if he were with the stiltspear singing, Judah sees in time gone thick. He watches the descent of the billy clubs, the fumbling of the boy who covers his head and his chitin embellishments. He has time to watch the moving of birds above them. He has time and a fascination for the faces of the crowd.

They are stricken and cannot look away. The piped Remade man who was the boy's protector has his teeth set, the track-layers are opened up with pity, the tunnel-men stare in the shadow of the rockforms with bleak astonishment, discomfort, and everywhere Judah looks as the cuffs land and the gendarmes hold back the crowd he sees a *hesitation*. Everyone is hesitating and tensed and looking at each other and at the howling Remade boy and the batons and looking at each other again and even the gendarmes are hesitating, each blow taking a moment longer to land than the previous, and their colleagues raise their weapons in uncertainty and there is a swelling of voices.

Judah sees Ann-Hari, held back by her friends, scratching the air, and she looks as if she will die of rage. And people hover as if steeling to dive into something cold, look to each other still, wait, wait, and Judah feels the thing in him reach out, the oddness and the good in him reach out and push them, and it makes him *smile* even in this blooded heat, and they move.

It is not Judah who moves first—he never moves first—or the Remade with the pipes, nor Thick Shanks nor Shaun but someone quite unknown in the forefront of the tunnel-men. He steps out and raises his arm. It is as if he pushes through a tension that has settled on the world, breaks it and pours out into time like water breaching its meniscus and others come with him, and there is Ann-Hari running forward and the Remade intervening to hold back the nightsticks and whips of the gendarmes, and Judah himself is running now and wrapping his work-hardened arms around the throat of a uniformed man.

Judah's ears are stopped with a hot tinnitus, and all that he can hear is the beat of his own rage. He turns and fights as he has learnt to fight in brawls along the sides of the rails. He does not hear but feels the firing of guns as shoves in the air. Energy boils in him in hexes, and when he grips a gendarme, in a moment of instinct he makes the man's shirt a golem that wriggles on his body. Judah runs and fights, and what he touches that is lifeless he gives instants of ablife and makes obey his orders, to struggle.

The gendarmes have flintlocks and whips, but are outnumbered. They have thaumaturges, but they are not the militia: there are no spit gobbets of energy or transformations on the strikers, only base charms the railroaders can match and survive.

There are more cactus-men among the track-layers than there are cactus overseers. They run huge through the TRT guards and lay green fists on them, breaking them easily. They shield their friends; the gendarmes are not carrying rivebows that can slice them apart.

The piped Remade man drags the body of the insect-altered boy. The man pulls coal from his pocket and smears it into his mouth, leaving his lips black. He runs. The gendarmes who can still move are retreating. Others litter the ground, beside broken Remade and free men. It is so fast.

Judah is running. He drips. Gendarmes swing their weapons and are overcome by Remade out of shackles. They shoot and Remade fall. By the train, the gendarmes are regrouping.

—We have to—Judah shouts, and the piped Remade man is beside him and nodding and shouting too, and there are those who obey him: Remade and free whole men and women, there is Ann-Hari, there is Shaun, and they take their orders from this nondescript Remade man.

—You, he says to Judah. —With me.

They round the curve through dead trees and there is the perpetual train. It breathes its smoke and it spits steam as they come closer in mangy army. Its cowcatcher is splayed like ruined teeth. Its chimney flares, seems a funnel sucking up the energy of the sun.

And all over figures jump from it and to it, from the bunks on its roof, from the trucks where the free men sleep, from all of it, staring as those who approach, gendarmes and strikers, shout. The two sides try to win them over as they run.

—they, they—

—get *down*, it's the bastard Remade—

—they shot us *down*, they beat us—

—disperse you bastards or I'll godsdamned shoot—

—stop them, Jabber, fuck *stop* them fuck's sake—

The gendarmes fringe the train in raggedy formation, guns out, and the surge of the curious and the angry strikers—tunnellers, prostitutes, Remade—skitters to a stop. The gendarme retreat to their teetering guntower.

Now there is a long moment between a standoff and a confusion. Ann-Hari and the piped man approach. He looks emotionless. Ann-Hari does not. Behind them is a pitching army of Remade. They do not march, they shake their legs, some still ringed by the fringes of shackles opened with stones and stolen keys. They do not march, they almost fall with every step, and the sun makes them vivid in mongrel colours. The sun cuts sharp edges around the weapons they have made.

They raise slivers of the fence that has contained them. They swing the chains that tethered their feet. They grip shivs, pot shards embedded in wood. There are scores, and then hundreds of them.

—Jabber who let *them* out, what you *done*? someone shouts hysterically.

The thing in Judah swells up to see them. It bloats him; it moves like a baby in his belly. Judah shouts for them, a welcome, an alarum.

Men on all fours become bison-men, carrying men wrapped about with limbs, and women walking on elongated arms made of animals' parts, and men stamping on piston legs like jackhammers come alive, and women all over whiskers, or with finger-thick tendrils feeling through their skin, and tusks stolen from boars and carved from marble, and mouths become interlocked gears, and switching tails of cats and dogs frilling waists like skirts and sweating in inks from Remade glands and astream with a rainbow mess, and this aggregate of criminals, this motley comes closer in freedom.

The gendarmes have withdrawn. They are in their armoured cab, in the guntower. Some have grabbed mules and horses from the tracks'-end corral and gone.

—No no no.

Many among the tunnellers and the track-layers are aghast at the freeing of the Remade. No one is sure who did it, how. Some stolen keys, a moment that went through the kraal of tethered criminals (though still there are a few who will not emerge, who cling to their irons).

—This ain't what we're here for. This ain't what this was. A tunneller is shouting at Shaun Sullervan, disdaining to speak to Ann-Hari or the host of Remade stretching their limbs. —I didn't want that boy to be beat, it ain't nothing he'd done, but this is *stupid*. What are you going to fucking do? Eh? We have . . .

He looks at the blinking Remade, who stare at him. He twists a little.

—No offence, mates. He is speaking to the Remade now. —Look, it ain't my fucking business. You seen we won't let them beat you down no more. But, but, you can't, you got to go back, this is . . . He indicates the guntower.

It is late. There is a siege and a strange siege calm.

—People have fucking *died,* the man says. —They've *died.*

The boy with the insect additions is dead. Other Remade were dropped by bullets. A cactus-man was split by a moment of flying wood. Gendarmes have been piled up, broken on mallets, on spikes, on the ersatz weapons of the railroad. There are dazed mourners by trench graves.

Hunters return. Prostitutes sit on rocks in that deserted middle

of the world and watch the train. Its firemen and brakemen agitate
as the giddy Remade fill the boiler and pull levers and those with
boilers of their own steal the high-grade coke. People mill bewildered and ask each other what has *happened*. They look at the sun
and the shifting tree corpses and wait for someone to come into
control.

A strange angst because there is such calm here now and it cannot sustain. The gendarmes have taken the guntower and one other
car: the Remade have the rest of the train. The iron tower cracks in
the heat, and the weapon at its top swivels.

The free men want to treat Shaun and Thick Shanks as leaders
of a Remade rabble, but Ann-Hari stands with them, and with the
pipe-woven man, whose name Judah learns is Uzman, and with
other Remade.

—Take your boys back in. What you think they're doing
in there? the free workers' speaker says. He points at the tower.
—Getting ready is what. To take you. Now, we made our point.
If you go back now, they'll pay us up, and there'll be no, no penalties . . .

He speaks to Shaun, but it is Uzman answers.

—You'll get your money, and you're telling us to give this back?
The train?

He laughs, and the craziness of what the free men are asking
is very evident. They want these Remade to unfree themselves.
Uzman laughs. —We ain't decided yet what we do here, he says.
—But we decide.

There are shouted arguments like street meetings, out of the guntower's lines, between Remade with Remade, layers, rust-eaters
together, the tunnel-men. From the guntower come noises of industry. The strikers watch from behind blockades. The moon is
split near exactly in half. It is waning. In its light and the lanterns'
and the phosphor of lux hexes, the men and women of the perpetual train gather.

—We can't just wait, says Thick Shanks. —People are running already. Gods know how many gendarmes got out—too many horses are gone. Hand-trucks. And it ain't just the overseers leaving, Uzman. We have to make them give in.

—Give in *what*? Ann-Hari speaks. The thing in Judah moves. —Give in what? What do you want from them, chaver? They've nothing to give us. They're still scared—that's why they're in that tower—but when they start having to throw their shit out over the parapets, they'll come out gunning.

They raise their voices. The crowd turns to them, slowly.

—We make *demands,* Thick Shanks says. —They'll bring reinforcements. We have to have demands ready.

Shaun says, —Like what? You want them to free the fucking Remade? Ain't going to happen. Recognise the new guilds? What is it we want?

—We have to link it up, Thick Shanks says. —We send our *own* riders back to New Crobuzon, talk to the guilds there, make *joint* demands. If we can get them to back us—

—You're dreaming. You think they'll do that? For us?

—We have to take control of this. This is *ours, now,* says Uzman.

Someone jeers and makes a noise about the godsdamned Remade. Ann-Hari shouts, and in her agitation her arcane hill Ragamoll asserts itself.

—Shut up, she says to the heckler. —You curse the Remade, as if it make you better. Why we here? You fought. You—she gestures at the tunnellers—you struck. Against *us.* Her lieutenant prostitutes nod. —But why did you fight the gendarmes? Because *they,* they Remade, wouldn't scab. They *wouldn't.* They took beating for you. To not break *your* strike. And they did it for *us.* For *me.*

Ann-Hari reaches out and grips Uzman and pulls him to her, he acquiescing with surprise. She kisses him on his mouth. He is Remade: it is a vivid transgression. There are shocks and exhalations, but Ann-Hari roars.

—These Remade strike for *us*, so *you* won't be broken. You strike against us and we against you, but these Remade are on *both* our damn sides. You *know* it. You fought for them. You scorn them *now*? They *won* you your damn strike, and *ours too,* even though we strike against each other. She kisses Uzman again. Among the prostitutes, some are aghast and others are cheering. —I tell you, Ann-Hari says, —if anyone deserves service on *credit,* it's the damn Remade.

The prostitutes closest to Ann-Hari and most militant seek out Remade ostentatiously to touch.

—We have to link up, shouts Thick Shanks, but no one is listening to him. They are listening to his friend Ann-Hari. Judah makes a golem out of the dust.

It is deep night but very few are sleeping. Judah's golem is taller than he, held together with oil and dirty water. The old man become the Weaver's prophet stands behind Ann-Hari and shouts obscure praise to her while she and Thick Shanks argue.

A gendarme comes to them from the direction of the train. He waves a truce flag. —They want to talk, says a woman on chitin wheels.

—Wait, he shouts as he walks. —We want to end this. No recrimination. We'll talk to the TRT, get the money through. Everyone wins. You, Remade, we can talk. End your peonage early, maybe. We can talk about everything. Everything's open.

Ann-Hari's face is a joy of anger. The man cowers from her and she passes him and runs in the direction of the train, followed by Remade, Thick Shanks and Uzman, and Judah, who slaps his golem on its arse as if it is a baby and shocks it, hexes it into motion. It astonishes those it passes.

Shanks is shouting to Ann-Hari, —Wait wait, what are you going to do? *Wait.* And Uzman is urging something too, but where the Remade besiegers hide behind their stockades she simply steps into view of the gendarmes in the tower. She takes a man's flintlock.

Uzman and Shanks are shouting at her but she is walking on into the no-man's-land by the train. Only Judah's golem goes with her. The tower's guns swivel toward her. Inexpertly she brings up the flintlock. She stands with the oily dirt man, the two of them alone.

—No deal with you bastards, she shouts, and pulls the trigger, though bullets cannot penetrate the cladding. As the shot sounds, Remade run forward to protect her and Judah hears the captain at the tower's top screaming something at his own men and it could be *hold* or *fire*. Judah has his dirty golem step before Ann-Hari as first one and then a sudden percussion of the gendarmes' guns sound.

Everyone drops but Ann-Hari and the golem, and there are screams and blood. The gunshots dwindle. Three people lie unmoving. Others, mostly Remade but whole too, are shouting for help. Ann-Hari is still. The golem is pitted where bullets have stopped in its dense substance.

—No no no, the captain is shouting. —I didn't—but the Remade will not wait now. They roar. Someone pulls Ann-Hari back, and Judah sees her, and she is *smiling,* and he feels himself smiling too.

There is a little war. —What are you *doing*? Shanks screams at Ann-Hari but it is a pointless question now. Gendarmes, free workers, prostitutes and Remade skirmish, and two sides assert: the Remade and their friends; the gendarmes and those opposed to this exultant hysteria. Judah is afraid of it, but he never unwishes this violent child's birth.

Remade attack the tower with guns, crude bombards and their swing-hammer limbs. They fire stone slabs and track-ends that make the tower ring. A man beside Judah, whose chin wears a fringe of crabs' pincers, dies suddenly from gendarme shot. Judah has his golem move slowly around the belfry, disaggregating in bullet-slugs of its earth flesh.

He does not hear the shot from the heavy gun above. An over-turned curricle is at one moment a cart with men and women lean-ing between its spokes and then is an eruption, a fire expansion of burnt knife-edged wood and blood uncoiling above a cavity bleed-ing smoke. Judah blinks. He sees detritus. He sees that the dark thing acrawl toward him leaving a mollusc trail is a woman, her skin blacked and redded, ink craquelure on meat. He wonders that she does not make a sound as her hair burns then knows he cannot hear. His ears sing. The barrel of the gun exhales like a languid smoker.

It turns. The rebel Remade, prostitutes, and those of the free who are with them run to escape its range.

Judah stands. Slow. Steps up, and makes his golem move. The gun motors with unoiled imprecision. The golem presses its filthy self against the freightcar. It reaches up, echoing and exaggerating Judah's little motions, pulls itself up, leaving a smear of its corpus.

The towertop gun fires again. It stabs oily smoke, and the rail-road cut and the people on it, yards away, bloom. The golem as-cends the tower, stamping on buttresses, on gutters. It uses the very guns that gendarmes angle down at it as handles and steps. It disre-gards itself, as no sane or sentient thing could, sheds itself in scabs and diminishes as it rises, but it is near the top now, weakened with sticks and railway spikes protruding from its gravel-grease skin, its very legs falling from it to land formless as excrement. The gun swivels and Judah has the golem probe its arm deep into the barrel.

It reaches to its shoulder. The gun is blocked by hex-bound golem dirt. It fires and there is a strange motion, a shuddering backward. The barrel splays in strips, the golem is a rain of filth. Ig-nited air and smoke fill out, the tower rocks, its tip glows and is punched brutally open, its roof unclenches into metal fingers.

Rank billows plume in a great cough, and a dead man falls from the shatter. The corpse of the gun sways. Judah is spattered with his golem's remnants. The rebels are cheering. He cannot hear them but he can see.

* * *

The renegades take the train. The gendarmes throw out their guns and come out bloody, eyes seared and dripping.

—No, no, no, Uzman shouts. He is eating coal, and his biceps are swelling. With Shanks and with Ann-Hari, and with other faces that Judah now knows, the Runagaters try to stop the beatings when they look like becoming killing. They take away knives. People shout but cede to them. The gendarmes are chained where the Remade were.

—What now? Everywhere Judah goes he hears it.

It is the Remades' train. They make flags for their new sudden country and wave them from the burst guntower. No one sleeps that night. The tunnellers' overseers disappear into the barrens, and many men go with them, and some prostitutes.

—Send word back for gods' sake, Thick Shanks says. —We have to make links, he says, and Uzman nods. Around them are other leaders of the sudden mutiny. They make their points in untrained passionate language. They decide things.

Ann-Hari tells everyone, —Not backward, we don't go back, we go out. And she points into the wilderness.

They choose messengers. Riders. A Remade sutured to steam-and-piston legs like spread-out fingers that run with tremendous shuddering up slopes of rock, his man-torso aflail like an unwilling passenger. Another, a muscled man made a strange six-limbed thing: he is joined below his abdomen to the neck of a great bipedal lizard, one of those the badland nomads half-tame to ride. He stands high on two back-bent legs before a stiff tail, clawed fore-arms just below his human skin. He has been a scout for months, ridden by a gendarme with a gun to his back.

—Go, says Uzman. —Stay by the tracks. Out of sight. Get to the towns. Get to the workcamps, get to Junctiontown. And Jabber and fuck, get to New Crobuzon. Tell them. Tell the new guilds. Tell them we need help. Have them come. If they support us, down tools for us, we can win this. Remade and free—bring them all.

—Uzman, they say and nod, as if his name itself is an affirmative.

The horse riders go in wheels of dust, the steam-insect man in an instant of scuttling speed. The gnarled and reptile-paced man accelerates over shreds of heather by the roadbed. Birds and other things that fly watch them. The ones that are not birds veer with the zigzag spasms of fish in the sea.

The prostitutes let some men come to them in strict conditions, unarmed, guard-women nearby. Since Uzman and Ann-Hari, some of them have even been with Remade.

—New Crobuzon's full of it, Ann-Hari says. —Whole-and-Remade fucking. What happens when someone gets the punishment factory, what, always his wife leave him?

—Supposed to. It ain't decorum.

—They doing it all over the city, like they doing cross-sex, khepri, human, vods.

—True, Judah says. —But you ain't supposed to admit it. These women . . . your women . . . they're letting us see.

She looks to the moon. She lets the moon go over her. She watches its last light over the skeletal bridge. —City guilds can't help us here, she says. —This is new.

Torches move on the girders below them. The bridge builders have returned to work, without overseers.

—What did you tell them? says Judah.

—The truth, says Ann-Hari. —Told them they can't stop. Told them this is a Remaking.

Sunup, after three days, the steam-spider Remade returns. He sucks up water before he can speak.

—They're coming, he says. —Gendarmes. Hundreds. In a new train. A commandeered passenger train, he tells them, emptied of the sightseers and chancers come to explore the continent's interior.

Most of the freeandwhole have run. Some are members of this new town, resentful of the Remade suddenly their equals but held by a deep query, by *What will happen?* They are part of this train-assembly, a gathering. There are some as committed as the Remade, part of the sabotage crews who go back to tear up the tracks behind them. Those drivers, firemen and brakers left teach the Remade.

They reverse through landscape they have altered. It was never stable, afflicted with life in hex tides. They go over places where the ground, when they cut it, was stone and that is now dappled lizard's skin, bleeding milklike blood where rails are spiked. There are places where the earth has become like the cover of a book, and shards of paper spurt from the spike-wounds. They dismantle the rails to block their pursuers.

A reversed industry. They turn their expertise to the road's dismantling, levering up spikes, shouldering rails and ties piles, scattering the stones. They plough up the roadbed and return home.

But—They took the barricade down, the scouts soon come and tell them. —They brought rails and sleepers. They're building the track again. Within three days the gendarmes will reach the camp.

There are lights in the tunnel; there is industry.

—What did you do? Judah says.

—We're finishing the tunnel, says Ann-Hari. —And the bridge. We're almost through.

Her influence is spreading. Ann-Hari is more and less than a leader, Judah thinks: she is a person, a nexus of desires, of want for change.

The last yards of rock are being ground through in the dark wet mountain. Judah looks down at the bridge. The new work is something laughable, a quick flimsy lattice of metal and wood thrown up beyond the stumps of proper construction. It is ersatz; it is only just bridge.

Judah is one of a conclave—it surprises him—struggling for strategy. They meet in the hills: Shaun, Uzman, Ann-Hari, Thick

Shanks, Judah. But parallel to them, something raucous and collective is emerging.

Every night in the gaslamps the workers gather. First it was convivial—liquor, dice and liaisons—but as the gendarmes come closer, and as Uzman debates strategy in the overlooking ground, the parties change. The men of the train name each other *brother*.

Ann-Hari comes to the meeting and invades a man's rambled contribution. A wedge of women push into the men. There are those who try to shout Ann-Hari down.

—You ain't a worker on this road, a man says. —You ain't nothing but a mountain whore. This ain't your damn congress, it's ours.

Ann-Hari speaks something base. She talks in ragged rhetoric of thrown-together exhortations—a speech that stops Judah. It seems as if it is the train that speaks. The fire holds still.

—not to speak. she says. —If I am not to speak who has the right?—What but on us? What but on the backs of me and mine have we built these rails? We are become history. There's no backward now. No way back. You know what we have to do. Where we should go.

When she is done no one can speak for seconds, until someone mutters respect.

—Brothers, let's vote.

Uzman tells them that whichever way they see it, whatever they claim to themselves, Ann-Hari is telling them to run. That's not the answer. Are they afraid?

—Ain't running, Ann-Hari says. —We're done here. We're something new.

—It's running, he says. —Utopian.

—It's something new. We're something new, she says, and Uzman shakes his head.

—This is running, he says.

*　*　*

They unbolt the guntower and guide the train into the tunnel. They take up the tracks behind them. There is still blasting and scraping from inside the hill, and construction on the strange new bridge. The work is frantic.

In the heat of the morning the sound of other hammers and steam comes. The gendarmes' train. They see smoke over the heat-dead trees.

The workers gather in the tunnel, among the cleavage of chiselled edges, minutely variant planes. The light makes shadows where vectors of stones meet.

Uzman, the grassroots general, gives orders they choose to obey. A hundreds-strong army of Remade and the freeanole now committed: those few clerks, scientists and bureaucrats who have not run; weak geoempaths; a few others—the camp followers, the mad and unemployable, and the prostitutes whose exhaustion started this. They come out into the night, ready. The train hides in the hole in the hill.

It is cool before dawn. The gendarmes come over ridges and around the bend. They come on foot, in plated carts pulled by Remade horses, in single-person aerostats, balloons above them and propellers on their back. They career through the air, and bear down on the track-layers' hides.

They drop grenades. It is astounding. The train people are shrieking. They cannot believe that this is how it starts. They are deafened and bloodied. This is how it begins. A cascade of clay splinters and sooty fire.

Those with guns fire. One, two gendarmes snap and bleed out of the sky, haul their strange aircraft out of range, or loll in death in their harnesses, flying or coming down at random. But they keep coming. They roast the air with firethrowers.

—Crush them, Uzman urges, and his troops roll down logs and boulders as the gendarmes regroup and fire arbalests. Thaumaturges on either side make the air oscillate, make patches of grey swim up from nothing to stain the real, send arrows of energy spitting like water in fat that hit and do strange things. It is a chaos of fighting. A constant coughing of shot and screams, and gendarmes fall, but the strikers do in many greater numbers.

There are moments. A troupe of cactacae step forward and only wince as bullets break their skins. They terrorise the gendarmes, who run before the huge flora, but though the officers have no rivebows they have caustics that scorch the cactus skin.

—We're rabble, Uzman says, and looks in despair. Ann-Hari says nothing. She looks beyond the gendarmes, beyond the tower of smoke where their train is coming.

Judah has made a golem. He sends it out toward the gendarmes. It is a thing made of the railway itself. It is made of handcars, the odds of rails and ties. Its hands are gears. It wears a grill for teeth. Its eyes are something of glass.

The golem walks out of the tunnel. It is impervious. It treads with the care of a man.

As it goes, the fighting seems to quiet. The ugly and incompetent warfare pauses. The golem passes the dead. Only the railway thing seems to move.

And then it stops walking, and Judah shudders in shock because he has not told it to. A new cart comes, carrying an older man and protectors. The man halloos them kindly. Weather Wrightby.

One man beside Weather wears charms. A thaumaturge. He stares at the golem and moves his hands.

Is it you who stopped it? Judah cannot tell.

Weather Wrightby stands amid the fighting. Of course he must be cosseted in hexes to turn bullets, but it is a powerful thing to see. He talks to the hills. The golem stands yards from him, as if facing him in a gunfight, and Weather Wrightby talks to it, too, as if he is talking to the railroad.

—Men, men, he shouts. He pats the air. Slowly his gendarmes lower guns. —What are you doing? he says. —We know what's happening here. We don't need all this. Who ordered firing on these men? Who ordered this?

—We must fix this, he says. —This mess. It's money, they tell me. And it's the harshness of the overseers. He lifts a sack from the cart. —Money, he says. —We have payment for those free and whole still here. It's time you all were paid. It's been too long, and I'm sorry for that. I can't control the flows of cash, but I've done all I can to bring you what's yours.

Judah says nothing. He makes the golem move its head, a little piece of theatre.

—And you Remade. Weather Wrightby smiles a sad smile. —I don't know, he says. —I don't know. You are indentured men. I don't make laws. You have debts to the factories that made you. Your lives are not your own. Your money . . . you have no money. But understand. Understand that I don't think ill of you or blame you for this. I understand that you are reasonable men. We will fix this.

—I cannot pay you: the law will not allow me. But I can put money aside. The TRT cares for its workforce. I will not have my good Remade men suffer the needless harshness of ignorant foremen. I blame myself for this predicament. I was not listening hard enough, and I apologise to you for that.

—We will put structures in hand. We will have an ombudsman to listen, who can punish overseers not worthy of the badge. We will fix this, understand?

—I will put aside money that you would earn if you were free, whole men, and there will be a place for you when this railroad is done. A retreat. In the city if they'll have it but in these wild lands, near your road, if New Crobuzon is so damned deaf as not to hear what is needed. I will not have you worked to death. There'll be a cabin for you, and baths, and good food, and you can see out your days there. Think I'm a liar? Think I lie to you?

—No more of this, now. The road's stalled. Would you halt it?

Men, men . . . You aren't blasphemers I don't believe, but this is an unholy thing you do though your reasons are understandable. I don't blame you, but you're holding back something the world deserves. Come now. An end to this.

Judah stands. He has his golem come nearer Weather Wrightby in its stuttering railway walk.

—Don't be *fools,* comes Uzman's voice from his hide. —Are you soft, you fucking *soft?* You think Wrightby gives a damn? But he is cut off by other shouts. Someone is shooting. Someone is screaming.

—We can't win this, says Judah aloud, though no one is listening. He stands on the rocks and makes his traintrack golem run.

He makes it run like a steam man, with the metal chewing sound of its gear-thighs. It stamps through an increasing bullet-rain leaving huge footprints, and it runs and leaps, throws itself, falls in a punitive wood-and-metal mass, breaking the bones of the gendarmes. Judah cannot see Weather Wrightby, but he knows, as he watches the golem make its swimming motion and crush as it disaggregates, that Wrightby is alive.

—Fall back fall back, Shanks or Shaun or someone, some thrown-up general is calling, but fall back where? There is nowhere to go. The gendarmes scatter under the punishment of black-powder, but their weapons are so much the stronger, they cannot be held off. It is a desperate, desultory standoff, the gendarmes moving in desert-fight formations, the Remade across the hills from rock to rock hiding place, half-ordered, half-routed.

But there is ruckus from around the curve. Something.

—What, what the, what is . . . ? Judah says. The TRT men are pulling back toward their train, and now there is the sound of other fighting.

From the way they have come, from the history in the roadbed, come noises Judah has never heard before. Something is approaching in a staccato onrush, a drumming on the flattened stone. A cavalry of striders. The borinatch. Moving at a speed that awes, their legs taller than the tallest men, unhinging, stiff unguligrade motion of spasms and lurching, turning by pinpoint acrobatics, twisting on their hooves.

They lurch with inhuman grace closer, their faces masks between baboons and wood-carvings, and insectlike and haunting. They come among the gendarmes, dwarfing them and spinning and sending their bone-stiff legs among the axles, tottering but not falling as vehicles veer and crash. The borinatch grasp down, and their arms and hands manipulate in space and vectors other than those Judah can see.

They grope through dimensions, their limbs become unseen, reaching across gaps of space much too wide and grabbing gendarmes or punching them through their skin. The striders attack with weapons extant in whatever other plane it is they touch, that are visible for instants only as purple flowers or silver liquid faces, and where they strike the gendarmes are cut and crushed and diminished in complex ways and scream without sound and stumble over angles of earth that should never trouble them.

There are scores of the striders, a fighting band. Riding among them is the Remade scout on the lizard's body, sent from the train and ordered to reach New Crobuzon.

The gendarmes are pulling back, killed and wounded in grotesque ways by the striders' spectral maces. Judah cannot see Weather Wrightby. The Remade scout moves with the highstep of the plains lizard. The striders jostle him and mutter with their stringy mouths, and he laughs and slaps them and shouts, —Ann-Hari, I done it. They come with me. They done like you said they would. I found them.

When did she have time? Judah cannot imagine. When did she have time, when did she know, when did she go to those who might be chosen as scouts, when did she know she had another agenda, when

did she suspect the gendarmes would attack, and send for reinforcements? How did she know where to send him?

The lizard-mount scout has not been on the mission he was
given; he has been on a different task, on Ann-Hari's instructions.
He has saved the train.

—See, see? Ann-Hari is delighted. —I knew them strider hate
the rails, the TRT.

—I told them like you said, the lizard-man says. —I told them
what TRT was doing, begged help.

—You went against the council, Uzman says to her. She holds
his look and waits until the silence is discomfiting, and then in her
accented Ragamoll she says, —We go.

—You went against the *council.*

—Saved us.

People are gathering.

—This ain't your queendom.

Ann-Hari blinks. She looks wonderingly at him, *How stupid are
you?* her face says, but she waits a moment and speaks again slowly.
—We, go, *now.*

—You went against the council.

Judah speaks. His own voice shocks him. Everyone looks at
him. The legs of a golem in earth shift behind him and drum their
unfinished heels in mild tantrum. —Uzman, he says. —You're
right, but listen.

—Without the council, what are we? Uzman says.

Judah nods. —Without it what are we? I know, I know. She
shouldn't have gone against it. But Uzman, you seen what they
done. They ain't going to hold back. They've come to end us,
Uzman. What we going to do?

—We needed others, Uzman says. —We needed the city guilds.
We could have had them . . .

—It's too late now, Judah says. —We won't know, will we? We
won't find out. We have to go. We can't beat them now.

—You want us to go fReemade? Uzman says. He is loud. —I'm

a fucking insurrectionist, Judah. You want me to run like a bandit? He is raging. Shooting still sounds. —You want us to take off into the damn hills like we're afraid? That what you want? Fuck you, and you, Ann-Hari . . . Everything we have—

—We have nothing, says Judah.

—We have everything, says Ann-Hari.

They look at each other.

—We don't give up what we have, says Ann-Hari. Judah's golem's legs shudder. —We give up nothing. All our blood and muscle. All the dead. Every hammer blow, the stone, every mouthful we eat. Every bullet from every gun. Each whipping. The sea of sweat that come from us. Every piece of coal in the Remade boilers and the boiler of the engine, each drop of come between my legs and my sisters' legs, all of it, all of it is in that train.

She points into the darkness of the tunnel where the work continues. —All of it. We unrolled history. We made history. We cast history in iron and the train shat it out behind it. Now we've ploughed that up. We'll go on, and we'll take our history with us. Remake. It's all our wealth, it's everything, it's all we have. We'll take it.

The strikers of the iron council join her. Even Uzman can do nothing else.

Waving many-planed hands, the striders go. —Thank you thank you, Judah shouts.

In the mountain's stomach, the train punches through the last veil of stone. The tunnel that has been so hadal dark is gusted full of light.

The train rolls on to the skeletal bridge that has been so quickly made to meet it. The train shudders and lists. The bridge moves. The train reels, drunkard. Judah does not breathe.

It moves firmer, continues across that so-spindly accretion of girders. The train passes high over the dreadful valley, breathing smoke above it, over the yards of swaying make-do bridge to the original structure, and the movement stops.

The train crosses. It is on the earth, on the other side of the mountain.

The rebels step over the awful trellis, children crying as their mothers hold them. With each wind the people are still, but they all of them come across, and no one falls.

They are the cactus-men, the freeanole humans, one two scarab-head khepri, camp followers and drifters, a flock of the wyrmen low in the sky staring with the enthusiasm of dogs, stranger races, renegade llorgiss and a mute hotchi, and hundreds and hundreds of the Remade, in every shape of flesh. They are firemen, engineers and brakemen, those who were clerks, the few overseers who changed sides early enough, the hunters, bridge-builders, the scouts and scientists who will not leave their laboratory, the prostitutes, tunnellers, plebeian magicians, verity-gaugers and low-grade hexers, the workless nomads who scavenge the tracks, now become something, and hundreds, hundreds of the track-layers.

Their wealth and history is embedded in the train. They are a town moving. It is their moment in iron and grease. They control it. Iron council. The motion of the council begins.

It is the same motion that has brought them so far. It is exactly the same. The carts full of rails and ties unload and the crews drop them in position and they are spaced and the rails are taken out and hauled and dropped and hammered with careful rhythm, one two three, down. Ahead race the grading crews; but this long flat land has only a few extrusions that are cleared easily, and they do not sweep away all the bric-a-brac of stones and nature that they would have done before.

It is just the same motion, and it is utterly new. The urgency is drunken. The pace faster by orders of magnitude. The ties are thrown down much farther apart, only just enough to hold the train. These rails will not last. They are not meant to. The road-bed they are building is only a sketch, a ghost in the land. The train creeps like a child.

As the rails come clear, ground clean by the weight of the train, the men and women take them up again. They are pulled by mules past the storage and workshop cars where hundreds more are stacked, past the railroad and the train itself, to the front, into the glare of the engine's lamp eyes. And there they are unloaded. And the track-layers lay them down again.

Miles of track, reused, reused, it is the train's future and its present, and it emerges a fraction more scarred as history and is hauled up again and becomes another future. The train carries its track with it, picking it up and laying it down: a sliver, a moment of railroad. No longer a line split through time, but contingent and fleeting, recurring beneath the train, leaving only its footprint.

They move at speeds that eclipse anything they have achieved. A mile a day has been their benchmark, and this is many times that. Now the huge Remade woman who was freakish and kept from the tracks before is welcomed with her one-blow hammering. The tracks lay down, come up, lay down, come up. They protrude hundreds of yards before and behind the train.

—The gendarmes are coming.

Judah goes back with the demolishers.

—I want to do this with a golem, he says. He touches the flimsy bridge, sends his power out conducted by the metal, makes it ab-live. No one is listening to him. —I want to make this rail a golem. I want to make the rails conductors for it.

He can hear the crack of unsettling metal as the tracks try to stretch and become a giant man. He shudders. He has not the strength for this. His companions climb the shaking bridge, cross into the darkness of the hole. It is not golem they prepare but it is an intervention.

Judah rejoins the train shunting on the flat, toward Cobsea. It is turning. Some popular committee, some delegated or loudly insistent group squatting on the weather-hood, directing the track-layers. They turn from the invisible line to where that fickle town waits. With taps from the mallets, with their expertise, the perpetual train veers. Judah helps the crews take up the final rails and return them to the front. The tracks are turning.

The perpetual train deviates, west-northwest. Into wilderness where there is nothing, a new unmapped place. The train is going feral. Judah cannot breathe.

(Much later he hears the crack and billow of explosions. He imagines the poorly built bridge folding and become spillikins. He imagines the gendarme's train jackknifing to kiss its own tail, voiding men and ordnance, uncoiling to the chasm floor. He thinks of Oil Bill's plan, and of the detritus that will scud across the dried-up river. The train and the skeleton of the bridge will settle, become wood-and-metal fossils.)

The perpetual train has gone wild. The iron council is renegade.

S PRING IS STARTING TO SING SUMMER, AND THE PERPETUAL TRAIN IS buzzed by insects Judah has never seen before, like folded paper lanterns, like tiny hooded monks. Their ichor is bloodred.

Judah hauls rails. He hauls them up, unbuckling the past. Behind him the army of camp followers are suddenly full of mission. They carry hoes and break up the earth where the tracks have been.

It is ineffective camouflage. They cannot pass without indelible marks. It will take years of earth shucking and rock rabbits and rock foxes crisscrossing ruts with their own paths, years of rain and winds before the scab left by the perpetual train is gone.

There is so much to do. It is not easy to run away.

Miles every day. Sharp turns of the reused and reused rails, and the snatch of railroad skirts impediments—pools, rock snarls. Crews of graders throw rubble into sinkholes. Behind the train is a track of dust. The train is in a sparse wood that has waited for the railroad to fill it, and the iron council meets.

—We got to get more planned. We need scouts, hunters, we need water. We have to track a route.

—Where we going then?

—Brothers, brothers . . .

—I ain't your brother, a woman shouts.

—All right bloody hell *sisters* then, and everyone is laughing.
—Sisters, sisters . . .

—They won't stop, you know. It is Uzman. People quiet. —It
ain't a joke. It ain't safe. Brothers . . . sisters . . . We crossed Weather
Wrightby. He won't forget. They'll hunt us down.

Steam rises from his pipes. *You never wanted us here,* Judah
thinks. *This isn't what you wanted. You wanted us to hold. Your pretty
runagate dreams were of making a line to the guilds, as if they'd run
come save us. Now you're still trying. Though you'd not have chose it
thus.*

Uzman is a good man.

—It ain't just the gendarmes. TRT'll put a price on our head.
We stole their train. We stole their *railroad*. Think they'll let that go?

—Every bounty hunter in Rohagi's coming for us. And godspit,
you think the *city*'ll let this go? It is quiet but for the snap of insects
against the lantern. —It's New Crobuzon's railway too, and we took
it. You think they'll let Remade walk away, find a place in the wilds?
The *militia* are coming for us now, too. The militia.

—They'll come in airships. They'll come over land. Think
they'll let us go to ground, some fucking fReemade arcadia? They'll
bring the train back wearing our heads. We can't just find a little
valley ten, thirty, a hundred miles from here. If we do this . . . we
have to *go*.

—We have to be *gone*. Bring me a damn map. Do you realise
what we've done here? What we are now?

A scattered mess of Remade. A town of Remade and their xenian and freeanole friends. These thieves and murderers, rapists,
vagrants, embezzlers, liars. —You look carved, Uzman says with a
wonder they can suddenly hear. —Bits of wood, man-sized, whittled by gods. They blink up at him in the shadow of the train they
have stolen.

* * *

Only three days' deviation from their plotted route, the iron council is beyond the details of maps. These are strange lands. These are the Middling Sweeps. The Rohagi wilds.

The more intelligent wyrmen are sent out over empty geographies that make them nervous, little urban things that they are. They are charged with finding the hunters still away, the water-carriers in their carts, looking for springs. Those reconnoitring, who will return to find nothing but carnage where the tunnel once was. They will look over the moulding and sunburnt corpses of the gendarme train, and will say, —What happened here? The wyrmen are sent to gather the iron council's own.

Systems grow. They find springs, and the water car is kept full, caulked where it bleeds. The guntower is welded and hammered into a seared approximation of its old shape. Remade are trained, hurriedly, by the scientists who have stayed, are shown how to draw charts.

—Where will we go?

At night the renegades play banjos and pipes, the train's warning bell is struck, its boiler made a drum. Women and men lie together again. Some Chainday nights Judah goes to the wordless trackside man-meets for release, but Ann-Hari and he fuck one night and stroke each other with the most sincere, the most close affection.

The slowly stranging place delights Judah. On the sixth day of the iron council, as the mile-long track-stretch swallows its own tail and moves, as the train enters a dreamish landscape of bruised succulents and the summer comes down on them, a posse of gendarmes and bounty hunters arrives.

They underestimate the council by a gross degree. They are no more than thirty men and xenians, in cracked leather and spikes, their very clothes made weapons. They come out of the vein-coloured undergrowth under the standard of the TRT, creatures like scurrying mushrooms running from them.

The band fire, scream through their loudhailers. —Comply! Lawbreakers, surrender!

Do they think the iron council will be cowed? Judah watches in awe at their stupidity. Twelve of them are shot fast, and the others ride away.

—Get them, get them, get them, shouts Ann-Hari, and the fastest Remade take off with their weapons. —They know where we are!

They can only kill six more. The others escape. —We're marked, Uzman says. It is less than a hundred miles since they have escaped. —They'll come for us.

They leave traps. Barrels of blackpowder, complex batteries and fuses. They send the train between stone overhangs, and the geo-thaumaturges and what hedge-mancers there are cut diaglyphs into the mineral walls and lay down primed circuits so that the weight of a cart will make the rock deliquesce and pour down in cold magma to set again with the outriders of the gendarmes or militia drowned. That is the plan.

Judah sets golem traps. Batteries, somaturgic turbines of his design, so the fallen wood or the bone-heap or the earth or split discarded ties will stand and fight for iron council.

At night he walks the renegade railroad with Uzman and Ann-Hari, who are chary but need each other. Strategist and visionary. The perpetual train does not stop at night. The train is full of skills. Remade fix what flintlocks can be fixed, and make new weapons. In the furnaces they melt down older rails for cutters and armour. They are making their wheeled town a war-machine.

—It won't be long, Uzman says. —Time'll come we probably have to abandon the train, have to run.

—We can't, Ann-Hari says. —Without it we have nothing.

A group of councillors in the clerk's car lean over vague maps— sketchy composites of myths. The darkwood desks and inlaid walls are carved and graffitied from the first days, when the drunken rebels rendered savage art.

—Here. Uzman presses the map. —What's this?

—Swamp.

Uzman moves his finger.

—Unknown.

—Salt flats.

—Scree.

—Unknown.

—Tar pits.

—Unknown.

—Smokestone. Smokestone gulleys.

Uzman chews his knuckle. He looks out of the window. Councillors haul the rails from one end of their stolen track-mile to the other.

—Do we have any meteoromancers?

—There's a girl Toma. Someone shakes their head. —Can whistle up a gust dries her clothes but, you know, parlour hex really . . .

—We need someone can raise a gale—

—No. One of the researchers speaks. He is a young man who has grown his beard and wears the sweaty clothes of the workforce. He is shaking his head. —I know what you're wanting. You're thinking, through the smokestone? No. You saw what happened when Malke was caught in it? He nearly died. You saw what it was like.

—There must be ways to know when it's coming . . .

The young man shrugs. —Pressure, he says. —Cracking. A few things. From geysers. He shrugs again. —We looked it up when it trapped us. It's too many things.

—But there are ways of telling . . .

—Yes, but Uzman, you're not thinking. These maps are best-guesses. We're in the Middling Sweeps. And there's one thing we *do* know that's there. The man runs his finger up the map. The car sways. —See? What this is?

It is a crosshatched patch of land, inked in red. Two hundred miles from them, less than a month at this absurd pace. It abuts the smokestone, or where the old cartographers thought the smoke-stone might be.

—You know what that is?

Of course Uzman does. They all do. It is the cacotopic stain.

—You ain't taking us to the stain, Uzman.

—I can't take you anywhere. The council goes where it decides it will. But I'm telling you the only thing we can do. You decide if it's what you want or not. And if not I'll stay and fight, and we die.

—It's the *stain*.

—No, no it ain't the stain. It's the edges. It's the outskirts.

Uzman has a look on him. He stands and seems to glimmer. He sweats from the heat of his own pipes, eats coal. His lips are black.

—It ain't the stain. We have to go through the smokestone flats—

—If they're there.

—If they're there. We have to go through the smokestone flats, and beyond that's the *outskirts* of the cacotopos. Even if they got through the stone, no one'll follow us there.

—And you know why, Uzman, right? For good damn reason.

—We got no choice. No, that ain't so. We run. Leave the train to rot. Run be fReemade. Or we can keep it. All our sweat. The road. But if we keep it, we have to go do this. We have to make it out, far away, or we die. We have to go west. And west of here? He prods the waxed chart. —The cacotopic zone. Just the edges.

He sounds as if he is pleading.

—People've dipped in there before. We'll be all right. We have to. He pleads.

—Just the edges.

It opened a half millennium before, a rift through which spilt great masses of the feral cancerous force, Torque. A badland beyond understanding. Where men might become rat-things made of glass and rats devilish potentates or unnatural sounds and jaguars and trees might become moments that could not have happened, might become impossible angles. Where monsters go and are born. Where the land, and the air, and time are sick.

—It's no matter, anyway, someone says. —We ain't got no meteoromancers, and we ain't got anyone can call up air elementals, and we ain't going through smokestone without someone can push wind.

Judah leans on the table; his fringe dances before his eyes. He looks down at the ink landscape.

—Well, he says. —Well now.

Somaturgy, golemetry, is an intervention. Making servants from unlive matter is about persuasion, insinuation. A strategy of life-giving.

—Well now.

I can make a golem out of air, thinks Judah. *A clutch of air in the air. Have it run with us. Air running through air.* It will exhaust him. But he knows he can get them passage through the smoke.

Judah knows that they will go.

HE WALKS WITH UZMAN, AND A GOLEM WALKS WITH THEM. SHAM-
bling vegetable pulp. They are a strange troika: the Remade sending
steam from the pipes that burrow him; Judah tall and bony, his
beard like a furring of dirt; the golem putting down its shapeless
feet. The train slips forward in tiny motions.

The moonlight is the colour of lipid fluid, as if the night has an
unclosing wound. Behind them Judah sees the train and the train
and the train farting smoke, clanging, like some lumpen orchestra
of drums and bells. A half mile ahead are Remade laying track, and
ahead of them the teams performing a cursory groundbreaking.
Behind the railroad is disassembled, and there are hundreds of followers like pilgrims.

Judah sees everything as a city. New Crobuzon has taught him
that. He watches the train skirt a curling crust of land and sees the
curve and edge of river walls, the warehouse walls by the Tar. He
sees a half-fallen tree and remembers a drunken New Crobuzon
man leaning at the same angle.

We don't choose what we remember, Judah thinks, *what stays with us.* He carries New Crobuzon with him, even now he is a citizen of this new vagrant sanctuary.

—Smokestone won't do it, Uzman says. The perpetual train sighs. —The militia'll break that down, fly over that. It ain't about the smokestone, it's the cacotopic stain. That's what'll hide us.

The next day a sortie of the gendarmes kills fifty of the council's stragglers and are gone before any Remade can counterattack. Wyrmen scream that they were shot at. In their rough inventive grammar they say what they have seen, spread their wings to show bullet holes in their tough skin.

It is hot. They come into a stretch of space, an upland of good thick earth.

—What are they? There is a panic. —Something's come for us!

Animals are keeping pace with the train, snapping at the wheels. No not animals or if animals ones that melt and re-form and emerge from the ground and through which light shines. Bullets go through them ignored.

Judah watches them with building pleasure once his fear goes. Each time the train moves on again the little length of its track, the things return.

Demons of motion. They are not attacking but playing. Delighting like porpoises, they dive out of the earth and roll around the turning wheels. They eat the rhythm, the *ka ka ka* of turning iron on iron. After millennia of snapping up only the quickstep of plains hunters and prey, the demons are drunk on the heavy beat. They evanesce out of colours in the near-shapes of foxes and rockrats, the only animals they have seen. They learn the newcomers, and as hours pass the motion demons mimic humans and cactacae inexpertly, to the track-layers' delight.

—Look, lookit, it's you, that's your ugly bonce, that is.

The skittish things manifest and dive wheelward to eat more. If

Councillors detrain, demons pullulate about their feet, eating the echoes of their steps. One woman dances, and the air goes alive with the rapture of motion-demons now-seen-now-unseen gorging on her tempo. Soon the perpetual train is girdled with shuffling figures: Remade, the freeanole women who were once whores, cactacae overcoming their grimness. They dance by the train, keeping pace in capers, in barley-mows and lilly-gins. Their feet are thronged by demons catching the light. It is a contest: the most complex, repeated, perfect rhythms are the best food.

The sunlight is the colour of the grass it dries. Judah smiles at the train and the dancers, and at the motion demons. It is a strange pastoral, a harvest procession it looks like, amid scruffs of pampas grass and the dead creeks, the big train shunting in spasms toward worshippers who lay down its way. As if the tracks are a leash, they haul it in like some tamed wilderness animal, and around the suddenly docile iron beast are hundreds of celebrants kicking up summer dust. The kinetophages tremble around their ankles like spume. Judah thinks of the energy they find in rhythm. Pulse-magic. What strange calories there are in repeated sounds.

Judah looks and loves the iron council. He unfolds a tripod. He is not a good heliotypist, but he knows as he frames the shamble of legs and iron and late sun that this one will come out clean. Movement-blurred and developed crudely in the tiny darkroom, but above what will be a ghost-mass of legs and demons he knows that the perpetual train and the smiles and bodies of the dancers will be clear. He has fixed them in sepia ink, frozen them like the stiltspear with their golem song.

An aerostat comes out of the east. It approaches with its sedate, predatory bobbing, makes its way fatly toward them.

The thuggish wyrmen yelp and blather obscenities as they fly. They become specks against the distended whale of leather; they buzz its gondola, make it sway a little. Judah hears flat sounds like paper bags bursting that must be gunshot, and the wyrmen scatter. They drop. They fall where they are, folding their wings and plummeting in unison, curving toward the train, and there is a crumbling sound, a huge clearing of the throat, and glass and black smoke gust out of the aerostat windows.

—Yes, Uzman says.

The dirigible rocks. Gunpowder smog swells from the underbelly. It will limp home to New Crobuzon, or to the base over the horizon, where attack squads of militia are waiting for directions. Where other airships are stationed. Bigger warflots with bombs to drop. With windows that clay-pot grenades won't breach.

New Crobuzon has found them. That night there is a meeting, and it is beyond chaos. Ideas clamour with ideas. It is all shouting. The women who had been whores have delegated Ann-Hari to speak for them.

Others find them. Out of the grasslands come figures. The iron council is shedding word of its own self along songlines no one can see. It draws the dispossessed, the outlawed.

FReemade. A little tribe. Escapees from New Crobuzon, feral a long time. The leader is a man without arms, with useless ornamental beetle wings. There is a man with rubberised pincers, a man who wears a crocodile's snout, a huge cur with the head of a pretty woman. The dog's is a male body. By the skins they wear and the jewellery of holed stones on sinews, by their complexions like wood and tea, Judah knows they have been fReemade for years.

—We heard about you, one man says. He and his family are staring at the train. They are not looking at the guards, nor at Judah, nor at his golem made of the bones of meat-birds. —You're going west, they say. You're crossing the world.

—They say, he says, —you're building a new life. Out of sight.

—We come to ask, he says, and pauses. —We come to ask . . . the man says.

And Judah, mandated by the council, nods: *yes you can join us.*

* * *

Nomads in numbers. Criminals and runaways. Plains races and outsiders—striders who wordlessly lope trainside, even a garuda easing out of the sky and made air marshal over the quarrelsome wyrmen. The iron council absorbs them.

They are surrounded by strange, unlikely truces between armed fReemade toughs and the borinatch braves who swing by the train with their unlikely grace. *We are protected,* Judah thinks. *They're here to give us gods-speed. To help us go.*

The bounty hunters harry them three more times in quick, vicious raids. The gunmen ride away before there can be much retribution.

—This ain't nothing, Uzman says to Judah. —We got more coming. He harangues the iron council at night in the headlights. Ann-Hari takes his side, and though the stokers and the engineers complain that they can see their stocks of coal dwindling, though the workers are exhausted, the council agrees to more speed. The tracks are laid all night and day, by men and women in an anaesthesia of tiredness, dreaming while they swing their hammers.

The iron road eats the miles. At night the train's moving illumination makes the rockforms shift, as if they are trying to get away. Insects and things the size of insects perform a rhythm of their bodies on lantern glass, become flame-bursts where they find a way inside. The train is a line of dark light on the night plains.

THE EARTH FEELS UNEASY. THE COUNCIL TENSES. NEWCOMERS ARE targeted, are told they are spies. Judah helps an intervening crowd stop one terror-struck angry man beating a fReemade newcomer to death, and in their admonishments and the counter-beating they give him, neither Judah nor any other person acknowledges that the man might be right, that there are spies with them.

At the edge of the plain is the landform they want. A smoke-stone range. The unmoving brume shapes grow slowly clearer. A posse treks on to blast a path through the solid mist.

The perpetual train is a fortress. Its strange guntower is scabbed with new metal. All the councillors carry clubs, sharpen them into spears, splints of stone with rag handles. Crude and eccentric rifles. The council is waiting.

Inside Judah the thing shifts, and he knows that though it is not the time yet, he will leave.

They pass the outskirts of the smokestone hills. An abrupt change of landscape into something dreamish and unsettling, where wisp-shapes rise in basalt-hard congelation, clotted clouds on which the tough fauna of the smokestone run. There are plumes, fountain-heads where geysers of smoke have poured and set near-instantly. The roadbed goes between them, through a solfatara of vented gases.

The iron council graders have blasted passage. The elegance of set smokestone is interrupted with the base simplicity of jag-edged holes.

Mostly the stonemass is caught as billows, but there are pillars that corkscrew faintly and become wisps at their peak, where leaks of smokestone have gusted in very still air. The train passes under arcs where currents have blown smokestone up from the ground and down again.

The roadbed is extended, the tracks laid through, taken up again. The uncanny landscape is beautiful and discomfiting. The ground could crack and gush at them, a mist that would set in their lungs and statue them in agony. There is no smoking, no cooking; the train moves only in sudden lurches, clearing its exhaust as fast as it can: there can be no smoke distractions. Judah waits ready to release an air golem. The stone around them might evanesce again, as smokestone sometimes does, after an hour or a thousand years of being rock.

Out of the horizon the army comes on Remade horses, camels, steaming jitneys that grind on many wheels. They come in forma-tion into the smokestone. The wyrmen of the iron council track them, flying higher than smokestone might set.

The graders blast the capricious geography. They watch anxious and inexpert for any sign that they have split a smokestone seam.

Other crews lay huge charges in holes they carefully dig, di-rected by the crawling geoempath. She licks the dirt with animal sounds, in some crude ecstatic trance. Hers is not a strong or fo-cused talent, and trying for such powerful prehension of the earth debases her to it.

Iron Councillors build barricades in a yardang between set faces of cloud. A mile off are the smoke and downlaid and uptaken rails of the perpetual train. Uzman and Ann-Hari are on board, while Judah and Thick Shanks and hundreds of others are ambushers.

They can see the army now. Judah is drained after his preparations. He is already so tired that his dreams are slipping into his thoughts. He must return to iron council as soon as he can. It needs his protection. He has built a golem trap on the cowcatcher, has told them how to trip it should the silicate mist appear, but a golem of air will not last without his shepherding.

—There must be other attacks, he says, as they have all said. This cannot be the only front New Crobuzon will open. But there is no time to think of that now as the attackers come close enough, and before their first guns sound to destroy the ramparts, the iron council attacks.

The wyrmen hammer the air with their thick wings, wheel through shots and drop their clay grenades. Bullets snatch them out of the air.

Bomblets drop, made of whatever the council has: gunpowder, the shrapnel of torn-up tools, vials of crude acids, unpleasant thaumaturgic compounds, oil. Naphtha, caustics, hot smoke unfold and the militia break a little, but they re-form fast, break again at a second sortie of wyrmen. The sun is bright but seems suddenly very cold to Judah.

—It ain't far, he is muttering. He hears himself. —Ain't got to do this long.

He leans out, field glasses to his eyes. Wyrmen defecate their contempt on the enemy as they let their missiles go. One bursts: Avvatry, a truculent bull Judah knows enough to greet, taken apart with fusillade so he reaches the ground more rags than animal.

The Councillors fire arbalests made in iron council's foundries. They light fuses and send rockfall down on the invaders. Judah knows this is his fight to win or to lose.

Judah stands. He stands on the rampart. Wires trail from him, to batteries, to a transformer. He trembles with bravery.

The men and women with him in his hide—all with some vestige, some trace, of hex, all joined together—cut their hands and wrap wire tight around the wounds. It is a crude engine that links them, to require so vulgar and literal a bleeding, something battered together from found materials. —Give it me, Judah shouts, and Shaun shoves the leads home, and the gutter-motor moans, and those amassed all stagger as it siphons out their strength and funnels it into the clips that puncture Judah's chest.

A sound comes from him that is impossible to describe. His skin tightens and moves as if someone is pressing their fingers to him. From the dust, men stand. They are in the army's path. Judah sweats. It spews from him. He moves his hands. The men, the golems, walk in ponderous stride.

There are a score or more. Bigger than humans. Premade and waiting. They walk toward the New Crobuzon Militia. Judah shakes. The weaker of his comrades are passed out. Judah is sweating blood.

The black golems stalk on. One is kicked apart by militia horses. Its torso twitches and tries to claw itself on farther, and Judah quivers as if hit with stones. He hauls on the air, pulls something immaterial into place. The dirt men-things walk into the melee, and the mounts shy around them. Bounty hunters and uniformed militia veer as the golems reach for them. Some golems stand cruciform. Some wrap their arms around struggling quarries. Where he can see to direct them, Judah has them push with their abnatural strength through bodyguards to embrace officers. Crowds of the fighters surround each one, hacking the mineral bodies, levelling their pistols.

—Shoot dammit! Judah gasps. And though his enemies cannot hear him they obey. A bullet grinds into one of the figures. The golem is made of flint and gunpowder.

There is a tremendous bay of ignition and the golem disappears in a pillar of explosion. It is a man-thing then a wind of dirt-coloured fire, the stones that were embedded in it suddenly out-rushing and laying down the bounty hunters in a circle; and its heat touches one of its fellows and it too goes up, and when the smoke they have become is gone Judah sees soot-stains where they were, and around them ripples of dead men, black and bloody, becoming more solid, becoming more like bodies farther out, and those at the circumference of each crater still move, still shriek.

—Shoot, Judah says again. Gunshots, flaming arrows from bal-listae. The hot missiles come in and transform the made figures into vortices of combustion.

One by one they stumble into the attackers, hug them, bury them in blackpowder and then in fire. The gunpowder golems, shambling bombs, sear holes in the army. Judah stands and hears a rhythmic roar that is his heart. His comrades shout in his honour. Blood drips from his face. The last of the golems runs into the in-vaders, scattering soldiers with every ungainly step. It is gone in the flame from some marksman's arrow, and dusty fire is unrolling.

There are still hundreds of bounty-men and militia but they are reeling, their commanders screaming, their mounts' hooves slip-ping on the mulch of their dead. And the wyrmen come back, and the Councillors make more rockfalls, and the arbalestiers send their huge bolts.

—Low! the men shout. —Yes! And Judah Low roars back at them.

Iron council raiders descend, the hugest Remade, cactacae braves with picks and heavy hatchets. Judah is tugged back and kissed. His comrades are sallow, trembling and cold from the en-ergy he borrowed, but they are stronger than he. Judah closes his eyes.

He passes out, manhandled to safety. He dreams of gunpowder golems, and the sun, and then he is suddenly awake.

—What, what? he says, lurches up. —What, what?

Thick Shanks and Shaun point east, up, into the air. —There are more of them. They've attacked the train.

Judah and Shaun ride on a horse reconfigured for speed. Judah is numb. The loud and random bounty-men-and-militia army was an unsubtle distraction.

What will you do, golemist? he asks himself. *What will you do to stop them? You ain't going to stop them; you're going to die.* To die with his council. *You're too broken to do anything now. Look at the blood come from you.* But he does not think he will die. Judah would not go if he thought he would die.

There are men in the sky, militia swinging under taut spheres. He sees the smoke of the perpetual train and he can hear explosions. The aeronauts seep bombs, breaking apart the scud-sculptures of the smokestone in a line of craters, drawing a gully toward the council.

What will you do, golemist? Judah asks himself. He will do something. The thing in him, the oddity, the good in him flexes.

People are scrambling away. Refugees again: men, the old, the terrified and wounded, newcomers without loyalty to keep them, women carrying their children, running over the ridges of hard cloud. Judah and Shaun career past them by the tracks. They ride into the battle.

There is the train, firing from its riveted-together guntower. Militia and the Councillors who outnumber but are outfought by them. The sky ahead is unnatural, a matted pewter, stained with colours that should not be there.

Out ahead, protected by cactus and Remade guards, is a track-laying team. They move frenetic, in a sped-up mumming of their usual work, over a rubble of nimbostratus stone. They are picked off by militia targeteers, falling wounded or killed over the rails, and their comrades push them aside and continue their urgent work.

Judah comes in fighting.

The militia will not stop the train: they will kill many but there are only yards left, and even with the cull of track-layers (another man down with a blood-blossom) the train will go through. It is the oncoming aerostats that make Judah afraid. There is the sound of rain in the west, but no rain appears.

Shaun relaxes. Judah feels him lean backward and puts his arm around him and feels his front slick, too wet for sweat, and Judah knows his friend is dead. The horse stumbles and stops and Judah dismounts, dragging Shaun with him, his sternum all ruptured. Judah hauls him until volleys disturb him and he must let his dead friend go and run through the lines of his comrades and along the train, staying low, grabbing a bow from a pile as he goes. A rivebow it is—he curses its weight, its limited range, but he tries to level it as he runs the length of the battered cars, toward the steaming chimney where his golem trap is set.

He fires a scalpel-edged chakri; he hunkers by Remade and edges toward the cowcatcher. There are thaumaturges among the militia, and darts of baleful energy spit at the Councillors and do arcane damage. The wyrmen perform brave and dangerous raids on the militia, and the militia begin to withdraw.

—We make them run! We make them run! screams a wyrman, hysterical with pride, but she is wrong. The militia are leaving because airships are coming.

—Move! There is a shout. —We're through! And the segmented edifice lurches and trembles and crawls through the stone mist and up, looking as if it will derail any second, on smokestone shards. The scree moves uneasy but holds, and the carriages progress, bullets typing on their iron skin. The train pauses at the apex of the shard hill, descends. The train finds a pothole—a track cracks, carriages list, but somehow the rutted wheels keep traction and shuddering like something wounded the train rolls into the land beyond.

—Keep going! Judah shouts, as hundreds of the Councillors run to rejoin the train. —Come *on*. The sky and the land are not as they should be. There is a sound like something hollow being struck, way off, before the sun.

The geoempath stands by a chasm in the rocks, by the powder-monkeys cutting fuses. She is smeared with the earth's filth and her eyes retain something of the degradation of her hex, but she looks at Judah and nods before he can ask, points into the ground. —There, she says. —I think.

The train gushes steam and hisses impatient. —Get on, get on get on get on, Ann-Hari shouts from the cab. Wyrmen race across the reefs of stone to where the last Councillors hold out at the crevice. The Remade run. They are such little things. Can no one see it? Judah looks west and up. Can no one see the sky? The land?

A panorama like and unlike everything they have passed.

What are you? Miles to the west, a moment's distance in this great stretched landscape—*Gods we're in the middle lands, we're out of all maps, we're nowhere*—here stony ground becomes something more rippled, something rilled as if the earth were poured wax, its parameters unclear as Judah tries to focus. The land dips away. Trees puncture the plain, but they change, they are less like trees, they flicker, is it? Like some dark flame, they flicker, they phase in their substance, or is it only the eye trying to see so far off, no, there is something about these trees or are they some other thing? There is a mountain but it may be a mirage, rippling as it does, it may be a barrow and much closer, it may be a fleck in Judah's eye. Nothing is as it should be.

Things that are not birds fly like birds above, birds like rain. While the council gathers its lost Judah looks at the sky. It moves like a baby.

Drained and bleeding fighters climb for the train. —Get *on*, Uzman shouts. He is standing on a crest, looking down the splits in rock at the Councillors struggling to get home. —Come on come on, Uzman says, as more find their way through, but his voice tells

Judah that time will not allow them all, as the militia regroup. It is already too late. Uzman is looking to the powder-men, to the geoempath. The perpetual train moves, the track-layers continue, it crawls on, away from the last smokestone.

—This is only the edge, Judah says, looks at the sky, —of the cacotopic stain. We're only at the outskirts. But he can feel the ground; he feels its energy in a way he should not. He sees Uzman's despair.

In their desperation to save the last of their comrades they delay bursting the seam so late the re-formed cadres of militia catch up with the stragglers of Remade. At last there is a stuttering of three explosions, and a huge squall of smokestone kecks up from porous earth and uncoils in a smog that expands fast to clog the channel the graders have made, and moves slower as it begins to set.

Uzman cries miserably out as it enfolds the slower Remade. He looks down at the gaseous rock expanding.

In the ropes of his gut Judah feels a newness, a constructed non-life, a giant anthropoid wind come to him, as Ann-Hari releases his golem trap. Judah flexes inside, spits out an effort and grabs control of the thing, reaches up as if he would hold its hand and together Judah and his golem run for the unfolding stone. The golem walks into it, stretches out its air arms, pushes back wafts, tries ineffectually to clear a hollow.

Judah is scores of yards from the now sluggish vapor, which is smothering as it indurates. From within its setting stone Judah hears choked calls. In resentful unfolding gusts the cloud pushes its innards out and Judah sees movement inside, not wind-driven or random, and arms, supplicant, emerge from the obscurity and a man comes out, greyed by wisps that cling to him and become silicon chitin, crusting him as he falls, and behind is another belching of mist and another figure pushes through smokestone visibly harder now, wading through dough, scabbed with it, labouring under matter.

Judah reaches them. The first man through is militia, they see through a ragged epidermis of stone, but it is impossible to feel hate or anger for him as he shivers and fights to breathe through a mouth thick with mineral curd. The other is council. There is no saving him. His comrades try to break the boulder that has settled over his face but by the time they do their efforts have cracked his skull.

—We have to go, Uzman shouts from above. He is stricken but controlled.

An enormous boiling of rock is where the train came through. The rails disappear into it, embedded forever or until it desolidifies again. Judah has his golem disaggregate, and the air currents around them change.

There is motion, and Judah's face curls to see in the mid of the new rock geography a forearm protruding, jutted like some horizontal cliff plant, still clutching or trying to clutch as the nerves of the corpse within the smokestone die.

Though they shatter aspects of the train with their bombs the aeronauts are uncertain. The ballooners swivel to see the sudden blockage, rock all full of their colleagues. They are shot down by boldened Councillors. One falls as Judah watches, gas venting from his split globe.

In sudden formation the aeronauts hornet away over the new low hills. Uzman shouts instructions and Councillors run to strip the fallen ballooner of his equipment, to salvage the cloth of his dirigible. —We have to be scavengers, says Uzman. —We have to learn that, from now on. He looks up at the sky.

—There'll be more, he says, before Judah can even feel relief.

But it comes, the relief, on the day and night of setting out into the uncovered wilderness. Relief and a desperate sadness and a mourning of the many lost.

—They didn't all get trapped, says Uzman. Judah winces at his tone, the eagerness to find respite. —Some of them was still on the other side.

Where the militia were. It is no comfort. Judah imagines what it must have been for them, militia and council, to watch that thundercloud become rock and eat their friends.

Now as new inhabitants of that place the Councillors attend to their environs. In the torchlight they shudder as the geography shifts. They see other lights that move quite wrong in the distance, and hear shouts they do not recognise, or that they recognise as their own, echoes held captive for hours and released distorted.

The escapees gather. The tracks shift a little. North a shade, a whisper. Uzman is taking them into the cacotopic zone. They are at its very edges, but closer than anyone should ever come.

THEY HAVE CLOSED A HILL DOOR BEHIND THEM, AND WITH SUNRISE they see the new landscape for the first time. Miles of scrub in ordinary colours rich after the grey rock. The ground pitching, yawing, becoming wilder. Tremendous numbers of trees, and stone teeth to guard them, and vines fruited with flowers in gewgaw colours. And little lakes and other earthscapes, and in the direction the train and its tracks are heading, a tremendous alteration in the land. Judah can feel it. They all can. Through the wheels.

The shadows do not all lie in the same plane. —We're only snipping in, Uzman says. —Only putting our toes in. The shadows are wrong, and Judah feels winds blowing in contradictory directions. When the ground is not watched it skews.

They have left so many of their dead behind them, unburied. Shaun is somewhere, lying like a sleeper.

One last day Judah hauls rails. He digs them up from by the new rock, under the mummying hand, and leads the mule carts to the front of the train to lay them down again. Two nubs of iron remain poking from the stone fog.

They are watched by animals, by plants with eyes. The second night Judah speaks to his friends around a fire that by some arcana burns white. Uzman, Ann-Hari, Thick Shanks and those others new elected, mandated by engineers, dowsers, brakemen, waterboys, the ex-whores and the followers.

—You've done it, Judah says. Uzman and Ann-Hari are unblinking at his praise. —Got us out. And now you're in this strange place.

—It isn't finished yet.

—No, it ain't. But you'll be all right. You will. You *will*. There must be a place beyond this. A place far enough. They won't follow you. You'll cross, right across the world. Where there's fruit and meat. Where the train can stop. You can hunt, fish, rear cattle—I don't know. You can read, and when you've read the books in the library car you should write others. You got to get there.

—But what's here? What'll come for us here?

—I don't know. It'll be hard, but you'll get through. Judah does not know why he is speaking like a prophet. It is not him who speaks; it is his thing inside, his innard good. —They won't follow you in. I'll lay money.

They laughed at that. Money was ornament now. There were those who still hoarded it, but it was notepaper for the children. It was jewellery.

—And Uzman was right, even though he was wrong, Judah says. —We should have got word to New Crobuzon. Think on it. No one might know.

There is silence. —You might tell no one, just disappear, and all they'd say is that once, when they was building the railroad, the train just went. The Remade went fReemade and took the train with them. You want more than that. The Remade in the city, waiting, they deserve more.

—There's those as know what happened . . .

—Yes but will they do it right? You'll be rumour—that can't be altered—but what kind of rumour? Do you want to be a rumour that won't die? That matters? Do you want them to shout the council's name when they strike?

Ann-Hari smiles.

Judah says, —I'll go back. I'll be your bard.

Some of them say at first that it is cowardice, that he is afraid to come with them across the little purlieu of the cacotopos, but none of them really believe him cowardly. They are sorry that he is leaving them.

—We need your golems, a woman says.

—How can you go? Don't you care for the council, Judah?

Judah rounds at that.

—You ask me that? he says. —You ask me that? He shames them.

—I'll be your bard. I'll tell them. Stay still. The powderflash goes and each of the gathered blinks.

In so alien a place, with the foreboding of the Torque, with the unnatural sky and the alterity of the cacotopic zone, even with the smokestone behind them there are some leaving the council.

—Some'll make it, Judah says. —Go fReemade—they won't go back to New Crobuzon, not Remade like that.

—You will, you'll get through, sisters. He looks at them without even uncertainty. —Take it, he says. His voxiterator. They are quizzical. —Here. This is how you make it keep what you say. They watch him load the wax and take what spare cylinders he has. —One every year, he says slowly. —Send me one back. Wherever you are. By boat, horse, foot, whatever. We'll see if they get through. I want to hear your voices. He looks at Ann-Hari. —I want to hear your voices.

One by one he holds them. He grips each of his comrades very hard, even those whose names he does not know. —Long live iron council, he says to each of them in turn. —Long live, long live.

With sudden mischievous love Judah tongues Uzman, and the Remade jerks and is about to pull away and then does not. Judah does not kiss him for long. —Be gentle to the Chainday-night boys, he says in the Remade's ear, and Uzman smiles.

And Judah holds Ann-Hari and she kisses him as she did when first they were lovers, and he pulls her close by the hips and she holds his face for seconds. —Long live, he whispers into her mouth. —Long live.

H E HAS FORGOTTEN HOW MUCH FASTER IT IS TO TRAVEL ALONE. IT is not a day before he is returned to the smokestone. The hand of the trapped man, egressing the rock, has been gnawed down to red bone.

Judah walks across the tops of the swells as if over the sea. He sees detritus from the fight and a scattering of corpses. At noon he feels shadows, and over him is a school of airships, moving toward the perpetual train. Judah shields his eyes and leans against his staff.

He supposes that perhaps he should be afraid for his comrades, but he is not. He reads the changing formations of the dirigibles. He smiles, alone on the ground, as they pass like slow barracuda. They seem to hesitate. He sits, his back to a granitic coil, and watches.

Judah can see the smoke of the train. One midsize warflot edges nervously into the air of the cacotopic zone. From here, the land-scape seems utterly quotidian, but Judah can feel something bane-ful welling below the world's skin.

The airship lets its bombs fall as it approaches the perpetual train. Judah sees little explosion-flowers over the hills. Even now he is not afraid.

In the distance the sky convulses. A bolus of something moves, a coilsome organic thing—not a cloud but an aspect of the sky itself become palpable and squidish across the land not quite seen. Sound is strange. Judah does not breathe. There is a stutter. The dirigible falters and comes clear again and then it is different—it is a splinter different, it is lower in the sky—and it turns, it removes itself with a speed that Judah would swear was panicked.

The train continues, into the stain, into the cacotopic zone that has beaten New Crobuzon back.

JUDAH WALKS FOR MONTHS. HIS LIFE BECOMES A FUGUE OF WALKING. Over creeks, quagmire, over rockland, through forests of vitreous trees, through forests that he thinks are fossil trees then sees are great skeletons. He walks a bonescape, an ossein ecology with its own undergrowth and scavengers.

He passes lakes that bubble with the fighting of vodyanoi tribes. He sees chimneys extruded from mountainsides where there are troglodyte villages. Judah is the guest of neglected priest-tribes. He is robbed by fReemade. He joins a fReemade band.

His body becomes a traveller's body again. The startling muscles of his arms and chest subside and he is once again a thin mannequin tempered by travel. Garuda come to feed him, dropping from the sky with wordless charity. He checks his just-adequate maps, his compass. He does not retrace his steps the long route he has gone but goes directly east.

Judah passes through a storm, in a basalt place hundreds of miles from New Crobuzon, by blitzbaums, miles-high lightning trees. Bolts held still by cryptic forces, forking into boughs, a magnesium-bright forest.

The low rust skyline of a time-eaten iron town. And a swamp of thaumaturgically jinxed mud that degenerates his boots into worms. And a barrow and a buried church, and fields of wild berries, and beautiful hills. Five times he fights animals and three times he fights sentients. Judah runs or kills.

He is a quieter man. He moves with effortless expertise. It has been many weeks since he made a grass golem to walk with him, for him to talk to until the wind picks it apart. Judah passes cattle that were once domestic and are now feral. The ruins of fences, deserted pastures, miles by miles.

And then at last Judah comes down from the sudden hills and stands quiet like an idiot. At last he comes forward and now he stumbles. Judah goes to his knees. It is cold. What seasons have passed? Judah crawls forward and touches the rails.

It seems impossible that he can touch this metal, these iron sashes that wind around the weather and geography, that for all the blood and salt he spilled on them, the bones of all the men and women they press upon, are nothing, are a nothing, are made nothing by time and dust.

They are scavenged. Imperfect. Sections are gone. The tracks look out from the dirt and hide again. It has been a time since any train came this way.

Judah looks north along the cut. He remembers the carving of the roadbed. He is a long way north of the swamp.

When he goes back Judah will learn why the rails are still. How the money at last choked up in its sluices and died when the malfeasances grew so great that to ignore them would have shamed the state too far. That the money faltered when degraded news of the revolt, of the iron council, reached the railway's backers. And how after panicked attempts to salvage the TRT through raised wages and a merciless expansion of Remaking the capital flight was so great that Transcontinental Railroad Trust was punctured, and the tracks became bones.

Soon, when he reaches the city again, Judah will learn that. For now he only smiles. He picks up his fallen pack, and as he stoops he strokes a rail as if it were a cat. He strokes it with affection, even with a melancholy.

He steps up and walks on over the dead rails. Around him the angles of the banks enclose him. He cannot see the wider land. This road tunnels his vision and leads him back to New Crobuzon. It has been waiting for him.

—New Crobuzon, he says, he whispers. It is the first time he has spoken for days. —New Crobuzon, I'll always come back to you.

Not a lover's promise, not a challenge, not resignation or pugnacity. Something of all of them.

He walks on. Helios of the iron council are in his pack. The truth, escape, a new life, a rolling democracy, Remade arcadia. —I'll make you legend, he says and the birds listen, —and it will be true.

Judah walks on the iron road, back, to the city, back to the towers of New Crobuzon.

part four

---◆---

THE HAINTING

CHAPTER FOURTEEN

THE CROWD WERE CHASING A MAIMED MAN. ONE OF THE SOLDIERS or sailors from the Tesh War. They seemed to be on every street: they had welled up as if from under stones.

No papers would say that the war had gone bad but the upswell of the wounded and ruined bespoke disasters. Ori imagined the New Crobuzon ironclads upending and sliding under water made hot by war, imagined slicks of men on the waves, gorged on by sea-wyrms, by sharks. There were terrible rumours. Everyone knew something of the Battle of Bad Earth and the Fight in the Sun.

The first wave of wounded were treated with fear and respect. They were militia and so not trusted, but they had fought and been ruined for the city, and there was true rage for them, and a fashion for New Crobuzon–loyal songs. What few Teshi there were in the city were murdered or went underground. Anyone with a foreign accent risked a beating.

Increasingly, criminals were conscripted instead of being Re-made and jailed. Many of the cripples begging and screaming about the Tesh soulcannon and the efrit winds had been press-ganged and recruited solely for the war. They were not career militia. They were discomfiting, shambling reminders.

The veterans were welcomed and then not welcomed, unwelcomed, spurned. The militia, their erstwhile comrades, cleared them from the parks and squares uptown. Ori had seen them take a man from the petally Churchyard Square, his skin erupted and splitting from beneath with dental wedges, as he screamed about a toothbomb.

New Crobuzoners gave alms to charities that tended the thaumaturgically afflicted. There were still speeches and marches in support of the war: *freedom parades* they called them with their trumpeters and military floats. But the strangely wounded returnees found they were jinxes.

And those whose hurts were simple and somatic, unhexed? Scarred, stumped rather than too-limbed, blinded, with signs TESH WAR VETEREN, BROKEN FOR N. CROBUZON. Many were doubtless the everyday maimed giving their old injuries a spurious soldier's glamour, and the resentment and anxiety of Crobuzoners about their city's war had an outlet.

Only one voice had to raise a jeer—*you was born that way, you lying fucker*—and a mob might gather, and run the orthodox wounded down. It was for New Crobuzon that they did it, of course, they said—*you bastard comparing yourself to our boys fighting and dying.* The Murkside crowd approached the burly armless man they accused of lying, said had never been on a ship. He shouted his rank while they threw stones. Ori walked.

Other victims knew better than to raise complaint. The Remade, slave-militia built for war, survivors of their tour. Their integrated arms were decommissioned before their release on the streets of New Crobuzon. If they tried to claim that these Remakings themselves—forgetting even the wound-cut flesh, lost eyes and ill-splinted bones—were war injuries, they would be jeered at the very best. Ori walked.

It was cool summer, and he passed under lush trees until he could not hear the shouts of crowds or the man they were beating and accusing of treachery. Breezes came with him under the arches of Dark Water Station. Streets were tight like veins, houses of dark-wood and white daub next to those in brick, and here one burnt-out with carbon bones jutting from uncleared ash. The walls of Pincod, in New Crobuzon's west, drank water from the air and sweated it out, making plaster bulge like cysts. Their damp was coloured and shining.

North to where streets widened. The Piazza della Settimana di Polvere was a trimmed garden of fox-rose and tall stones, looked on by the stuccowork bay windows of Nigh Sump. Ori did not like it here. He had grown up in Dog Fenn. Not the gang-jungle of Bad-side, not so bad as that, but the child Ori had run through rookeries of buildings reshaped by the ingenuity of the poor, over planks looking down on washing and outhouses. He had scavenged pen-nies and stivers from roadside dirt, squabbled and learned sex and the fast-spat performative slang of the Dog Fenn Dozens. Ori did not understand the geography of Nigh Sump and the uptown parts. He did not understand where children here would run. The austere houses cowed him, and he hated them for it.

He felt cocky challenge at the glances from the well-dressed lo-cals. Night was coming. Ori fingered his weapons.

At the junction he saw his contacts. Old Shoulder and the oth-ers did not acknowledge him, but they walked at the same pace under the willows that softened each corner and on to Crosshatch Avenue.

It was one of the city's prettiest places. Shops and houses pil-lared, studded with fossils in the old Os Tumulus style. They were fronted for a stretch by the famous glasheim, a facade of stained glass centuries old whose designs ranged across the divides of the buildings. Guards protected it, and no carts could pass over the cobblestones outside it and risk shards. Once, Ori had suggested trying to break it, as a provocation, but even Toro's crew had seemed shocked. They were not here for that. Old Shoulder slouched toward an office.

And then the careful ballet that they had walked through so many times in the deserted warehouse: two steps, one two, Ori was by the door, and bumping, three four, into the woman Catlina; they shuffled as rehearsed; Ori tripped; Marcus slipped into the office with Shoulder as Ori and Catlina yelled, decoying.

Elyctro-barometric lights were spitting all around them, making the glasheim incandesce and staining Ori and Catlina ghost colours. They abused each other, and he watched the door over her shoulder, ready to call her *dog,* the signal for her to draw attention with screams should anyone seem ready to look inside the office where their comrades were. They must be interrogating their quarry. *Who've you sold out?* Shoulder would be saying.

The glasheim guards approached but did not look anywhere but at him and Catlina. The shopkeepers watched wary and amused, and the uptown shoppers stared from café fronts. Ori was astonished. Didn't they *know* that things were happening? How did Nigh Sump shield itself?

Soon—and the thought was uncomfortable though he strained for ruthlessness—soon Old Shoulder would kill the informant. He would do it quickly, then stab his deadness with a double-horned cestus that left marks like a bull's gore.

There's a war, Ori wanted to shout. *Outside the city. And inside too. Does it tell you that in your papers?* Instead he performed.

Toro gave them instructions, was not bitter or vicious but stressed what was necessary. This was necessary. Toro had linked the man suddenly to arrest-chains, to the towers of the militia, to the snatch-squads who predated on guildsmen and activists. The man in the office was a militiaman, a backroom-man, a nexus of informers. Old Shoulder would find out what he could, and then he would kill him.

Ori thought of the first time he had seen Toro.

* * *

It had been down to Spiral Jacobs' money. *I want to make a contribution,* Ori had said, and let Old Shoulder know that this was not just another week's hoardings. *I want in,* he had said, and Old Shoulder had pursed his green lips and nodded and come back to him two days later. *Come now. Bring the money.*

Over Barley Bridge, out of Dog Fenn to Badside. An apocalypse landscape of long-deserted slag and stagnant shipyards, where the keels of vessels poked from their internment in shallow waters. No one salvaged these sculptures in rust. Old Shoulder led Ori to a hangar where dirigibles were once built, and Ori waited in the shade of its mooring mast.

The gang came. A few men and women; a Remade named Ulliam, a big man in his fifties who walked carefully, his head backward on his neck, staring behind him. More waiting. And the late light refracted by the city came through glass-fringed panes, and into its corona came Toro.

Little dusts came up with each of Toro's steps. *Toro,* Ori thought, stared hard, with awe.

Toro moved like a mime, an exaggerated padding so unbullish Ori almost laughed. Toro was slighter than he, shorter, almost like a child, but walked with a precision that said *I am something to fear.* The thin figure was surmounted with a massive headpiece, a great bulk of iron and brass that looked too heavy to be carried by such tight little muscles, but Toro did not totter. Of course the helmet was a bull's head.

Stylized, made from knots of metalwork, gnarled by the residue of fights. The myth, that helmet. More than dumb metal. Ori tasted hex. The horns were ivory or bone. The snout ended in a grille mimicking teeth; the exhaust pipe was a nose ring. The eyes were perfect, round, tiny portholes in tempered glass that glowed white—whether backlit or hexed, Ori could not see. He could not see human eyes behind them.

Toro stopped and raised a hand, and spoke, and from that little body had come a profound bass, an animal vibration so low that Ori was delighted. Little wisps of steam gusted from the nose ring, and Toro threw back its head. It was, Ori was astounded, it *was* the voice of a bull, speaking Ragamoll.

"You have something for me," Toro said, and eager as a pilgrim Ori threw the sack of money.

"I counted it," Old Shoulder said. "Some of it's old, some of it'll be a bitch to shift, but there's a lot. He's a good lad."

And he was there, in. No more tests, no more fool's jobs to prove himself.

Still junior, he was lookout or distraction, and that was enough for him. He had made himself part of something. He had not considered holding back some money, though he could live on it for a long time. Some of it came back to him anyway: they paid him to work at their crimes and insurrectionary revenge.

New Crobuzon became a new city for him. Now where he looked at streets he saw in them escapes, routes for incursions: he remembered the urban techniques of his childhood.

He had come to a more fierce existence. His heart quickened past any militia; he watched for signs on the walls. With the scatology, pornography and insults were more important marks. Chalked devices, runes and pictograms, where base thaumaturgy occurred (wards, preservers, pranks to turn milk and beer). There were sigils that were spreading by some memesis, that he saw now in all quarters: cochlear swirls and many-edged ideograms. He looked for the graffiti by which the gangs communicated. Calls to battle and parlay in terse paint slogans. Apocolypse cultism and rumour: *Ecce Jabber, Vedne Save Us!, IC's steaming home!* Toro was in a hinterland between factions like the Proscribed and the Runagates, and the thief-gangs, the murderers of the east city. Toro's crew were known to both sides.

Twice Ori negotiated with gangsters. He went with Old Shoulder and the Remade Ulliam to beg-threaten the crew of razor-eyed boys called the Murkside Shrikes, asking them to stay away from the docks where their nihilist depredations risked bringing the militia. Ori looked at the Shrikes with naked hate but paid them off as Toro had instructed. Once he went alone to Bonetown, and in the sight of the huge age-cracked chest-cage he made a careful deal with Mr. Motley's vizier, buying a bulk quantity of shazbah. He did not know what Toro did with it.

He rarely saw Toro. For stretches it was a dull and insular life. They did not read as the Runagaters had read. His new comrades played games in the Badside warehouse, went "scouting," which was walking without aim. No one ever quite spoke their ultimate plan, their target; no one ever quite said what they wanted to do. No one ever said the Mayor's name or even the word *mayor*, but instead *chair-of-the-board* or *pigboss*: speaking the truth had become a shibboleth. *When d'you suppose we might ah help our-friend-at-the-head-of-the-meeting take a permanent sabbatical downstairs?* one of them might say, and they would debate the Mayor's routine and check their weapons.

Ori did not always know what his comrades were doing. Sometimes he would learn only when he heard or read of another heist, the freeing of prisoners from a punishment factory, the murder of some rich old couple in Flag Hill. That last outraged the papers, who excoriated Toro for the killing of innocents. Ori wondered sourly what it was the victims had done, how many they had Remade or executed. He rummaged in the gang's box of militia spoils, the badges and contracts of office, but could find nothing of the uptown couple to tell why they had been targeted.

With Spiral Jacobs' contribution they had money to bribe, and bribe well, though the bulk of the cash Toro took for some expensive mysterious project. The Toroans trawled for information and contacts. Ori tried to rebuild his own network. He had neglected his old friends. He had not seen Petron for weeks, or any of the Nuevists. He had felt with a new dissident aggression that they were too frivolous, their interventions mannered. Eventually he sought them out, and realised how much he had missed their savage play.

And he learnt from them. Realised how fast he uncoupled from rumour when he spent all his days with the crew. So once a week he went back to the Griss Fell soup kitchen. He decided he would return to the *Runagate Rampant* meetings.

He had tried not to neglect Spiral Jacobs. The man was not easy to find. He disappeared for a long time, and Ori only found him after leaving messages with the shelters and the vagrants who were the old tramp's family.

"Where did you go?" Ori said, and Spiral Jacobs was too vague to reply. The old man's fog lifted when he spoke of his old life, of Jack Half-a-Prayer.

"How'd you come to know so much about Toro's plans, Spiral?" The old man laughed and bobbed his head.

Are you a friend of Toro? Ori thought. *Do you meet and talk about the old times, talk about the Man'Tis?*

"Whyn't you just give them the money yourself?" Nothing.

"You don't know them, do you?"

No one among the Toro-run recognised his description of Spiral. Ori asked Jacobs to tell him about Jack Half-a-Prayer. *I think you like me,* Ori thought. The mad old man looked at him with a familial care. *I think you gave me the money to help them and me both.* The weakness of Spiral's mind came and went.

"Not seen much of you," Petron had said in a louche cabaret pub of Howl Barrow. They ignored the gyring striptease and illicit dealings at the other tables.

"Doing things."

"Running with a new crowd?" There was no accusation or

venom in Petron's tone—allegiances were fast among the bohemians. Ori shrugged.

"We're doing good things, if you want to come back. The Flexibles are doing another show: 'Rud and the Gutter and the Devil's
Embassy.' Can't use Rudgutter's name, obviously, but it's about the
Midsummer Nightmares, years back: there's rumours they tried to
make some wicked deals to fix it."

Ori listened and thought, *You'll do a show of* me *in years to come.*
"Ori and the Toro-Gored Mayor." Things'll be different then.

Two Chaindays running he went to The Grocer's Sweetheart.
No one was there the first night. The second, the trapdoor was
raised to him and he was let back into the *Runagate Rampant* meeting. The Jacks were not all the same as they had been. The Remade
man he had met months back was still there. There was a vodyanoi
stevedore and a crippled cactus-man Ori did not remember, a few
others looking through the literature.

A woman led the meeting. She was small and intense, older
than he but still young. She spoke well. She eyed him, and when her
face took on an uncertain expression he remembered her: she was
the knit-machinist.

She spoke about the war. It was a tense meeting. Not only
did the *Runagate Rampant* not support the war's aims, stated or
interpreted—that position was common to the tiny dissident
groups—they said they fought for New Crobuzon to lose.

"You think Tesh is any better?" someone said, angry and in-
credulous.

The knit-worker said, "It ain't that we think it's better, it's that
our prime opponents are here, right here."

Ori did not speak. He watched her and tensed only a second
when it seemed one man's anger at what he called her Tesh-love
would make him violent, but she calmed him. Ori did not think she
convinced everyone—he was not sure of his own feelings for the
war, beyond that both sides were bastards, and that he did not

care—but she did well. When the others had gone he waited and applauded her, and he was only half mocking.

"Where's Jack?" Ori said. "The Jack who used to take these?"

"Curdin?" she said. "Gone. Militia. Snatched. No one knows."

They were silent. She gathered her papers. Curdin was dead or jailed or who knew what.

"Sorry."

She nodded.

"You did well."

She nodded again. "He told me about you." She did not look at him. "He told me a lot about you. He was disappointed you weren't coming no more. Thought a lot of you. 'Boy's got the anger,' he said. 'Hope he knows what to do with it.' So . . . so what's it like on the wild side, Jack? How's it with, with the Bonnot Gang, or Toro, or Poppy's lot or whoever you're with now? Think people don't know? So, so what is it you're doing now?"

"More than you." But he hated his petulance and did not want to fight, so he said, "How'd you take over?" He meant *You know so much, you argue well, you've risen to this.* When last he saw her he would have been the experienced dissident, with insurrectionist philosophy: and now he had been present at deaths and was harder, and had been cut by a militia knife and knew how to talk to the danger-scum of the east city, but she knew more than him, and it had only been some weeks.

She shrugged.

"It's the time," she said. She tried to be dismissive, then met his eye. "Do you . . . How could you do this now? Now? What d'you think's happening? Do you know what's going on? Do you feel it? Five foundries went out last week, Jack. Five. The Rétif Platform of the dockers' guild's in talks with the vodyanoi for a *cross-race union.* That's *our* chaverim pulling that, that's *Double-R.* The next march we have we'll make into a meeting, and we won't have to moulder like this." She waved at the close walls, brought her fists down on her thighs. She almost stamped. "And you've heard the stories. You know what's returning? What's coming back to us? And you choose now to go be an adventurer? To turn your back on the common-alty?"

The word made him breathe a sneer. The jargon of it, *the com-monalty, the commonalty* that the *Double-Rs* spoke of so relentlessly.

"We're doing things," he said. Her tirade made him uneasy—or perhaps melancholic, nostalgic. He did not know of the actions and the changes that she spoke of, that he would once have been part of. But all his excitement, his pride came up in him and effaced anxi-ety, and he smiled. "Oh Jack," he had said. "You don't know what we'll do."

The door of the office opened and Old Shoulder and Marcus emerged, seen only by Ori. The cactus-man held Ori's eyes and then was gone behind the curious crowd.

Carefully, not too sudden, Ori let Catlina know they were done, and they let their voices down like two people tired of arguing. Ori walked under the skyrails and the arches of the Dexter Line, the trains over his head lit up by gas, under skies awash in brown dusk, toward Badside where Toro was waiting. He walked back to his masked boss, whom he saw so rarely, whose face he never saw, leav-ing a dead man behind him.

CHAPTER FIFTEEN

Ori went to the docks of Kelltree. There was a congregation, made to look spontaneous, which the Caucus and its factions
had spread word of for weeks. They could not have listed it in *RR* or
The Forge so had relied on graffiti, handslang and rumour. The
militia would close them down: the question was how long they
had. A mass milled in the forefront of the Paradox Warehouse,
dockworkers and a few clerks, human mostly, but all the races were
there; even Remade, carefully at the edges of the crowd.

From canals that linked the docks to the river, vodyanoi
watched the gathering. A few score yards away, hidden by roofs, was
the Gross Tar, the meet of the Tar and the Canker, the wide river
that bisected the east of the city. When tall ships passed, Ori could
see their masts move behind the houses, their rigging over the
chimneys.

Airships went over. *Quick now,* Ori thought. A wedge of men
and women came through the crowd, coalescing out of random-
ness and moving with sudden purpose. They bundled around one

man whom they pushed to the brick shed become a stage, where he vaulted up and was joined by someone Ori recognised, a Caucusist, from the Proscribed.

"Friends," the man shouted. "We've someone wants to talk to you, a friend of mine, *Jack*," and there were humourless smiles. "He wants to tell something of the war."

They had so little time. Militia spies would be running to their contacts. In the thaumaturgic listening post in the Spike, the echelon of communicators and communicatrices would be blinking fast and trying to decipher from the city's welter of cognition which illicit topics were being spoken. *Quick now,* Ori thought.

Looking behind him to gauge the size of the crowd, Ori was surprised to see Petron. The Nuevist was lacing his art activism with real dissidence, was risking more than late fighting in Salacus Fields. Ori was impressed.

There were Caucusists everywhere. Ori saw someone from the Excess, from the Suffragim; he saw an editor of *Runagate Rampant*. This speaker was not affiliated, and all the factions of the unstable, chaotic, infighting and comradely front had to share him. They were vying for the man.

"He has things to say," the Proscribed man was shouting. "Jack here . . . Jack here is back from the war."

There was an utter sudden hush. The man was a *soldier*. Ori was poised. What was this, this stupidity? Yes there was press-ganging and military Remaking, but whatever his history, this man was, formally at least, militia. And he had been invited here. He stepped forward.

"Don't fret about me. I'm here, I'm here to tell you, of, of the real," the man said. He was not a good speaker. But he shouted loud enough that all could hear him, and his own anxiety kept the crowd there.

He spoke fast. He had been warned he would not have long. "I ain't spoken before to people like this," he said and they could hear his voice trembling, this man who had carried guns and killed for New Crobuzon.

The war's a lie (*he said*). I got my badge. (*He drew it out by his finger-tips as if it were dirty. City finds that he's a dead man, thought Ori.*) Months on them ships, we went through the Firewater Straits, on till landfall, and we thought we'd have to fight on the seas, we was trained to, sailor-soldiers, 'acause them Tesh ships were out for us, we saw them and their weapons in flocks circling but they ain't seen us, and it ain't all city-loyal, the militia, not now, us from Dog Fenn on that ship were there because there ain't no other jobs to do. Let loose and told to go liberate them Tesh villages.

They don't want us. I seen things . . . What they done to us. What we done back. (*There was a restive stirring somewhere in the streets and a brief incoming of Caucus scouts handslanging frantically to the Proscribed man and he whispered to the speaker. Ori got ready to run. The militia renegade gabbled in anger.*) It ain't no war for lib-erty, nor for the Teshi, they hate us and we, we fucking hated them I tell you, and it was a, it's *carnage* there, just plain murder, they sending their children out stuffed full of hex to make us melt, I had my men *melt* on me, and I done things . . . You don't know what it is, in Tesh. They ain't like us. Jabber, I done things to people . . . (*The Proscribed man hurried him, pulled him to the shed's edge.*)

So screw the militia and screw their war. I ain't no friends to the damn Teshi after what they done but I don't hate them half so much as I hate *them*. (*He pointed at the basalt column-palace of Parlia-ment, prodding the sky with tubes and tuskish jags, profane and arro-gant.*) Anyone needs dying it ain't some damn Tesh peasant, it's them, in there, who got us here. Who'll take them out? (*He cocked his thumb, shot his finger several times toward the Parliament—a Re-making offence.*) Screw their war.

And at that someone from *Runagate Rampant* barked, "Yeah, so fight to lose, fight for defeat," and there was angry calling from those who saw stupidity in this. They yelled at the Runagaters that they supported Tesh, that they were agents of the Crawling Liquid, but before there were fists between the factions, the whistles of the guards went, and the crowd began to scatter. Ori wrote fast on a tear of paper.

Militia were coming. People were prepared, and they ran. Ori ran too, but not for the doors or the broken fence. He went straight for the speaker.

Pushed past the bickering Caucus members who surrounded him. Some recognised Ori, stared at him with greeting or query stillborn as he went past them to the raging soldier-Jack. Ori put his name and his address into the speaker's pocket, and whispered.

"Who'll take them out?" he said. "We will. These lot won't. Come find me."

And then there was the burring of propellers and an airship protruded over them. Ropes spilled down and dribbled armoured militia. There were the sounds of dogs. The gates of the Paradox Warehouse were too full of people, and there was a panic. "Men-o'-war!" someone shouted, and yes there slowly rising to swell over the walls were the grotesque gland-bodies contoured with extrusions and organic holes, ridden by militia manipulating the exposed nerves of the giant filament-dangling things, flying them sedately toward the crews of Caucusists, the toxin in their tendrils dripping. Ori ran.

There would be other militia squads on the street: shunn-riders, plainclothes infiltrators. Ori had to take care. He itched at the sense that some sharpshooter might target him from the airship. But he knew the ways through these streets. Most of the audience had already disappeared in New Crobuzon's brick tangles, careering past startled shop holders and corner-hanging vagrants to stop suddenly and walk like everyone else was walking, a few streets on. Later, a mile away on the other side of the river, Ori heard that no one had been captured or killed, and was savagely delighted.

* * *

The soldier's name was Baron. He told Ori without any sense of the
secrecy and care with which the dissidents did their business. He
turned up two nights later. When Ori opened his door to him,
Baron was holding Ori's paper. "Tell me then," Baron had said.
"What is it you'll do? Who the fuck *are* you, chaver?"

"How come they ain't got you yet?" Ori asked. Baron said there
were hundreds of militia gone AWOL. Most of those planning to go
into hiding were keeping their heads down, readying for the black
survivalist economy of New Crobuzon, staying out of sight of their
erstwhile colleagues. With the chaos in the city, he said, it would be
impossible for the militia to keep track of all their men. No day
passed without a strike or riot: the numbers of the unemployed
were growing, there were attacks on xenians by Quillers and on
Quillers by xenians and dissidents. Some in Parliament were arguing for compromise, meeting the guilds.
    "I ain't hiding," said Baron. "I don't care."
    They approached The Terrible Magpie in Riverskin, near the
cactus ghetto. Ori would not go to The Two Maggots, or any place
so known as a dissidents' hole that it would be watched. Here in
Riverskin the roads were quiet gullies between damp wood houses.
The worst trouble they were likely to find was from the gangs of
drugged cactus youth who lounged and carved keloid tattoos into
their green skins, sitting on the girders at the base of the Glasshouse
as it loomed eighty yards high, a quarter of a mile across where it
cut streets out of New Crobuzon like a stencil. The cactus punks
watched Ori and Baron but did not accost them.
    Something had happened to Baron. He said nothing explicit to
make Ori wonder about his experiences, but it was in his pauses, in
the ways he did not say things. A rage. Ori supposed there were as
many unspeakable stories as there were men come back from war.
Baron was thinking of something, of some *one thing*, a moment
of—what? blood? death? transfiguration?—some atrocity that had

made him this angry fighting man, eager to kill those who had once paid him. Ori thought of dead friends and of pain.

Each of the Caucus groups was courting Baron and the other renegade militia. With careful scorn Ori explained the agenda of the various factions. He told stories of Toro's adventures, the crew's works, and pulled Baron to his orbit.

Baron was a prize. The Toroans were delighted. Toro came the night Baron joined them, put a bony hand on the militiaman's chest to welcome him.

That was the first time Ori saw how Toro travelled. When Old Shoulder and the gang were done talking, Toro lowered that carved and cast metal head and horns and pushed. The helmeted figure was leaning against nothing, against air, and then driving, straining forward, until those hexed horns caught at something, caught on it and the universe seemed to flex and stretch at two points, and Ori felt the air crack with thaumaturgy and Toro's horns pierced the world and Toro stomped suddenly through. The split skin of reality closed again like lips, back into position, and Toro was gone.

"What does Toro *do*?" Ori asked Ulliam the Remade that night. "To make boss? I'm not complaining, you know that, right? I'm just saying. What does Toro do?"

Ulliam smiled.

"Hope you never find out," he said. "Without Toro, we're nothing."

Baron brought a military savagery to the gang. When he was talking of the war he shook and barked rage; he became etched with veins. But when he went on jobs, on revenge-raids against informers, on punishment beatings against the drug gangs encroaching on Toro's land, in the action itself he was utterly cold, mouth barely twitching as he worked without emotion on someone.

He frightened his new gang-comrades. His machinish drive, the ease with which he gave out punishment, the way his eyes switched off and the life in them sank very deep. *We ain't nothing*, Ori thought. The Toroans had thought themselves hard desperados—and yes they had done violent, murderous things in the name of change—but their anarchist anger was a vague floundering next to the cool rageless expertise of the soldier. They were in awe of him.

Ori remembered the first execution he had seen, of a captain-informer. The roughhousing had been easy. They had found the proof, the blacklists of names, the executive orders. But even with all their hatred, even with the memory of fallen brothers and sisters, even with Ulliam's memory of the punishment factories themselves, the execution was a difficult thing. Ori had closed his eyes so as not to see the shot. They had given Ulliam the gun saying it was for his Remaking, but Ori thought it was also because Ulliam could not look at his quarry. His backward-facing head focused on nothing. And even then, Ori bet he closed his eyes when he pulled the trigger.

By contrast Baron walked in anywhere he was bid and fought who he was told to fight and killed if told to implacably. He moved like the best constructs Ori remembered from his youth: like something oiled, metal, mindless.

When the Murkside Shrikes again, with pissy provocation, started to spread into Toro's streets, Ori, Enoch and Baron were sent to finish the incursions. "One only," Toro said. "The one with the harelip. He's the planner." Ori, always the best shot, had a flintlock, Enoch a double-crossbow, but neither had a chance to fire. Baron had checked and cleaned the barrels of his repeater with effortless expertise.

Young men and women, the hangers-on of the youthful Shrikes, lounged over the stairs to the Murkside attic drinking very-tea and smoking shazbah. Ori and Enoch followed Baron. Twice he was challenged by some junkie nominally on guard: twice he dismissed them with a look, a whispered threat. Ori was still turning the cor-

ner on the last mezzanine when he heard the quick-kicked splinter-
ing of wood, shouts.

Two shots had sounded already by the time he reached the
door. Two boys about seventeen were fallen on ruined legs and
screaming. While others ran and dropped their guns Baron kept
moving. Someone shot Baron, and Ori saw blood flower on his left
arm: Baron grunted and his face flashed a moment of pain and was
impassive again. Two more quick shots disabled or terrified those
firing, and then he was closing on the harelipped young man who
gave the gang its ideas, and he shot him as Enoch and Ori stared.

He doesn't care if he dies, Ori thought that night. Baron terrified
him. *He'll kill if we tell him. He'll kill if we let him.*

That ain't a man who learnt his fighting in the wilds. The quick
and brute expertise with which he swept a room, the one-two-three
taking in of all corners. Baron had done this many times before, this
urban violence. Baron was no recent recruit, a jobless man found a
job, a rushed soldier.

What can Toro do? Ori wondered. He had never seen his boss
fight.

"What's that helmet?" he said, and Ulliam told him that Toro had
come out of the punishment factories or the jail, or the wilds, or the
undertown, and gone on a long and arduous search to find a crafts-
man and the materials, had had the helmet made: the rasulbagra it
was sometimes called, the head of the bull. Ulliam told him the unbelievable stories of its powers and the way it had been made, the
long dangers of its forging, the years. "Years in jail, years hunting
the pieces, years wearing it," he said. "You'll see what it can do."

Each of the crew had their own tasks. Ori was sent to steal rockmilk
and hexed liquors from laboratories. He knew a plan was coming.
He could see its glimmers in his instructions.

Get a plan of the lower floors of Parliament. Get what? Ori did not know how to start. *Make friends with a clerk at the magisters' offices. Find the name of the Mayor's undersecretary. Get day work in Parliament, wait for more instructions.*

The air of strikes and insurrection was growing: Ori felt it, detached, excited.

Spiral Jacobs came back to the soup kitchen. Ori felt a strange unburdening at the sight of him. Jacobs was lucid, shrewd that night, staring at Ori with stoat eyes.

"Your money keeps helping us," Ori said. "But I got instructions now I can't do nothing with." He told. "What's that, then?"

They were at the river wall in Griss Fell, just down from the confluence, with Strack Island and the spires of Parliament sheer out of the Gross Tar. Its lights shone grey in the evening; their reflections in the water were drab. A cat was mewing from Little Strack, stranded somehow on the stub of land in the river. Spiral Jacobs spat at the waterpillars that had marked the limits of the Old Town. They were tremendously ancient stone carvings, a winding path of stylised figures ascending, depicting events from the early histories of New Crobuzon. Where they met the water they were defaced by delinquent vodyanoi.

"They trying for different things, ain't they?" Jacobs took Ori's cigarillo. "They ain't got a strategy, have they? They're trying for all different things. Lots of ways in." He smoked and thought and shook his head. "Damn, but this ain't how Jack would have done it." He laughed.

"How would Jack have done it?"

Jacobs kept looking at the glow-end of his smoke.

"Mayor can't stay in Parliament all the time." He spoke with care. "Someone like the Mayor, though, can't just go walking, or riding. Has to have protection, yes? Has to trust them. Wherever they go—Jack told me this, Jack watched for this—wherever they go, Mayor's Clypean Guard take over. They're the only ones trusted."

He looked up. His face was not impish or playful. "Imagine if one of them were turned. Imagine if one could be bought."

"But they're chosen just so's they *can't* be bought . . ."

"History . . ." Jacobs spoke with terse authority. Brought Ori to a hush. "Is all full. And dripping. With the *corpses.* Of them who trusted the *incorruptible.*"

He gave Ori a name. Ori stared while the old tramp walked away. He hobbled into view in each puddled streetlight until he reached the end of the alley and leaned, a tired old man with chalk on his fingers.

"Where do you go?" Ori said. His voice was flat by the river, did not echo between brick walls and windows but spread out and was quickly gone. "And dammit, Spiral, how d'you know these things? Come to Toro," he said. He was excited and unnerved. "How do you do this? You're better than any of us, come to the fucking Bull, come join us. Won't you?"

The old man licked his lips and hovered. Would he speak? Ori saw him deciding.

"Not all Jack's paths is dried up," he said. "There's ways of knowing. Ways of hearing things. I know." Tapped his nose, comedically conspiratorial. "I know things, ain't it? But I'm too old to be a player now, boy. Leave that to the young and angry."

He repeated the name. He smiled again and walked away. And Ori knew he should go after him, should try again to bring him into the orbit of Toro. But there was a very strong and strange respect in him, something close to awe. Ori had taken to wearing marks on his clothes, coils mimicking the spirals Jacobs left on walls. Spiral Jacobs came and went in his strange ways, and Ori could not deny him his exits.

CHAPTER SIXTEEN

O LD SHOULDER WAS DELIGHTED WITH ORI'S INFORMATION, THE name, but cheerfully disbelieved his claims to its provenance.

"Drinking in the right pubs in Sheck my green arse, boy," he said. "This is insider stuff. You ain't telling. You've a contact you're guarding. You hoarding him? Her? Some officer's tart? You been doing some horizontal recruitment, Ori? Whatever. I don't know what you're doing but this is . . . this is gold. If it's true. So I ain't going to push it.

"I trust you, boy—wouldn't have brought you in if I didn't. So whatever you're keeping this for, I'm thinking it's for reasons that make sense. But I can't say I like it. If you're playing some game . . ." *If you're on another side* he did not say. "Or even if you're doing it for the right reasons but you're just *wrong*, even if you just make a wrong call and mess us all up, you got to know I'd kill you."

Ori was not even intimidated. Old Shoulder was suddenly vastly annoying to him.

He stood up carefully to the cactacae, met his eyes. "I'll give my life for this," he said, and it was true, he realised. "I'll take the Mayor down, take off the fucking head of this snake-government. But you know, tell me, Shoulder. If I was playing you? If this information I got for us—that's going to let us damn well do what we been wanting to do—if it *was* me setting you up, how'd you go about killing me after, Shoulder? Because you're the one who'd be dead."

It was a mistake. He saw Old Shoulder's eyes. But Ori could not regret his provocation. He tried but he could not.

Baron frightened them all. They had seen that he could shoot and fight, but they were not sure if he could persuade. They briefed him with great anxiety, until he snapped at them to shut up and trust him. There was no choice.

"We need a man who knows how to speak militia to militia," Toro said. The mechanisms or thaumaturgy of the helmet turned the words into lowing. Ori looked at the body so dwarfed by that helmet but somehow not ridiculous, dancer-tight and hard. The lamps of those featureless round eyes sprayed out light. "We're crims," Toro said. "Can't talk to the militia—they'd see into us. Need someone who has no guilt. Who's one of them. Knows barrack slang. We need a militiaman."

There were militia quarters about the city. Some were hidden. All were protected with hex and firepower. But near each one were militia pubs, and all the dissidents knew which they were.

Bertold Sulion, the man whose name Spiral Jacobs had given Ori, and which Ori had given to his comrades, was, Jacobs said, a dissatisfied Clypean Guard, loyalty becoming nihilism or greed. He would be stationed in Parliament itself, by or in the Mayor's quarter. And that meant the pubs below the skyrails and the militia tower at the wedge of Brock Marsh, where the rivers converged.

Brock Marsh, the magician's arrondissement. Oldest part of an old city. In the north, with pebbled streets and yawing wooden lean-tos full of charmed equipment, karcists, bionumanists, physicists and all-trade thaumaturges lived. In the south of the borough, though, the elixirs did not so fill the drains; there was not such a pall of hex-stench in the air. The scientists and their parasite industries petered out below thrumming skyrails and pods. Strack Island and Parliament emerged from the river close-by. It was in this region that the Clypean Guards would drink.

It was a drab few streets of concrete blocks and girders, industrial, distressed by age and unkempt. In the pubs of the area—in The Defeated Enemy, in The Badger, in The Compass and Carrot— Baron went to be a frequenter, to find Sulion.

The headlines of *The Quarrel* and *The Beacon* told of slow triumphs in the Firewater Straits, the defeat of Teshi shunboats and the emancipation of the serf towns in Tesh's demesne. There were unclear heliotypes of villagers and Crobuzoner militia exchanging smiles, the militia helping rebuild a food store, a militia surgeon tending a peasant child.

The Forge, a Caucus paper, found another officer like Baron, on the run. He told the war differently. "And even with all the things we're doing that he's talking about," Baron said, "we ain't winning. We *ain't going to win.*" Ori was not certain that was not the main basis of his anger.

"Baron reminds me of things I seen," said Ulliam. "And not in a good way." It was night in Pelorus Fields, in the south of New Crobuzon. A quiet little haunt of the clerks, office men, with enclaves like prosperous villages, garden squares unflowered in the cold, cosy fountains, fat churches and devotionals to Jabber. Bucolic hideouts jutted off from the busyness of Wynion Street, with its shoe markets and tea dens.

Ulliam and Ori took a risk in being there. With the growth in strikes and unlaw, Pelorus Fields felt sieged. As Parliamentarians met with the guilds, whose demands became more organised, as the Caucus spoke out from its unsubtle front organs, Pelorus Fields was anxious. Its respectable citizens patrolled, nightly, in Committees for the Defence of Decency. Frightened copywriters and actuaries running down xenians and the shabby-dressed, Remade who did not show deference.

But there were places like Boland's. "Show a bit of care, ladies, gents," was all Boland would say to the Nuevist poets, the dissidents, who came for his coffees and to hide behind ivy-lush windows. Ori and Ulliam sat together. Ulliam's chair faced away from Ori's so his backward face was forward.

"I seen men take a room like that before," Ulliam said. "It was men like that done this to me.

"It's why Toro didn't send me to Motley's—I used to work for him. Long, long time ago." He indicated his neck.

"What did they Remake you for? Why that way?" It showed trust to ask. Ulliam did not blench at the query, showed no shock. He *laughed*.

"Ori, you wouldn't believe me, boy. You can't have been more than a baby, if you was even born. I can't tell you it all now; it's done and gone. I was a herder, of sorts." He laughed again. "I've seen things. Oh, the animals I guarded. Nothing scares me no more. Except, you know . . . when I saw Baron come into that room. I won't say I was scared again but I remembered what it was, to feel that way.

"Do you think about what we'll do, when we do this?" he asked later. "This job? The chair-of-the-board?" Ori shook his head.

"We'll change things. Push it all the way." Excitement rose in him as it always did, with speed. "When we cut off the head and watch it fall, we'll wake people up. Nothing'll stop us." *We'll change everything. We'll change history. We'll wake the city up, and they'll free themselves.*

When they left and walked a few careful feet apart (whole and Remade could not fraternise in Pelorus Fields) they heard screaming from a few streets away, heard a woman running, her voice coming over the nightlit slates of Wynion Street. *It just come, it just come,* she shouted, and Ori and Ulliam looked at each other tense and wondered if they should go to her, but the sound became crying and then faded, and when they turned north they could not find her.

On Dockday the twelfth of Octuary, something came in front of the cold summer sun. Later Ori could not remember if he had seen the moment of its arrival or if he had only heard it so many times he had made it a memory.

He was in a train. On the Sink Line, passing over the shantytown of Spatters, toward the incline and grand houses of Vaudois Hill. Someone farther on in the carriage gave a shriek that he ignored, but others came then, too, and he looked up through the window.

They were raised, the train on arches, so they pushed through chimneys like little swells, minarets, towers with damp-splintered skins like swamp trees. They saw clearly across to the east and the morning sun spreading shadows and thick light, and at its centre something was swimming. A figure tiny in the core of the sun's glare and made of the deepest silhouette, neither human nor ciliated plankton nor rapid startling bird but all of them and other things, in turn or at one instant. It moved with an impossible crawl, straight out, emerging from the sun with a swimming motion that used all of its contradicting limbs.

A spit of chymical fear hit Ori's face from the khepri woman beside him, and he blinked till it dissipated. Later he learnt that wherever people stood in the city, from Flag Hill north, to Barrackham seven miles south, every compass point, they all saw the thing swim straight for them, growing in the heart of the sun.

It came closer, occluding the light so the city was drabbed. A dancing, swimming thing. The train was slowing—they would stop before Lich Sitting Station. The driver must have seen the sun and stopped in terror.

The sky over New Crobuzon shimmered like grease. Like plasma. The thing stuttered, palsied between sizes, was dwarfed by the sun around it and then for one dreadful instant was *there* above the heads of everyone in the city so looming, so massive it dwarfed New Crobuzon itself and all there was that moment was an eye with starred iris in baleful alien colours looking straight down between all the buildings, onto all the streets, into the eyes of everyone staring up at it so there was a tremendous, city-wide scream of fear, and then the thing was gone.

Ori heard his own shout. His eyes hurt, and it took him seconds to realise the sun was burning them, that he was staring where the thing had been, and now there was only the sun again. All that day he saw through the ghost of green colours, where his sight was burnt.

That evening there were riots in Smog Bend. The raged workforce of the factories ran for St. Jabber's Mound, to assault the militia tower for something—failing to protect them from that dreadful haint vision. Others ran for Creekside, and the khepri ghetto, to punish the outlanders there, as if they had sent the apparition. The stone idiocy of this had the Caucusers in the crowd screaming, but they could not hold back the armed few who went to punish the xenians.

Word was quick, and across the city Ori knew of the attacks while they were still occurring. He knew, only minutes after it had happened, that a hard wall of militia faced the rioters from the base of their tower, and that they had been ready with men-o'-war, and that the jellyfish things had come at the crowd.

He feared for the khepri of the ghetto. "We need to get there," Ori said, and while he and his comrades disguised their faces and pulled on guns he saw Baron look at him with cool incomprehension. Ori knew Baron was coming not because he cared about the khepri of Creekside, but only because this organisation to which he had allied himself had made a decision. "Toro'll find us," Ori said.

In a commandeered carriage they went fast through Echomire,

under the colossal Ribs of Bonetown, across Danechi's Bridge and through Brock Marsh, and the sky was dark-studded with dirigibles, many more than usual, black and lit against the black. There were militia on the streets, shielded, their faces hidden behind mirrors, specialist squads with hexed truncheons and blunderbusses for crowd control. Enoch whipped the pterabirds. Through the fringes of The Crow, where crowds were running to and from broken-open shopfronts and hauling away calico, jars of food, apothecaries' remedies.

Over the roofs scant streets away was the Spike, the bleak splinter from where the militia ruled, tugged seven ways by skyrails. And beside it, its colossal paradox roofscape soaring, disappearing, soaring again into view, was Perdido Street Station.

They tore under the arches of the Sud and Sink Lines, listening to militia whistles. *Stupid blind* idiots, Ori thought, of the mass, the rioters out that night. *Fighting the* khepri, *for Jabber's sake. This is why you need us to wake you up.* He checked his guns.

The first and worst flare of violence had ended when they arrived, but the ghetto was unquiet. They went through streets lit by rubbish fires. The century-old houses of Creekside had been made by and for humans, with poor materials and no care, and they sagged in toward each other like the sick. They were held by the wax and exuded byssus of the home-grubs, colossal maggoting larvae that the khepri used to reshape their dwellings. Ori and his comrades walked under houses half-seen through solid sputum that glowed fat-yellow in torchlight.

In a nameless square there was a last offensive. There were no militia, of course. Protecting the khepri was not their agenda.

Twenty or thirty men were attacking a khepri church. They had stamped to broken pieces the figure of Awesome Broodma that had stood by the entrance. It had been a poor, pathetic work, an oversized marble woman stolen or bought cheap from some human ruin, its head sawn off, supplanted with a carefully constructed headscarab in wire, thick with solder, bolted to the neck to mimic she-khepri shape. This chimera of poverty and faith lay scattered.

The men were battering at the door. Staring down from the first-floor windows were the congregation. Emotion was invisible in their insect eyes.

"Quillers," Ori said. Most of the men wore the New Quill Party's fighting outfits: dark business suits with trousers rolled, bowler hats that Ori knew were lined with steel. They carried razors and chains. Some had pistols. "Quillers."

Baron moved in. His first shot pushed a hole through the hat of one New Quill attacker, flaring the armoured lining into a crocus of felt, blood and metal. The men stopped, stared at him. *Gods, will we get out of this?* Ori thought as he ran where he had been directed, to where masonry gave him some inadequate cover. He dropped a New Quill man and hunkered behind the stone as it pattered viciously with shots.

For a dreadful half minute the Toroans were pinned. Ori could see Baron's implacable face, could see where Ruby and Ulliam crouched, Ulliam's face in an anguish as he fired according to Ruby's whispered commands. Some of their enemies had scattered, but the hardcore Quillers were focused, those with pistols covering those without as they crept closer.

And then as Ori prepared to shoot on an approaching corpulent and muscular New Quill man bulging from his inadequate suit, he heard an ugly tearing, and the air between him and the suddenly stupefied New Quillers was interrupted. As if a film of skin was stretched, the fabric of things bowed at two close points, distorting light and sound, and then the warp was a split and from out of the gash reality spat Toro.

The world resealed. Toro shouted. Crouched and pushed through the intervening feet with one shove of those horns and there was a stammering and Toro was close up to the fat Quill man whose billy club was shattering on the strange-refracting darkness that spilt from Toro's horns. And then the horns were through the fat man, who gasped and gouted and dropped, sliding like meat off a hook.

Toro shouted and moved again that uncanny goring way, following the horns that bled the toughened dark, and was then by another man and gouged him, and the horns seemed in the night's dim to soak up blood. Ori was astounded. A bullet from a New Quill gun pushed through the half-seen integument the horns shed and drew red, and Toro lowed, staggered back, righted and horned at the air and sent the gunman sprawling, feet away.

But though Toro took three men fast, the New Quillers still way outnumbered them, and were stoked with rage at these race-traitors. They danced in avoidance. Some lumbered, and some were consummate pugilists and gunmen. *We ain't going to get them khepri out,* Ori thought.

There was the noise of fast footsteps and Ori despaired, thinking another corps of street-fighters was about to attack them. But the New Quillers were turning, and began to run when the newcomers arrived.

Cactus-women and -men; khepri with the two sputtering flails of the stingbox; raucous, frog-leaping vodyanoi. A llorgiss with three knives. Perhaps a dozen of mixed xenian races in startling solidarity. A broad cactacae woman shouted orders—"Scabeyes, Anna," pointing at the running Quillers, "Chezh, Silur," pointing at the church door—and the motley xenian army moved in.

Ori was stunned. The New Quillers fired but ran.

"Who the fuck are *you*?" one of the Toroans shouted.

"Get up, shut up," Toro said. "Drop weapons, present yourselves."

A vodyanoi and the llorgiss shouted to the khepri in the church, and held open the doors as the terrified captives ran out and home. Some embraced their rescuers. An unclotting drizzle of khepri males—mindless two-foot scarabs seeking the warmth and darkness—scuttled back from the door. Ori shivered. It was only now he could feel the cold. He heard the fires that gave Creekside a shifting skin of dark light. In their up-and-down illumination he saw children come out of the church with their mothers. Young she-khepri with their headscarabs flexing, their headlegs rippling in childish communication. Two khepri women carried neonates, their bodies like human newborns, their little babies' necks shading into headgrubs that coiled fatly.

He dropped his gun hand, and a khepri, one of these militant newcomers, was running at him, the spiked flails of her stingbox leaving spirals of sparks in the air. "Wait!" Ori said.

"Aylsa." The cactus-woman stopped her with her name. "He's got a gun, Thumbs Ready," said a vodyanoi, and the cactus-woman said: "I know he's got a gun. There's exceptions, though."

"Exceptions?"

"They're under protection." Thumbs Ready pointed at Toro.

In the fight-anarchy, it was the first moment that many of the xenians had seen the armoured figure. They gasped in their different racial ways, stepped forward with camaraderie. "Bull," they said, and made respectful greetings. "Bull."

Toro and Thumbs Ready conferred too quiet for Ori to hear. Ori watched Baron's face. It was immobile, taking in each xenian fighter by turn. Ori knew he was working out in what order he could take them, if he had to.

"Out, out, out," Toro said suddenly. "You done so well, tonight. You saved people tonight." There were no khepri left in the tumbledown church. "Now you got to go. I'll see you back there. Go quickly." Ori realised he was breathing hard, that he was bloodied from wounds, exhausted and shaking. "Go, get back, we'll debrief. Tonight, Creekside's protected by the Militant Sundry. Humans with weapons are legitimate targets."

* * *

In the Badside hide. Dawn was pushing at the walls. They lay and fixed each other with unguent and bandages.

"Baron don't care, you know," Ori said. He spoke quietly to Old Shoulder while they made nepenthe-spiced tea. "I saw him. He didn't care if them khepri women died. He didn't care if them Quillers got them. He don't care about anything. He scares me."

"Scares me too, boy."

"Why's Toro *keep* him? Why's he here?"

Old Shoulder looked at him over the pot, spooned resin in and honeyed it.

"He's here, boy . . . because he hates the chair-of-the-board more than we do. He'll do whatever he has to, to bring you-know-who down. It was *you* brought him, Jabber's sake. You was right to. We can keep an eye on him."

Ori said nothing.

"I know what I'm doing," Old Shoulder said. "We can keep him watched."

Ori said nothing.

Fires in Howl Barrow, in Echomire, in Murkside. Riots in Creek-side and Dog Fenn. Race-hate in the ghetto, ineffectual powder gre-nades thrown from a Sud Line train at the Glasshouse, cracking two more of its frames. The Caucus put out posters deploring the at-tacks.

"What happened at the tower in Jabber's Mound?"

"Three sallies: first time they got the militia running, made it into the base. Then got beat back. Same as always."

Some weird thaumaturgy in Aspic Hole; self-defence commit-tees of the terrified respectable in Barrackham, in Chnum, in Nigh Sump where they were attacked by what everyone said was a mob of Remade.

"What a damn night. Gods." Things were breaking.

"And all because of that thing, that sun-thing."

"Nah, not really."

A critical mass of fear was what it had been, what it had released—a terror and a rage that found outlet. *Protect us,* people had shouted, tearing at the mechanisms that claimed to look after them. "It was just a catalyst," Ori said.

"What in the name of Jabber and his godsdamn saints *was* that thing?"

"I know." Whenever Baron spoke his comrades were quiet. "I know, or at least I know what I think it is, and I think so because it's what the militia and the Mayor think too.

"What they call a witnessing. Remote viewer. Tesh camera. Come to see what we're about. The state of us."

They were aghast.

"I told you. We ain't winning the war. It ain't as powerful as that—it didn't touch us, did it? The war ain't over yet. But yes, they're spying on us. And as well as all them normal spies they must have, they ain't afraid to show us, now, they're watching. They got strange gris-gris, the Tesh. Their science ain't ours. They've eyeballed us. There'll be more."

At the other end of the world, around the corners of coastlines, where physics, thaumaturgy, geography were different, where rock was gas, where settlements were built on the bones of exploration, where traders and pioneers had died at the savage justice of the western Rohagi, where there were cities and states and monarchies without cognates in Crobuzoner philosophy, a war was being fought. The militia exerting New Crobuzon's claims, fighting for territories and commodity chains, for theories, they said. Fighting for something unclear. And in response to bullets, the powderbombs, the thaumaturgy, burncurs and elementalists of New Crobuzon, Tesh, City of the Crawling Liquid, had sent this witnessing, to learn them.

"How?" Ori said. "New Crobuzon . . . It's the strongest . . . ain't it?"

"You going to swallow that?" Enoch jeered. He sounded tired.

"New Crobuzon, greatest city-state in the world, and that? Horse-shit . . ."

"No it ain't," said Baron, and they were quiet again. "He's right. New Crobuzon *is* the strongest state in Bas-Lag. But sometimes it ain't the strongest wins. And especially when the stronger thinks, because it's stronger, that it ain't got to try to fight.

"We're getting outfought. And the government knows it. And they don't like it, and they're going to try to turn it into a victory, but here's the thing: they *know* they have to end this. They're going to sue for peace."

The sun kept rising, and its light through the warehouse windows reached at sharper and sharper angles and took them one at a time, tangled in their hair and shone from Old Shoulder's skin. Ori felt warm for the first time in hours.

"They're going to *surrender*?"

Of course they would not. Not explicitly—not in the speeches they would give, not in their history books or in the loyal newspapers. It would be a historic compromise, a nuanced strategy of magnificent precision. But even many of those loyal to the Mayor's Fat Sun Party and the partners in the Urban Unity Government would balk. They would know—everyone would know—what had been done. That New Crobuzon, however the Mayor put it, had been defeated.

"They're trying to now," Baron said, "but they don't even know how to speak to the Teshi. We ain't had contact with our mission there for years. And gods know there must be Teshi afuckingplenty in New Crobuzon now, but they ain't got no clue who, where they are. The embassy's *always* been empty. Teshi don't do things that way. They're trying thaumaturgy, message-boats, dirigibles . . . they'll do whatever they bloody have to. They'll try pigeon before long. They want a meeting. No one's going to know what's damn-well being done till they turn round and tell us 'Good news, the

Mayor's brought peace.' And in the meantime the poor bastards in the boats and on the ground'll keep fighting and dying."

Under alien skies. Ori felt vertigo.

"How do you know?" said Old Shoulder. He was standing, his legs locked, his arms folded. "How do you know what they think, Baron?"

Baron smiled. Ori looked down and hoped he would not see that smile again.

" 'Cause of who I'm talking to, Shoulder. You know how I know. After all them bloody pints I sunk in Brock Marsh, I know because I been talking to my new best friend, Bertold Sulion."

part five

RETREAD

CHAPTER SEVENTEEN

"HERE. THIS IS IT, HERE. THE EDGE OF IT. THE EDGE OF THE CACO-topic stain."

Long before that the arc-flight of buzzards was disrupted. They scattered. The coy unfolding walk of a jaguar faltered and the cat erupted, was gone. Dust and black smoke sent animals away. Hundreds of years changed at the arrival of that crude loudness.

Through an opening-up of earth, like a bacillus, some little organic thread sullying blood, infecting landscape, came the Iron Council. A steaming and sniffing metal animal god. As once they did years before, figures before it laid down rails, and others cleared its tracks, and others recycled them, took the left-behind path and hauled it in the path of the sounding engine.

Wherever it went it was intruder. It was never part of the land. It was an incursion of history in stubby hillside woodland and the thicker tree-pelt of real forest, valleys between mountains, canyon-plains horned randomly with monadnocks. It intruded in uncanny places, dissident landscape, creeping hills, squalls of smokestone and fulgurite statues, frozen storms of lightning.

An apparition. A town of men and women hacked at the ground, rendered it just flat enough to lay tracks. They were invaders.

Like their ancestors the first Councillors, some of whom were their own younger selves, they were muscled, weathered, expert. Remade, whole, cactus, alien other, a consummate industry, the rail-carriers with their tongs, the dropping of sleepers, hammer-blows tight enough to dance to.

They wore skins; they wore smocks and trousers made from sacks resewn. They wore jewels made of railway metal, and sang mongrel songs, bastards of decades-old construction chanties, and new lays telling their own story.

> West *we came to find a place to*
> Rest *to go without a trace and*
> Live *our lives Remade and free to*
> Give *ourselves our liberty*

In the centre of the swarm, hundreds of figures attending to its complex fussy needs, protected by guards, lookouts at the hills and treetops and in the air, came the cause of it all, the train. Marked by time. It was altered. The train had gone feral.

The abattoirs, the bunks, the guntower, the library, the mess hall, the work-cabs, all the old carriages were there, but changed. They were crenellated, baroque and topped with dovecots. Rope bridges joined new towers on different carriages and sagged and went tight at the slight curving of the Iron Council's path. Siege engines were bolted to the roofs. New windows were cut into the carriages' sides. Some were thickened with ivy and waxy vines, spilling from them as if they were old churches, winding the length of the guntower. Two of the flatbeds were filled with kitchen gardens full of herbs. Two others were also earth-filled, but only grass grew on them, between gravestones. A little pack of half-tame motion demons bit playfully at the Council's wheels.

There were new carriages, one built all of water-smoothed driftwood, caulked with resin, tottering on spare, newly smelted or reclaimed wheels. Cars for alien Councillors, mobile pools for water-dwellers. The train was long, pushed and pulled by its engines. Two in the back, two at the front, their smokestacks all amended with metal flanges, painted and stained in crushed-earth colours to mimic flames. And at the very front of the train the largest, behind its flaring guard-skirt, was so amended and reshaped with crude art that it looked to have distended over the years, almost buckled with gigantism.

Its headlamps were eyes now, predictably, bristling with thick wire lashes, its cowcatcher a jawful of protruding teeth. The huge tusks of wilderness animals were strapped and bolted to them. The front nub of its chimney wore a huge welded nose, the smokestack ajut from it in nonsense anatomy. Sharpened girders gave it horns. And behind that enormous unwieldy face the engine was crowded with trophies and totems. The skulls and chitin headcases of a menagerie glared dead ferocity from its flanks: toothy and agape, flat, eyeless, horned, lamprey-mouthed with cilia-teeth, bone-ridged, shockingly human, intricate. Where they had them the trophies' skins were tanned, drabbed by preservation, bones and teeth mazed with cracks and discoloured by smoke. The befaced engine wore dead like a raucous hunter god.

They cut their way on the echo of another path. Sometimes it was gone from view, or geography had twisted in the decades. They might spend hours splitting rocks by the side of hill-shadowed lakes to reach a fissure and, hacking through bramble and the outskirts of bosk, part crabgrass and uncover the ghost of a roadbed, the root-claimed ridge on which years ago they had come the other way. They found caches of rails, savaged by years, and sleepers, some still laid, covered in greased tarpaulin that had stained the earth. They placed their tracks to meet the ends waiting for them.

We left these, the oldsters who had been there at the laying said. *I remember now. To make it easier. You never know, we said, when we · might have to come back.* The left-behind rails sped them. Gifts from their young selves, wrapped in oilcloth in rock-toothed country.

Judah Low taught Cutter to lay tracks.

They had come quietly, the draggled party, into the grasses, when first they had come. They had reached their destination stunned by their arrival. Pomeroy and Elsie quite silent. Drogon the whisper-smith pulling his brimmed hat down. Qurabin invisible and felt, tired and diminished by the exertions of scouting, secret-finding. Cutter standing by Judah when he could. When he could, holding Judah's hand.

Under uncoiling clouds in a grassland were miles of garden. Dense crops abutting each other, bounded by an iron ellipsis of tracks. Beyond the rails other fields were scattered, dissipating and merging with wild flora.

The guides led them there, the grass unsealing and sealing again. They watched all the figures working at their husbandry. A farmland, out here where there was nothing. Most of the party was mute. Judah smiled without ceasing, and muttered *Long live.* Men and women came along the paths, by sod huts that fringed the railroad, all the topography of normality, an everyday farmstead village, passed through by a train.

Judah watched the locals, and when they came close enough he would laugh and shout *Long live,* and they would nod in response.

"Hello, hello, hello," Judah said as a very young child neared, its father half-watching from where he sharpened a scythe. Judah squatted. "Hello, hello, little comrade, little sister, little chaver," he said. He made a benediction with his hand. "What's it like, hey?"

And then he stepped back and simply sounded in happiness. The noise he made had been without syllables or shape, was nude delight, as he heard metal wincing and saw clouds of soot spoor, and as the train, the Iron Council, came through the grass. As the towering and shaking iron wood rope and found-sculpture wheeled town rolled out of the grasses and came at them.

They dropped what they carried. "Iron Council." "Iron Council." Each of them said it as the tusked train came.

It came, repeating its few-miles, as it had for so long, neither sedentary nor nomadic, describing its home. It was stopping.

"I'm Judah Low," he shouted. He went toward it as if it were drawing in to a station. "I'm Judah Low." Someone had stepped from the engine cab, and Cutter had heard a shout, a greeting whose words he could not pick apart but that had made Judah run and scream and scream a name. "Ann-Hari!"

CHAPTER EIGHTEEN

THERE HAD BEEN MARSHLAND. CAMOUFLAGED FENS WHERE WHAT seemed earth and crabgrass became suddenly only a layer of plant on thick water. The Iron Councillors laid down rock fragments, pontoons, sunk pillars quickly cut from woods. They saw copses of stumps weathered by more than two decades and interspersed with neonate trees, where they had taken timber on their way out. The Iron Council moved slowly on rails just above or just below the water. The train became a sedate creature of the shallows. Below it, around it, came noises of bolotnyi and bog-things.

Pomeroy laid tracks. Elsie went with the foragers. Qurabin came at night to the travellers and told them things she or he had found in the hills and swamps. Secret things. In the monk's slow surrender to the cost of revelations, Cutter sensed a sadness, a coward's eagerness to die. Qurabin had lost everything and was dissolving into the world with pointless worship.

Drogon the whispersmith was a guard. One of the gunmen who watched the Council in its gushing steaming progress. Cutter was with Judah—he would not let him go. They put down tracks together.

Judah was a fairy tale. The children would come to watch him, and not only them but men and women who had not been born when the Iron Council crossed the world. He was kind. He would make golems for them, which delighted them. They had all heard of his golems. They sang to him once, around a fire, as vaguely animal trees tried to shy from the sound.

They sang Judah a story of Judah. They sang in chanty counterpoint about when he fixed the soldiers with a mud monster and saved the Iron Council, and then how he went into the desert and made an army, and then how he went to the under-hill court of the king of the trow and made a woman out of the princess' bedsheet and how the sheet and trow had swapped places and how Judah Low had eloped with the troglodyte princess and gone across the sea.

At night Cutter pressed himself to Judah and the older man would sometimes respond, with his beneficent restraint. Cutter would push into Judah or open to him. On the nights they were not together, Judah was with Ann-Hari.

"I got your message," Judah had said, the first night, when they arrived. "Your cylinder. Rahul's voice. About Uzman. Long live."

"Long live."

Uzman died suddenly, she told him, a swift shutdown, of his organic or pipework tubes they never knew.

"You still have the voxiterator?"

"How many messages you got from us?"

"Four."

"We sent nine. Give them to someone going to the coast to trade, to give to a ship, that says it's going south, that might go through the straits, that might get past Tesh, that might get to Myrshock, and then to New Crobuzon. I wonder which ones you got."

"I have them with me. You can tell me what I missed."

They smiled at each other, a middle-aged man and a woman who looked much older, sunburnt and effort-lined, but whose energy was as great as his. Cutter was awed by her.

At the long first evening of introductions they met Thick Shanks. He was dethorned, and Judah hugged the brawny, greying cactus-man hard. There were others the golemist recognised and greeted with joy, but it was Shanks and Ann-Hari who filled him.

Others he knew lived quiet as farmers, had become nomads, trappers, hunters bushed with beards. There were newcomers at the head of the Council, with Ann-Hari.

Where she walked she was greeted. Thin and hard, lined, uglied perhaps by time but an astounding ugliness, vivid and passionate. As the train travelled it came to the factories, farmsteads, silos and halls that in the years had spread beyond the train. Ann-Hari would fetch down to walk wherever they stopped.

People gave her fruit, cakes of spiced game she shared among her entourage, a patrol of women, some seventy, some in their teens. Cutter saw the strange love in which she was held. She took Judah's arm. They were a stately couple. The Iron Councillors would cheer and tell Judah how welcome he was, give the others food and drink, kiss their cheeks. They shouted in strange accents: New Crobuzon gone skewwhiff.

The perpetual train was town hall, church and temple. It was the keep. It whistled as it went, prowling the perimeter of its land of peasants, hunters, surgeons, teachers, drivers of the train. There were cactus-men and a very few cactus-women, and a handful of vodyanoi, the dowsers and diviners and their children. The sky was full of scudding wyrmen. The oldest of them had forgotten New Crobuzon; the youngest had never seen it.

Other races were there in little clutches: though New Crobuzon Ragamoll was the main tongue, there were those who cough-talked in arcane tonal systems. Immigrants to this track-layers' land. The young were whole, of course, born without Remaking, but of those humans in their forties and above, most were Remade. They were the first Councillors. Those who had made the Council.

The spectre of the roadbed climbed slopes. *Look, there.* Veins through the stone. *Ain't this where we lost Marimon? On the crag yonder? It went up too fast and*—They paused, respectful, where topography reminded them of the long-dead.

Most hill animals fled the Council, but there were those airborne and rock-running predators who picked off stray travellers— mouthed things the size of bears that stalked sheer walls on pads or adhesive pulvilli, skin-winged tentacular masses on goat legs. Cactacae, with no meat smell to goad carnivores, were the best guards.

Where they could they retraced the Council's path. Sometimes they had to cut new paths. With powders synthesised in their made laboratories they broke through the matter of mountains. There were crag-ends and cliffs where the bridges they had made years before remained. Councillors would clamber out to test them, their footsteps echoed by crepitus as boards moved against each other. Many were fallen. Split wood lay weathered, mulched by insects, while above plank girders stubbed from hills.

They moved on quickly thrown-down tracks, on tracks already waiting scrubbed of rust. Where they reached cliff walls, they might see the scar of the old roadbed meander miles out of the way, while before them was a tunnel, crude but tall enough to take them. Over the years of the Council, battalions of tunnellers had come, in shifts, to cut passages, in case a quick return might one day be needed.

On the third day after their arrival, there was a trading. Striders raced in their stiff-legged, dimensionally disrespectful way through grass that did not move as it should at their approach. They laid before the Council's traders their arcane wares: a coagulum of hairs, phlegm and gemstones, some earth-spat bezoar.

"All sorts of ju-ju in that," a Councillor muttered to Cutter. Iron Council was privy to alien magics.

"If you can find us, you can trade with us." Grain, information, meat and engineering know-how. Above all Iron Council traded its experts' knowledge, selling them for a time, to dealers from The Brothers, from Vadaunk, from travelling tribes.

There were no cognates of this life. There was nothing like this. Cutter was agitated. He could not remember a time he had not known of the Council. As a child it was a strange story, as an older boy an adventure, as a man come to politics it had been some kind of possibility. And now he was here and though he could not have quite expressed his disappointment, he felt it.

He could not map the alterity he felt. He raged silently that he could see little in this life he had not seen before, and that yet each moment those he watched were farming, looking after animals, writing, arguing and helping children and performing a thousand actions he had seen all his life, they looked and felt like new things. He could not understand why this man stripping and repainting the train was doing something Cutter had seen before.

Except for some used for trading beyond the rails, there was no money. That angered him somehow. He had never seen why insurrectionists should want to mimic those old village fiefdoms in the badlands where landworkers never saw coin but took what the local big-man gave them. The cashless economy irritated him as an affectation. It made no difference whether it was for coin—painting was up-down with a brush, money or not.

It took him days to know that he was wrong. Something was very not the same. The painting was different, and the ploughing, knife-grinding, bookkeeping. *These are new people,* he thought. *They ain't the same as me.* Cutter was terribly troubled.

For a horrible day he almost despised what he saw. He hated it for how it kept him out. For being not strange enough and being so strange. And then he knew that it was not the Council, it was—of course, of course—it was him.

I weren't here when this was made. I didn't make this like the old ones did; I weren't born to it like the young. I didn't make this place, so it didn't make me.

"Was a long time coming here." The travellers, Ann-Hari, and others of the guiding committee had spent an evening in the mess hall. A hammer-rhythm song telling the story of Iron Council's journey west, recorded in snips on the antiquated voxiterator, was given to Judah: "Songs for the golem man."

"I'll tell you some real Council stories," one man said when the eating was done. "Not that those was lies, but they left off some things. You should know everything." It grew late and cold, and they picked at their flatbread as they listened. "Was a long time coming here," he said and told them of the cacotopic stain, though he would give no details. "We got off light" was all he'd say. "Near a month by the edge of the madlands."

He told them of more than two years sending out scouts across unknown unmapped land to be lost and many to die, squabbling over routes, learning techniques. The Council laying down tracks, blundering into wars. They had taken their train without intent between the ranks of feuding forest things that pattered them with darts and stones: animal-men accused them of invasion. The renegade train met representatives of half-heard-of countries: Vadaunk the mercenary kingdom; Gharcheltist, the aquapolis. The Iron Councillors learnt new languages, trade and politesse with brute and urgent efficiency. "Land went open after the cacotopos."

Poor bewildered little New Crobuzoners. They felt, Cutter sensed, a kind of pity for their younger selves traipsing dogged across places they could not comprehend. They felt their pasts gauche. At the time they must merely have blinked and kept walking, kept hammering, apologising where they realised they trespassed. There had been sacrifices—severe, dreadful prices to pay when they passed unknowing into this or that little despotism, crossed some potentate or quasigodling thing. "We took the Council once into that forest and there was that magma-horse took all our coal. Remember? Remember when we lost them boys to that ghast thing that left glass footprints?"

A landscape that punished outsiders. They were picked off by animals, by cold and heat. They starved, were sent to shivering deaths by illness, died of thirst when their watercarts got lost. They made themselves learn, constructing their absconder railway.

And they had warred themselves, when they had to, against tribes who would not take offerings for the right to pass into their lands. There was a time, which the Councillors described briefly in shame—The Idiocy, they called it—when the train itself had been ripped by civil war, over strategy, over how to continue. The generals of the caboose and those of the foremost engine had lobbed grenades at each other over the long yards of train between, a week of guerrilla actions on the roofs of the cars, butchery in corridors.

"It was a bad winter. We was hungry. We was stupid." No one could look up during that story.

But at last the grassland. They had mapped and made peace with the neighbours they found. "We got more maps than the New Crobuzon Library." The train kept moving. At very last, way west, their scouts found the sea.

"The train's our strength. We have to keep it strong." They could never have the train stand still. It would have been a betrayal. They knew—they always knew—that when they found the place where they could rest, where the land would support them, even then they would never let the train fall still. They worshipped it, in a profane way. They reshaped it, made it monstrous, kept its engines primed, able to power on anything that would burn. They had built a life.

Years. Throwing up structures as they needed them. Their town had grown. And nomads and lost adventurers of all races came to join the renegopolis. The Iron Council.

The town and its government were one. Its delegates, its committee were voted on by catchments based on work and age and random factors. There were vicious arguments, methods of persuasion not always admirable, a hinterland of democracy, patronage and charisma. There were those who advocated moving; those who said the wheels should stop. There had been factions within factions in the early years, over methods of industry and agriculture. They had continued to build life, delegating, being delegates, arguing, voting, disagreeing and making things work.

"Before, I was an oiler," the storyteller had said. "I oiled the wheels."

"And you know why I'm here," Judah had said. "Now it's time for you to reach a new decision. It's time for you to leave. To move again."

CHAPTER NINETEEN

CIVILISATIONS HAD BEEN IN THE TABLELANDS THROUGH WHICH they passed, in this strange puna. The Iron Council, tracking back in head-on collision with its own history, passed through ruins.

Something that had perhaps once been a temple, a town of temples. In the shadow of a cratered ziggurat they laid their tracks, and the vent of their engines rose over the vines. They drove home spikes and split corroded marble gods in the rootmass. The Iron Council made the dead home shiver with hammer-blows. It sooted the bas-reliefs of battles in heaven. The Iron Council cut through the ivy-clotted city, towers gone to moulder.

"I know a man from a long time gone," Judah had said to the committee. "We used to be partners. He was a government man for a time, works for some big concern now, but still has his ears open. He and me have history, and sometimes he needs golems for his work. And when he comes to me for that, we talk."

Judah had told Cutter of these strange conversations, Pennyhaugh half-crowing at Judah, become his enemy, but them still drinking together. Not debates but performances. "I only see him because he gives me information, and I can give it to the Caucus," Judah said. "And I don't know . . . I don't think he's stupid enough just to sound off. It's some kind of *gift*."

The committee listened. There were the middle-aged, and Re-mades who remembered New Crobuzon, women who had once been the camp's whores: but more than half the delegates were young, had been children or unborn when the Council was made. They watched Judah speak.

"There are always rumours. I asked him, like I know how to do, so he thinks he's offering it to me. He told me what was happening. You know there's war against Tesh." They did not know the details, but so big a war as this made Bas-Lag shudder, and stories reached the Iron Council by bush-adventurers.

"There's slaughter in the Firewater Straits: they call it the Sanguine Straits now. They broke the Witchocracy's thalassomach hex, and the navy's pushing ships through, all the way around the coast. Thousands of miles. But another expedition set off, weeks back. Below the warships. Ictineos. Maybe grindylow-led, I don't know. But they're coming. It'd take a long time, but they must be nearly here. Might have made landfall.

"They never forgot you in the city, you know. They never forgot Iron Council. Long live. People whisper the words. Your name's on walls. Parliament never forgave you, never forgot what you done. And now they know where you are."

He had waited for their alarm to subside.

"You couldn't stay hid forever. You knew it. I don't know how they know. Godspit, it's been more'n twenty years, it could be anything. A wanderer tells another tells another tells another: it could have been one of your own, finding their way back to New Crobuzon, caught and interrogated. It could be a spy." He spoke over the noise that spurred. "Far-seeing on a new scale. I don't know. Point is they *know where you are.* They found you. I don't even know how long they've known. But *they'd* never get a troop across the cacotopic stain, or through the Galaggi Veldt and forests and whatever—*we* had Qurabin." *But we didn't at first, Judah,* Cutter thought. *What were you planning to do?* "But with the war, that's changed. Because the Firewater Straits are open.

"They're coming *all the way round,* by sea. They're trying to get past Tesh, up past Maru'ahm, and they'll land on the edge of the grasslands. They'll come at you not from the east but the *west.* They could never do that till now.

"Sisters, Councillors, comrades. You're about to be attacked. And there'll be no quarter. They're coming to destroy you. They can't allow you to continue. You *got away.* And sisters . . . now more than ever they need to finish it."

It was hard for Judah to make the Councillors understand about the chaos in New Crobuzon. The older ones remembered their own strikes and the great shucking off in which they culminated, but New Crobuzon itself was an old old memory and thousands of miles away. Judah tried to make the troubles live to them. "There is something happening," he said.

"They have to bring you back in pieces. So they can say to the citizens, *See what we done. See what we do to them as tries to rise. See what's been done to your Council.*

"They're coming to destroy you. It's time to move, to relay the tracks. You have to go. You could go north—I don't know. Take it up to the tundra. An ice-train with the bear-riders. Up to the Cold Claws. I don't know. Hide again. But you have to go. Because they've found you, they're coming for you, and they won't stop till you're gone."

"*Yeah, they could hide,*" Drogon said in Cutter's ear, sudden and insistent. "*Or there's another possibility. They could come back. Tell them they have to come back. Tell them.*"

He did not whisper it as an instruction, but he spoke so urgently, with such sudden fervour, that Cutter obeyed him.

* * *

For days the Council was stunned enough that it could not plan. It had no sentimentality about its sedentary town. They had always insisted that the train was where they lived, that other buildings were only annexes, cabs without wheels. But the resources they had accrued over years, hard-won, would be missed.

"We should stay. We can take whatever comes," the younger Councillors declared, and their parents, the Remade, strove to tell their children what New Crobuzon was.

"This ain't a band of striders," they said. "This ain't horse-thieves. This is a different thing. Listen to Low."

"Yeah, but we've techniques now, that, no disrespect to Mr. Low, he don't know about. Moss-magic, cirriomancy—does he know about them?" Thaumaturgy learnt from arcane natives. Their parents shook their heads.

"This is New Crobuzon. Forget that. It ain't like that."

Judah unwrapped the braced mirror that Cutter had brought him. "There's only one," he said. "The other's broken and without it this isn't a weapon. But even if we had another, it wouldn't be enough. You have to go."

They had sent the cleverest of the wyrmen to watch the coast hundreds of miles off. A week passed. "Found nothing," the first said when it came back, and Judah had grown angry. "They're coming," he said.

He refused to advise anything specific. Drogon, though, had become maniacal in his desire for the Council to return. He told the Councillors again and again that it was their duty to return. It was a strange fervour.

Cutter went to dances. The raucousness of them calmed him, the drunk young men and women kicking to peasant waltzes. He swapped partners and drank and ate their drugged fruit. He went with a tough young man he could grab and handfuck and even kiss so long as it was some kind of boys' play, not sex but wrestling or somesuch. Afterward, wiping his hand, he found the man talkative about what Iron Council should do.

"Everyone knows we'll leave," he said. "What, we going to ignore Judah Low? And some say go up and some say down, and no one's sure which way we'll head, but me and more and more others, we've another plan. We been thinking. We say don't go north or south, we say go *east*. Back along the tracks we left. We say it's time to go home. Back to New Crobuzon."

It was not Drogon's doing, Cutter realised. It was a native desire.

"I think something is coming," Qurabin said, a disembodied voice.

Drogon said, *"They know it's coming. And more and more of them want to head for New Crobuzon."*

"No," Judah said. Cutter saw many things in him: a pride, a fear and anger, exasperation, confusion. "No, they're insane. They'll die. If they can't face one New Crobuzon battalion, how'll they face the city? It don't make any sense to run from the militia to the militia. They can't come back."

"That ain't what they're banking on. You fired them up, didn't you? With all your talk about what's happening. They think they might tip the balance, Judah. And I think they might be right. They want to return to crowds, throwing petals at the rails. They want to come home to a new city."

"No," said Judah, but Cutter saw excitement in Pomeroy, in Elsie. He felt something of it through his own sardonics and reserve.

There was a clamour to go back. "It's a matter of speed," one old Remade woman said. "When we come here we laid down spare iron, so as if we needed to get away, they were waiting. Well, we've people coming for us now, and we've a lot of miles between us and safety, and we need speed. Them tracks is waiting. A mile here, two there. Be idiocy not to use them." She pretended pragmatism.

Judah argued, but he was proud, Cutter saw, of his Council's desire to return, to be something in this New Crobuzon moment. He wanted to dissuade them out of fear, but he wanted not to—Cutter saw this—for a sense of history.

"You don't know," he said, and he spoke gently. "You don't know what it'll be, what'll be happening there. We need you to survive. It's more important than anything. I've been your damn bard, and I need you to survive."

"This ain't—forgive me, Mr. Low, with all respect—this ain't about what you need but what we need. We can't take the bastards on their way, so if we're to run, let's make our running something. Let's get word to New Crobuzon. Tell them we're coming home." That was a young man born five years after the Council, raised in the grasses.

Ann-Hari stood. She began to declaim.

I am not New Crobuzon born, she told them, and expounded her life in brute oratory. "I never knew I could have a country: Iron Council is my country, and what do I care about New Crobuzon? But Iron Council is an ungrateful child, and I ever loved ungrateful children. New Crobuzon deserves no gratitude—I been there and I know—and we are the child that freed ourselves. No other did. And all the other children are ungrateful now, and we can help them."

To Cutter it was as if Judah's party had liberated the Iron Council, had uncoupled it from some restraint, that it was taken by a tendency long immanent. Whatever reasons they gave, the Councillors arguing to go back seemed to voice something embedded, that they had wanted a long time. They were avid at the insurgency Judah described.

When he tried to think it in words, Cutter could not make it clear. They had come—he had come—so far, at such cost, to warn the Council that it should *flee:* how could it possibly face the city?

But though he could not express it, Cutter felt the logic of re-turn. He felt it swell as Ann-Hari spoke, and he was not the only one.

The Councillors cheered her and shouted her name, and shouted "New Crobuzon."

Elsie and Pomeroy exulted. They had never expected this. Qurabin made a sound of pleasure, no more supportive of New Crobuzon than of the Tesh who had betrayed the monastery, and impressed by the Councillors and their welcome. Qurabin was glad to be part of whatever exertion this would be. Drogon was delighted. Judah was silent, proud and frightened.

Cutter saw Judah's fear. *You need it to be a legend, don't you?* he thought. *This troubles you, this it-coming-back. You love it for want-ing to, but you need it safe, the thing you made. Something we can dream of.* Judah would do anything for the Iron Council, anything at all. Cutter saw that. Judah's love for it was complete.

They took the town down, broke their mud-and-wattle, their meet-ing houses, turned them to dust. They gathered what crops they could. There were plenty of those among the Councillors who were outraged.

The perpetual train, even with its new rolling stock in the strange materia of the wide lands, its rough wood and mineral cars, could not contain all the Councillors. There were hundreds who would be, again, camp followers, nomads in the train's trail. A few would not come. Some went for the hills, or insisted they would stay as farmers in the settled land, surrounded by remnants of the torn-up iron road.

"You'll die," Judah told them, "when they come." And they re-sponded with bluff and bravado. It would come to nothing, Cutter thought, when the New Crobuzon Militia appeared, its most pow-erful and well-armed squads, to where they thought they would find their quarry and instead met fifty aging farmers. He watched them, knowing they were dead. *May they kill you quick.*

Cutter did not know if Ann-Hari and Judah were lovers, but they loved one another in a deep and simple way. He was jealous, yes, but no more than of the other people Judah loved. Cutter was used to this thing so unrequited.

Judah was with Ann-Hari the night before the Iron Council left its grassland sanctuary. Cutter was alone, holding himself and remembering the night he had tussled with the muscular young man.

The next day they gathered: there was Cutter in the outskirt land where wild grass was crushed by the train and by the farmers. And there brawny Pomeroy swinging his weapon playfully, like a scythe, and Elsie her arm around her man's waist, and Drogon in his brimmed hat leading the mount he had persuaded the horse-husbanders of the Iron Council to give him, his lips moving and Cutter not sure to whom he spoke, and there the grass fluttered as Qurabin moved along secret ways revealed by his or her strange godling, and out ahead arm-in-arm walked Ann-Hari and Judah Low, investigated by the insects of the morning.

Behind them the Iron Council came. They would fall into line soon, would help lay tracks, help break the stone and wind through the sarsen blocks of the lowlands, but for now they walked ahead. The ellipse of iron was unwinding, the Councillors were track-layers again. And scouts and water dowsers, hunters and graders, but above all layers of track, who uncoiled the edge of their town and put it down again in a straight line, back along land that bore still the faint trace of their arrival.

Way to their west came predatory militia, soldiers wanting only to destroy them. The Iron Council shuddered, and went on, went east, headed for New Crobuzon, home.

* * *

That was how it had been. And then to this edge, this most literal badland.

"Here. This is it, here. The edge of it. The edge of the cacotopic stain."

part six

———✦———

THE CAUCUS RACE

CHAPTER TWENTY

THE MONSTROUS WITHOUT—AND WITHIN. NEW CROBUZON'S TWIN ENEMIES: THE WATCHER AND THE TREACHEROUS. NIGHT OF SHAME.

The newspapers declaimed. They brought out extra-large fonts for their condemnations of the EyeSky Riots. There were heliotypes of the dead barricaded in shops and smothered by smoke, crushed in falls from windows, shot.

In The Grocer's Sweetheart on the Chainday after, Ori expected the *Runagate Rampant* meeting to be overflowing, but no one was there. He came back the next night and the next, looking for a face he remembered. At last on Dustday he saw the knit-worker, gathering money, whispering in the landlord's ear.

"Jack," said Ori. She turned, untrusting, and her face only opened a very little when she saw it was him.

"Jack," she said.

"It'll have to be fast," she said. "I have to go. Wine, then, go on.

"Spiralling down, eh?" she said, pointing at the coil-marks on his clothes. "I see them all over now. They've gone from walls to clothes. Cactus punks are wearing them, Nuevists, radicals. What do they mean?"

"A link," he said carefully. "To Half-a-Prayer. I know the man who started them."

"I heard of him, I think . . ."

"He's a friend of mine. I know him well." There was silence. They drank. "Missed the meeting."

"There ain't no meetings now. You mad, Ori . . . Jack?" She was horrified. "I'm sorry, Jack," she said, "really sorry. Curdin told me your name. And where you live. He shouldn't have done, but he was keen I be able to get *Double-R* to you, if need be. I told no one."

He contained his shock, shook his head.

"The meetings?" he said, and she forgot her contrition quickly.

"Why would we have meetings?" she said. "When it's going on?" Ori shook his head, and she gave a sound almost a sob. "Jack, Jack . . . Jabber's *sake*. What are you *doing*? Weren't you *there*?"

"Godsdammit, of course I was. I was in Creekside. I was . . ." He lowered his voice. "Who are the Militant Sundry, any damn way? I was trying to stand up for the godsdamned khepri your bloody brainless *commonalty* were busy trying to butcher."

"The Sundry? Well, if you was xenian and all you'd had in your corner were the comprador bastards in the Divers Tendency, wouldn't you turn somewhere else? And don't you *dare*. Don't you dare scorn people. You know the Quillers take up the human dust. Even your friend Petron knows that—and don't bloody look at me like that, Jack, everyone knows his name, he was in the Flexibles. And I ain't sure of all the bloody lunacies the Nuevists do, faddling about dressed as animals, silly bloody games, but I'd trust him. I don't know as I'd trust you, Jack, and that's a sad thing, because it ain't that I think you don't want what I want. I know you do. But I don't trust your judgement. I think you're a fool, Jack."

Ori was not even outraged. He was used to the arrogance of the Runagates. He looked at her with cool annoyance, and, yes, a residue of respect, a due she had inherited from Curdin.

"While you're playing prophets, Jack," he said, "keep your eyes open. When I move . . . you'll *know*. We have plans."

"They say Iron Council's coming back."

Her face had taken on such joy.

"It's coming back."

All the things Ori could think to say were obvious. He did not want to insult her, so he tried to think of something else to say, but could not.

"It's a fairy tale," he said.

"It ain't."

"A fable. There's no Iron Council."

"They want you to think that. If there's no Iron Council, then we ain't never took power. But if there is, and there *is*, we did it before, we can do it again."

"Good Jabber, listen to yourself . . ."

"You telling me you never seen the helios? What do you think that was? You think they built the bloody train by marching alongside each other, women, *whores*, at the front? Children riding the damn cab hood?"

"Something happened, of course it did, but they were put down. It was a strike is all. They're long dead—"

She was laughing. "You don't know, you don't know. They wanted them dead, and they want them dead again, but they're coming back. Someone from the Caucus set out for them. We got a message. Why'd they be going, if not to tell them to return?

"Haven't you seen the graffiti?" she said. "All over. Along with all them coils and spirals you're wearing. *IC You*. Iron Council, You. It's coming back, and even just knowing that's a godsdamned inspiration."

"People want them, they'll find them, they'll believe in them, Jack . . ."

"What you don't know," she said, and didn't even look angry anymore, "is that we're moving. If you could hear the Caucus." She sipped her drink. She looked at him, some kind of challenge. *She's sitting on the damn* Caucus. The cabal of insurrectionists, the truce of the factions and the unaligned.

"There are those in Parliament trying to cosy up, you know. They can't admit it, but there are factories where *we* decide if people go to work or not. They want to negotiate. Parliament ain't the only decider in New Crobuzon anymore. There's two powers now."

The knit-worker stretched her hand across the table.

"Madeleina," she said deliberately. "Di Farja."

He shook her hand, moved by her trust. "Ori," he said, as if she didn't know.

"I tell you something, Ori. We're in a race. The Caucus is in a race to get things ready. It'll be weeks or months yet. And we won't just go round and round—we're making it a race *to* something. We ain't stupid, you know. We're racing to build what we have to, chains of—" She looked around. "—chains of *command*, communication. Last night was the start. There's a way to go, but it's started. The war's going sour, they say. The maimed'll fill the streets. If Tesh could send over that—" She closed her eyes and held her breath, retrospectively aghast. "—that thing, that sky-born witness, what else might they do? Time . . . we ain't got much time.

"And the Iron Council's coming back," she said. "When people hear that, it'll go off."

Maybe we're all together, Ori thought with a plaintiveness that troubled him. *Maybe the Caucus race is our race too . . .*

"We're all racing," he said.

"Yeah, but some of us in the wrong direction."

He thought then of what it would be. Of that moment when the dispossessed, the toilers, the, yes if she wanted, yes, the commonalty heard that the *Mayor*, the head of the Fat Sun, the arbiter of New Crobuzon, was *gone*. What that would be.

"You want to talk inspiration?" he said. He was angry again, at her monomaniac prescription. "That I'll give you," he said. "You'll thank me, Jack. What we're doing, what *we're* doing . . . we need to *wake people up.*"

"They're already awake, Jack. That's what you don't see."

He shook his head.

Bertold Sulion the Clypean Guard had lost his commitment to New Crobuzon, to the Mayor, to the law he was pledged to. Baron told them.

"It's bled out of him," he said. "You ain't trusted to much when you're a Clypean. The oath you take says it all: *I see and hear only what the Mayor and my charges allow me to.* Bertold don't know so much. But he knows the war's being lost. And he's seen the deals they'll do while them he trained with fight and die. It's all gone rancid. His loyalty's bled out of him and there ain't nothing left.

"That's the thing," he said. He spoke with care. "It's in you like your blood." He patted his sternum. "And when it goes bad, when it goes septic, you might say, you bleed it out and then either something else fills it, or it leaves you empty. Sulion ain't got nothing in him anymore. He wants to grass, and for form's sake, he's asking a lot of money for it, but it *ain't* the money he wants. He wants to betray because he wants to betray. He wants us to help him go bad. Whether he knows it or not."

They were not in Badside. *Here are keys for you,* the note had said, pinned by one of the two-horned cesti to the wall. *We have a new meeting house.* An address. Ori had read the note with Enoch, and they had stared at each other. Enoch was a stupid man, but this time Ori shared his confusion. "Flag Hill?"

At the edge of the city, at the end of the Head Line unrolling north from Perdido Street Station, Flag Hill was where the bankers and industrialists lived, the officials, the wealthiest artists. It was a landscape of wide-open ways and sumptuous houses sheer onto the streets, backing onto shared gardens. There were flowering trees and banyans spilling their knotting creepers and making them roots and trunks, emerging from between black paving.

There had been a slum in Flag Hill for years, like an abscess: an oddity of city planning. Mayor Tremulo the Reformer, two centuries past, had ordered some streets of modest housing built on the slopes of the rise that gave the area its name, so that the heroes of the Pirate Wars, he said, could live by those they had defended. The Flag Hill rich had not welcomed the newcomers, and Mayor Tremulo's schemes for "social merging" had been made risible. Without money what had been modest became a slum. Slate and brick went sickly. The little community of Flag Hill poor came in and out by train, while their neighbours disdained the raised rails for private hansoms, and waited for squalor to reach a critical mass. It had done so fifteen years before.

The poor had been removed from their collapsing houses, settled in ten- and fifteen-floor blocks of concrete in Echomire and Aspic. And then their once-neighbours had moved curiously into the deserted, hollowed rookeries, and money had at last come. Some buildings had been made into houses for the new wealthy, shored up and two or three holed together: to live in reconfigured "base cottages" became a fashion. But several streets at the heart of Flag Hill's nameless poverty district had been preserved, architecture as aspic, and made a slum museum.

It was through this that Ori and Enoch came. They had cleaned themselves, worn their better clothes. Ori had never been to this street-long memorial to poverty. There was no rot, of course, no smell, nor had there been for more than a decade. But the windows were still broken (their shard edges reinforced by subtle braces to prevent more cracking), the walls still bowed by damp and discoloured (thaumaturgy and joists holding them at the point of their collapse).

The houses were labelled. Brass plaques by their doors told the history of the slum, and talked of the conditions in which the in-

habitants had lived. HERE, Ori read, CAN BE SEEN SCARS OF THE ARSON
AND ACCIDENTAL CONFLAGRATIONS THAT PLAGUED THE STREETS, FORC-
ING THE LOCALS TO ENDURE LIFE IN THE SPOILS OF FIRE. The house was
smoked and char-dark. Its carbonised skin was sealed under a
matte varnish.

There were front rooms and outhouses that could be entered. A
FAMILY OF SIX OR EIGHT MIGHT CROWD INTO SUCH TERRIBLE SURROUND-
INGS. The detritus of slum life was left in place, sterilised and dusted
by attendants. IT SEEMS UNBELIEVABLE THAT IN MODERN TIMES SUCH
SQUALOR COULD GO UNCHECKED.

The house to which they had been directed was a classic of Flag Hill
architecture: big, beautiful, mosaiced in painted pebbles. Ori wondered if he had misread the address, but their keys worked. Enoch
was frowning. "I been here before," he said.

It was empty. It was a sham house. Its rooms were bone-
colourless, as were its curtains. Enoch's awe at the house and the
gardens annoyed Ori.

There were people on the Flag Hill streets, men in tailored jack-
ets, women in scarves. Mostly it was humans, but not only. There
were canals here, and a community of wealthy vodyanoi who
passed with their jump-crawl, dressed in light waterproof mumming of suits, chewing the cheroots that humans smoked and the
vodyanoi would eat. There might pass a cactus now and then, some
rare uptown achiever. There were constructs here, jolting steam-
figures that gave Ori nostalgia for his childhood when they had
been everywhere. The Flag Hillers were wealthy enough to afford
the licences, to have their equipment pass the assiduous tests insti-
tuted in the aftermath of the Construct War. Mostly, though, even
the rich had golems.

They walked with inhuman care, empty-eyed clay or stone or
wood or wire men and women. They carried bags, they carried
their owners, looking from side to side in mimicry of human mo-

tion, as if they could see through those pointless eyes, as if they did not sense mindlessly and abnaturally to follow their instructions.

When the other Toroans arrived, they all asked the question: "What are we doing here?"

When Baron came he was dressed as smartly as a local. He wore the lambswool, the fine sifted cotton and silk easily. They gaped.

"Oh yes," he said. Shaven, cleaned, smoking a prerolled cigarillo. "You're my staff, now. Best get used to it." He sat with his back to the wall in their new, huge, empty room, and told them about Bertold Sulion.

Toro was with them. Ori realised it. He did not know how long that strange-silhouetted figure had been standing at the edge, with the oil-light drawing the edges of its horns. It was evening.

"Why are we here, Bull?" he said. "Where's Ulliam?"

"Ulliam can't come often. Remade would be a rarity on these streets. You're here because I told you to be. Shut up and learn why. I'll give you money. You get clothes. You're servants now. Anyone sees you, you're butlers, footmen, scullery maids. You keep yourselves clean. Got to fit in."

"Was Badside compromised?" Ruby said. Toro did not sit, but seemed to lean, to be resting held up on nothing. Ori could feel the hex in those horns.

"You know what we aim to do. You know what we've wanted, what we build for." Toro's unnatural deep tones were a constant shock, a static charge. "The chair-of-the-board is in Parliament. On Strack Island. In the river. Vodyanoi militia in the water, cactus guards, officers in every chamber. Thaumaturges, the best in the city, putting up buffers and orneryblocks, charmtraps, all sorts. We ain't getting into Parliament.

"And then there's the Spike, and Perdido Street Station. You-know-who has to spend a lot of time in the Spike. Commanding the militia. Or in the station. In the embassy wing, in the high-tower." It was more than the hub of New Crobuzon's trains. It was a town, in three dimensions, encased in brick. The vastness of its mad-made architecture disobeyed not only rules of style but, it was said, of physics.

"When our quarry's there, it ain't as if it's just the Perdidae we got to face." Not that they would be easy to defeat. The dedicated submilitia given over to protect the station were well-armed and trained. "Wherever the chair-of-the-board goes, the Clypeans go. They're our worry.

"What about in town? When did you last see any Fat Sun bigwig give a speech? They're too scared, too busy trying to make secret peace with Tesh. So we need another strategy." There was a long quiet.

"You-know-who is very close, intimate with one particular magister. Magister Legus. Weekly they meet. There's all rumours, if you know who to ask. At Legus' *private* house. Where he lives as a citizen, takes off his mask. They settle down in private. Sometimes they don't part again until the morning.

"Happens every week, sometimes twice. In the magister's house.

"The house next door."

Tumult. *How do you* know? someone was shouting, and *You can't,* and *Whose is this place? How did you get this?* and on.

Ori had a memory. Something in him flinched from an understanding, unsettling, that veered close and was gone again and then was back. Ori saw others remembering, not sure what it was they remembered, not threading things together.

"It was hard to find out the true name behind a nom de jure," Toro was saying. "But I did it. Took me a long time. Tracked him down." Ori heard through gauze.

"This is the house . . ." Ori said, and then said nothing more. No one heard him and he was glad of that. He did not know what he wanted to do. He did not know what he felt.

This is the house where the old couple lived. That I heard about, the job you did, months ago, soon after I gave you the money. That the papers railed at. You killed them, or Old Shoulder did or one of us, and it weren't that they was militia at all. They was rich, but you wouldn't do them for that. It weren't because they was rich but because of where they lived. You needed them gone so you could buy this house. That's what you did with Jacobs' money.

Ori felt gutted. He swallowed many times.

He sat hard on his own instincts. Something welled in him. All the uncertainty, the desperate lack of knowledge, then the weight of knowledge but vacillation of ideas, the shameful hash of theory that had sent him to the Runagaters, to all the different sects and dissidents, looking for something to ground him, a political home, which he had found in the anger and anarchist passion of Toro. His uncertainty came back. He knew what he felt—that this was a dreadful thing, that he was aghast—but he remembered the exhortations to *contextualise,* always to have context, that the Runagaters above all had always stressed.

If one death'll stop ten, ain't it better? If two deaths'll save a city?

He was still. He had a sense that he did not know best, that he had to learn, that he was a better man in this collective than out, that he must understand why this had happened before he judged. Toro watched him. Turned to Old Shoulder. Ori saw the cactusman set his face. *They can see I know.*

"Ori. Listen to me."

The others watched without comprehension.

"Yes," Toro lowed. Ori felt like a schoolchild before a teacher, so disempowered, so ill-at-ease. He felt truly sick. Toro's thaumaturged drone felt through his skin.

"Yes," Old Shoulder said. "This is the house. They were old, rich, alone, no one to inherit, it'd be sold. But no, it ain't good. Don't presume, Ori, that there's no guilt and pain.

"We get in that house beside us . . . we're done. We *win.* We *win.*" Under the cactus's words, Toro began to roar. It was a sound that went from beast-noise to the cry of elyctricity and iron under strain. It lasted a long time, and though it was not loud it took over the room and Ori's head and stopped him thinking until it ebbed again and he was staring into Toro's phosphorescent glass eyes.

"If we win, we take the city," Old Shoulder said. "Take off the head. How many do we save then?" One by one, the other Toroans were understanding.

"You think other things weren't tried? The magister's house is closed. We can't lie in wait there. The boss can't push in, even with the horns. Some ward blocks us. Weapons won't go through: not a bullet, a blast, a stone. It's packed hard with charms. Because of who comes to visit. The sewers are stuffed with ghuls—no way in there there. It's what we had to do. Think about it. You want out of this, now?"

How did I become the one to be asked? Don't the others have to decide? But they were looking to him. Even Enoch had come to it now, and was open-mouthed thinking of what he had acted as lookout for, that night. Old Shoulder and Baron watched Ori. Tension drew the cactus-man up and stiff. Baron was relaxed. They would not let Ori walk, of course. He knew that. If he did not go along with this, he was dead. Even if he stayed, perhaps. If they thought they could not trust him.

Everything that was necessary was *necessary.* It was a tenet of the dissidents. And yes of course that *necessary* had to be fought over, debated and won. But they were so close. That they had found egress to a place their target would be alone, unwarded, vulnerable, where they could finally give their gift to New Crobuzon, was a towering thing. If it took two deaths to make it happen . . . could Ori stand in the way of history? Something in him blenched. *It was necessary,* he thought. He bowed his head.

On the top floor, the wall adjoining Magister Legus' property had been precisely excavated. Inches of plaster and thin wood were swept away. The wall was dug out.

"Deeper'n that, hexes kick in," Old Shoulder said. He touched the exposed surface with tremendous care. He was looking at Ori. Ori made his face unmoving. He listened. Toro had been preparing for weeks. *Do you have other gangs?* Ori thought, with an emotion he could not come close to identifying. *Or are we your only ones? Whose name is this house in? It ain't as if you bought it as yourself, is it?*

Baron was talking, with his instrumental precision. *I better listen,* Ori realised. *This is the plan.*

"Sulion's close to caving. We're buying two things: information, of who's where and what their tactics are, and a first move. Without him at the door, we're dead."

This is militia techniques, Ori thought, *that's what I'm learning.* Once again, Ori wondered how many militia there were who had been to the war and had come back with such bitterness as this, so full of it. What they would do. He watched Baron and realised that everything in Baron led him to this, that he had no plans beyond this, that this would be his revenge.

An epidemic of murders. That's what we'll see. If those AWOL and back from the wars don't have outlets. And the New Quill will recruit, too. They'll recruit men like this. Jabber help us. And Ori's eagerness to take off the head of the government came back strong. *Soon,* he thought. *Soon.*

He felt as if he might lose himself. He had to tell himself several times, until he was sure of it, that he was where he was meant to be.

CHAPTER TWENTY-ONE

Ｐ

EOPLE COULD NOT WALK NEW CROBUZON'S STREETS WITHOUT looking up. Past the aerostats and the wyrmen, the hundreds of lives—alien, indigenous, created—that teemed the city's skies, they looked at the cold white and the austere sun, and wondered if another of those searing organic shadows would come.

"They're still trying to parley," Baron told the crew. He had it from Bertold, who had inferred it from the Mayor's forays to the embassy wing with diplomats and linguists.

Ori returned to the shelter. Ladia welcomed him, but she was wary. She looked so exhausted he was shocked. As ever there were men and women the colours of dirt lying where gravity huddled them, but now the hall itself was scarred. The walls were tattooed with splinters and ripped-up paint; the windows were boarded.

"Quillers," she told him. "Three days ago. They heard we were . . . affiliated. We were slack, Ori, left papers around. With what's going on in Dog Fenn, I suppose, we've been distracted: it's been impossible to be so careful. We got cocky."

He made her lie down, and though she bantered with him she cried when he laid her out on the old sofa, cried and held onto him for seconds, then sniffed and patted him, made a last joke and slept. He cleaned for her. Some of the homeless helped him. "We had a play yesterday," one broken-toothed woman said to him as she wiped the tables. "Some Flexible troupe. Come to play for us. Very good it was, though not like nothing I'd seen before. I couldn't really hear what they was saying. But it was nice, you know, good of them to come and do that for us."

No one had seen Jacobs for days. "He's been around, though. He's been busy. You seen? His mark's all over."

The chalk spirals that Jacobs left wherever he went, that had given him his name, continued to disseminate, gone viral. They were in all quarters, in paint and thick wax colour, in tar; they were carved onto temples, scratched on glass and the girders of the towerblocks.

"You think he really started it? Maybe he's just copying someone else. Maybe no one started it at all. You heard how it's turning? People are using it as a slogan. It's been adopted."

Ori had heard and seen it. Spirals that tailed into obscenities levelled at the government. Shouts of *Spiral away!* when the militia appeared. Why that and not another of the symbols that had defaced walls for years?

The old man's corner was grey with spirals. Ink and graphite, in different sizes, the angles and directions of the curves variant, and here were spirals off spirals in intricate series. It could be a language, Ori thought. Clockwise or widdershins, stopping after so many turns, in differing directions and numbers; derivatives budded from each corkscrew whorl.

For nine nights, Ori came. He volunteered the night shift. "I got to do this," he told Old Shoulder. "I'll do what you need in the day, but I got to do something."

The Toroans granted him a kind of sabbatical, without trust. As he walked, Ori would stop, fasten his shoe buckle, lean against a wall and look behind him. If not Baron, someone would be following him, he was sure: he knew that the first time he spoke to someone that his unseen watcher, his fellow Bull-runner, did not trust, he was dead. Or perhaps there was no one. He did not know what he was to his comrades.

In The Two Maggots, Petron Carrickos gave Ori a book of his poems, self-published as Flexible Press.

"Been a long damn time, Ori," he said. He had a shade of wariness—his mouth twitched to ask *Where've you been? You disappeared*—but he bought Ori grappa and spoke to him about his projects. Petron held *Runagate Rampant*—not quite openly, but with the new bolshiness of the times.

Ori read a stanza aloud.

"A season here/In your flower/Petals of wood and iron/Lockstock stonedead shock of a Dog Fenn frown." He nodded.

Petron told Ori about the Flexibles: who was doing what, who had stayed part of something, who had disappeared. "Samuel's buggered off. He's selling stuff in some tarty gallery in Salacus Fields." He snorted. "Nelson and Drowena are still in Howl Barrow. Of course everything's changed now, you can imagine. We're still trying to do the shows when we can. Community stuff, in churches and halls and such."

"And just how does the Convulsive New go down with the commonalty?" It was a keystone concept from the second Nuevist Manifesto. Ori was sardonic.

"They like the Convulsive New just fine, Ori. Just fine."

There was an illicit congress of all the underground guilds, the militant factory workers of Smog Bend and Gross Coil, spreading, Petron said, to other industries. Delegates from foundries, shipyards, dye plants, in a secret Dog Fenn location, discussing what demands to put to Parliament.

"Caucus is talking to them, too," he said, and Ori nodded. He did not say, as he thought, *More talking, talking again, that's the problem, ain't it?*

At a crowded canalside market in Sangwine they reached, as part of the aimless walking that Petron theorised as a reconfiguration of the city, they came to sudden screams. "What in gods', what in gods', " someone was shouting, and there was a strange back-forward surge of crowd, people running to see what was happening and fleeing again past the stalls of books and trinket jewellery.

A woman lay in shudders by the lock and the watergates, her skirt puddled, her hair crawling like worms in static that made the air shake. People stared at her and tensed, made to run in and grab her and pull her away, but they blenched at the manifestation above her.

Vapour, a slick and sickly bruise-blue—a purpling as if the world itself, the air, was bleeding beneath its skin. The air souring and, like badness in milk, particles of matter coagulating from nothing, clots of rank aether aggregated into organising shape, and then there was a moving insectile thing made of scabbed nothing and sudden shade that twisted in the air as if suspended by thread and glimmered visible and invisible and then was unquestionably there, a hook-legged thing in the colours of rot, as large as a man. A wasp, its waist bone-thin below a thorax that refracted light like mottled glass, its sting like a curved finger beckoning from its abdomen, extending and adrip.

It cleaned its legs with its intricate mouth. It turned ugly compound eyes and looked at the aghast crowd. It unfolded its limbs one by one and shuddered and was moved, though not it seemed by the motion of those legs, but still as if it dangled and some giant hand holding its line had shifted. It came closer.

The woman was seizing. Her face had gone dark. She was not breathing. There was a gasp, a choking in the front of those watching. Two others fell. A man, another woman, fitting epileptically, flecking with spittle and vomit.

"Get out of the way!" The militia. From the entrance to the mar-

ket. They came firing, and the sounds of the guns broke the cold
that had held people, and they scattered screaming. Ori and Petron
ducked but did not run, pushed away from the noisome apparition
and watched the militia fire into its corpus.

Bullets went through it, to break glass and china beyond. The
woman in its shadow spat and died. In a fever of shot, the wasp
trilled and scissored its limbs like a trap. The lead was taken into it
with a bare ripple in its uncanny flesh, and some emerged and some
was eaten. The thing was dancing in the officers' fire. The leakage
from the dead woman's mouth was dark, her innards turned to tar.

An officer-thaumaturge cracked his fingers and made occult
shapes, and filaments spun into sight between his fingers and the
wasp, plasm made hexed fibres and webbing, but the predatory
thing passed through the mesh, suddenly far-off or side-on or
blinked closed like an eye, and in a spatter of unlight was there
again and the net was evanescing. The others stricken by the wasp
were still, and a seasick green was coming to the faces of the militia.

But then the wasp was gone. The air was clean. In a moment,
the militia began slowly to straighten, Ori braced himself, dropped
with a cry when a ghost image of the wasp returned in air again
momentarily varicose, and went, and came back once more, now
nothing but a vespine insinuation, and was, finally, all gone.

"It's not the first of them," Petron said. They had run back to The
Two Maggots, where they sucked at sugared rum tea, craving warm
and sweet. "You not hear about them? I thought it was stupid rumours, at first. I thought it was nonsense."

Manifestations that killed by toxic ambience. "One was a grub-
thing," Petron said, "in Gallmarch. There was one was a tree. And
one was a dagger, up Raven's Gate way, I heard."

"I heard of the dagger," Ori said. He remembered some strange
headline in *The Beacon*. "And weren't there others? A sewing machine? Wasn't there a candle?"

"Goddamn Tesh, isn't it? That's what it is. We got to end this war."

Were the conjurations Tesh weapons? Each must cost countless psychonoms of puissance, especially if called from Tesh, and each took only a handful of victims. How could they be effective?

"Yeah but it isn't just that, is it?" Petron said. "Not just the numbers. It's the effect. On the mind. On morale."

The next day Ori heard of another manifestant. It was in Serpolet. It was two people gripped together and fucking. No one could see their faces, he heard. Just saw them adangle, turning on twine, mashing their lips, their hands pushed into each other's flesh. When they went—driven out by the attacks of the locals or not, who knew?—they left five dead, leaked and spilled on the cobbles, turned bitumen.

When at last Spiral Jacobs came to the soup-house, Ori could not believe the look of him. The old man was twisted under the weight of his own bones; his skin was rucked and wretched on him.

"Gods almighty," Ori said gently as he ladled food. "Gods almighty, Spiral, what's happened to you?" The vagrant looked up at him with a wonderful and open smile. There was no recognition at all. "Where you been? All this time?"

Jacobs heard the question and pulled his brows together. He thought a long time and said carefully: "Perdido Street Station."

It was the only thing he said that night that evidenced sanity. He murmured to himself in a foreign language or in children's noises, he smiled, drew ink spirals on his skin. At night amid the grunts and the draughts, Ori came to where Jacobs sat chattering to himself. He was nothing but silhouette when Ori spoke.

"We've lost you, ain't we, Jacobs?" he said. He was stricken. He could almost feel the rise of tears. "I don't know if you'll come back. Where you've gone. I wanted, I wanted to find you to tell you thank you, for everything you done." *You can't hear me but I can.* "I got to tell you this now, because I'm going places and doing things that might, might make it so I won't get to see you no more, Spiral. And I want you to know . . . that we took your money, your gift, and we're doing it *right*. We're going to make you proud. We're going to make Jack proud. I promise you.

"What you done for me. Gods." Spiral Jacobs jabbered and drew swirls. "To know someone who knew Jack. To have your blessing. Whether you come back or not, Spiral, you'll always be part of this. And when it's over and it's done, I'll make sure the city knows your name. If I'm here. Got my word. Thank you." He kissed the crumpled forehead, astonished at the fragility of the skin.

That night there was no moon, and the gaslamps of Griss Fell gave out. In the dark the New Quill Party attacked the kitchen again. Ori woke to chants of "scum" and the tattoo of missiles on the wooded windows. Through a slit between boards he could see them massed. Ranks of men, studies in shadow, the brims of their bowlers low, making their eyes belts of dark. A streetful of carefully suited malignance, rows of black-cottoned shoulders padded with fighters' muscle, tipping their hats, straightening the dark ties noosed from their white shirts. They brushed imagined dust from themselves and swung weapons.

But the vagrants' fear was brief. Was it Militant Sundry who came for them? Was it the mixed ranks of the Caucus? Ori could not see. He only heard shouting and shots, saw the Quillers start and turn like a pack of feral clerks, and run to fight.

Ladia and the residents scattered. Ori ran for Jacobs, but to his surprise the old man walked past him with purpose but no urgency. He did not look at Ori or anywhere but ahead. He walked quickly past the last milling homeless, while at the street's end was the sound of battle and in the dark only a rapid and ugly mass of black figures. Jacobs turned the other way, toward Saltpetre Station and the raised arches that climbed north over the city.

Ori hesitated, thinking that there was perhaps nothing left to speak to in that shell, and then realising that he wanted to see where the man would go and what he would do. In the very dark of New Crobuzon without its lamps, Ori followed Spiral Jacobs.

He did not stalk him like a hunter but merely walked a few steps behind. He tried to place his shoes down soft enough that his step was only a ghost-echo of the mendicant's shuffling. They were the only people in the street. They walked between a fence of wood and iron on one side, damp bricks on the other, rising scores of feet above their heads. Spiral Jacobs skipped, treaded forward singing a song in an alien key, wandered back some steps, ran his fingers, poking from the cutoff ends of his gloves, over the corrugated iron and rubbed at its rust, and Ori came behind him as respectful and observant as a disciple.

With a thumb of chalk, Spiral Jacobs drew the shape that had given him his name, whispering while he did, and it was of astonishing perfection, a mathematical symbol. And then there were curlicues, smaller coils coming from its outer skin, and Jacobs ran his hand over it, and walked on.

It began to rain as Ori reached the mark Jacobs had made. It did not smear.

Past the tumbledown brick arch of Saltpetre Station and on toward Flyside into a place where the gaslamps had not given out, where guttering dirt-light returned to tan the walls and doors into grotesques. The old man wrote his shapes. He wrote on window, once, the grease of whatever he was using gripping the shine. A rut of street closed up to Ori and funnelled him through a brick arch after his idiot guru, into a wider zone of pallid light where the gas was effaced by the elyctro-barometrics, cold lurid colours, red and gold made ice in knotted glass.

They were not alone now. They were in some dream-dark landscape. Ori wondered when his city was taken, made this.

A succession. The loud sound of fiddles. Wealthy men slum-ming it with downtown whores fell out of the doors of drinkhalls, walking oblivious past tsotsis who eyed them and fingered ill-concealed weapons. Up now toward a militia tower, the thrum of the skyrails as a lit pod passed over. Crowding under slowworms of lit glass spelling names and services, simple animations—a red-mouthed lady drawn with the light, replaced stutteringly with another who had raised her glass, and back again in autistic illumi-nant recursion. Narcotics on the corners sold in twists by macer-ated youths, militia in aggressive cabals, their mirrors sending the light back around the street. Anger, drunk and stupid fights, and se-rious fights, too.

North to Nabob Bridge, approaching Riverskin. At the edge of Flyside they passed a series of lots, open and strewn, and Ori saw the last blows of some gang-pummelling, and there was a crowd of Quillers approaching in their suits, natty and baleful, but they did not harass him, instead sneering at the students who ran by laugh-ing, chasing motes of thaumaturgic light flying drunken as butter-flies; and a catcall, and there was the lit brazier of a picket outside a chymical plant, the numbers of the strikers swollen by supporters carrying billy clubs and forks to protect them from the Quillers who eyed them but ran the numbers and walked on.

A scarred cactus-boy begging for coins even so late while his monkey danced, the boy's head scratched with friendly condescen-sion by the big cactus-man leading a gang of, that must be the Mili-tant Sundry, not quite with weapons on display (militia were near enough to see) but making a presence in that late-night decadent street and nodding in some wary camaraderie-cum-challenge to a Caucus man, who shucked handslang at a passer and disappeared into an old cold alley when a panicked militia patrol ran past, and there was a fire in the back of the alley, and huddled junkie figures, and a wyrman called and came down to land and flew again.

Men and women passed. There was drink-smell and smoke, drug residue and the shrieks and calls like birds.

Spiral Jacobs walked through it all shielded by his madness. He stopped, drew his shapes, walked on, stopped, drew, walked, on to the spired old-century cragginess of Nabob Bridge, and over quickly through Kinken where the richer khepri moieties, older money and arriviste, preserved their dreamed-up culture in the Plaza of Statues, kitsch mythic shapes in khepri-spit. The air tasted, with the ghosts of khepri conversations in wafts of chymical.

Spiral Jacobs walked the tight streets of the Old Town, the first-born part of New Crobuzon, a V in the mud between rivers, now spilt over into metropolis dimensions. He shuffled and crooned and drew his spirals on the dark brick walls, on through Sheck, a grocertown of shopkeepers and a stronghold of New Quill, where Ori walked carefully. He saw not the bowlered Quill foot soldiers but the nervous paunchy men of defence committees, in agonies of pride at their own bravery. Through the outer edge of Spit Hearth where the prostitutes worked, streetwalkers eyeing him. Spiral Jacobs drew his coil. On one side was the window of a brothel advertising outré relaxations: on the other a mouldered poster, some radical group trying to recruit women it coyly called "those of unorthodox service professions."

The Crow, New Crobuzon's commercial heart, was not full. There were only a few walking so late. Spiral Jacobs, with Ori behind him, passed the arcades, tunnels through buildings neither open nor closed. They were curlicued in spiralled iron that the old man fingered with appreciation, their windows full of trinkets for the burghers.

And then Ori stopped and let Spiral continue toward the shadow, light-dappled, of the core of New Crobuzon: a castle, a factory, a town of towers; a god, some said, made by a madman intent on theogenesis. It was not a building but a mountain in the materials of building, a mongrel of styles united with illicit intelligence. The city's five railway lines emerged from its mouths, or perhaps they congregated there, perhaps their motion was inward and they coiled together like a rat-king's tails and knotted and made the edifice that housed them, Perdido Street Station. A ganglion of railroad.

Spiral Jacobs headed under the arch that tethered it to the militia's central Spike, was bunking down in the brick concrete wood iron temple great and charged enough to alter the weather above it, to alter the very night.

Ori watched the old man go. Perdido Street Station did not care that the city was surging. That nothing was the same as it had been. Ori turned and for the first time in hours his ears cleared, and he heard the calls of fighting, the swallowing of fires.

CHAPTER TWENTY-TWO

*A*LL HANDS, THE MESSAGE SAID. *IT'S NOW.* PINNED TO ORI'S DOOR.

Old Shoulder and Toro were the only ones not there. Baron explained the plan.

"Near a week," he said. "That's what we got. This information's from Bertold. We have to be careful. This"—a square of chalk—"is the top room. This is where they'll be.

"Remember. They ain't expecting attacks, but the Clypeans are tough. Each of you'll be told exactly what you have to do. Understood? Remember how you get in, and what you do, and how you get out. And—listen to me—don't alter your plan no matter what you see. Understand me? You do what you're told, let others do what they're told."

Are we a cell? Ori thought. *Are there others we don't know of?* Ori's companions shifted.

Baron drew more and more lines on the plan, repeating instructions until they had become mantra. His cadences did not alter; he was like a wax recording.

There was a cache of new weapons. Repeaters, blunderbusses, firespitters. Ori watched his comrades cleaning and oiling them. He saw whose hands shook. He saw that his own did not.

Baron taught them how to take point, secure areas, with the instrumental efficiency of the militia. They walked through their parts as if blocking a play. *Step up, swing, step, step, raise, secure, two three, say two officers, two three, step, turn, nod.* Ori recited his strategy to himself. *How are we going to do this?*

"We got surprise," said Baron. "Get through that one moment, that chink. They got nothing to hold us back. Tell you something though, Ori." He leaned in without even gallows humour. "Won't all of us get out. Some of us'll die there." He did not look afraid. He did not care if he came out.

You can feel it, can't you? Ori thought. His untethering. Ori was stretching out as if on a stem. It might snap. He still felt in that strange nightscape with Spiral Jacobs, his valedictory to the old man, when he had walked unmolested through a city turned into some psychotic, louche, broken thing. That was where he was.

There was no urgency in him. It was not a bleak feeling. Ori was only untethered. Things troubled him distantly. Uncertainties rose in him, distantly.

There were commotions. On the warming street, criers and journal-boys ran past, far from their usual grounds, called head-lines. *Convocation in Dog Fenn,* they shouted. *Demands to Parliament. Xenian Gangs, Seditionist Caucus.* The Toroans sat in the house they had bought from the estate of those they had killed. They ignored the news-vendors, the anxiety on the streets. They began to spread mess, to live in a kind of aggressive squalor. They hung their cesti on their belts; they sharpened the horns.

Magisters, even the top-rank doges, were citizens, it was always stressed, citizens like anyone. They worked masked for justice's sake, for the anonymity of justice. Any dwelling, in any part of town, could house a servant of law. The Flag Hill house next to the gang was elegant but nondescript.

Incongruously, at last, one early evening, with gunshots far off south—a noise New Crobuzon had grown used to, which no longer called the militia down from their dirigibles, was only part of the nightsound now—visitors began arriving. Cooks and maids and footmen left, given the night off. Not knowing their master's job, not knowing who it was who came to him. Fops and uptown dandies arrived, dressed for a sedate party. A cactus-man in smart clothes.

Probably the staff think he's an orgiast, Ori thought. *They think their master's up to shenanigans, peccadilloes or drugs.* The guests were militia. Clypean. Preparing for the mayor's arrival.

Ulliam put on a helmet. He strapped it tight and sighed. It jutted mirrors before his eyes. "Never, ever thought I'd put this on again," he said.

"I'm not clear," Enoch kept saying to Ori. "I'm not clear how it is I leave."

"You heard him, 'Noch, through the scullery window, over into the gardens, away." *You'll never leave.*

"Yeah, yeah, I, I know. It's just . . . I'm sure that's right."

You'll never leave.

"You'll know when it's time to go, Ori," Baron had said, and Ori waited. He leaned against the cracked plaster, put his head on the thin ribs of board. *Step step secure aim aim shoot.*

"You understand what you've to do, Ori?" Baron had said. "What's asked?"

Why this . . . this honour? Ori wondered. Why was he placed at the mission's heart? He was—after Baron—the best shot; and he did not expect to live, yet had not run. Perhaps that had decided Toro. *None of us will live,* he thought. *I'd still do this a thousand damn times.* He felt himself anchor.

"You know where I've got to be, and you know where Shoulder's got to be. We need someone at the top, Ori."

Ori's on point, he thought. *Ori, take point.*

He felt a weight of city below him, as if New Crobuzon were shackled to him as he dangled. He closed his eyes. He imagined he felt things burrowing in the house walls, through his skin. He looked over what he had done, over years. A churchbell sounded. A wyrman shouted from the sky. In Dog Fenn his friends kept fighting.

He heard Old Shoulder come and go below. Ori did not take his head from the wall. He heard trunk-legs, the surprisingly gentle touchdown of the cactacae's elephantine pads. Some time later reality pricked; there was a rending. He did not look round. "Evening boss," he said. Toro had come.

Between two and three o'clock in the morning, with the sky squid-ink dark, clouds occluding the stars and half-moon, they began.

Toro tremored and said, "The house-hex flickered."

Sulion, their treacherous contact, had left one key in one lock, turned one powerful ward charm upside down and rubbed it with hexed salt, cut one clutch of wires. It was all they needed.

With Toro's murmured reportage, gleaned from the horns that antennaed in the ripples of thaumaturgy, Ori tracked progress.

The gang were inside. "There's an empath," Toro said. "They know we're in." *Of course there's a damn empath,* Ori thought. *There's an empath and a shockjack and a cryomance, there's everything.* He stopped because he could feel the edge of hysteria.

There was the diversion. Ori could feel something. Steps on the stairs? Someone just beyond the wall running up and others running down. *First sign of entrance, they'll split: inner core'll go to the Mayor, the outer squad'll go to the incursion. They'll move fast to get the Mayor out.*

As the militia descended, Kit must be running the first set of stairs, sweeping whatever came at him with sticky flame, running fast past the fires he started. And as behind him came Ruby and Enoch with their own weapons, laying their traps, at the same time as that first wave—that diversion—came and the bodyguards rushed to its point of entry, Ulliam was funnelling gunpowder at the base of the door, leaving a tide-mark of explosive. And *there,* evidence of their breach. Ori heard shooting.

He imagined the guests moving with murderous militia grace. He hoped his comrades had surprised them enough to take some down. He even let himself hope they might get away.

Ulliam blew the door. Now the street would know. But in that fearful time, perhaps they would not intercede too quickly. Some of the Clypeans must be veering to deal with this new incursion. The ground floor would be thronging. And finally, Baron would be going in.

Ori pictured it. Such daring. He wished he could see. Swinging a line out from the first-floor window to that of the adjoining house, and Baron, in his new armour and helmet, brachiating across, letting the stepped rope drop for Old Shoulder to climb. Baron must be in the hall, attaching his charge to the banister and lighting that long fuse. And spraying oil on the stairs and lighting it so that the bulk of the militia were trapped beneath, Baron would let out a bellow, and now with Old Shoulder beside him, rivebow cocked, spitbolt ready, he must be treading up the stairs.

The inner guard would have to look, would send a scout-squad to the top of the stair, and oh Ori could just imagine the shock and the determination when they saw Baron. He would fire and back away, drawing them out. They would be so astonished to see him, his guns poised, bunching his shoulders, in his armour and his new helmet, cast so carefully in mimicry, his rivet-scarred bull's head.

Toro! they would cry. *Toro!*

Were they shouting that now?

Even the Clypeans would be afraid to have so famous a bandit with them, the perpetrator of such inventive death and rebellion. They would have to attack. Ori put his ear to the plaster-dusted wood. There was scuttering beyond. "They're going," said Toro behind him.

"It's time," said Toro.

There was running—Ori could hear it. He drew his pepperpot revolver and saw that his hands were absolutely unshaking.

"It's time, now," said Toro. The Clypean Guards would be running past the charge Baron had laid, seeing only fires below and the retreating, shooting figure of Baron in his bull's head disguise, slamming his horns from side to side so they rang against the walls. Ori had strapped on Baron's headgear. *Can you see?* he had said, and Baron had answered, *Enough to kill.* And enough to die. Ori did not think Baron cared.

Old Shoulder must be firing his rivebow at any cactus militia before turning to the others; and with him, shooting with the expertise of the specialist, Baron the ersatz Bull. Drawing the militia out. Toro said again that it was time.

It was, it was almost time, it would be time in any moment. Ori strained. *Step step two three quickly quickly step fire.*

"Now," Toro said, and this time it was true. There was a flowering of explosion. The sound of fire unfolding and the judder of masonry; dust pounced from the wall around Ori and in a chorus of downward raging housematter the stairs adjoining the topmost room to the melees below were blown by Baron's bomb. The room beyond Ori's wall was cut off.

"Now," Toro said, and stepped up beside Ori, who moved his gun into place, stood beside his boss as Toro crouched and charged, with a distorted rage-noise, pushing horns ajut and piercing this time not the world with hermetic techniques but in the most base way the wall itself. It gave without restraint. And Toro was through, and Ori was through, and standing in the wall's lime and laths detritus in a bedroom, with men and a woman staring at them.

Ori's calm held. It slowed time. Motion was languid. He moved as if in water.

A warm room, tapestries and paintings, ornate furniture, a fire, a woman and man on a chaise, another man standing, no, two men, looking at the dusting hole and at Ori and Toro. There was music. Someone was moving: a man in evening dress, his coat-tails flapping as he came with cat-grace, levelling a cane that unfolded organically into a weapon like a metal claw. He was very close and Ori was curiously without fear raising his pistol and wondering if it would reach its apogee in time, if he could interrupt the oncomer.

Toro grunted. Toro was goring forward and spitted the man from a distance, two boreholes opening in the bodyguard's chest so he was sodden in blood and his eyes closed and he died at Ori's feet.

Ori moved his gun: *step step, aim, one two, corner, corner.* He heard shouting. The other standing man had his hands up, was shouting, "Sulion! Sulion!" Ori shot him.

The body of their contact lay bleeding from the clean headshot. The man and the woman sat quite still and stared at the corpse. Toro raised a snubbed pistol to them, and looked through those white-shining glass eyes at Ori.

Of course there was no expression to the cast head. No one had given Ori the order to kill Sulion. He looked at the body and did not feel vindication. Had it been a panic? Had he meant to do it? For what was this revenge? Ori did not know. He was still not shaking.

Toro nodded at the door: *Secure the room.* Ori stepped over Sulion's wet corpse.

The corridor ended in a charred and guttering interruption. There was fighting below. He wondered which of his friends were still alive. Oily fire slathered the walls like ivy. They had only minutes before the house became conflagration or militia thaumaturgy breached the black hole they had punched in the house.

"We ain't got long," Ori said. He stood by Toro, before the last two people in the room, still sitting by the fire, watching them.

From a voxiterator a cello suite sounded, spitting momentarily with a crack of the wax. The man was in his sixties, broad and muscled under flesh, wearing a silk robe. He had a still, clever face. He kept his eyes on Ori and the Bull with such precision Ori knew he was trying to plan. He held the hand of the woman.

She must be close to his age—history evidenced that—but her face was almost without lines. Her hair was down-white. Ori recognised her from hundreds of heliotypes. She carried a long clay pipe as slender as a fingerbone. Its bowl still smoldered. It smelt of spice. She wore a shawl with nothing beneath. She did not cringe or glower or stare defiance. She watched with the same calm probing look as her lover.

"I can pay you," she said. Her voice was absolutely steady.

"Hush," Toro said. "Mayor Stem-Fulcher, hush now."

Mayor Stem-Fulcher. Ori was curious. More even than angry, or disgusted, or murderous for revenge, he was curious. This woman had ordered the Paradox Massacre, had sent the rate of Remaking higher and higher. This woman did backdoor deals with the New Quill Party, let their pogroms against xenians go uninvestigated. This was the woman who had stuffed the official guilds with informers. Presiding over a rotting polity on which countereconomies of hunger and theft grew like fungus. This woman perpetrated the war. Mayor Eliza Stem-Fulcher, La Crobuzonia, the Fat Sun Mater.

"You know you won't get out," the Mayor said. Her voice was steady. She even raised her pipe, as if she would smoke. "I can give you passage." She did not sound hopeful. She looked at her lover, and something went between them. *A valediction,* Ori thought, and for the first time felt a swell of something in him, a compound emotion he could not begin to parse. *She knows.*

"Hush, Mayor."

The Mayor and her magister looked again at each other. Eliza Stem-Fulcher turned to Toro, and though she did not take her hand from the man's she sat up some, as if formally, and she *did* take a draw from her pipe. She held it and closed her eyes a moment, breathed it out in a great flow from her nostrils, and she looked at Toro again and, gods, Ori thought awed, gods, she smiled.

"What do you think you'll do?" she said. Indulgent as a kindly schoolma'am. "What do you think you're doing?"

She turned square to Toro and gave another smile, drew again from the pipe, held her smoky breath, and she cocked her face quizzically and raised an eyebrow—*Well?*—and Toro shot her dead.

Her lover jumped as the bullet took her, and bit his lip hard but could not control his voice, could not stop himself letting out a mew, a cat-sound that became a moan. He sat and held her hand while she emptied out, her head back on blood. Smoke uncoiling from her open mouth. Gunsmoke joined her head and Toro's hand in a moment's sulphur umbilicum. The man breathed out sobs and held her hand. But he made himself be done, and made himself look up at Toro.

Ori was deep and dreamishly stunned, but he felt in him the tremors of the knowledge that they were *done,* and not dead. He raised the thought that gods, they might get out, they might yet. *Let's go then.*

"Watch him," Toro said and Ori raised his gun. Toro began to unbuckle the straps that held the huge metal head in place. Ori did not understand what he saw. Toro was removing the iron. "Watch him." The voice came again, this time uncoupled from whatever mechanisms made it so orotund, and it seemed to falter and become human.

Something went out of the air as Toro pulled the helmet away and broke a thaumaturgic current. Toro lifted the metal off, like a diver removing the heavy brass helmet. Toro shook out her sweaty hair.

* * *

Ori looked at the woman and his gun did not waver from the magister's chest. He had not felt capable of surprise for a long time.

Toro was Remade, of course. She turned her head. She was turned to wire by her middle years and by whatever traumas had made her Toro. Her face was set and animal hungry. She did not look at Ori. She sat, on a footstool, in front of the magister, laid her bull helmet to one side.

A child's arms emerged from her. One from each side of her face. One over each brow. A baby's arms that moved listlessly, tangling and untangling in her lank hair. They had been stretched out, one inside each horn, in the helmet. They waved next to her face like spiders' pedipalps.

She sat and closed her eyes, stretched out her arms and the baby's arms. She was quiet some moments.

"Legus," she said. "I know you're grieving now, but I need you to listen to me." Without the distortion, Ori could hear her accent from the southwest of the city was strong. She pointed at the magister's eyes and then at her own: *Look at me.* She held her gun gently at his belly.

"I'll tell you my story. I want you to understand why I'm here." A little sucking sound came out of the Mayor as gas or blood moved. She stared at the ceiling with the concentration of the dead. "I'll tell you. Maybe you know already. But listen.

"It's hard to find out your true name, like it's supposed to be, but it can be done. There's a black market in onomastics. But if it's consolation, yours stayed hidden well. Magister Legus. I been trying to find out a long time.

"I came out of jail more than a decade ago. Graduated, we called it. The rumours, what we learn inside. We had something on every magister there is. You hear things. Drugs, boys, girls, blackmail. Nonsense, some of it. *Legus,* they said to me, *Legus is a wily sod. You know he fucks the home secretary?* As she was then." She nodded at the cooling Stem-Fulcher. "That was information that never went away. Heard it often enough from those I trusted, inside and outside.

"Know how hard I been working on this, Legus?" She would not use his real name. "Getting myself ready. Had to fight to get my helmet made." The child-arms patted her forehead. "I made myself; I been readying for years. To be exact, Legus," she said, "you made me. Do you remember?"

"More than two decades gone. You remember those big old towers in Ketch Heath? Yes, you remember. That's where I lived. I killed my darling. You remember, Magister? My girl Cecile.

"She cried and cried and cried and I was crying too and then I took her and I think maybe it was that I was shaking her to make her shush, I don't remember, but she was gone when I remember again. And I took her down held close to keep her warm, to a sawbones worked gratis every other Blueday, but of course that didn't work.

"And then there you were." She leaned in. "You remember now?"

He did not. Of the thousands he had sentenced to Remaking, how could he remember one? Ori watched Legus. Toro reached up, tugged with a parent's unthinking gentle playfulness at the child's hand.

"You told me it was so I didn't forget. I didn't forget." She leaned forward again and Cecile's arms stretched out, toward Magister Legus holding the Mayor's dead hand. There was noise. Their bomb-cavity was being breached. Toro pulled on her cestus. "It was her birthday just two weeks gone," she said. "She's older now than I was when I had her. My little girl."

She stood and put her gun to Legus' temple. Legus gripped Stem-Fulcher's hand and opened his mouth but did not speak.

"From me," she said. She did not sound angry. "From the men you made machines, the women you made monsters. Tanks, snailgirls, panto-horses, industry engines. And from all them you locked away in the toilets you call jails. And from all them on the run in case you find them. And from me, and from Cecile—and yes it was me, my hands done it, and that's mine to feel. Cecile don't grow, and she don't rest. My girl. So this is from her too."

She kept her pistol barrel to his head and punched him once then many times with her spiked cestus, and he grunted and gave out a blood retch and his face went ugly and he put up his hand not to ward her but in a reaching for something, not to interrupt the bi-horned jabs—those he took, gripping his lover's hand so hard her dead fingers splayed. He could not stop himself barking at the pain and spilling more blood down his front as Toro punched him in a miserable repetition, shoving horns into his gullet and heart, and her baby's hands reached out above her onslaught and played with the dying magister's hair.

Ori stood still while it was done and for a long time afterward. He waited for Toro to move—this small woman, with her south-city accent, her old grudge. After a minute or more when she did not, only sat with her head down while the magister put out his blood around her, he spoke.

"Come on," Ori said. There was the sound of approach. "We have to go."

She did turn to him, though he thought at first she would not. She looked with the effort of one waking and shook her head as if she did not understand his language. She did not speak, but she gave him to understand that she was going nowhere, that she was done.

"And, and . . ." Some pride or respect meant Ori would not have himself sound plaintive or aghast, and he spoke only when he knew his voice would level. "And this was the only way, then, eh? Us?" *Ruby,* he was saying, *Ulliam, Kit, all of them down there, did they have to be part of this? Baron, godsdammit, and Old Shoulder. Gods know who's died for you.*

She gestured at the stiffening Mayor.

"We done what they wanted. We done what they come here to do."

"Yes." *Yes but it isn't the same. It was a sideshow, it wasn't what you were here for, and that's different, it makes it different.*

Does it? Didn't we win?

A middle-aged woman from the working-class estates of south-west New Crobuzon sat by two blood-glazed corpses. A young man from Dog Fenn held a gun uneasily and listened to his enemies getting closer. Everything was different.

"I want to *go*," he said, shaking suddenly as all the anxiety he had dulled welled in him. He felt himself want again, for the first time in many days. And what it was he wanted, was to get out.

"So go."

From the bitten-out hole through which they had come in he could hear hammering, sledgehammers taken to the doors of their empty house and echoing up its stairwells.

"You've *killed* me!"

"For Jabber's sake, Ori, go." She kicked her helmet at him. It jerked, rocked on its horns. He looked at it, at her, at it, picked it up. "Hexes are down. Go." It was very heavy.

"I don't know how to use this. What do I *do*?"

"Just push. Just push."

There were shouts from the approaching militia.

"You're giving me your helmet?"

She screamed at him. She said *Go!* but it stopped being a word, was quickly more animal than that, was only misery. He backed away and looked at the sticky emitting dead who kept her company, the way she sat, too tired even to tug her baby's hands.

"You shouldn't have done this," he said. "You shouldn't have used us like this. You used us hard. You had no right." He lifted the mask, faltered under it. He hated how he sounded. "You killed them. Probably me too. It was . . . Was an honour to run with you." He heard what must be grapples. Militia climbing. He heard them shout the Mayor's name. "You shouldn't have done this. I'm glad you . . . you got what you wanted. Shouldn't have done it this way, but we got what we meant to, too." He lowered the mask to his shoulders and tried to effect some militant salute, but Toro was not looking at him.

When the helmet settled it lightened. It felt like cloth. He had no talent for thaumaturgy, but even he could feel the metal thick with it. He looked through crystal that lightened the room, brought edges clear; he pulled the buckles tight under his shoulders, felt himself enhanced.

He gasped. Little needles spoked into his neck; his fingers gripped the metal. The sacrifice, the blood to power this iron head. *How do I do this?* he tried to shout. He felt extrusions of metal under his teeth and tried to bite or push them one way or another, feeling them still wet with the woman's spit. His voice dinned in his own ears.

Push. Ori stood as he had seen her do and shoved with new-powerful thighs, jerked forward, staggered, balanced, tried again. He braced the tips of the horns against the wall and strained and only embedded them in the wood. People were running toward the door. *Push,* she had said. *Where am I pushing to?*

In his eagerness, his desperate sudden want to be alive, he reached for an urgency, envisioned his home, his little room. He thought of it and alchemised the want into a focus, and when he ploughed forward again he clenched his eyes and teeth and felt the hankering coalesce in two blistering nodes where the horns met his forehead, and he pushed again and felt something catch, a sensual rupture like splitting taut wax paper. He gasped, and the substance of the air began to part for him and like water tension it tried to draw him in.

Ori paused at the edge of the little ontic abomination, the hole, while the universe strained. Ahead of him was distressed darkness. He twisted, keeping the horns in the wound he had made, and tried to catch the eyes of the woman with the child's arms playing pat-a-cake on her cheeks. She did not look at him. She did not look at the corpses she had made.

The militia were at the door. Ori pushed, let the momentum take him, into the rift he had made, out of that room where the most notorious thief and murderer of a generation quietly wept, where the ruler of New Crobuzon grew stiff, and he was for a moment a long moment in a wrinkle, in an innard of time, of the world, his synapses gone sluggard so he felt his back-wash of panic like slow clouding water as he thought what if he had the strength to break the surface of the universe and slip grubbish into the mortar between instants between cells of the real but what if he did not have the power to emerge again and was lost in the flesh of dimensions, a microbe in the protean, in spaceandtime?

What then?

But his push continued, and a long long time and an instant after the first split, he felt another; the membrane parted for him again, on the other side, and disgorged him like a splinter. He fell through and to the ground slippery, wet with reality's blood, his inexpert passage having done trauma in its passing, blood that evanesced in iridescent skeins, a pavonine moment in the air that was gone, and left Ori disoriented and dry again, and in an alley scattered with rubbish.

For a long time he lay bleating weakly, until the feeling like overwhelming motion sickness subsided, and strength seeped back to him.

He could not fathom where he was. He was giddy. In his Toro getup, aware that it made him a target. *I'll rest soon,* he thought through fog. His forehead hurt, in points at the bases of the horns. He had come through, but nowhere near where he wanted to go.

Ori could feel a chill, but it did not trouble him. He stumbled and looked up as he came through entangled alleyways, and there was a line intersecting his path, nightblack arches that even Toro's eyes could not see into, the brick and the dorsal crest of the elevated railroad. And beyond, tooth-yellow in the gaslamps that underlit them, the soffit of the Ribs. Ori was in Bonetown.

He lay for hours. The sky was grey-lit when he woke. When he removed the helmet he almost blacked out, and had to lean and breathe in a cavity below the railway. Silence unnerved him. He heard a few of the sounds that made the city whisper, but the bricks against which he leaned were still. They conducted no vibrations. The New Crobuzon trains should run all night, but there were none.

Ori made his jacket a kind of satchel for the helmet, he pocketed his pistol, and stumbled out toward the Bonetown Ribs.

The air seemed sultry, wire-tight. *What's happening?* He could not believe word had spread so fast, in fact he did *not* believe it. With a gust his excitement turned bad, and foreboding filled him. *What has happened?*

There was no one on the streets, or freakishly few, and those who there were went heads down. Past tarred houses by the Ribs, he kept the bricks of the raised railway to his left, went south, stumbling through Sunter, ready to turn on Rust Bridge to Murkside and from there to Syriac, but he saw the lights of fires and heard drumming, bugles. Nothing should be so loud at these predawn hours.

They grew louder; he felt himself going into shock, shaking hard, the weight of the helmet dragging him. South down High Chypre Hill, a street of florists and trinketeers by whose roofs the trains should come. There was a fork in the lines, where the tributary of the Dexter Line went down to Kelltree and veered east over the river to Dog Fenn. There, something was blocking his way.

Blinking till he teared in exhaustion, Ori saw in the glimmer of fires a rough barrier. He could not make sense of it. Its silhouette in that warm light was like something wild, something geographical in the city. People were moving at its top.

"Stop," someone shouted. Ori kept walking, did not understand that the word could be meant for him.

It was a barricade of paving slabs and rubble, carts, chimneys, old doors, the overturned remnants of stalls. Tons of urban detritus had gone to make a little mountain ridge, a ten-foot-high debris cordon planted with flags. The marbled arm of a statue jutted from its flank.

"*Stop,* fucker." A shot, a shard of concrete sounded with the ricochet. "Where you going, friend?"

Ori put his hands up high. He approached, waving.

"What's happened? What's going on?" he shouted, and there were jeers from the blockage. *What is he some fucker from Mafaton back from holiday?* "No papers, no kiosks, no criers where you been then, mate?" the sentry shouted. He was a man-shape in black, backlit. "Piss off home."

"This *is* my home. Syriac. What's *happened*? Godsdammit, how long was I between . . . This is about her, ain't it? You've heard? The Mayor?" And all his excitement was back again. So much that he could hardly speak. *I might've been days,* he thought. *What's happened while I've been gone? Did we do it? It happened. It woke them. The inspiration. Gods.* "Dammit, chaverim, let me in! Tell me what's gone on." He forgot cold and tiredness and stood up straight in the licking yellow light of the fires. "It's all *happened* . . . How long ago did she die?"

"Who?"

"The *Mayor.*" Ori creased his brow. There were more calls, more shouting. *She dead? The bitch is gone? Who's this fool, he's a madman, I wouldn't set your store . . .*

"I don't know what you're talking about, mate. I think you should go now." He heard the sound of gun-preparation.

"But what . . ."

"Listen, friend, someone can vouch for you? Because without that there's no in, no out. You're in no-man's-land, and that ain't a safe place to be. You'd best bugger off back to the Old Town, unless you give me a name. Give me a name, and we'll check you out." More heads were rising now; the man was being joined. An armed band, humans and other races, weapons hefted below snapping flags.

"Because you're on the threshold now, mate, and you're either on one side or the other. It ain't like we just got here. Been two powers in the city for days, boy. You've had days to make up your mind. You're either north"—and there were pantomime boos—"back in the old days and old ways: or you're in here, Kelltree and Echomire and Dog fucking Fenn, in the future, which is now.

"Walk toward me slow, and keep your hands like that. Let's have a look at you, you gormless fool." It was almost kindly. A bottle smashed. "Come a bit closer. Welcome to the Free Territories, mate. Welcome to the New Crobuzon Collective."

part seven

STAIN

CHAPTER TWENTY-THREE

"I HATE THAT WE RUN FROM THEM."

"You heard, though. You heard how it was. We have to play safe. They're armed to take us out."

"But if we have to run from them, why by gods are we heading back to the city? It'll be way worse."

"It doesn't work like that, though, does it? That's not the idea. We send out word. By coming back, we change things. By the time we get back, it won't be them waiting for us. It'll be a different city."

Cutter and the man lounged against a wall after another dance, in a cab reconfigured. It was a punitive journey, and night after night the Iron Councillors kicked against the darkness to improvised rhythms.

There had been deaths, of course, to footholds lost, to viruses and bacteria of the hinterland, and to the depredations of the inland predators, animals that unfolded in claws, teeth, cirri, and killed. Drogon went hunting with the Council's forces, came back with the heads of strange predators, with new wounds and stories.

That one phases, so we trapped it when it went icy and I took it through the heart. That one sees with its teeth.

Cutter saw some of the new thaumaturgy the Iron Council had learned. It would not have saved them from the militia. The Council tried to make things hard for their pursuers, blowing up bridges behind them, filling trenches with rubble. Judah laid golem traps behind the Iron Council, set to be triggered only by a company of men. He laid as many as he could—each one ate at his energy. Cutter imagined the earth buckling and unbuckling become a rock figure, a figure made of fallen trees, water of the stream, wherever Judah had laid the trap. Its one instruction indelible and simple in place of a brain: *fight.* The substance of the inlands themselves gone not feral but organized, interceding and pounding down the militia with its blows.

If the militia reached that far, which Cutter thought they would. Some of them would die, but most would likely not. When they made landfall, found the Council's trail, even the power of Judah's great golems could not stop them coming. The militia would close on the stragglers of the Iron Council, those left behind by the train. Iron Council relied on the cacotopic zone. That was what would hide them.

"Didn't think I'd see this again," Judah said. They were on a crag peering over the tracks, the long dotted-out spread of men and women, riding pack mules or walking hard and fast, surrounding and joining the graders.

What if the Council changes its policy on the way? Cutter thought. *What if we get halfway across and enough people disagree and want to go back?*

There. The sun moved behind them. Its vividness seemed to green slowly as it sank, as if it were verdigrising. In the ill-seeming light they looked north and east into the cacotopic stain. They had come hundreds of miles, in weeks, and here they were, at the edge.

Cutter went white to see it. "Qurabin," he said, "tell us a secret. What is it? What's happening there?" Something sounded in the air like scuttling.

The monk's voice came: "Some secrets I don't want to know."

There, a Torque landscape. Mussed by that ineffable bad energy, the explosion of shaping, a terrible fecundity. Vistas. *We ain't seeing what this really is,* Cutter thought. *This is just one idea. One way of it being.*

Even there in the outskirts of the cacotopos land was liminal, half-worldly geography, half some bad-dream set. It was merciless, stone horns and trees that looked like stone horns, forests of head-high mushrooms and ferns that dwarfed runt pines and, a way off, the flat of some delta where the sky seemed to push in between too-tall extrusions. Cutter could see nothing moving. That unplace extended to the horizon. It was many miles to pass through.

Cutter did not know if he was seeing hills or insects flying close to his eye: that could not be, he knew, but the impossibility of focus confounded him. Was that a forest so far off? That went for many miles? Or was it not a forest but a tar pit? Or now perhaps not a tar pit but a sea of bones or a grid, a wall of tessellated carbon or scab-matter the size of a city.

He could not make it out. He saw a mountain and the mountain was a new shape, and the snow on its top was a colour snow should not be and was not snow but something alive and tenebrotropic. The distant stuff extended cilia that must be the size of trees, toward oncoming darkness. Lights in the sky, stars, then birds, moons, two or three moons that were the bellies of acre-wide lightning bugs and then were gone.

"I can't do the sense of it." Qurabin's voice was terrible. "There are some things the Moment of the Hidden and the Lost doesn't know, or's scared to say."

The Torquescape was insinuatory, and fervent, and full of presences, animalized rock that hunted *as granite must of course hunt* and spliced impossibilities. They had all heard the stories: the cock-roach tree, the chimerae of goat and ghost, reptilian insects, treeish things, trees themselves become holes in time. There was more than Cutter could bear. His eyes and mind kept trying, kept straining to contain, encompass. "How could they *do* this? Travel through this?"

"Not through," Judah said. "They didn't. Keep remembering that. They went just round the outside. Close enough to scare."

"Close enough to die," Cutter said, and Judah inclined his head.

"What things live here?" Cutter said.

"Impossible to list," Judah said. "Each is its own thing. There are some I suppose—there are shunn, there are inchmen in the out-skirts . . ."

"Where we'll be."

"Where we'll be."

They would be three weeks, perhaps, in the edges of the cacotopic zone. Three weeks pushing as close as they dared into the viral landscape. There must have been those who had passed through it before, in the half-millennium since it appeared in a spurt of patho-logical parturition. Cutter knew the stories of Cally the winged man; he had heard rumours of adventures in the stain.

"There must be another way," he said. But no, they said there was not.

"*It's the only way to be safe from the militia,*" Drogon whispered. "*The only way to be sure they won't follow us. They'll be stranded out-side. It's basic orders: never go into the zone. And anyway—*" His in-tonation changed, the breath of his words faster. "*—this is how they found their way. The Council, I mean. A passage through the conti-nent. You know how long people tried for that? A passage? Through the smokestone, the cordillera, the quaglands, the barrows? We can't risk changing it. This might be the only way.*"

A few miles in, Judah disappeared for hours in the train's wake, returned exhausted. Cutter screamed at him not to go off alone, and Judah gave one of his saint's smiles.

Camouflaged with brush were segments of the tracks. The scouts and graders joined them, section to section, and the train went through the outlands of the stain. Cutter clung to the perpetual train and let the wind refresh him. There were a few demons of motion left, all domesticated now, the children or grandchildren of the first wild pulse-eating dweomers who had chewed the wheels. The ethereal little fauna were cowed. Cutter watched them.

He watched the rocks and the trees, heard below the grind of the gears and flywheels the bleatings of unseen animals. There were fights as people tried to take their turn sleeping in the cabs. The camp of graders was a tight little tent-town, in circles for safety. Still, nothing could prevent some of the effects of the cacotopic stain reaching out.

Water was rationed, but still every day crews led by the council's few vodyanoi dowsers would set out to find potable streams—they went south, always, away from the Torque and the danger. And still every few days one or other would return ragged and stammering, carrying the remnants of someone lost, or bundling someone who had changed. Torque touched at night with its fingers of alterity.

"She was fine till we headed home," the hunters might shout, holding a Remade woman who shook so ceaselessly hard and fast that the blur of her limbs and head half-solidified and she was a faintly screaming mass of quasi-solid flesh. "Shadowphage," they might say, indicating the terrified boy from whom light shone too brightly, the inside of his open mouth as clear and illuminated as the crown of his head. People came back who had become gnawed by the radula of impossibly fast vermiform predators. The Iron Council passed over footprints: the stiletto holes of an echinoid rex, the strange tracks of an inchman, pounded earth in clumps four or five yards apart.

Of the Torque- or animal-wounded they saved those they could, in the cattle-truck become a sanatorium. Others they buried. In their tradition, they laid them ahead of the tracks. Once, digging a grave, they disturbed the bones of one of their ancestors, one of the

Council dead on the outward journey, and with tremendous respect they begged her pardon and laid the newly died down with her forever.

"This can't be right," Cutter raged. "How many will this take? How many have to die?"

"Cutter, Cutter," Ann-Hari said. "Hush you. It's a terrible thing. But if we stayed, faced militia, we all die. And Cutter . . . so many more were killed the first time. So many more. We're getting better at this. The perpetual train sends out safety. It's charmed." Every day the heads of new predators were hung from the train. It became a grotesque museum of the hunt.

When Cutter saw Drogon, the whispersmith was in a state of constant amazement. He relished the hunt even in these badlands, and everywhere they went he watched so closely, tracking their passage through splits and rockways, watching the movement of the cacotopic zone. He was committing it to memory, trying to understand it. That was one way. Cutter preferred another: wanted this time to be done, wanted only to have it end.

He went with crews scavenging for wood and ground-coal, peat, anything for the boilers. He went with his companions, searching for water.

The diviner emerged from the water-tank car given over to the vodyanoi. His name was Shuechen. He was sour and taciturn as stereotype said vodyanoi always were. Cutter liked that. His own brusqueness, cynicism and temper predisposed him to atrabilious vodyanoi.

As they rode, Shuechen swinging in his water-filled saddlesac, the dowser told them about the debates, the factions among the Councillors, the argument over the Council's new direction. Ex-Runagaters, cynics, the young, the fearful old. There was uncertainty growing as to whether this was the best strategy, he said.

Shuech would put his big palms flat and sniff the earth, slapping it and listening to its echoes. He led them three hours from the train. Clean water came out of the rocks and gathered in a basin surrounded by roots so minimally touched by Torque that Cutter could imagine he was back in Rudewood. When he did, loss broke him a long moment.

They filled their water-sacks but then it was night, fast as a rag thrown over the sun, and quickly they made camp. They did not light a fire. "Not near the zone," Shuech said.

Gripped together against a punitive rocky cold, the two Remade made Cutter's party tell them about New Crobuzon. "Rudgutter's dead? Can't say it's a shock. That bastard was Mayor forever. And now it's *Stem-Fulcher*? Gods help us."

They were stunned by the changes. "The militia patrol *openly*? In uniform? What in hell happened?" Pomeroy gave a brief history of the Construct War, the attack on the dumps, the rumours of what was within. It did not sound real, even to Cutter, who remembered it.

For a long time they straight refused to believe what Cutter told them of the handlingers.

"We was *chased* by one," he said. "I'm telling you. During one of the riot crises a few years back Stem-Fulcher announced that they've, whatever, *made contact*, and that they were all misunderstood." The handlingers, figures of terror for centuries, the feral hands come from corpses (some said), who were devils escaped from hell (some said), who took over the minds of their hosts and made their bodies into something much more than they had been. If the condemned are to die anyway, Stem-Fulcher had said, and the city is in need of help the handlingers can give, it is foolish sentimentality not to draw an obvious conclusion. And of course they would be tightly controlled.

Even so the announcement had spurred new riots out of disgust, the abortive Handlinger Revolt. The crowd who would have taken boats across the Gross Tar to assault Parliament were defeated by those they were protesting, men and women suddenly rising from their masses and spitting fire, dextrier handlingers wearing the meat of the condemned.

Cutter talked late. He was very afraid of changing. "What if Torque gets out here?" he kept saying, and the Remade reassured him differently, one saying that if your number was up it was up, the other that they were far enough that they should be all right.

That night they were attacked.

Cutter woke to ripping and opened his eyes into grey moonlight and a face staring at his own. He thought it had come with him from his dreams. He heard shooting. He hauled himself away from the expression bearing down on him, a quizzical and monstrous look.

When adrenaline hit him he was already moving, was already out and running, thinking, *Where are the others, what's happening, what will I do?* Emerging into the camp he saw more clearly what had come and what was happening and he stumbled and fought hard not to fall.

His party were around him, running, firing, and there was someone's scream that made Cutter cry out himself. He saw the stirrings of the tent like a rag-beast as the thing that tore it flapped fragments like wings. He saw a looping, spastic move and there was the impact of something hurled to the ground, and then another. The percussions were around him everywhere.

"Inchmen!" he heard Elsie shout. "Inchmen!"

The creature threw the rippings of his tent apart and the wind spiraled them into the air and emerging from their centre as if by cheap stage effect was what had come for him with brute and hungry enquiry, what had smelt him through the cerecloth. In the swirl of rag-ends came his predator. Spangrub. Kohramit. *Homo raptor geometridae.* An inchman.

* * *

Cutter stared. The face of the figure leered at him and came forward very suddenly, snapping up and down in a motion Cutter did not for some moments understand.

Taller than he but all torso, its trunk seeming to extend from the ground, its head twice the size of his, long arms scrawn and bone, hands splayed or knuckle-dragging, clutching as it moved. Near-human, its mouth opened by teeth black and long, spike-sharp. He could not see its eyes. Two sinkholes, a mass of wrinkled skin and shadows: if it saw it did so out of darkness. It turned and sniffed, throwing back its bald head and opening and closing as best it could that toothed mouth. And then it shifted and Cutter saw its hindquarters.

Colossal and grossly tubate, a caterpillar body studded with tufts, ventricles opening and closing sphincters, dun and specked with warning colours. The man torso congealed into the front of that yards-long body, hip bones into larval flesh. The inchman moved.

It had a clutch of little pulsing legs at its front below its pale torso, and two, three stubby pairs of prolegs at its very rear. It pulled its rear up in a great arch, vised its prolegs into the hard earth, took the weight of its forebody, and with a flail lifted it, straightening the tube of bodiness, the humanish torso high at the end of outstretched grub physiognomy that batted uncertainly at the air, then onto the spongy caterpillar forelegs.

It sniffed again. It arched again, gripped and opened itself out, put its forebody down closer. Inchworm motion. A groping walk, a spanning toward him.

Cutter fired and ran. The inchman accelerated. The Iron Councillors tried to fight. There were several inchmen at the camp's corners. There was the bray of a mule, and shouting.

In the moon's glare Cutter saw another of the loopworm men champing, blood black in the half-light all over its front and mouth, a huge hand pressing down on the shuddering animal beneath it. It made an open-mouthed parody of chewing.

One inchman emitted an elyctric roar. The others joined in, spilling grots from their mouths.

The mules and runt camels were screaming. Shuech fired and the fist of buckshot sheared off skull and brain mass, but the inchman hit did not drop, too stupid or stubborn to die. It lurched in with its grotesque larval swaying, and with a leather-skinned hand grabbed a man and punctured him. The man screamed but stopped very fast as the inchman took him apart.

Shuech threw flaming cacodyl, and the caustic spread over one of the caterpillar figures, which batted without urgency at the fire. It sounded again, that throat noise, and as it reared on its hind pro-legs it became a torch, illuminating them all.

The things blocked them. They were caught by a shelf above a canyon, which went to scree too loose to run. Cutter backed against rock and fired. Someone cried. Judah was murmuring.

The rearmost inchman chattered slab teeth. Its head burst. Matter spattered its fellows. Pomeroy refilled his smoking grenade shot.

In the wake of one Iron Council thaumaturge Cutter saw simple plantlife growing in footprint shapes, the spoor of moss-magic. The mossist growled and a mass of blots mottled an inchman's skin, a bryophyte coating clogging its mouth and the holes of its eyes. It reared, retching, clawing the plant pelt and drawing its own thick blood.

The Iron Councillors fired chakris, fat flat-blade disks or scythe-bladed arrows. The inchmen bled in gouts, but did not stop coming. Judah stepped up with a near-holy fury in his face. He touched the ground. His crooked hand spasmed.

For a second nothing and then the inchmen were padding on moving earth that began to unfold in the shape of a vast man, a so-matic intervention in the rock and regolith—and then something stammered in the aether and broke. Judah staggered and sat hard on the loose stones, and the ground settled. The human shape that had begun to disaggregate from it became random again.

Cutter cried Judah's name. Judah was holding his head. An inchman was one step away from him.

But Pomeroy was there, his blade in his hand. With a psychotic doomed bravery while Elsie screamed he hacked into the human-form abdomen of the inchman.

He was a very strong man. The inchman even stopped a moment at the impact, and Pomeroy let go the sword and stepped back, standing in front of Judah, who gathered himself, looked up as the inchman snatched Pomeroy's head. Its enormous palm pressed over the man's face, swung him by his head with the absent savagery of a baby.

Cutter heard the shearing of Pomeroy's neck, and Elsie's scream. The inchman flailed Pomeroy's body. Judah was crouched again, drawing up the golem from the earth. This time it came all the way. It stamped, shedding its earth-self, swung at the nearest inchman. The enormous strike sent the thing off the rock, into the air. Its inchworm arse flexed; it dropped and hit the ground with explosive wetness.

Elsie was weeping. The other inchmen were closing, and Judah crooked his fingers and the golem interceded. It stamped with a walk that was Judah's walk, Cutter would swear, performed by earth. It stood before the Councillors and tore into another of the geometrid things.

After a moment of indecision while the exhausted Councillors fired, the inchmen retreated from the towering golem. Two descended head-first down the sheer uneven rock. The third was trapped in a last ugly blood-mud wrestle, and the collapsing golem rolled with its opponent to the edge and over.

Judah kneeled by Pomeroy, and the Iron Councillors ran to help their comrades. Cutter, shaking, stared over the edge. He saw the inchmen descending the vertical surface. On the rock floor were the bodies of the two who had fallen, and the red earth of the golem.

Cutter went to Pomeroy and gripped his dead friend. He gripped Elsie, who was wailing, who sobbed on him. Judah was stricken. Cutter tried to grab him too, pulled him close. They hung on together. The three of them held as Elsie cried, and Cutter felt Pomeroy go cold.

"What *happened*?" he whispered in Judah's ear. "What *happened*? You . . . are you all right? You stumbled . . . and Pom—"

"Died for me." Judah's voice was perfectly flat. "Yes."

"What happened?"

"Something . . . A remote. I weren't expecting it. A golem trap was triggered. I'm saving chymicals and batteries—it took its energy mostly from me, and I didn't have the focus. It shook me, made me fall." He closed his eyes, lowered his head. He kissed Pomeroy's face.

"It's a golem trap I put in our path," he said. "The militia triggered it. They've made landfall. They're coming."

CHAPTER TWENTY-FOUR

O N THE COAST HUNDREDS OF MILES AWAY (JUDAH SAID) AN ICTI-neo, one of New Crobuzon's experimental ichthyscaphoi, must have come to land. A behemoth fish come out of the ocean crawling on fins that became leg-stubs that stamped forward until the stumpy limbs shattered under their own weight and the enormous Remade fish-thing lay down and shuddered. This was what must have come.

A mongrel of whale-shark distended by biothaumaturgy to be cathedral-sized, varicellate shelled, metal pipework thicker than a man in ganglia protuberant like prolapsed veins, boat-sized fins swinging on oiled hinges, a dorsal row of chimneys smoking whitely. The fish-ship's mouth (Judah said) must have opened with a grind of industry, anchored by chains, drawbridge-style, as the flange of lower jaw descended and the men of the New Crobuzon militia emerged, bringing their weapons, and coming for the Council.

* * *

"It weren't so easy for us when first we came through. We found ourselves wandering, trying to get away from the stain, and then the path would coil and we'd be going straight into the Torque's innards, sky like guts or like teeth. We lost so many to it then," the man said.

He was, from long ago, a Dog Fenn Remade. His hands were gone, the left a mess of bird's feet congealed in talon-mass, the right a snake's thick tail. He was a scald, an Iron Council balladeer, and the apparent halting of his delivery was a game: he told in a complex, arresting syncopation mimicking novicehood. His story was a kind of lay for those dead by the inchmen.

"We lost so many. They went to glass and then was just gone, on a hill that was a bone and then a pile of bones and then a hill again. We learnt ways of passing through this in-between." There was no scientist in the world of Bas-Lag who knew more about Torque, about the cacotopos, than the Iron Council.

"Now we come back, the land's shucked and the Torque's done what it's done. Some of the rails we hid is gone, some's corkscrewed, some are holes the shape of rails, some are lizards made of stone. But there are enough to get us out again. To come out on the other side, with only the plains between us and New Crobuzon. Hundreds of miles, weeks maybe months, but not the years it would once have taken."

Many miles west, the New Crobuzon Militia tracked them.

Inchmen came again. This time they attacked the train itself, and were repelled but at cost. They drag-crawled and with their wavering spanworm walk stomped toward the train and even touched it and gnawed at it, marked it with stone-hard teeth and caustic spit. Councillors died pushing them away. There were other creatures: shadows shaped like dogs, simians with hyaena voices pelted with grass and leaves.

The ground defied the Council. It changed in sped-up corrasion, in the buckling of tectonics at some psychotic rate as if time was untethered from its rules. The ground crawled. There were patches of sudden and extreme cold where frost-heave buckled rails, and then temperate places where the rockwalls came closer and creeping hills stalked them.

They laid tracks on ground just smooth enough for their passage, on ties just strong enough, just close enough together. It was a just-railroad, existing in the moment for the train to pass, then gone again. Hauled by the Remade and by young Councillors who had never seen their parents' former home. Over a spread-out swamp, a quag that ate the tracks.

Cutter would look up, time to time, from his hammering or earth-laying, and see the glowering of the cacotopic stain in the near-distance: the snarl of sky and scene, a baby's face, an explosion of leaves, an animal in the uncertainty in the air and the hills. *We don't even see it no more,* he thought, amazed, and shook his head. The sky was clear, but a serein drizzled onto them. *You can get used to the most monstrous absurdity,* he thought.

With the knowledge that the militia followed them was a calm. "They'll stop at the stain," Judah said, but Cutter realized he was no longer sure. Cutter took heliotypes from the stationary train, of the unstable landscape and creatures that were not insects nor lizards, birds nor metal cogs but something Torque-random that seemed inspired by all these things.

Judah was quiet. He was in himself. He came to Cutter one night and let the younger man fuck him, which Cutter did with the urgency and love he could not ever control. Judah smiled at him and kissed him and stroked his cheek, gods, not as a lover but like some kind of priest.

Judah spent most of his hours in the laboratory car wedged full of witchy detritus. He wound his voxiterator. Listened over and again to the recordings of the stiltspear songs. Cutter saw his notebooks. They were filled: musical scores slashed through with colours, queries, interruptions. Judah muttered rhythms under his breath.

Once Cutter saw him, standing in half-light at day's end, at the front of the perpetual train. He heard Judah mutter a song-rhythm and pat his own face with one hand, clicking a syncopation with the other. There were motes around Judah's head, unmoving, a scattered hand of specks, flies and mountain midges that did not eddy with the wind: an unnatural and profound inertia. When the train shucked and rolled a few feet on, Judah left the gust of immobile insects behind.

Wyrmen Councillors flew. They looked for the end of the zone. Some of course did not return, vanished in a fold of air or suddenly forgetful of how to fly, or ossified, or become wyrmen cubs or tangles of rope. But most came back, and after many days in the outlands half-bred from the monstrous and quotidian, they told the Iron Councillors that they were near the end.

They built their last rails along a path their geoseers said was ambulatory, would wander and confuse pursuers. With the engine newly coated with predator heads, newly charnel, and the carriages scratched and marked by their passage, the Iron Council jackknifed up a slope. Cutter found it impossible to imagine land untouched by Torque.

They crested the rise, hammers laying down last tracks, behind them the crews hauling away the iron of their passage. Cutter stared at a windblown landscape of smokestone. It was a vivid and strange place, but without that pathology, that dreadful cancer fertility of the cacotopic stain.

"Oh my gods," Cutter heard himself say. There was cheering, spontaneous, absolute with delight. "Oh my gods and Jabber and godsdamned fuck, we're out, we're out."

They took a route on the very edge, the littoral ridge that divided the fringes of the Torque from the healthy land. They hammered the metal home on the smokestone flat and came back into natural land.

The perpetual train went through the smokelands. The winds had gusted great roils, rock cumulonimbus on the anvil-tops of which they laid tracks quickly, nervous that they might revert. "Somewhere down there's where we came in," Judah said. The split path they had made had long been effaced in scudding stone.

Judah, Cutter and Thick Shanks walked in the lee of the solid cloud, by the edge of the cacotopos.

"Some of us are afraid," Thick Shanks said. "Things have run away from us. Feels like we ain't got a choice of what we're doing." His voice was thin in the warm wind.

"Sometimes there are no choices," Judah said. "Sometimes it's history decides. Just have to hope history don't get it wrong. Look, look, isn't that it?"

They found what they were looking for: a vertical uncoil of rock drooled with ivy and on which shrubs were stubbled. There was something different about the ground, a remnant of gouging, long-ago explosive-ploughing. A path visible under two decades' growth.

"This is where we came through," Judah said, "the first time."

He stood by the cloudlike wall and tugged at a rockplant, and Cutter saw it was not a rockplant but a bone come from the stone. A sere wristbone, time-bleached leather still ragging it.

Judah said: "Was too slow."

A man encased. Caught by a tide of smokestone. Cutter looked with wide eyes. Around the wristbone was a circle of air, a thin burrow, where the arm-meat had been, and had rotted. And inside, it must hollow in a body's contours, emptied by grubs and bacteria. A flaw, an ossuary the shape of a man. Silted with bones and bonemeal.

"Councillor or militia. Can't remember now, can you, Shanks? There's others. Dotted through. Bodies in the rock." They clambered to the top of the range. The Iron Council moved, its hammers ringing, the wyrmen like windblown leaves above it through the gushing of its smoke. Cutter watched the train progress. He saw the strangeness of its contours, its brick and stone towers, the rope bridges that linked its carriages, its carriage-mounted gardens and the smoke of its chimneys, echoes of the smokestacks at its head and tail.

A way east, long-rusted barrels of militia ordnance protruded from the stone.

In the land beyond, the land that extended to New Crobuzon itself, it was a prairie autumn. The Councillors looked carefully at the water and the woods and hills and at their charts. They could not believe where they were.

The maps they inherited from when Iron Council was the TRT train became useful again. The perpetual train was still embedded in the loosest ink, the crosshatched beige that indicated uncertainty, but eastward the drawings grew more clear; stippling of brush, the watercolour wash of fen, contours of hills in precise line. This was not land on which tracks had been laid, but it was in the city's ken. The Council could track its route through the ink.

They checked and rechecked. It was a burgeoning revelation. They were heady and astounded. "Around the long lake here. We've Cobsea to our south. We should avoid them, get northside of the lake as fast we can. We'll bring Council justice to New Crobuzon."

Even knowing the militia followed them could not cow them. "They've come after us. They followed us into the stain," Judah told Cutter. "They've triggered a golem trap I put in the cacotopos." No militia had ever gone so deep. This must be a dedicated squad, who realised the Council was heading back for New Crobuzon.

"We'll go close to the hills." Days ahead, a backbone of mountains rose and extended half a thousand miles to New Crobuzon. "We'll skirt them; we'll take the train through the foothills. To New Crobuzon."

There were still months to go, but they went fast. Scouts went to see where bridges or fording were needed, where swampers had to fill wetland, where tunnellers and geothaumaturges would carve out passages. History felt quicker.

Drogon the whispersmith was alight with excitement, sounding in Cutter's ears, telling him he could not believe that they had come through, that they had achieved this, that they were so close to being home. *"Got to clock what we done,"* he said. *"Got to mark it. No one's ever done this, and plenty've tried. There's still a way to go, and it's still land no one knows well, but we'll do it."*

Judah sat on the traintop and watched this suddenly unalien landscape. "It ain't safe," he told Cutter. "Can't say it's safe at all." He spent much time alone, listened to his voxiterator.

"Judah, Cutter," Elsie said, "we should go back to the city."

She was silent in these days, with Pomeroy's death. She had found a calm that let her live in her loneliness. "We don't know what's happening there; we don't know what state they're in. We need to get them word that we're coming. We could sway things. We could change it."

It was a long way still, and there were many things that stood to stop them.

"She's right." Drogon spoke to each of them. *"We need to know."*

"It ain't no matter, I don't think," Judah said. "We'll go, nearer the time. We'll go and get a welcome ready, prepare for them."

"But we don't know what it'll be there . . ."

"No. But it won't make a difference."

"What are you *talking* about, Judah?"

"It won't make a difference."

"Well if he ain't going, no matter. I'll go alone," Drogon said. *"I'm going back to the city, believe it."*

"They'll find us, you know," Elsie said. "Even if we veer north, Cobsea'll likely hear of us."

"As if the Council can't deal with fucking *Cobsea* men," Cutter said, but she interrupted.

"And if Cobsea finds us, it won't be long before New Crobuzon does. And then we'll have to face them again. Them as follows us, and those that'll face us too."

One of the carriages of the perpetual train was changing. They thought they had got through the fringe of Torque without being marked too hard, that all they had to show was the sanatorium full of the uncanny ill or dying. But some of the cacotopic miasma was slow to show effect.

There were three people in the boxcar when its Torque sarcoma began. The train was juddering through a high land of alpestrine plants and stoneforms jawing the air. One morning while snow as fine as dust eddied and the hammerers had to warm their fingers with each strike, the door of the carriage would not open. The Councillors within could only shout through cracks in the wood.

They took an axe to it but it rebounded without scuffing paint or wood, and the Councillors knew that this was the cacotopic stain's last fingers. But by then the voices of those within had dulled with lassitude, a surrendering up.

Through the night they became more and more languid. By the next day the car was changing its shape, was bulbous and distend-ing, the wood straining, and the people within made contented cetacean sounds. The walls grew translucent and shapes could be seen, eddying as if in water. The planks and nails and wood-fibre opalesced then went transparent as the boxcar sagged, fat over the wheels, and the councillors inside grew more placid, moved oozily within air become thick. The debris from the store-cupboards lost their shapes and spun as impurities.

The carriage became a vast membranous cell, three nuclei still vaguely shaped like men and women afloat in cytoplasm. They watched and waved stubby arm-flagella at their comrades. Some Councillors wanted to decouple the grotesquerie, let it roll away and thrive or denature according to its new biology, but others said *they're our sisters in there* and would not let them. The long train continued with the corpulent amoebic thing rippling with the movement of passage, its innard inhabitants smiling.

"What in Jabber's name is it?" Cutter asked Qurabin.

"Not in Jabber's name anything. I don't know. There are things I don't want to trade myself for. And even if I did, there are secrets that have no meaning, questions without answers. It is what it is."

A fortnight after they had left the cacotopic zone, they met their first eastlanders for twenty years. A little group of nomads emerging from the hills. A fReemade gang, twenty or thirty strong. They were a wild mix, including a rare vodyanoi-Remade among the men and women reshaped for industry or display.

They came with wary courtesy to the train. "We met your scouts," their leader said. She was amended with organic whips. She stared and stared, and it took Cutter a long time to realise that what he saw in her eyes was awe. "They said you was coming."

The Remade of the Council looked at her and her brigands. "It's all change," the fReemade said that night at a meagre feast. "Something's going on in the city. It's under some siege. Tesh, I think. And something else, going on inside." But they were too far, had been too many years from the town that made them, to know details. New Crobuzon was almost the legend to them that it was to the Iron Councillors.

They did not go with the Council: they wished them their friendship and went on to their rootless robbing life in the hills, but the next fReemade the Council came to did join. They came to show respect, to worship (Cutter could see it) the self-made Remade town, and stayed as citizens, Councillors themselves. When the Iron Council came to the northern shores of the lake that would shield them from Cobsea, they were met by the first fReemade to have sought them out deliberately.

Word must be passing along the strange byways of the continent, the paths between communities and itinerants. Cutter imagined it an infection. Threads of rumour, a fibroma knotting Rohagi together. *Iron Council is coming! Iron Council is back!*

The Council was fracturing. Their momentum was such that they could not have turned away. The closer they came to the metropolis, the more anxious, hesitant the older Councillors were. "We know what it's like," they'd say. "We know what it is there." And the more certain, messianic, their children became. Those who had never seen the city were eager to visit on it something: what was it, a retribution? An anger? Justice, it might have been.

They would lead the track-laying, young men who might not have the enhanced strength of their parents but who swung their hammers with energy and hunger. The Remade put down tracks with them, but the older Councillors were the followers now.

Ann-Hari was different. She gloried. She was insistent, demanding they go faster. She would stand on outcrops, clamber with crude grace up overhanging hillocks and gnarls and gesture the perpetual train on as if she controlled it, conductor of a steam symphony.

It was so fast, suddenly: they carved on, scouts warning of this small gorge, that stream. Work-crews built hybrid forms of New Crobuzon traditions and oddities from the west—trellis bridges anchored with thick greenery, supports not of stone but of solid colour, that could only be crossed when light shone on them.

"There's war!" a fReemade told them. "Tesh says it's stopped its attacks, and then it hasn't. They say there's two envoys from New Crobuzon, asking different terms. New Crobuzon don't speak with one voice no more."

If the fReemade out here know we're coming, Cutter thought, *there's no way them in New Crobuzon don't. Word gets out. When will we face them?*

Every few days Judah would spasm as the militia following them triggered his traps. With each, a few more of the soldiers might be taken, but a few days later another of the traps would go and prove they were coming. Judah tracked their progress in his own moments of weakness.

"They're there," he said finally. "I recognise that one. They're definitely in the cacotopos. I can't believe they followed us there. They must be *desperate* to get us." What would a golem be, made of Torqued materia? With ablife channelled through that bleak matrix?

The stretched-out crew of graders and track-layers went north and east, and though they took their rails and crossties with them they left a land permanently tainted by their passage: a litter of metal parts, scars of railroad. The sky became colder, and through the darkness of the air massif became visible, leagues north. Dark drizzle came.

Here, perhaps three hundred miles west of the stub of the New Crobuzon railway, they were met by refugees. Not fReemade but recent citizens, come in a huddled rainwet congress out of the mist to run the last mile toward the growling engine, abasing before it like pilgrims. It was they who told Ann-Hari and Judah and the Iron Councillors what had happened in New Crobuzon, what was still happening, the story of the Collective.

"Oh my good gods," said Elsie. "We did it. It's happened. It's *happened*. Oh my gods." She was rapt. Judah's face was open.

"It rose in Dog Fenn," a refugee said. "Came up out of nowhere."

"That ain't the case," another said. "We knew you was coming— the Council. We had to get ready for you, some said."

They were terribly cowed before the Iron Council. These runaways were speaking to the figures they had seen so many times, for years, in the famous heliotype. They had to be cajoled into talking.

"So there's no wages: people are hungry. There's the war, and ex-militia telling what it's really like, and there are Tesh attacks. We feel like we ain't safe at all and the city ain't keeping us . . . And we hear that someone's gone to find the Iron Council." Judah's face moved to hear it.

"There are Tesh attacks?" Cutter said. The man nodded.

"Yes. Manifestations. And you know, the government's saying it's going to sort out the Tesh, going to end the war, but it's chaos, and no one knows if they're doing what they say. There's another demonstration to Parliament to demand protection, and there's them in the crowd yelling for more than that, giving out their leaflets. Caucus people, I think. But out come the men-o'-war, and the shunn, and the militia come down on us.

"And someone starts saying there's a *handlinger* at the front. And people started fighting.

"I wasn't there—I heard about it, is all. There was dead all over the streets. And when people got the militia on the run . . . All over the city come up barricades. Time for us to do what we needed, on our own. We didn't need the militia. Keep them out.

"It was after that we heard the Mayor was dead."

Delegates from all the districts had gathered in a collective, called and recalled in excitement and panic as the downtowners re-alised there was no suffrage lottery, that each of them had direct power. After some days the anti-Parliament had curtailed that rude democracy; but only, they swore, because they were in a double war. Most in the Collective were eager to negotiate with Tesh, not caring who controlled what in the seas south.

"Why are you here?" the Councillors asked.

The New Crobuzoners looked down and up again and said that the fierceness of the fighting had driven them away, that there were many exiles. They had been walking for weeks, trying to find the Iron Council.

They were not Caucusers nor collectivists, Cutter thought, only people who had found they were part of a dissident town-within-a-town and under fire, who had run with their possessions in their barrows. They had sought the Council not with a theory or politics, but with the awe of religious petitioners. Cutter disdained them. But Judah was all joy.

"It's happened, it's happening," Judah said. His voice was thick. "The rising, the second Contumancy, we've *done* it. Because of what we did. The Iron Council . . . it was an inspiration . . . When they heard we were coming . . ."

Ann-Hari was staring at him. He seemed to wear a halation in the last of the light. He spoke as if he were reading a poem. "We made this thing years ago and it laid its tracks through history, left its marks. And then we did this to New Crobuzon."

He looked astounding, a very beautiful thing. He looked transformed. But Cutter knew he was wrong. *We didn't do this, Judah. They did. In New Crobuzon. With or without the Council.*

"Now," Judah said. "We ride into the city, we join them. We aren't so far from the last of the rails. Jabber, gods, we'll ride into a changed city, we'll be part of *change*. We're bringing a *cargo*. We're bringing *history*."

Yes, and no, Judah. Yes we are. But they've got their own history already.

Cutter had come not for the Iron Council, but for Judah. It was a guilt he could never forget. *I'm not here for history,* he thought. Low mountain pikes looked down on him. In a cold river, the Iron Council vodyanoi were swimming, while the train idled in its strath. *I'm here for you.*

"And there'll be no militia now," Judah said. "They know we're coming, but with the city in revolt they won't spare anything to face us down. When we come, there'll be a new government. We'll be a . . . a coda to the insurgency. A commonwealth of New Crobuzon."

"It's been hard," said one of the refugees, uncertainly. "The Collective's under fire. Parliament's come back hard . . ."

"Oh oh oh." No one saw who spoke. The sounds ebbed up suddenly. "Oh, now.

"What's this?"

The voice was Qurabin's. Cutter looked for the fold in air, saw a flit of gusting.

"What's this?" The pilgrim-refugees were open-eyed in fear of this bodiless voice. "You said there were attacks, Tesh attacks. Manifestations? What kind? And what is *this*? This, this, this here?"

A buffeting, the stained leather of a newcomer's bag belling with Qurabin's tug. The woman moaned at what she thought some ghost, and Cutter snapped at her as Qurabin repeated, *"What is that mark?"* She looked in idiot fear at the complex gyral design on her bag.

"That? That's a sign of freedom. Freedom spiral, that is. It's all over the city."

"Oh oh oh."

"What is it, what is it, Qurabin?"

"What are the Tesh attacks?" The monk's voice was calmer but still very fast. Cutter and Elsie stiffened; Ann-Hari's concern grew; Judah slowly folded as he saw something was happening.

"No, no, this . . . I remember this. I need to, I have to, I'll ask . . ." The monk's voice wavered. There was an infolding sense, colours. Qurabin was asking something of the Moment of Secrets. There was silence. The refugees looked fearful.

"How is Tesh attacking?" Qurabin's voice came back strong. "You said manifestations? Is it colour-sucked things, presences? Emptinesses in the shape of things in the world—animals, plants, hands, everything? And people gone, sickened by them and dead? They come out of nothing, unglow, is it? And they're still coming. Yes?"

"What *is* it? Qurabin for *Jabber's* sake . . ."

"Jabber?" There was a hysteria to the monk's voice. Qurabin was moving, the locus of his sound bobbing among them. "Jabber can't help, no, no. More to come, there's more to come. And he has you thinking those are signs for freedom. The spiral. Oh."

Cutter started—the voice was right up close to him. He felt a gust of breath.

"I'm Tesh, remember. I know. The things that are coming in your city, the haints—they aren't attacks, they're *ripples*. Of an event that hasn't yet come. They're spots in time and place. Something's coming, dropped into time like water, and these have splashed back. And where they land, these little droplets come like maggoty things to suck at the world. Something's coming soon, and these, these, these spirals, these curlicues are bringing it.

"Someone is loose in New Crobuzon. This is ambassadormagik. The little manifs are nothing. Tesh want more than that. They're going to end your city. These spirals—they're the marks of a hecatombist."

Qurabin had to explain several times.

"Who left that mark is a purveyor of many thaumaturgies. Of which this is the last. This is the finishing of the law. This will take your city and, and will *wipe your city clean*. Understand that."

"These are *freedom* spirals," said a refugee, and Cutter all but cuffed him to be quiet.

"They say Tesh is talking? They say there are negotiations? No no no. If there are, they are ploy. This is the final thing they will do. Their last attack. Months of preparation, huge energy. This will end everything. No more wars for New Crobuzon. Not ever again."

"What is it, what will it be?"

But Qurabin did not answer that.

"There will be no more wars and no more peace," Qurabin said. "And more ripples will come, spattered, on the other side of the event. The last drops. Manifestations in the nothing left after your city's gone. They'll wipe it out."

It was very cold, and the wind that ran down from the chines snatched smoke from their food-fires. Before and behind them, Councillors bunked in their ironside town. There were the noises of mountain animals. There was talking, and the settling metal of the sleeping train.

"What can we do?" Judah was in horror.

"If you want . . . if you want to fix it, you have to find him. The one who's doing this, who's calling things. We have to find him. We have to stop him.

"You—we—have to get back to New Crobuzon. We have to go now."

part eight

THE REMAKING

CHAPTER TWENTY-FIVE

THE BATTLE OF COCKSCOMB BRIDGE STARTED EARLY. A SUN THAT looked watered-down lit amassing troops on either side of the river. Cockscomb, a thousand years old and built up with houses, joined Riverskin on the south of the Tar to Petty Coil north. The Collective fought very hard for Cockscomb Bridge. After the first astonishing days, when for a brief moment most of the south of New Crobuzon had been at least officially in Collective control, their zone had been eroded. Now, weeks later, Cockscomb Bridge was the westernmost point controlled by the Collective's Dog Fenn chapter.

Lookouts from the Flyside Militia Tower, long occupied by the insurgents, verified the movements of militia units before dawn, and the insurrectionist tacticians mobilised forces from several boroughs. The militia came from The Crow, through Spit Hearth where those renegade hierophants who had not left or gone into hiding said prayers for one or other or both sides, and on to the dé-classé collapse of Petty Coil. There in the decaying baroque of Mis-direct Square, looked on by architecture once sumptuous now a little absurd with its blistered paint and falling-down facades, the militia fanned out. Light went in thousands of directions from their mirrors. They wheeled cannons and motorguns to point at the old stones of the Cockscomb, and waited.

Across the water the Collective's troops came, battalions named for their areas. "Wynion Way, to me." "Silverback Street, left flank." Each corps identified by a scrap of coloured cloth, a sash, green for Wynion, grey for Silverback. Each officer wore a bandana in their colour, though their men and women would recognise them, having voted them in. They were mixed platoons, of all races. And Remade.

Rumours about militia tactics abounded. "There'll be men-o'-war." "There'll be handlingers." "There'll be drakows." "They've done a deal with Tesh—there'll be haints on the bridge." Heading each Collective unit were ex-militia, who had trained their new comrades as quick and thorough as they could. Where populist enthusiasm had resulted in someone utterly callow, untrained or useless voted in as officer, and where misplaced loyalty let them retain their position, some ex-soldier was quietly installed as advisor, to whisper tactics.

Dirigibles gathered like carrion fish at the edges of Parliament airspace, overlooking the Collective, beyond the reach of explosive harpoons, of grenades or squads of Collectivist wyrmen. The lookouts on the south watched carefully for signs that the aerostats would do a bombing run.

The standoff continued. There was anxiety among the Dog Fenn chapter that this was a decoy, that some other great attack was about to occur somewhere else. Runners went to Sheer Bridge and the barricades south of Bonetown and Mog Hill, the shanties east of Grand Calibre Bridge, but they found nothing. In the midmorning the hand-claps of explosions began—the day's bombardments against each of the Collective's three chapters.

"Howl Barrow'll fall today." The isolation of the three sections from each other had crippled them. After the first excitement-frenetic weeks, the militia had cut the street-corridors linking Fly-side to Howl Barrow, had taken Kinken, separating Howl Barrow from Skulkford and the Smog Bend chapter. There had been some attempts at air-corridors, but the Collective's dirigibles could not defeat or bypass those of Parliament. The three rebellious areas were separated, and messages passed between them by desperate and unreliable means.

"Howl Barrow's gone." It was the smallest of the chapters, one without industry, without factories or armouries. Howl Barrow was the revolt of the bohemians, and while their fervour was real, they had little beyond enthusiasm and some weakling thaumaturgy to resist the militia. At one time Dog Fenn would have sent troops through the sewers and buried roads of the undercity to join their comrades in Howl Barrow, but that would be a luxury now. They could only listen to bursts of masonry as the area was attacked. "Maybe Smoggers'll go help them," some said, but it was not a real hope. Smog Bend could send no one. The artists' commune was doomed.

Before noon one of those who had refused to leave Cockscomb Bridge emerged from his cellar waving a white flag, and was shot by the militia. There were screams just audible from other houses. "We have to get them out," Collectivists muttered. These citizens had been in their care.

Perhaps the militia were trying to draw the Collective onto the bridge. Perhaps those who had idiotically stayed behind had ceded their right to protection. Still, the officers tried to plan rescues.

A messenger came with orders from the tactics council. The leader of Wynion Way was a fierce young woman who, like other officers, carried a shield on which was nailed the torn-off streetsign for which her troop was named. She moved her men and women toward the bridge with their aging cannon, and opposite the militia began also to approach. From the south came the Glasshouse Gunners, a platoon of cactacae men.

So many debates over the pure-race squads! When the gangs of khepri guard sisters had come and said they would fight for the Collective, when the cactus squads had offered themselves as heavy infantry, some of the officers argued hard against it. "We're Collectivists!" they had said. "Not cactus or human or Remade or vodyanoi or whatever! We stand and fight together." And it was an impressive, even moving position, but it did not always make sense. "Would the chaver," a vodyanoi delegate had, to laughter, asked one of the most strident human ultraequalitarian anarchs, "like to join me tonight as we trawl the riverbed for militia bombs?"

And if the vodyanoi had to be given the freedom to operate together (though each corps, the equalitarianists insisted, contained one symbolic and powerless officer from another race, as a comradely reminder), was it not absurd to deny that to others? Wouldn't a crew of khepri trained in stingboxes be less likely to inadvertently hurt their own?

In the case of cactacae it became expedient: squads of the very strong were needed. Only the most augmented Remade could join them, with their agreement. The Glasshouse Gunners had agreed: with the tens of cactacae were two Remade, swollen with grafted muscle and oiled metal. "Rescue raid," they were told, and under cover of Collective attack, lobbing powderbombs, pyrogenics and thaumaturgic compounds, the Glasshouse Gunners went onto the bridge. They swept the houses for inhabitants, and where they found them they funnelled them to safety through holes they blew in the walls between the terraced buildings.

There was little movement on the militia side. Though they fired, burst holes in the stone, shearing off faces of houses to display subsiding rooms, the militia were waiting for something. The Collective began to advance, emboldened, and laid down suppressing counterattack while their scouts (hotchi, wyrmen, acrobatic humans) went rooftop or airborne to watch what was coming. Then the militia ranks parted and there were three men adangle, clots of handflesh clamped to their throats. Handlingers.

There was no washing on Cockscomb Bridge, but there were still lines drooped over the street studded with pegs like wizened fruit, and they shuddered as the shelling continued. At the sight of the flying men the line of Collectivists almost broke.

Parliament's handlingers were dressed in suits and bowlers, their trousers a shade too short. A strange scare tactic. Were these the bodies of condemned New Quillers? Could they be volunteers, about whom there were rumours? Men and women whose loyalty to New Crobuzon's government was so absolute they sacrificed themselves to be vessels for the handlingers? A holy rightist suicide. Probably these were just the executed dressed in costumes to cause foreboding.

Seeing them loom, thaumaturgicked and fire-spitting, stronger than cactacae, they seemed supra-Quillers, nightmares of reaction. The costumes raised memories of the Night of the Kinken Shards, when the New Quill Party had overrun the khepri ghetto in a storm of murder, shattering spit-sculptures in the Plaza of Statues, stamping the mindless males and butchering the women until they trod a ground of glass needles, ichor, blood. After that attack, so frenzied that respectable uptown opinion was horrified, the militia had come in to protect those few khepri not fled or murdered. But the Quillers did not have to flee: they were allowed to leave in an orderly and triumphant way.

Now Quillers or what looked like them were bearing down from the sky. The Collectivists stepped quickly into the lees of the bomb-shaken houses. They coughed in the dust of millennium-old bricks.

From the south, running the length of the bridge unnaturally fast to join them, came a thin and naked man. Clamped not to his neck or his head but to his face, fingers spread over his eyes and nose, was a dark left hand. A sinistral.

Civil wars made for unlikely allies. There were those few handlingers that for whatever reasons opposed their brothersisters—

whether odd altruism or a politic calculation, the Collective's negotiators never knew. It may have sickened the negotiators to do deals
with these symbols of corruption and parasite cunning, but they
would turn nothing down now. Especially as several of the handlinger turncoats were sinistrals.

The three militia handlingers were dextriers, warriors, but for
all their power they veered when they saw it was a sinistral on the
man's face. They tried to get out of range, but the Collectivist handlinger jumped up higher than a human should and snapped his fingers. One dark-suited man spasmed as the sinistral shut down the
dextrier's assimilation gland. It became nothing but a blind five-
fingered beast clutching a brain-dead man who fell out of the sky,
his bowler hat a coda behind him, into the slow and dirty river Tar.

A second snap from the sinistral's fingers and the nude handlinger sent another of the flying men palsied and down, to spread
out red on the cobbles. The Collectivists cheered. But the third loy-
alist handlinger had flown in fast under eaves unseen, and as the
sinistral began to turn its host away from its burst victim, the dextrier opened its man's mouth and spatseared.

Inky gusts of flame uncoiled and rolled over the nude man's
skin, darking him and sending his fat spitting, and the sinistral
screamed in its host's voice and psychically in its own, making re-
ceptives for a half mile wince. It dropped and burnt up, fire-ruined.

The militia motorguns opened and the air became a shred-
der. The Collectivists dropped behind stone as the dextrier flew
unconcerned through the firing, its body jerking, protecting its
hand-body with the contingent flesh it borrowed.

On the roofs at the north end of the bridge a thaumaturge rose,
a Brock Marsh rebel come to defend the Collective. His body was
aglow with corposant. It flared without sound in cobalt, and he
barked and a gob of the colour sputtered, flew with butterfly flight
to the frontmost militia gun, and it arced and took over the can-
noneers who staggered and pulled their masks from faces gone
bleached and blind.

The men and the gun brittled, cracks spread across them, and one by one gun and men shattered. The ground where they had been was dusted with shards of them, quite dry.

Another cheer, and the leader of Wynion Way came forward firing a musket, but the handlinger flew down, spinning as it did, heavy black boots flailing. It flew into a column of Collectivists with a kind of angry playfulness, smashing them and spitting fire in an incandescent spiral, leaving brutalised dead and dying and fire-stained walls.

"Fall back! Now!"

The Glasshouse Gunners emerged on the streeted bridge and started to retreat, firing rivebows into the militia, who were no longer waiting, were beginning to advance dragging carronade with them. Their motorguns started again. The handlinger and the Collectivist thaumaturge faced each other. The man raised his fists to send out a bolt; the handlinger sent him burning out of the air.

"Get the fuck back now!" The militia were coming. The Glasshouse Gunners turned and in a sudden rage stormed them. The ranks of huge thorned fighters were tremendous. The militia faltered.

The dextrier spat but too early. It burned through several clotheslines. A cactus-man sent a machete into the host, shouted triumph. It was a huge knife; it ground deep into the human meat, sent him down. The cactacae kicked and stamped the parasite and host with tree-trunk feet. The Gunners' random line was enfiladed and, even armoured in crude-cast metal, the motorgun bullets tore at them.

The weary cactus fighters began to retreat, toward their approaching weapons. The last of the Gunners was a Remade human. He wore a mottlesome thing on his foot. His cactus comrades turned to him, and he spat fire across their faces. They had killed the host but not the handlinger. It had crept onto him.

A train came tearing over the city on the close-by rail-bridge, within a few yards of the Cockscomb. At the north shore the rails were blocked by a barricade, but south of Petty Coil Station, the Sud Line was the Collective's. The train stopped beside the bridge, and from its windows Collectivists fired grenades, directed by a shantytown garuda on updrafts over the bomb fires. The missiles ruined more and more of the Cockscomb Bridge skyline, and broke apart the militia lines.

But it was not enough. The militia were taking Cockscomb Bridge, firing back at the train. In the east, the black spine of Parliament stabbed up, an inselberg of dark architecture, watching this and the other fights (an airship raid on the Kelltree Docks, shunn-cavalry riding their bipeds into Creekside, a Mamluk regiment of loyal Remade fighting in Echomire while the Collectivists screamed and called them traitors).

It's time. A whisper from the Collective's Riverskin commanders. Under the railway arches by Saltpetre Station, a command headquarters, Frengeler, ex-militia, trained in tactics and turned to the radicals, the outstanding military thinker of the Collective, was screaming: *Decide if you want to fucking win or not. We're out of time, do it. Blow the bridges.*

There were few bridges left that crossed from Parliament territory directly into the Collective: each was a conduit they could not afford to cede to the militia. Below the surface of the Tar, the vodyanoi Collectivists guarding the sewer entrances sent out aquatic sappers.

None of them liked the job they had to do. None of them wanted to destroy these loved old things. They felt they must.

They found their way through the murked waters to where the arches of the bridge rose from mud, they groped, but with growing anxiety could not find their demolitions. They gripped at each other and barked their submerged tongue, but out of the dark water came enemy shapes. *Betrayal,* someone shouted, as militia vodyanoi came at them, shamans with roiling patches of clean water, undines that gripped the Collectivists and squeezed.

*   *   *

A rump escaped. Their information came through: *We can't explode the fucking bridge.*

Sheer Bridge, then. But though this time the vodyanoi swimmers were careful of ambush, it was the same thing—their explosives were gone. Found gods-knew-when and removed. The plans of the Collective to cauterise the ingress of militia had been stymied.

"It'll be the same on Mandrake Bridge, and Barrow. They've got *ways in.*"

And now here they were coming. With the suppressing fire of the Collective's guns, the thanatic foci of their hexes, their booby-traps, it took the militia hours to advance through what they made a monstrous landscape, of jags that had been walls and windows without glass or purpose. But they were advancing. Cockscomb Bridge belonged to Parliament again.

As the Collectivists fell back, more barricades went up. The rubble from bombed buildings was hauled as foundation and *anything* went above it, slag from factories, sleepers, furniture, the stumps of trees from Sobek Croix. The Collectivists had to sacrifice a few streets west of Sedilia Square to focus on main streets. They sent word to the defenders of the south bank itself to prepare for invasion if the militia veered east over the bridge.

They did not. They crossed the river; and in the square they halted, commandeered buildings (one only just vacated by Collectivists, whose effects the militia began systematically to defile, throwing pissed-on heliotypes out of the windows).

In Griss Twist, the insurrectionists took decades-old rubbish from the dumps to block Sheer Bridge. Badside was being shelled, its desolate population and the token Collectivist units left to guard it conserving their ammunition. No one wanted Badside itself; but as a conduit to Echomire and Kelltree, and as the riverbank facing Dog Fenn, the Collective's heart, it had to be defended.

In the city's northwest, where the Dog Fenn Collectivists could not go, their sister chapters were in trouble. Something was being prepared in Tar and Canker Wedge, surely an attack on Smog Bend. Break it, with its machinofacture and its organised workers, and that chapter of the Collective was gone.

Howl Barrow was easy. "We can flatten a bunch of inverts, perverts and painters quicker than scratching our arses," one captured militia commander had said, and his disdainful claim had become notorious. The Howl Barrow chapter would not last long, with its Nuevist squads, its battalions of militant ballet dancers, its infamous Pretty Brigade, a group of Collectivist grenadiers and musketeers all of them dollyboy man-whores in dresses and exaggerated make-up, shouting orders to each other in invert slang. At first they had been greeted with disgust; then with forbearance, as they fought without restraint; then with exasperated affection. No one wanted them to be overrun, but it was inevitable.

The militia took Cockscomb Bridge, broke the Glasshouse Gunners, and were camped on the south bank of the River Tar. They were poised to push east into the heartlands of the Dog Fenn chapter, the stronghold of the New Crobuzon Collective. There was a sense that no Collectivist would voice, that this was the start of the end.

It was into this atmosphere, this war, that Judah, Cutter and their party entered the city.

CHAPTER TWENTY-SIX

"GODS. *GODS.* HOW IN THE NAME OF JABBER DID YOU *GET* here?"

Entering and leaving the New Crobuzon Collective was hard. The barricades were guarded by the tense and terrified. The sewers were patrolled. With the Parliamentarian aeronauts savaging any dirigibles not their own, with hexes protecting each side, coming in and out had become epic and dangerous.

There were lurid folk tales: the heroic guardsman who slipped out without fanfare to execute militia; the Parliamentarian unit that took a wrong turn in a backstreet maze to emerge in the middle of Collectivist territory. Now there was a story of the crusade coming, to take all the poor starvelings in the Collective away.

Of course hundreds *had* entered and left the Collective, through ill-guarded barriers, through thaumaturgy. The Mayor's city was full of those who took the Collective's side: in Chimer, in the industrial fringe of Lichford, areas under martial law but from which guilders, seditionists and the curious sometimes made their way into Dog Fenn or Creekside, begging entry. And the Collective itself contained many who passively or actively wished it ill, and crept out uptown or stayed as spies.

So arrivals were feted, but suspiciously. Judah and the others came from the east of the city, through the ruinous landscape by Grand Calibre Bridge. With Qurabin's help they found hidden byways, more and more of the monk eroding with each journey. Past the barricadistes. Along brick gulches to the post office in Dog Fenn where the delegate council met. They addressed the representatives of the Caucus.

Cutter felt emptied out. So many months since he had been in New Crobuzon and now it was so new, so tremendously not as it had been. It made him think of everything, it made him think of Drey and Ihona and Fejh and Pomeroy, of the bones under the railroad tracks.

What city is this? he had thought as they entered.

The towers of Grand Calibre Bridge, ajut and centuries broken in the water of the Gross Tar, now crowned with guns puffing lazily to send shells uptown. Badside, always squalid, reshaped and broken now by more than poverty.

Everywhere. Over the girders of Barley Bridge, the streets concatenate with the everyday, the monstrous and the beautiful. They were not quite empty. There were bandaged soldiers who watched the party from broken buildings. Members of a quickly running, now ratlike populace bent under sacks of food, under furniture and nonsense they took from one place to another. They were cowed.

The trail-dust on Cutter and his comrades meant they took curious looks—everyone was dirty but their dirt was different—but no one seemed to find it strange that they travelled together: two Remade, with four whole humans (no one could see Qurabin) pulling their exhausted mounts.

The Remade were mounts themselves. The lizard-bodied man,

Rahul, was one: Ann-Hari's agent when the Iron Council was born, whose voice Cutter had heard telling of Uzman's death. He was in late mid-age, but still ran on those backbent legs faster than any horse. Judah had ridden him across the wildlands to the city. The other was a woman, Maribet, whose arcane Remaking had put her head on the neck of a carthorse studded with avian claws. Elsie was her rider.

Many of the young freeborn Councillors had been desperate to see New Crobuzon, but Ann-Hari had insisted that the Council itself needed every hand. They would see the city soon enough. Iron Council had sent only these emissaries.

The two Remade stared like farmboys from the Mendican Foothills. As if the geography awed them utterly. They were walking in a broken dream of their own pasts.

There were children in the streets. Wild, they made playgrounds out of destroyed architecture. Bombs had taken large parts of the city away, recast others in a bleak fantastic of pointless still-standing walls, rubble wastes, girders and thick wires uncoiled arm-thick from the ground: gardens of ruin. And amid them new kinds of beauty.

Hexes had made sculptures of brick, stained breakdown, strange colours. In one place they had made an ivied wall only half there, a glasslike brick refraction. The cats and dogs of New Crobuzon ran over this reshaping. They were tense, prey animals now: the Collectivists were hungry.

A strange parade. A children's play performed on a street-corner to an audience of parents and friends desperate and ostentatious with pride and enjoyment, as bomb sounds continued. Spirals on the walls. Complex, arcing and re-arcing. Qurabin, unseen, made a hiss, a *yes* sound.

Once there was a panic, someone as they walked past screaming and running from a patch of moving colour, crying "A haint! A haint!" But it was fresh graffiti, ink sliding down, that had shocked the woman. She laughed, embarrassed. A klaxon sounded and an aerostat had hauled piscine over the Collective and drizzled bombs with coughs of collapsing mortar; those on the streets started and looked wary but more resigned than afraid.

There were countless styles on the streets. A last flowering of impoverished dandyism.

What is this *place?* thought Cutter. *I cannot believe I'm here. I cannot believe I'm back. We're* back.

He saw Judah. Judah was destroyed. His face was absolute with misery. *Is this what we won?* Cutter saw him wonder.

In the later days of their journey, close to the city, Iron Council's emissaries had met scores of refugees, poor and not-poor, from downtown and uptown. Out in the open land, they were only the lost. "Too much terror," one had told them, not knowing who they were, assuming them explorers. "It ain't the same," the Crobuzoners said.

"It was something in the first days," a woman said. She held a baby. "I'd have stayed. It weren't easy, but it was something. Empty- ing the prisons and the punishment factories, hearing Tarmuth had gone, getting messages from its Collective, till it fell. The food run out and next thing we're eating rat. Time to go."

A terrified shopkeeper from Sheck claimed the Collective had gathered all the rich from the south of Aspic when they had taken it, stolen their houses, shot the men, raped the women and shot them too, and were raising the children as slaves.

"I'm gone," he said. "What if they win? What if they kill Mayor Triesti like they did Stem-Fulcher? I'm gone for Cobsea. They ap- preciate an industrious man."

Through streets Cutter had once known now made strange by mortars, with neglected bunting in the colours of factions, with signs proclaiming idiot theories or new churches, new things, new ways of being, split and peeling. The raucousness and vigour were gone from the streets but still sensible in echo, in the buildings themselves: palimpsests of history, epochs, wars, other revolts embedded in their stones.

There were sixteen Caucusers in the delegate council. Five could be found. They stared. They hugged the newcomers. They wept.

"I can't believe it, I can't believe it."

They each gripped Judah for what he had done, finding Iron Council, and Cutter and Elsie for finding Judah and bringing him back. They greeted Drogon. Judah told them Qurabin was with them, described the monk as a renegade from Tesh, and they looked in unease and waved at the air.

And then the Remade. The Iron Councillors.

One by one, the Caucusers of New Crobuzon's Collective gripped the hands or tail-like limb of the Councillors, awed, abject, let out murmurs of solidarity. "Decades," one whispered, holding Rahul, who reciprocated with unexpected gentleness in his lower, reptile arms. "You came back. Chaver, where you been? Gods. We been *waiting*."

There were too many things to ask. *What has it been? Where have you been? How do you live? Do you miss us?* These questions and others filled the room in ghost unspoken form. When at last someone spoke, it was to say, "Why have you come back?"

Cutter knew some of the delegates. An old cactus-woman called Swelled Eyelid, a Proscribed, he remembered; a man Terrimer, whose affiliation he did not know; and Curdin.

Curdin, a leader of the Runagates Rampant, had been Remade.

There were fashions in Remaking. Cutter had seen this shape before. Pantomime horses, people called them. Curdin had been made quadruped. Behind his own, another pair of legs shuffled uncertainly, bent at their waist, their human torso horizontal and submerging into the flesh above Curdin's arse as if he were opaque water. Another man had been embedded in him.

"They broke me out," he said to Cutter quietly. "When it started.

When the Collective took over. They emptied the punishment factories. Too late for me."

"Curdin," Judah said. "Curdin, what is this? What's happening? Is this the Collective?"

"It was," Curdin said. "It *was.*"

"Why's the Council coming *back*?"

"We're being targeted," Judah said. "New Crobuzon fought its way through the Firewater Straits for us. They found out where we are. They've wanted us for years. Curdin, they're chasing us *through the cacotopic stain.* The Council's a way off yet, but it's coming. We came to tell you, and to see—"

"You sure you're still being followed? Through the stain? How did you *come through the damn stain*?"

"We've not shaken them off. They may be depleted, but they're still coming. Even if Parliament doesn't believe that the Council's returning, their assassins are after us."

"But why are you *here*?"

"Because of you, of course. God*damn,* Curdin. I knew something was happening when I left. I knew, and when the Council heard about it, they knew it was time to come home. To be part of this."

But you wanted to stay away, Judah. Cutter looked at him, with a strange sense.

"We're coming back. We're going to join the Collective."

Though there was joy in the faces of the Caucusers, Cutter swore he saw something ambivalent in all of them.

"There ain't a Collective."

"You *shut* your damn *mouth,*" said others instantly, rounding on Curdin, and, "The *fuck* you say." Even the other Runagaters looked shocked, but Curdin raised himself up on four tiptoes and shouted.

"We *know* it. We've weeks, at the most. We've nothing left. They've cut us off, they're killing Smog Bend, Howl Barrow's probably gone. We're less than a fifth of the committee—half the others don't know what they want, or want to *make peace,* for gods' sake, with the Mayor, as if Parliament wants that now. We're *over.* We're just living out days. And now you want to drag the godsdamned *Iron Council* into this? You want to bring it down?"

"Chaver." It was a young woman who spoke, a Runagater. Her voice shook. "You won't like what I'm going to say."

"No this *ain't* because of what's done to me . . ."

"Yes, it is. You been *Remade,* chaver, and it's a sick thing, and it's made you despair, and I ain't saying I'd do it any differently, and I ain't saying we'll win for sure, but I am damn well saying that you don't decide now that we're done. You better godsdamned fight with us, Curdin."

"Wait." Judah's mouth moved with a panic of collapsing plans. "Listen listen. Whatever the, whatever it is, whatever's happening, you have to know that ain't the reason we're here. We have a job to do. Listen.

"*Listen.*

"New Crobuzon will fall.

"We heard—listen, please—we heard about the manifestations, your haints. They haven't stopped, have they?"

"No but they grow smaller . . ."

"Yeah. For the same reason there aren't droplets just around a splash. Because something's getting close. Tesh *ain't suing for peace.* Whether they're talking to you, or Parliament, or both or whatever . . . they ain't making peace, they're preparing for the end. The haints ain't the weapon. Something else is. It's in the spirals."

When at last they understood, they thought him mad. But not in fact for long.

"You think this is a whim?" Cutter raged at them. "You got any idea what we went through to get here? Any idea at all? What we're trying to do here? The spirals are calling down fucking *fire* on you. On Parliament, Collective, all."

They believed him, but Curdin laughed when Judah asked for help.

"What do you want from us, Judah? We ain't got troops. I mean we do, but who's 'we'? I can't control the Collective's fighters. If I try to tell them what we need, they'll think—even godsdamned now— that it's a sodding ploy from a Runagater, trying to take over the Collective. I ain't a military commander; I couldn't control them. Or do you want *Runagaters*? Specifically?" He looked at his factionists.

"There's a few left. Kirriko Street Irregulars is ours, but who the fuck knows how to contact them? The others are at the front. They're on the barricades, Judah. What would you have me do? You think we can call a godsdamned meeting of the delegates, explain the situation? We're breaking down, Judah—it's each district for itself. We have to hold off the militia."

"Curdin, if we don't stop this there won't be a damn *city,* let alone the Collective."

"I understand." The Remade man's eyes looked rubbed with sand. He was scabbed from fighting. He swayed. "What would you have me do?"

A standoff, as if they are enemies. A silence.

"The city needs this."

"I *understand,* Judah. What would you have us *do?*"

"There must be someone, some thaumaturge, some of the kithless . . ."

"I know who makes the spirals," someone said.

"Maybe there is, but you'll have to find them, and don't look at me like that Judah of *course* I'll do what I can, but I don't know where to go. It's the end now: there ain't no one giving orders."

"I know who makes the spirals. I know who makes the spirals."

Quiet, finally. It was the young woman Runagater who spoke.

"Who makes the spirals. Who's calling something. The Tesh agent."

"How?" Judah said. "Who?"

"I don't know him, not really . . . but I know someone who does. He used to be a Runagater, or nearly. I know him from meetings, Curdin. You do too. Ori."

"*Ori*? Who went to Toro?"

"Ori. He's still with Toro, I think. It was Toro killed Stem-Fulcher, they reckon, for whatever bloody good it did. Toro disappeared after, but he's been seen again. Maybe Ori's with him. Maybe Ori can bring Toro to help.

"Ori knows who does the spirals. He told me."

CHAPTER TWENTY-SEVEN

Toro was a dog now, a stupid and brutalised dog following a master it hated, unable to stop. Ori considered it that way.

We did it! he had thought. For a very short time. For less than one night. Even in the sadness and the shock of learning the first Bull's motives and her manipulations, even uncoupled as he felt himself from the movement he had thought defined him, he had been proud that the killing of the Mayor had been this great catalyst.

He thought that for a few hours, against the evidence: the rebels who had no idea Stem-Fulcher was gone, who learnt it with a cruel excitement but no great renewal of purpose, no upsurge of fight spirit. They had enough of that in those early barricade days, irrespective of what the Toroans had done. A few hours with the Collective, and Ori had known that the operation against the Mayor had been irrelevant to its birth.

Ori, Toro, pushed against the world with his helmet and split through again and again. He could move easily. He went skulking from the Collective to Parliament's city and back again, disdaining the traps and barriers between them. He followed his quarry, like a dog. He followed Spiral Jacobs.

Well then, he had thought, the execution of the Mayor will be part of the movement. It was of the moment. The world was changed. It would be part of the momentum. Ugly, yes, but a freeing, something that would drive things forward. The Collective would be inexorable. Uptown would fall. In the Collective, the seditionists would win the delegates, and the Collectivists would win against Parliament.

The militia imposed lockdown law across what of New Crobuzon they controlled. The populace convulsed in sympathy riots, fought in some places, to join the Collective, and failed. Ori had waited. With a tumour of anxiety, he found in himself a drab certainty that the killing of the Mayor had done nothing at all.

When he was Toro, Ori moved in the darkness between reality's pores, to emerge in the quiet of uptown, in the evenings, on Mog Hill, unseen behind the rows of sightseers. Uptowners from Chnum and Mafaton whooped as if at fireworks at the oily blossomings of explosives, at the unlight glow of witch fire from Parliament's thaumaturges, gave childish boos at the motes of glow from hedge-hexers of the Collective.

I could kill so many of you, Ori thought, time and again, *for my brothers and sisters, for my dead,* and found himself doing nothing.

He went to the Kelltree warehouse many nights running. None of his comrades came back. He thought that Baron might have escaped, but he was sure the militiaman had not tried for that. No one came back to the rendezvous.

Ori gave his landlady promissory notes, which she accepted in kindness. Within the Collective's bounds, everything was camaraderie. He sat with her at night and listened to the attacks. There were rumours that Parliament was using war constructs for the first time in twenty years.

He kept the armour under his bed. His bull helmet. He did not use it except to walk at night, and he did not know why. Once he horned his way through newly dangerous streets, past Collectivist guards who were drunk and others focused and sober, through the raucous night, to the soup kitchen. There was a debate among the derelicts.

Ori had been back again, in these most recent days. The roof was gone, replaced by the droppings of some masonry-riddling weaponworms Parliament had loosed. The kitchen was empty. The residues of seditionist literature, long unhidden, lay in wet scraps. Blankets were moulding.

Toro could have been a fighter for the Collective. Toro could have stood on the barricades, run boulevards between bomb-denuded trees and gored militia.

Ori did not. A lassitude took him. He was deadened by failure. In the first days, he tried to be in the Collective, to shore up its defences and learn from the public lectures, the art shows that initially proliferated: he could only lie and wonder *what it was he had done.* He had a literal sense of unknowing. *What is it I did? What did I do?*

He saw a haint in Syriac. A thick, unopened book in mottling uncolours, turning on spiderthreads of force. It sucked light and shade, killed two passersby before evanescing and leaving only a remnant of bookness that lingered another day. He was not afraid; he watched the apparition, its movements, its position, before the graffitied wall. Among the obscenities and slogans, the nonsense signs and little pictures, he saw familiar spirals.

I need to find Jacobs.

Toro could do it. Toro's eyes could see which of the painted helicoid marks were new. There was thaumaturgy in them: they could not be effaced. When he was Toro, Ori traced backward by the marks' ages, tracking Spiral Jacobs through a grand and ultracomplex spiral in the city itself.

Jacobs moved without difficulty between the Collective and Parliament's city, just as Toro did. The spiral, through its recombinant coils, veered toward New Crobuzon's core. Toro stalked at night, gathered in shadows the helmet snagged. A fortnight after the Collective was born, amid the noise of the popular committees for defence and allocation, Ori, unseen in his bull-head, came through Syriac Well and found Spiral Jacobs.

The old man was shuffling, his palette of graffiti tools in his hand. Toro followed him down an alley overshadowed by concrete. The tramp began to draw another of his coils.

Spiral Jacobs had not looked up. Had only murmured something like, "Boy, hello there, once a doubler eh, now kithless? You got out, did you then? Hello boy." The thaumaturged iron of the helmet did not confuse him. He knew who he spoke to.

"It didn't work like we thought," Ori said. Plaintive, and disgusted with himself for that. "It didn't turn out."

"Turned out perfect."

"What?"

"It turned, out, perfect."

He thought the old man's madness was asserting again, that the words were meaningless. He believed at first that that was what he thought. But anxiety rose in him. It swelled as he attended public meetings in Murkside, Echomire and Dog Fenn.

In Bull-guise, he found Jacobs again. It took him two days.

"What did you mean?" he had said. They were in Sheck, under the brick of Outer Crow Station, where he had tracked the convolutes of paint. "What did you mean it turned out perfect?"

The truth appalled him of course, but worse was that he was not surprised.

"Do you think you're the only one, boy?" Spiral Jacobs said. "I made suggestions all over. You was the best. Well done, son."

"What is it you wanted?" Ori said in Toro's guttural voice, but he knew the answer, he realised. Jacobs wanted chaos. "Who are you? Why did you make the Collective?" Jacobs looked at him with something it took Ori seconds to recognise as contempt.

"Go away, boy," the tramp said. "You don't *make* something like this. It weren't me done this. I been doing other things. And what you done—*frippery.* Just go."

Ori was bewildered then debased. Everything the Toroans had done was a sideshow. Toro, Baron, his comrades . . . he did not understand what they had been used for, but he knew they had been used. His insides pitched. He could not breathe.

Without anger—with sudden calm—Ori knew he must kill Jacobs. For revenge, the protection of his city—he was not sure. He came close. He raised a crossbow pistol. The old man did not move. Ori aimed at his eye. The man did not move.

Ori fired and air rushed with the bolt, and Spiral Jacobs was unmoved, staring with two unbloodied eyes. The quarrel was embedded in the wall. Ori drew a pistol with clustered barrels. One by one the bullets he fired at Spiral Jacobs hit the ground or the wall. They would not touch the old man. Ori put his gun away and punched at Spiral Jacobs' head, and though Jacobs had not moved Ori hit air.

Anger took him. He launched at the old man who had led him to Toro, had helped him, had had him kill. Ori kicked with all the power in him, all the strength given by the arcane helmet, gouged, and the old man did not move.

Ori could not touch Spiral Jacobs. He tried again. He could not touch him.

His anger had become despair, and even the Collectivists, even the militia a mile away who had grown inured to the noises of fighting stopped at his lowing. Ori could not touch the old man.

Spiral Jacobs was drunk. He was a real vagrant. He was just something else as well.

At last he walked away with slow near-rambling steps, and Toro, doglike, could only follow. Jacobs had walked to the centre of New Crobuzon, toward the vaults of Perdido Street Station, and Toro had followed. Ori was reduced to calling questions Spiral Jacobs would not answer.

"What were you doing?

"Why me?

"What about the others, what were they supposed to do? What's the real plan?

"What are you doing?"

The Collective. It was a Remaking.

At first, in the upsurge of resentment, violence, surprise and contingencies, revenges, motives altruist and base, necessities, chaos and history, in the first moments of the New Crobuzon Collective, there had been those who refused to work with the Remade. Necessity had changed most of their minds.

It had been fast. Those who had agitated for the overthrowing of Parliament were stunned. The militia abandoned their places, the spikes, the pitons of the government left empty in Collective territory. Skyrails stopped. As looters ransacked militia towers, as AWOL soldiers brought out their weapons, an old word began to change. In a speech to the strikers of the Turgisadi Foundry, an agitator from the Caucus waved at the Remade workers to join the main mass and shouted, "We're Remaking the damn city: who knows better about that than you?"

Ori knew his seditionist ex-friends, his erstwhile comrades, would be there as the commonalty rose. He could help them; as Toro he could be a weapon of the Collective.

He could not. Ori was broken. He could only find Spiral Jacobs and follow him, many nights. He felt he would remain unfinished until he had spoken to him, learnt what he had done.

"Where are the others?" he said. "What did you have us do? Why did we kill the Mayor?" Jacobs would say nothing, only walked away. *Why does he want chaos?*

Ori could always find him. The spirals glowed in Toro's eyes. Ori was pathetic.

"I'm worried about you, love," his landlady said. "You're falling apart, anyone can see. You eating? You sleeping?"

He could not speak, could only lie for days, eating what she gave him, until his anxiety swelled and he would rise and, as Toro, find Spiral Jacobs again. That was how it was. Nights behind the strange old man.

At first he tracked him in his bull gear, moving in and out of the real. Following him in that terrible disempowered way, Ori saw weird in the old man's own movements. He took off his helmet. Spiral Jacobs paid no mind.

Ori followed without Toro's thaumaturgy, and still they passed somehow between Collective and Parliament's city. In the gaslight, by vivid elyctro-barometric tubes, Spiral Jacobs walked his old-man walk on streets of night-stained brick, dark concrete, dark wood and iron, and Ori went after him, a desultory pilgrim.

Jacobs might start in Aspic, at the edge of the Collective, shambling past crowds of night-guards, turn under an arch of wattle. He might pass through a sooty alley between the backs of buildings, by shades of trees and the spires of saint-houses, and after a curve the passage might empty him and his follower into the streets of Pincod. Two minutes of walking but more than four miles from the starting point.

Ori followed Jacobs as the tramp kinked the city's geography. He went easily between areas that were not coterminous. Later, alone, Ori tried to retrace the routes and of course could not.

From Flyside to Creekside, from Salacus Fields to St Jabber's Mound, Spiral Jacobs made the city convenient. He quietly put this area by that, had a terrace (always momentarily empty of passersby) wind impossibly through far-apart areas. He passed in and out of the Collective without seeing barricades or militia, and Ori followed, and begged him to answer questions, and sometimes in his rage fired or knifed at the old man, and always his weapon met nothing.

I'm in trouble. Ori knew it. *I'm trapped.* There was something in him: his mind was rutting, he was not well, he was despairing. In the middle of this upturn, this upheaval, the Remaking of the city, he who should live this moment was stricken, was crying, was lying in bed days at a time. *Something's wrong with me.*

All he could do was track Jacobs through the byways he made: and sit alone, sometimes weep. He was crushed by a weight, while things changed, while the first days—of excitement, construction, arguments and street-meetings—became days of injury, of losses, became embattlement, became terror, became a sense of end.

The Collectivists' resolution grew for a last stand, for something they knew was coming. Ori lay, and walked the violent streets and saw the initial spreading of the Collective halt, and reverse. Saw the militia encroach. Nightly another barricade was lost. The militia took the kilns on Pigsty Street, the stables of Helianthus Avenue, the arcades of Sunter. The Collective was shrinking. Ori, Toro, lay alone.

I should tell someone, he thought. *Spiral Jacobs is trouble. He's the cause of something.* But he did nothing.

Was the city full of Jacobs' castoffs? Men and women lost, their tasks unfinished, their work for Spiral Jacobs interrupted before they knew they did it, or what it was at all. Was it better or worse to have succeeded?

"Hush, hush," Spiral Jacobs said to him as they walked at night. The old man's wall-paintings became more arcane, more complexly spiralled. Ori was not quite crying but like a lost thing, following and asking questions in a tone near begging. "What did you have me do, what are you doing, what did you do?"

"Hush, hush." Jacobs did not sound unkind. "It's nearly done. We just needed something to keep things busy. Not long now."

* * *

Ori returned home, and people were waiting for him: Madeleina di Farja; Curdin, whom he had not seen for months, Remade and broken; and a group of men and women he did not know.

"We need to talk to you," Madeleina said. "We need your help. We have to find your friend Jacobs. We have to stop him."

At that Ori cried, with the relief that someone else had come to this knowledge without him, that something would be done, that he did not have to do it alone. He was so tired. Seeing them, ranged and rugged by him, carrying their weapons with purpose, without the panic of those days, he felt something in him strain for them.

CHAPTER TWENTY-EIGHT

IN THE SOUTH, A SALVAGE SQUAD TOOK A DANGEROUS MISSION through the streets that separated Aspic from Sobek Croix Gardens. The park was a free-fire zone, inhabited by prison escapees and renegades from factions, not controlled by the Collective or by Parliament. The Collectivists needed fuel: they took axes and saws to the trees. But hauling through the streets under militia fire and returning weighed down by logs cost them. Men fell, shot on the corners of the park, lay on the cobbles, pinned and put down in the shade of walls.

Decisions were still made, but the overarching strategy that had made the Collective operate like a power, an alternative city-state, was breaking down. Some squads were commanded with strategic intelligence, but each action now was more or less its own end, part of nothing larger.

The Flyside Militia Tower had long been stripped of weapons, its thaumaturgic compounds deployed, its secret maps taken. Sky-rails, thick and thrumming wires, extended south and north from its top, each stretched taut to its terminus. In the south the last militia tower in the city, in the suburbs of Barrackham; to the north the rail angled up, hundreds of feet above the tangle of slate and iron roofs, over the ghetto of the Glasshouse and the intricately twisted River Tar, up to the centre of New Crobuzon. It went to the Spike, stabbed into the sky by Perdido Street Station.

In these savage last days, the Collectivists of the Flyside tower filled two pods with explosives, chymical and blackpowder. A little before noon, they released one in each direction, throttles jammed. The little vehicles of brass tubing and glass and wood accelerated very fast, screamed over the city.

Wyrmen scattered in surprise as the wires bowed under the pods' weight. They rose, shouted obscenities.

Perdido Street Station was the centre of the city, even more than Parliament, the atramentous keep now empty of functionaries (it was an irony of the time that the "Parliamentarian" government had suspended Parliament). The Mayor was making decisions from the Spike.

As the north-travelling pod careered over Riverskin the militia fired grenades. They landed short, with cruel billows, on Sheck or the riverside streets near Petty Coil. But the guards could not miss for long. The pod made the metal skyrail scream, and one two missiles sailed out, burst its windows and detonated.

The pod blew, its payload conflagrating in an apocalypse instant, and it plummetted in a smoke-described arc. It shattered across the shopkeepers' houses and terraces of Sheck, crumbling into melting metal and fire.

To the south, though, the explosive-crammed pod rushed over spivvy streets, directly above a barricade at the borders of Aspic and Barrackham. Militia and Collectivist looked up from either side of the wedge of rubble and brick.

The pod overshot open scrubland, sinking as the skyrail angled down, as the estate towers rose toward it. It rushed into the Barrackham Tower.

A one-two-three of explosions as dirty fire blared from the top of the militia spire. Its concrete bulged and split; it was eaten from inside by an unfolding plume; it went up, blew out and began to fall, and the stories below it subsided. In burning slabs like pyroclastic flow the top of the tower slewed off, militia pods falling out and tumbling.

The skyrail went murderously slack, whiplashed down across two miles of city. It coiled through slates, gouging a threadline fault and killing as it came. It dangled from the Flyside Tower and curved toward Aspic, where its hot weight tore buildings.

A spectacular kind of triumph, but one the Collectivists knew would not change the tide.

Most of the workshops by Rust Bridge were quiet, their staff and owners keeping out of sight or protecting the Collective's borders. But there were still some small factories doing what work they could, for what payment they could get, and it was to one of these that Cutter went on the day the militia tower fell.

The fires of the ancient street of glassworkers were cold, but with a scraped-together purse and political exhortations, he persuaded the seditionist workforce of the Ramuno Hotworks to restart their furnaces, bring out the potash, ferns, the limestone to scour and clear. Cutter gave them the housing with Judah's circular mirror that he had broken. At last they said they would build him a crystal-glass speculum. He went to Ori's rooms, to wait for him and Judah.

If Cutter had met Ori before, which was possible given the tight world of the pre-Collective seditionists, he did not remember it. Madeleina di Farja had described Ori, and Cutter had envisaged an angry, frantic, pugnacious boy eager to fight, excoriating his comrades for supposed quiescence. Ori had been something very else.

He was broken. In some way Cutter did not quite understand, but for which he felt empathy. Ori had shut down, and Cutter and Judah and Madeleina had to start him up again.

"It's getting close," Qurabin said. "It's getting near, we have to hurry."

The monk spoke more and more urgently: the mind behind the words seemed to degrade a little every day. There had been so many enquiries of that hidden Tesh Moment, more and more of Qurabin must have become hidden.

In her or his faintly decomposing way, Qurabin was anxious. The monk was troubled by each spiral they passed, felt the incoming of whatever the thing was, the purveyor of the coming hecatomb: the massacre spirit, the massenmordist, the unswarm, Qurabin called it. It was coming soon, he said, he felt it. The urgency infected Cutter, and the fear.

A ring of small haints beset the city. On the way to Ori's home Cutter passed a commotion a street away, and Qurabin suddenly dragged him toward it, gripping him with hidden hands and keening. When they got there they saw the last moments of an emission like a dog, tumbling in complex patterns, disappearing and seeming to gather the world's colour and light to it as it went. The small crowd of Collectivists around it were screaming and pointing, but none of them had died.

Qurabin moaned. "That's it that's it," Qurabin said as the world blinked and the thing was gone. "It's the endgame."

Cutter did not know if he believed that Ori had killed Mayor Stem-Fulcher. It was still incredible to him. To think of that poised, white-haired woman he had known from heliotypes, from posters, from brief glimpses at public events, who had taken so much of his hatred for so long, now gone, was hard. He did not know what to do with it. He sat in Ori's rooms, and waited.

Judah was with Ori, with Ori as Toro. He was clinging to him, pushed through the world's skin to his old workshop in Brock Marsh.

"What you got to go for anyway?" Cutter had said. "I'm going to get a mirror—we'll have that for the Council—so what is it you want? They'll have closed your workshop."

"Yes," Judah said, "they will have. And yes, the mirror's what's needed, but there are things I want. Things I might need. I have a plan."

The others were at the armouries. The Iron Council Remade were preparing to defend the Collective on the barricades. What must it be for them, this strange fight? Cutter thought.

He thought of the journey through the badlands and pampas, through the tumbledown rockscape, through hundreds of miles at a tremendous rate, directed by Drogon the horse-tramp who had explored these hinterlands before, until they had come to the city rising west of the estuary plain. They had come through ghost towns. Little empties, mean architecture desiccated by years of being left alone, inhabited only by squalls of dust.

"Yes," Judah had whispered. This was his past, these outposts, the remnants of fences, the little bough-marked graves. Less than three decades before these had been the boomtowns.

The revolt of the Iron Council, the renegacy of the perpetual train, had been the last part of the crisis of corruption, incompetence and overproduction that had destroyed Wrightby's Transcontinental Railroad Trust. The thrown-up towns and hamlets of the plains, and the herds of beef and crossbred meat-beasts, the gunfighters and mercenaries, the trappers, the populace of that mongrel of money and wild, had evaporated, in months. They left their houses like snakeskin casts behind. The waddies were gone, the horse-gangsters, the whores.

The Iron Council would be accelerating. It would eat the distance, even as each moment of track-laying seemed arduous and slow. Cutter had realised the Council must be in the open land. And the militia who tracked it, who had traced over the whole world to find it, must still be following, all the way back toward their home, gaining daily. The most absurdly roundabout trip, across the continent and back again, by a terrible route.

As the light began to glower and go out, the sense of the room buckled and ripped at two points, and from nothing, horns emerged.

Toro shoved through adrip with the energies that were reality's blood, carrying Judah, wrapped together like lovers.

Judah stumbled free and the colours dripped upward from him to sputter out of existence before they hit the ceiling. He was carrying a full sack.

"Got what you needed, then?" Cutter said. Judah looked at him and the last of the worldblood evanesced.

"Everything to finish this," he said. "We'll be ready."

The fact that there were Iron Councillors in the Collective had leaked. Even through the terror and the unhappiness of those bleak days, it was huge news.

Excited mobs ran through the byways by the Dog Fenn post office, looking for their guests. When at last they found Maribet and Rahul, the barricade they had joined became a kind of fighting shrine.

There were queues of Collectivists waiting while militia bullets went overhead. They trooped past the Councillors and asked questions—an unspoken politeness limited each person to three. "When will the Council come?" "Have you come to save us?" "Will you take me away with you?" Solidarity and fear and millennial absurdity, in turn. The line became a street meeting, with old arguments between factions rehearsed again while bombs fell.

At the end of the street, on the other side of the barricades, lookouts saw through their periscopes the approach of war constructs. Soldier-machines in brass and iron, glass-eyed, weapons welded to them, came walking. More constructs in one place than had been seen for years.

They stamped and their caterpillar treads ground on the rubble and glass-strewn street toward the barrier. At their head a great earthmover, fronted by a cuneal plough that would push the matter of the barricade apart.

The Collectivists tried grenades, bombs, sent frantic word for a thaumaturge who might be able to halt this ugly monster thing, but it would not be fast enough. They knew they must withdraw. This barricade, this street, was lost.

Snipers and witch-snipers appeared on rooftops over the no-man's-land, to lay down fire and hex on the constructs and the militia. At first they cut into the government forces, but a swivelling motorgun brought a score of them down in meat-wet and panicked the rest.

As the constructs sped, the Collectivists scrambled and their order broke down as they made for the backstreets. Rahul and Maribet did not know where to go. They headed toward secondary lines that did not take them out of the militia fire. Afterward, Cutter heard what happened: the two Remade had loped with their animal legs and skittered one way and another across the street, called by terrified Collectivists trying to help them. Maribet had turned her hooves on a bomb hole, and as she struggled to stand again and Rahul put out his human and lizard hands to help her, there was a grinding and the wedge-fronted construct began to push the barricade apart, and a militia-loyal cactus-man came over the rim of the tons of city-stuff, fired his rivebow into Maribet's neck.

Rahul told them about it when he made it to Ori's house. It was the first Iron Council death in New Crobuzon.

Posters had appeared throughout Collective territory, half-begging half-demanding that the populace stay. EVERY LOST MAN OR WOMAN OR CHILD IS A WEAKENING OF THE COLLECTIVE. TOGETHER WE CAN WIN. Of course they could not stem the refugees, who went out under the cordons, to the undercity or the collapsing suburbs beyond Grand Calibre Bridge.

Most ran to the Grain Spiral, the Mendican Foothills, the most adventurous into Rudewood to become forest bandits. But some, at risk, organised into guerrilla work-crews and made their way through the chaos of the city's outer reaches, past neglected militia crews, by low boroughs become feral without food, too mean for

Parliament to give them any notice. West of the city the escapees passed through the long-deserted hangars and goods yards where once the hub of the TRT had been. Rusting engines and flatcars were left deserted.

Offices were still inhabited and lit, where the remnant of Weather Wrightby's company clung to existence, maintaining a last crew, a few tens of clerks and engineers. It survived off financial speculation, off railroad salvage, off the security work and bounty hunting of the TRT's paramilitary guard-army, tiny and loyal to Wrightby's corporatist vision, disdaining the race-thuggery of the Quillers. The men were stationed across the sprawling TRT property, and they and their dogs sometimes chased the escapees away.

The refugees took tools, made their way out of the once-terminus to the cut from where the Cobsea-Myrshock Railroad had set out.

"It moves, under, it is, they are, the Teshi, are," said Qurabin. The monk's voice scuttered around. They were all there—Drogon and Elsie, Qurabin, Cutter, Judah and Toro. Rahul kept watch. They had mourned Maribet. Qurabin was anxious.

"Something happens very soon," the monk said.

In his strange and strangely broken voice Ori told them the history of his relations with the mysterious tramp: the money, the heliotype of Jack Half-a-Prayer. The help he had given Toro. "I don't know where the plans come from," Ori said. "Jacobs? No, no it was Toro's plan, I know that, because it wasn't the plan I thought it was. But it *did the job*. But Jacobs said, when I saw him . . . I don't think it mattered much to him at all. He's had other things on his mind. This was just . . . a distraction."

They had promised they would wait for Curdin and for Madeleina, hoping for help. That morning, Judah had begged them to persuade the delegates to aid them, but what could they do? The militia were eating their territory house by broken-down house:

there were rumours of punitive revenges against Collectivists in re-captured streets. "We have no one to give, Judah," Curdin had said.

They returned late.

"Came as soon as we could. It was hard," Curdin said. "Hello Jack," he said to Ori.

"We lost Howl Barrow today," said Madeleina.

She was hard; they both were hard. She was trying not to fall to her despair.

"It was something," Curdin said. "They lasted two days longer than they should have done. The militia came down over Barrow Bridge, and there was all the barricadistes, and out of nowhere come the Pretty Brigade. And they was *magnificent*." He shouted this suddenly and blinked. In the quiet after the word they heard bombs, at the battlefronts.

"A liability? They were *lions*. They came in formation, firing, in their dresses." He laughed with a moment's genuine pleasure. "They kept up the attack, they lobbed their grenades. Run forward skirts flapping, all lipstick and blackpowder, sending militia to hell. Hadn't eaten anything but stale bread and rat meat for days, and they fought like gladiators in Shankell. It took the motorguns to cut them down. And they went shouting and kissing each other." He blinked again many times.

"But they couldn't hold it off. The Nuevists died. Petron and the others. The militia went in. There was street-fighting, but Howl Barrow's gone. Got the last globe today." Howl Barrow had released sealed glass floats to drift down the River Tar, past Strack Island, till the Collective's bargers and mudlarks fished them and broke them to get the messages out.

"I tried, Judah, honestly, though your plan's madness. But there's no one spare. Everyone's protecting the Collective. I don't blame them, and I'm going to join them. We've a couple of weeks left, no more."

Madeleina looked agonised but she did not say anything.

"I can't help you, Judah," Curdin continued. "But I'll tell you something. When you left and there were rumours why, I thought you were . . . not mad, *stupid*. A stupid, stupid man. I never thought you could find the Iron Council. I would have bet it was long gone, nothing but a rotten train in the middle of a desert. Full of skeletons.

"I was wrong, Judah. And you, and all of you, done something I never thought could be done. I won't say the Collective is *because* of you, because it ain't. All I'll say is that word that the Iron Council was coming . . . well, it changed things. Even when we thought it was just a rumour, even when I thought it was a *myth*, it still felt like something was . . . it was different. Maybe we heard you were coming a little bit too soon. Maybe that's what happened. But it changed things.

"But I don't quite trust you, Judah. Oh, gods, don't get me wrong, I ain't saying you're a traitor. You always helped us, with golems, with money . . . but you watch from outside. Like you get to be pleased with us. It ain't right, Judah.

"I wish you luck. If you're right, and maybe you are, then you'd better win. But I ain't coming to fight with you. I fight for the Collective. If you win and the Collective loses, I don't want to live anyway." Though it must be hyperbole, Cutter drew himself up at that, in respect.

"How you plan on finishing this, Judah?"

Judah pursed his lips. "I'll have something," he said.

"You'll have what?"

"I'll have something. And there's someone here who knows what to do. Who knows Tesh magic."

"I know, I know," Qurabin said suddenly and loud. "The Moment I worship will tell me things. Will help me. It's a Tesh thing. My Moment knows the gods this consul might call."

"Consul?" Madeleina said, and when Judah told her that Spiral Jacobs was the ambassador of Tesh, Curdin laughed. Not a pleasant laugh.

"Yon Teshi'll know what to do, is that it?" Curdin came close on his clumsy four legs. "You're going to die, Judah," he said. He spoke with true sadness. "If you're right, you're going to die. Good luck."

Curdin shook each of their hands and left. Madeleina went with him.

CHAPTER TWENTY-NINE

THOUGH WINTER IT WAS SUDDENLY WARM. *UNSEASONAL* WAS NOT the word—it was uncanny, as if the city was in an exhalation. A warmth like that of innards took the streets. The party went with Toro.

Two nights they walked the streets, behind Ori, who stopped and stared at all the graffiti. Each night they did not find Spiral Jacobs, Qurabin's distress became animal. Toro would trace a finger along Spiral's marks, find signs, nod and lower his head, shove and be gone for long minutes, and then would return and shake his head: *No, no sign.*

Once he could not find him; once he found him but in the farthest north of the city, in the quiets of Flag Hill, scrawling his marks, unafraid of Ori as ever. There was no way for the others to get to him. Ori tracked Spiral Jacobs around the city, but until he came back to the Dog Fenn chapter, he could only be reached by Ori, who could do nothing alone.

Each day they had to live knowing the agent of the city's destruction was walking free, that they could not touch him. They tried where they could to protect the streets of the Collective. From the river's shores they saw a fight between two trains traveling alongside on the Dexter Line, a Collectivist and a militia, shooting into each other's windows as they went.

There was a lightning raid by dirigibles scattering leaflets. PEOPLE OF THE SO-CALLED "COLLECTIVE," they said. THE GOVERNMENT OF MAYOR TRIESTI WILL NOT TOLERATE THE MASS-MURDER AND CARNAGE YOU HAVE UNLEASHED ON NEW CROBUZON. AFTER THE OUTRAGE OF THE BARRACKHAM TOWER ALL CITIZENS NOT ACTIVELY SEEKING ESCAPE ARE DEEMED COMPLICIT IN THE DESPICABLE POLICIES OF YOUR COMMITTEES. APPROACH THE MILITIA WITH HANDS CLEAR AND UP, HALLOOING YOUR SURRENDER, and so on.

The third night. There they were, on the streets, with hundreds of Collectivists, a last wave of mobilizations, of every race. Little snips of magic, prestidigitation of light, chromathaumaturgy sending up pretences of birds made of radiance. The rebels made the night a carnival, as it had once been.

Everywhere people were running, according to news of a militia incursion, a moment's panic, a rumour, a nothing at all. They drank, ate whatever repulsive food had been mustered or smuggled through the militia's cordon. There was a millennial sense. Drinkers toasted Judah and Toro and Cutter and the others as they walked under half-lit gaslamps, raised mugs of poteen and beer and cheered the passersby in the name of the Collective.

Qurabin was moaning. Low but always audible.

"Something's happening," Cutter said to no one.

They passed Bohrum Junction where houses converged in a wedge of antique architecture, past dry fountains where war orphans played some catchpenny game and tied shell-casings to a dog too diseased to eat. Toro walked, making no effort to hide himself, and the children pointed and catcalled. *Hey Bull, hey Bull, what you going to do? Who you going to kill?* Cutter did not know if they thought Ori just a man in a strange uniform, or if they knew they had seen the bandit kithless himself that night. Perhaps in the exotica of the Collective, gods and the unique arcane were not worth awe.

Rahul came with saurian gait, knives in each human hand, his muscular reptile claws clenching. "Come come on," said Qurabin.

Each wall of graffiti Ori would stop and stare at with lightemitting Bull-mask eyes. With an effortful grunt he straightened his legs, poked into nothing, and then there he was again in a new rent scant feet away, so fast Cutter could not be sure his feet had not still dangled from the first hole as his head emerged yards off.

"He's here," Ori said. "Trauka Station. Come."

Not a mile off. They passed near the riverwall through longemptied markets, where the integuments of the stalls were left, metal ribs slotted together, a herd of skeletons.

They were just one of the running groups that night. Into Trauka through narrow old streets in a mix of ugly architecture, under paint proclaiming *Free Collective Territory* and *Fuck You Stem-Fulcher* written then crossed out and *Been done mate* appended in another hand. Toro disappeared, reappeared a street from them, beckoning, splitting worldskin to keep sure of his quarry's motion, coming back to the party to direct them. As if they were directed by a dozen identical bull-faced men throughout the city.

The smoke and miracle-colour blood that dripped from Toro's helmet was thick; the horns were sparking as if with friction. So much violence against ontology was straining the thaumaturgic circuits. "Come," Toro said again, and beckoned. "Just here, two turns from here, left left, he's moving, come now."

Judah stopped, quickly set down ceramic conductors and a funnel in the darkest part of a brick overhang. There was a snap of thaumaturgy. He sounded an invocatory whisper—no not an

invocation—he had told Cutter that the difference was crucial—
not an invocation but a creation, a constitution of matter or ideo-
matter. Cutter watched and Judah gathered. Cutter felt the creep of
awe on his skin, watching the man for whom he felt and had always
felt so animal an emotion, surely the most potent golemist in New
Crobuzon, its autodidact magus.

Darkness gathered. Judah's mechanism sucked the dark. It
shifted, a tenebrous plasma; it was dragged in a slow resentful mass,
the shadows become a cloud of unlight, and like water coiling down
a plughole they wound into the cone, condensing, becoming darker
as they went. The bricks it left were a catastrophe of physics, utterly
abnatural. No light fell on them, but with their darkness gone they
were clearly visible, as if harshly illuminated, but without colour, a
perfect-edged grey. The cul-de-sac had become impossible: un-
glowing, unlit, uncoloured visibility in the absolute dark.

Shadows emerged from the funnel's spigot to congeal in a shape
between a body and a puddle of oil, a presence of dark, unsolid but
profoundly there, a human shape of blackness. *Gods, is that what
you got from your study?* Cutter thought. He had seen Judah animate
hundreds of golems, but never one so uncorporeal. Judah raised
his hands. The darkness golem stood. Eight feet of silhouette. It
stepped into the night and became half-visible, a darkness on the
dark that moved like a man.

Judah gathered his equipment and whispered, *"Go!"* He ran,
and his companions, dumbed by what they had seen, let him pass
before they found their energy again. Beside him with utterly silent
steps was the golem, like a gorilla made of shade.

Left, left. Into alleys overlooked by the upreach of dark brown
masonry, windows without doors, doorless brick-and-mortar cliffs
that seemed a glimpse on something unfinished, the land behind
the facades.

There was Toro ahead, one horn on fire and vibrating. He called
to them, but his voice was drowned by the shuddering of the hel-

met, the unpeeling, the splitting of his horns. Screaming and with the metal itself spitting on fire, Ori scrabbled to undo the straps. He fought the helmet free and straightened, his face rivered with sweat. "There!" He pointed.

An old man at the far end of the street watched them, holding a paintbrush poised and dripping. He turned and shuffled with an incompetent run toward where the street curved away. Spiral Jacobs.

"Keep him in your sights!" Ori shouted, and ran, leaving his helmet to be eaten by blue fire. Cutter saw the thaumaturged glass eyes crack, the strange colours of fire and sparks as the heat ate arcana in the metal. It did not look like a statue's head anymore but a skull, a bovine skull on fire.

They tried to catch Ori, who ran as if Toro's strength were still in him. "Keep up, keep on him," he shouted.

At the limits of their vision, where the leftward curve shut off the long alley from their view, Jacobs moved fast despite his age and gait. Judah and Cutter followed Ori, the golem loping dark beside them, and Drogon behind, and the others in changing order. The alleyway was full of echoes, of the sounds of all their feet. There were no other sounds, no gunfire of the war, no horns or noise of the Collective or the mayor's city. Only footsteps on winter-damp brick.

"Where's he going?" Ori shouted. Cutter turned and saw Rahul, two three seconds behind him, disappear momentarily around the corner and not emerge. Where was he? He had slipped beyond the influence of Jacobs' reconfiguration, been tipped out into New Crobuzon; he would turn the corner into gods-knew-where.

Jacobs was still running, and was that, was he *laughing*? They ran faster, and from over the rooftops came light and sound again. Drogon was suddenly slow, and Jacobs was walking, his paint still dripping in his hand, and the alley was ended, and his footsteps were suddenly open as he emerged into a clearing. His pursuers ran out after him. They were in cold wind, in the city again, on the other end of that impossible alleyway.

Rahul was gone, and Drogon. They had stumbled and were lost somewhere in the errant geography. Cutter came forward. Judah walked and the darkness golem walked with him, step for step. Scores of yards away was Spiral Jacobs. He was not even looking at them.

Where were they? Cutter found the moon. He looked down between towers and walls. He was half enclosed. He struggled to make sense of it: this then that monolith spired, and here a minaret, and here one much fatter studded with lights, and above them the huge lines of airships. They were outside the Collective.

Above them an enormous column crowned with radial wires. The Spike. They were in an irregular courtyard. The walls were different stones, in different colours. A shaking came up at them through the concrete. They were high up. Cutter looked down over a spread-out skyline, over the city.

Perdido Street Station. Of course. They were in a huge and empty amphitheatre made by chance, floored with scrub, a little wilderness on the station's roof. Undesigned, a forgot space in the vastness. The passage that had brought them looked now not like a street but a kink in concrete.

The wall, an edifice of huge bricks that made them feel shrunk to dolls, was broken by the remnants of wooden floors where once this open place had been interior. It was surfaced completely with spirals. A thicket rising, as high as a canopy. Some as intricate and complex as tangled briars, some the simplest snailshell patterns. Thousands. Months of industry. Cutter breathed out. From the very top of the wall descended one black line, through the forest of helix pictograms. A spiral, pinpointing this place.

Across the brickdust and savage weeds was Jacobs, the Tesh ambassador. He was drawing marks in the air, and he was singing.

"He's hurried," Qurabin said. His disembodied voice was close. "Has to move. He weren't ready, but he's moving now, early . . . He'll try to force it, the thysiac, the murderspirit . . . feel! Quick," and the voice was gone.

Ori ran. Across waste through dead thigh-high grass that cracked with cold, the plateau open and the lights of New Crobuzon splayed beneath him. The others followed, though no one knew what to do.

Spiral Jacobs tremored, and the air all around tremored with him. A hundred shapes began to solidify from nothing. Cutter saw a patch of milky air, a cataract, that took lumpy shape, peristalsed maggotlike and was a pale ghost stool, a three-legged kitchen thing hanging over his brow. Beside it was an insect, impossibly big, and a flower, a pot and a hand, a candle, a lamp, all the haints that had beset New Crobuzon. They looked undercooked, not quite fine, without colour, hanging and spinning. And as Cutter came closer the haints began to turn and move around each other in decaying orbits, an impossibly complex interpenetration of silent spiral paths. The things never collided, nor touched anyone. The apparitions moved fast, centring over Spiral Jacobs. A vortex of the everyday, the uncanny quotidian.

Ori batted at the things. They had not yet come full; they were not murderously sucking his colour. He reached Spiral Jacobs. The old man looked at him and said something: a greeting, Cutter thought.

He watched as Ori swung his fists, and kept missing Spiral Jacobs, kept always missing, each punch consistently mistimed, misjudged. Ori screamed and went onto his knees. Judah was just behind him, and the darkness golem stepped up.

The great thing swung its enormous shadow hands and unlight swept over Spiral Jacobs as it gripped him. It obscured him a long moment. Jacobs faltered, went obscure and dimmed, and all the ectoplasm shapes faltered with him, waning in time like dimming lamps. They came back again as he regained strength and light, and then he growled, showed anger for the first time.

He moved his hands, and the school of moving haints changed, came together, gusted suddenly through the golem, and where they passed they left a light in the core of the thing. It staggered like a wounded man and reached to throttle Jacobs once again, mimicking Judah's motions. The light in the darkness golem's core was growing.

It fell back, it stood back on its fading heels as the lantern glow in its innards effaced it. Jacobs fought free of its shade hands. He bared dark-stained teeth. The haints swarmed. Jacobs was cobwebbed with darkness the golem had left; it was choking him. He retched up a gout of empty shadows. They spilled on the ground and crept away to their natural place below blockages of light. The darkness golem fell, and Judah fell with it, and while he lay flattened and unconscious for a second the golem disappeared.

Ori was crying, still trying to hit Jacobs, still missing. Spiral Jacobs did not look at him, turned away as the sobbing man flailed and lost his balance and flailed again. Jacobs pushed out his hand and Ori was yanked by matter and whipped to a wall. A clutch of the apparitions went through the air in a brief tentacle to slap Elsie without quite touching her, a moment's halo of spinning uncoloured shapes around her—a bowl, a bone, a scrap of cotton. Her face greyed instantly, choked off sudden, her eyes gone bloodshot but the blood without colour. She did not fall. With a care as if she were going to bed, she settled herself to the floor, lay down and died.

The haints were maelstroming so fast they lost visible integrity, seemed to melt to a kind of swirling oil. Spiral Jacobs drew another shape and everything convulsed. Ori was shuddering from the wall where he was embedded, making little sounds.

Judah woke. Spiral Jacobs moved his hands. There were no haints now; instead the air was a dilute milk of their residue tracked through with vapour trails. Jacobs was shaking with effort, hauling something out of nothing, vividly trembling. As if from behind a rock, from underwater, a presence began to insinuate.

It was very small, or very big and very far away, and then it was perhaps much bigger than Cutter had thought or much closer, and moving very slowly or tremendously fast over a huge distance. He could not make out its parameters. He could see nothing. He heard it. He could see nothing. The thing made sound. The thing Spiral Jacobs was bringing, the murderspirit, the citykiller, he heard it howl. It came round and round like a rising vine, growing or rising up as if uncoiling from a well. It made a metal howl.

Cutter saw the lights of the city change below them. As the unseen palpable thing approached, the buildings glowered. New Crobuzon's architecture glared. The streetlamps and the lights of industry became the glints in eyes.

The beast was manifesting in New Crobuzon itself. It was pushing itself into New Crobuzon's skin. Or was it waking what had been there always? Cutter could tell the thing was nearing them because the wall, the concrete beside them, did not change but looked to him suddenly like the flank of an animal tensed to attack. The Tesh thing was making the city itself a predator, rousing the hunt instincts of the metropolis.

How big, how big, when does it reach the top? Cutter thought. He felt a sleepiness, a bled-out emergent death.

"I know your gods," Qurabin said. The thing kept coming. The buildings tensed. Spiral Jacobs looked suddenly afraid.

Qurabin was only a voice, moving through the empty space. The monk sounded hysterical, aggressive, eager to fight. Qurabin taunted Spiral Jacobs. Had she or he still known Tesh, Cutter was certain that was what he would have heard, that glottal and interruptive language. Ragamoll was all that was left to Qurabin.

"Jinxing . . . it's easy to intimidate them as don't know what it is, yes? But what if you face one as does, eh? Another Teshi? Who can find out Teshi secrets? Your secrets?"

Spiral Jacobs shouted something.

"I don't understand you no more, mate," Qurabin said, but Cutter was sure the ambassador had said *traitor.*

"Know who I am?" Qurabin said.

"Aye, I know who y'are," shouted Jacobs, and he pushed out his hands sending a swirl of the buttery haint-stuff at where the voice came from, but the whirling air met no resistance. "You're a Momentist blatherer."

Judah was trying to stand, was burrowing his hands in dirt that shook with the incoming spirit-thing. He was trying to raise a golem, any golem, something.

"It's coming," Cutter shouted. It was coming out of its burrow into the real, it was unfolding into more and more impossible conjunctions. The dimensions of the bricks and the edges of the walls strained as it came close. Architecture stirred.

"Your godlings and demiurgii all live in the Moments, Teshman. And my Moment knows." Qurabin's voice was tremendous, louder than the oncoming of the murder-thing. Spiral Jacobs spat and his spit sent a cuffing wave through the milk-white disturbance. Qurabin roared, and began to shout.

"Tekke Vogu," the monk said, "please tell me—" and the voice disappeared as Qurabin slipped into whatever place it was where the Moment lived and listened.

Nothing moved; the oncoming spirit seemed poised. And then Qurabin sounded again with a gasp, a terrible pain, because these were huge secrets to uncover. What it cost, Cutter could not imagine, but the monk learnt something. As the twitching filigree of the Phasma Urbomach unrolled into regular space, making the bricks, the spires and weathervanes and night-slates of New Crobuzon terrible teeth and claws, waking the surrounds so that Cutter gasped in terror, Qurabin let loose hidden knowledge and the thing was *snatched* back down toward the nothing it had come from. It strained to emerge.

Judah sent a grass-and-earth golem stumbling toward Jacobs, but it was shuddered to dust before it got close. He reached out, tried to make a golem in the air, but whiteness clogged him.

Spiral Jacobs cursed in Tesh, and Qurabin screamed and the spirit began to crawl back again, but with a last plea, a last hollering for knowledge, Qurabin made the dire and mass-murderous visitant begin to slide away. As Spiral Jacobs cursed the thinning air that very air disgorged a figure. Blood-faced and exhausted, Qurabin the monk smiled through wounds, without language, only barking a seal's gasps, without *eyes,* Cutter saw. These were the cost of all the secrets that had saved them. Qurabin reached out and gripped Jacobs the ambassador and whispered what must be the last word left to the renegade Tesh, stepped back into a true secret, a hidden place, into the domain of Tekke Vogu. The air winked behind them, and they, and in a swallowing of space the Urbomach, were gone.

Only the opalescence in the air was left. It began to thicken, moving and congealing like eggwhite in hot water, into a stinking solidity. It inspissated, fell in clots, mucal rain, and the sky and air was empty.

A silence gathered, then ebbed, and Cutter heard the shoot-sounds of the war again. He rolled in the debris, saw Judah gather himself all groggy and sodden with the smell of haint-dissolution. Saw Ori, unmoving, tethered somehow to brick, bleeding. The body of Elsie, a greyed nothing. Saw nothing in the air. Cutter saw that Qurabin, Spiral Jacobs and his city-killing thing were gone.

CHAPTER THIRTY

Tʜᴇʏ ᴄᴀʟʟᴇᴅ ᴀɴᴅ ᴡʜɪsᴘᴇʀᴇᴅ ꜰᴏʀ Qᴜʀᴀʙɪɴ ʙᴜᴛ ᴛʜᴇ ᴍᴏɴᴋ ᴡᴀs definitely gone. "With the Moment now," Judah said.

Elsie was colour-bled and dead. Ori was sutured to a wall, his skin become brick where it met the brick. Blood crusted the join. He was dead too.

Ori's eyes were very open, would not close. Cutter felt huge sorrow for the young man. He tried to convince himself that there was peace in Ori's expression, something settled. *You rest,* he thought. *You rest.*

They worked their slow way around their enclosure and found a hole in the stonework. There was no wall in New Crobuzon without its flaw. Through back tunnels, through metal-floored walkways and ladders, they entered Perdido Street Station. They had to leave their dead friends in the hidden garden. They could do nothing else.

In the enormous girdered cavern of Perdido Street Station, its vast central concourse, Judah and Cutter discarded their weapons and tried to clean their haint-fouled clothes, milled with late-night travellers and militia. They took a train.

They ricketed over the middling townscape of Ludmead with late-shift workers. When the cupolas of New Crobuzon University rose in the windows to the north, they got out at Sedim Junction Station. When at last the platforms were silent, Cutter led Judah onto the forking trainlines, toward the Kelltree and Dog Fenn branches. With the half-moon weak above the city's lights, they crept onto the rails and set out south.

Some lines jutted into Collective territory—the Collective tried to run its own short services to match Triesti's, from Syriac Rising to Saltpetre, Low Falling Mud to Rim. The conventional trains and those waving Collective flags would approach each other on the same lines, would halt above the many-angled roofs, a few yards apart, each on its side of barricades thrown across the lines themselves.

The Ribs curled hugely into the sky. Halfway up their length, scores of yards above the train lines, was the ragged jag where one of the Ribs had been broken by firing. The sharded edge of the break was a cleaner white, already yellowing. In the streets below Cutter saw the torn hole in the terrace where the broken end had fallen, crushing houses. It lay there still in the hole, among bomb damage, tons of bone ruin.

They walked an empty stretch of unclaimed railroad, chimney-pots up from the street morass like periscopes peering curious, until they saw the piles of debris blocking the tracks. There were torches. Below in the alleyways was fighting, the incursion of the militia as the Collective's barricadistes withdrew and fell back a few streets, firing from street kiosks, voxiterator booths, from behind iron pillars.

A war train was approaching from beyond the barricade—they could see its lights and the gush of it. It fired as it came, sending shells into the militia in the streets. It came up from the south, from Kelltree's docks.

"Halt, you fuckers!" came from the barrier. Cutter was ready to beg entrance, but Judah spoke in a huge voice, coming out of stupor.

"Do you know who you're talking to, chaver? Let me through, *now*. I'm *Judah Low*. I'm *Judah Low*."

Ori's landlady let them in. "I don't know if he'll be coming back," Cutter said, and she looked away and thinned her green lips, nodded. "I'll clean up later," she said. "He's a good boy. I like him. Your friends are here."

Curdin and Madeleina were in Ori's room. Madeleina wore tears. She sat by the bed and did not make a sound. Curdin lay soaking blood into the mattress. He sweated.

"Are we saved?" he said when Judah and Cutter came in. He did not wait. "Got pretty harsh out there." They sat with him. Judah put his head in his hands. "We had some hostages, some priests, some members of Parliament, Fat Sunners, the old Mayor's party. And the crowd was . . . It got ugly." He shook his head.

"He's dead, or dying," Curdin said. He tapped his rear legs. "This one. The man inside me. That was the worst of it." He backheeled his own ruined hindleg.

"Sometimes it seemed to want to go somewhere. There's a knot in my belly. I wonder whether this was a dead man, or whether they left him alive in there. Whether his brain's in there, in the dark. He'd be mad, wouldn't he? I was either half-corpse, or half-madman. I might have been a *prison*."

He coughed—there was blood. No one spoke a long time.

"I wish, you know I really wish you'd been here in the early days." He looked at the ceiling. "We didn't know what we were doing. People on the streets were moving much faster than the Caucus. Even some militia were coming over to us. We had to run to catch up.

"We put on lectures and hundreds came. The cactacae voted to show people inside the Glasshouse. I won't tell you everything was all right because it weren't. But we was trying."

Silence again. Madeleina kept her eyes on his face.

"Chaos. Concessionists wanted to meet the Mayor, Suitors wanted peace whatever cost. The Victorians screaming that we had to *crush* Tesh: they thought the city'd gone pusillanimous. A core of Caucus. And provocateurs." He smiled. "We had plans. We made mistakes. When we took over the banks, the Caucus didn't argue hard enough, or we argued wrong, because we ended up *borrowing* little bits with *by your leave.* Never mind it should have been ours to start with."

He was quiet so long Cutter thought he had died.

"Once, it was something else," he said. "I wish you'd seen it. Where's Rahul gone? I wanted to tell him.

"Well he or his'll see something, I suppose. They're still coming, ain't they? Gods know what they'll face." He shook as if chuckling, emitting no sound. "The militia must know Iron Council's coming. It's *good* that they're coming. I'm sorry it's later than we'd have liked. We were thinking of them, when we did what we did. I hope we made them proud."

By noon he was in a coma. Madeleina watched him.

She said: "It was him tried to stop the mob, when they took revenge against the hostages. He tried to step in."

"Listen to me," Judah said to Cutter. They were in the hallway. All Judah's uncertainty was gone. He was hard as one of his own iron golems. "The Collective is dead. No, listen, be quiet. It's *dead* and if Iron Council comes here it'll be dead too. They've no chance. The militia'll amass on the borders, where the trains come in. They'll just wait. By the time the Council gets here—be, what, four weeks at least?—the Collective'll be gone. And the militia'll pour everything into killing Iron Council.

"Cutter. I won't let them. I won't. Listen to me. You have to tell them. You have to get back and tell them. They have to go. Send the train up north, find a way into the mountains. I don't know. Maybe they have to desert the train, be fReemade. Whatever. But they can't come into the city.

"Be *quiet.*" Cutter had been about to speak but he closed his mouth hard. He had never seen Judah like this: all the beatific calm was gone, and something stone-hard remained. "Be quiet and listen. You have to go now. Get out of the city *however you damn well can,* and find them. If Rahul or Drogon or anyone finds their way back I'll send them after you. But Cutter, you have to stop the train from coming."

"What about you?"

Judah's face set. He seemed wistful.

"You might fail, Cutter. And if you do, I might, just, be able to do something."

"You know how to use the mirrors, don't you? You remember? Because those militia . . . they've come all the way through the cacotopic zone. They'll reach the Council. And I ain't sure, but I bet I know what they are, what they'd have to be to be hardcore enough to take us, but travel quick and light like they've done. If I'm right you'll have to do what you can, Cutter. You'll have to show the Council. Do right by me, Cutter."

"And you? What are you going to do? While I'm off persuading the damn Council."

"I said. I've an idea—something for safety's sake. A last plan. Because by Jabber and by gods and by everything, Cutter, I will *not* let this happen. Stop them. But if you don't, I'll be here, with my plan. *Do right by me, Cutter.*"

Bastard, Cutter thought, tearing up, trying to speak. *Bastard to say that to me. You know what you are to me.* Bastard. He felt his chest hollow, felt as if he were falling inside, as if his very fucking *innards* were straining for Judah.

"Love you, Judah," he said. He looked away. "Love you. Do what I can." *I love you so much Judah. I'd die for you.* He wept without sob or sound, furious at it, trying to wipe it away.

Judah kissed him. Judah straightened, kind, implacable, held Cutter gently by the chin and tilted his head up. Cutter saw the damp on the wallpaper, saw the doorframe, looked at Judah's stubble all grey, the man's thin face. Judah kissed him and Cutter heard a sound from his own throat, and was enraged at himself and then also at Judah. *You bastard,* he thought or tried to think at the kiss, but he could not make himself. He would do what Judah asked. *I love you Judah.*

part nine

———❧———

SOUND AND LIGHT

CHAPTER THIRTY-ONE

A DIRIGIBLE FLEW FAST. IT WAS PUSHED BY WIND AND ITS ENGINE over stone fragments. The dead towns it overflew, the remnants of railroad boom, were like discolourations on heliotypes. Cutter watched from the little cockpit.

The Collective had got them out. First two decoy balloons had set out, piloted by dummies, and while the militia pounded them, the escape dirigible flew. The pilot went so low towerblocks rose around them. The ship had cut between the smokestacks of the slum factories, evaded hunter warflots.

They travelled in fear of air-pirates, but beyond the idiot aggressions of githwings and a few outlander wyrmen nothing attacked them in the wilds outside the city. Cutter thought of Judah all the time. In him moved a complex of anger, and a kind of need he could not exorcise.

"Be careful, Cutter," Judah said before he went, and held him. He would not say what he was doing, why he was staying. "You have to be quick. They're through. The militia, through the cacotopos, and they're hunting the Council down. Come back," he said. "When they turn away, or scatter, come back, and I'll be waiting. And if they refuse to turn away, come ahead of them, come to the city, and I'll be here, I'll wait."

You never will, Cutter thought. *Not in the way you know I want.*

The pilot was Remade, his arm a python that he strapped to him. He hardly spoke. Over three days, all Cutter learnt was that he had once worked for a crime-boss, that he was pledged to the Collective.

"We have to go fast," Cutter said. "Something's coming out of the cacotopic zone." He knew it must sound like some Torque-beast was hunting, and he did not correct the impression. "We have to find the Council."

He checked the mirrors he carried. The glassworks had built a beautiful replacement. He had shown them to Madeleina di Farja, explaining what they were for.

"How many times have you done it?" she said, and he laughed.

"None times. But Judah Low told me how."

Cutter stared down into the acres of air specked with birds and windblown scobs. They flew over raincloud like a smoke floor. At the limits of their vision, miles south, they saw people. A long spread-out column through the landscape, the vanguard of the rogue train, who went ahead even of the graders and the bridge-builders.

"Fly past, not too close," Cutter said. "Let them know we don't mean no harm." His heart went fast. It took them an hour to trace the scattered miles of Council back, to the graders sweeping aside debris, patting down and hammering down the ground, and then to the track-layers moving with precision that made them seem automata, and then to the perpetual train.

"There."

Cutter watched it. Its flatbeds, its carriages and its built-up towers, its bridges swaying, the mottled colours of its addenda, the skull and head adornments, smoke from all of its chimneys, those of the engines and those that specked its length. And all around it the hundreds of Councillors moving along it and on it, in the gap through which it travelled. A bolt of hexed gunpowder combusted below them.

"Dammit, they think we're attacking. Swing round, give them a berth, let's lower some flags."

The train edged forward along the unrolling tracks, the line behind it dismantled as it went. In its wake was debris, a cut of altered ground.

"Gods they're moving fast. They'll be at the city within weeks," Cutter said. *Weeks*. Too slow. Too late. *Besides*, he thought, *what can it do? What can it do?*

Cutter thought of the perpetual train deserted, growing old, made at last of age and weather as rain and wind turned its iron into red dust and the slates and thatch of its remade roofs slipped untended and mouldered, became mulch. In the shade of the flatcars weeds would pierce the hard floor of the train and its spokes and axles would be knotted with stems, honeysuckle, an empire of buddleia. Spiders and wilderness animals would run its nooks, and the boiler would grow cold. The last stores of coal would settle like the striae of ore they had once been. The smokestacks would clog with windblown loess. The train would be made of landscape. The rocks in which it sat would be stained with train.

The passage that the Iron Council had left would be a strange furrow of geography. And at last the descendants of the Councillors who had run as they had to, as he would persuade them they must, from the incoming militia and New Crobuzon's revenge, the children of their many-times children would find the remnants. They would walk it and excavate the strange barrow, find their history.

Miles behind the very last of the Council's stragglers, at the end of a wilder, wooded zone, was a line of fire, a crawl-motion that through the telescope Cutter saw was dark figures. Men were coming. Perhaps two days away.

"Oh Jabber they're there," Cutter said. "It's them. It's the militia."

When they descended, the leaders were waiting for them. Ann-Hari and Thick Shanks embraced Cutter. They turned to the pilot, and Cutter saw that the Collectivist had tears in his eyes.

The urgency of Cutter's mission filled him. The Councillors surrounded him, demanding to know what was happening in New Crobuzon. Ann-Hari was trying to control the situation, trying to bring Cutter to her, but he wanted very much not to be in her hands alone, did not want her controlling the message he brought. She was too powerful for him, her agenda too strong.

"Listen to me," he shouted until he was heard. "The militia are coming. They've come through the cacotopic stain. They're a day or two away. And you *can't* go to the city. You have to run."

When at last they understood him a gusty roar of *no* took them over, and Cutter climbed out of their arms and stamped on the train roof in frustration. He felt a wave of the bitterness, sadness and near-contempt with which Judah's politicking and that of the Caucus had always filled him. He wanted to save these people from their own desperate want.

"You *fools*," he shouted. He knew he should restrain himself but he could not. "Godsdammit, listen to me. There is a militia squad on your tail which has come through the *cacotopic godsdamned stain*, do you understand? They've crossed the world and back again *just to kill you*. And there are *thousands* more of them in New Crobuzon. You have to turn." He shouted over their anger. "I'm your *friend*, I ain't your enemy. Didn't I cross the fucking desert? I'm trying to fucking *save* you. You cannot fight them, and you godsdamned well can't fight their paymasters."

* * *

A clutch of Council wyrmen flew to see. The Councillors debated. But it was a one-sided argument, to Cutter's rage.

"We beat the militia before, years ago."

"No you didn't," he said. "I know the damn story. You blocked them just enough that you could run away—that ain't the same thing. This is the flatlands. You ain't got nowhere to run. You face them now, they'll kill you."

"We're stronger now, and we've got our own hexes."

"I don't know what the militia are carrying, but godsdammit, you think your fucking moss magic is going to stop a New Cro-buzon murder squad? *Go.* Get out. Regroup. Hide. You cannot do this."

"What about Judah's mirrors?"

"I don't know," Cutter said. "I don't even know if I can make them work."

"Better try," said Ann-Hari. "Better get ready. We haven't come this far to run. If we can't shake them off, we take them down."

Cutter had lost.

"The Collective sends its solidarity, its love," the pilot shouted. His voice was shaking. "We need you. We need you to join us, as fast as you can. Your fight's ours. Come be part of our fight," he said, and though Cutter was shouting, "Their fight is over," he was not heard.

Ann-Hari came to him. He was almost weeping in frustration.

"We were meant to do this," she said.

"There's no plan to history," he shouted. "You'll die."

"No. Some of us will, but we can't turn away now. You knew we wouldn't." It was true. He had always known. The wyrmen returned as the light came down.

"Enough to fill a carriage," one shouted. There were only a few score militia, it seemed, and at that the Councillors shouted deri-sion. They had many times that number.

"Yes but *gods* it ain't just about that," Cutter shouted. "You think they won't have something on their side?"

"So you better be ready," Ann-Hari said. "You better practise with Judah's mirrors."

The Iron Councillors gathered everyone who could fight. The laggers, spread out behind them, were called to catch up, for safety. They sped up their track-laying, to reach a point where a few igneous pillars jutted out of the earth, where there were some dry hills, so they would have a little shelter. With the expertise they had accrued over years, they readied to fight.

"He got gone," one wyrman said. He was talking about one of the others on the reconnoitre. "He got gone out the air. Something come pull him out the air, see?"

There were none of the chances Cutter had wanted, no opportunity to tell the stories of the Collective, to ask for the stories of the Council. It was rushed and ugly. He felt desperately angry as the Councillors prepared to die. He felt as well a sense of his own failure, that he was letting down Judah. *You knew I couldn't do it, you bastard. That's why you're still there. Getting ready some plan or other for when I fail.* Still, even though Judah had expected it, Cutter hated that he had not succeeded.

No one slept that night. Councillors came to the train throughout the darkness hours.

With the first light Cutter and Thick Shanks withdrew into position, each on a stele twenty feet high, yards apart, both facing the sun, holding one of Judah's mirrors. Before he went, Cutter found Ann-Hari, to try to tell her that she was having her sisters, the Councillors, commit suicide. She smiled until he had finished.

"Our hexers have what Judah gave them," she said. "We have our own thaumaturgy. And we have what Judah taught us. There are those'll be calling golems from the traps he gave us."

"Each time you trigger one, he'll feel it, you know. No matter how far he is."

"Yes. And we'll trigger all of them. One at a time. As the militia come. If we have to."

"You'll have to."

Cutter and Thick Shanks braced themselves each on their rock shaft. It was a little after dawn. The moon was still visible, pale and high. As the sun rose its light struck their mirrors, and Cutter angled his down, directing his beam at the cross-mark he had made on the ground. Thick Shanks did the same, as Cutter had shown him, and the spots of intensified sunlight roamed like nervous animals over scrub and dust, to blend on the X.

Hundreds of Councillors prepared to fight, spread out in waves to trenches and earthworks, propped rifles. Cutter turned west, to where the militia would come.

It was not long. At first he saw only dust. Cutter looked through his telescope. They were still tiny, and they did seem to be very few.

A flock of wyrmen set out to harass them, carrying acid and drop-knives. Behind them the dirigible followed with the snake-armed pilot and two volunteers as strafe-gunners. The militia came closer, over minutes and then hours, and the wyrmen crossed the grey nothing-land, and the dirigible flew low. The engines of Judah's golem traps were ready; the hexers sang incantations.

A frantic Councillor came out of the stony lands. He stumbled to them, could not speak for moments, silenced by exhaustion and fear.

"I got trapped," he said at last. "They took my missus. There was eight of us. They made something come out of the earth, *they made something come out of us.*" He screamed. People looked at each other. *I fucking* told *you,* Cutter thought. He felt despair. *I bastard told you that this weren't simple like it looked.*

Two miles off, the wyrmen came close to the militia on their horses. The riders carried no equipment anyone could see. Moved in formation. There was a strange instant, and the wyrmen were pulled one by one out of the air.

For a long few seconds there was no sound. Then—"What . . . ?" "Did . . . ?" "I think that, did you . . . ?" Not yet fear. Still incomprehension. Cutter did not know what had happened, but he knew that fear would come soon.

A last wyrman lurched in the air, wrestling, swaddled in a caul of dirty nothing. Cutter saw it by a smear of the particles it carried, a thrombus of feral air. Cutter knew what was happening.

"Where did they *go*?" someone shouted.

The wyrmen fought air that overwhelmed them, pulled them apart in marauding currents.

The dirigible was close to the militia, and a line of bullet-dust stretched out across the ground toward them. And then the bullets broke off, and with a sudden violent dancing the vessel tipped mightily up, pitching in the air as if a ship on an unstable sea. For seconds it paused, then began to fall, not as if with gravity but as if fighting, as if the turning motors and air-propellors were struggling. The airship was hauled out of the sky by some brutal hand, broke apart.

Shapes began to organise around the militia as they approached, out of the air or the earth or the fire of the torches they carried. Close enough now to see. All the officers were moving their hands in invocation. Cutter could see the ruins of their uniforms, the split and splintered helmets, scratches and Torque-stains where leather had become something else. The horses were dappled with blood and slather. Their passage through the cacotopic zone had marked them.

There were scores, despite what depredations must have culled them. Made mad by what they had suffered, ready to revenge against these renegades whose flight had dragged them into the cacotopos. No wonder they were so light-armed, no wonder so few. They did not need equipment or ordnance when they called up their weapons out of the surrounds and the matter of the world.

Cutter saw their arcane whips. He saw them shaping the air. He knew it was luftgeists that had brought down the wyrmen and the dirigible, air elementals of tremendous power. This was a corps of invocators, whose weapons were the presences they raised. Beast-handlers, of a preternatural kind. A cadre of elementarii.

Cutter was shouting at his chaverim. He saw some understood. Some were startled into fear.

There were no elementalists in the Iron Council. One man had a tiny captive yag that lived in a jar, a fire-spirit no larger than a match-flame. Those few vodyanoi with undines were bound to them by agreement; they could not control them. But there were some who understood what they were facing.

The elementarii were ranging out, each subgroup preparing its calling. *It had to be,* Cutter thought. *People who could fight without hauling weapons. It had to be either elementalists or karcists, and dæmons are too unsure. Gods damn, a cadre of elementalists.* That New Crobuzon would risk losing these men showed how profound was the government's desire to end the Council.

"Come on, let's do it," he shouted to Thick Shanks, and wound the metaclockwork engine as well as he could. He focused the reflected light, levelled the beam, could not stop staring over his shoulder at the attack coming.

Which will it be? Cutter thought. *Fulmen? Shudners? Undines?* Lightning or stone or freshwater elementals, but of course it might be others: metal, sun, wood or fire. Or one whose elemental status was uncertain or disputed: elements made by history, born out of nothing and become real. Would it be a concrete elemental, a glass elemental? What would it be?

He could see already the coils of dust moving against any wind, extending air limbs. The luftgeists. The militia began to bring into being other things.

Sun? Darkness?

They threw all their torches to the ground, and the fire enlarged as if each individual flame loomed much larger than it should, so the ground was impossibly alight, and from the prodigious fire, with a tremendous cry of pleasure, came things like dogs or great apes made of the flames. A pack of yags, fire elementals that bounded in a motion between loping and burning. Cutter saw unridden horses corralled and chanted over and giving out equine screams. One by one they shuddered and let out dying wet noises and unfolded from inside: out of their shuddering carcasses came leaping creatures of their sinew and muscle and their organs all reconfigured into bloody skinless predators: proasmae, the flesh elementals.

Air, fire, flesh ran and turned in animal excitement. A line of militia drew whips occult-tempered, and cracked them, sending the elementals rearing in fear, delight and challenge. The whips snapped like heavy leather and elyctricity, like shadows. When they cracked the noise made dark light.

The elementarii cajoled their charges forward. Air and fire and flesh came. Councillors screamed. They fired and their shells burst among the elementals. Without strategy, pushed by panic, they triggered Judah's golem traps.

With automaton motion golems unfolded out of the earth and the metal and wood debris of the railroad. There were not so many as there were elementals, and each of them drew on Judah's powers. Wherever he was, he must have felt a burst of sudden draining. *And soon he'll feel more,* Cutter thought, and tried to focus the mirror.

A bomb exploded in the path of the yags, and they disappeared amid its copse of high flames, and their cries were uncanny cries of pleasure. When the bomb settled, there were the fire elementals still running, bigger, through the smoke. A line of earth golems faced them.

Cutter felt the murmur of clockwork in the mirror, gears uncoiling in discombobulant dimensions. He felt the mirror moving as if it were a baby.

"Unlock your engine," he shouted, and when Thick Shanks did Cutter felt another tugging. He held his mirror hard and saw Thick

Shanks doing the same. The recombinant light their reflections made was waxing.

It was curling, growing around itself. It was something in itself, something real, with dimensions, something that moved. Cutter saw the fishlike swimming presence, a thing roaming out of nothing and made of the hard light, shining like a sun. He felt his strength haemorrhage from him. "We've got it," he shouted. "Take it to them."

Thick Shanks and he kept their mirrors angled at each other and moved them in time, and the presence of glutinous light followed, dragged over the ground as they turned to face the elementarii. Something terrible was happening. The militia whipmen had come forward, cajoling the elementals at the ends of their lashes, and though the outer lines of the Councillors were laying down fire with everything they had, the proasmae were coming.

Missiles tore into the creatures of slabbed-together muscle, burrowing into them so they refolded and spat out the nuggets of lead and the honed flint or iron blades. The proasmae, the flesh elementals, called up out of the stuff of the horses, reached the earthwork barrier.

They rolled up it, they were amoeboid, they were urchinlike, studded with bones they made limbs, they made themselves suddenly humanoid or like some unskinned and baying wildebeests, and they scrambled the height of the rise and paused at its top, then hurled down onto the screaming men, and Cutter saw what they did.

They dived into the men's flesh. They dived and poured themselves through the Councillors' skin, emptying into flesh-stuff, swimming in the innards while their victims, their new houses, looked suddenly stunned and grossly bloated, scrabbling for a brief second at their chests or necks or wherever the proasm had entered before exploding or infolding in a wet burp of blood and the flutter and flap of skin, and the proasm would run on again, its substance increased, built up with stolen flesh. They raced through the line, tugging the mens' insides out of them and leaving gory skin rags, growing bigger and more bone-flecked as they came.

"Jabber preserve us," Cutter said.

He pulled at the speculum, and felt resistance. He and Thick Shanks pulled their mirrors at different speeds and the thing between them began to pull apart, to split resentfully, strings of light-matter stretching out between its parts like mucus. Cutter shouted, "Back, back your end, pull it back together!" They struggled to reaggregate the light golem.

The strikes of the militia's gnoscourges reached much longer than it seemed they should. Yards up the luftgeists screeched and were galvanised into aggression as the elementarii corrected them. They swept down, invisible. They forced the Councillors who shot and slashed pointlessly to breathe them, shoved into their lungs and burst them.

A salvo of attacks, bombs, a rush of weak thaumaturgy, and the militia regrouped. One was hit; one only was killed. The yags faced the first of the golems, a huge figure of stone and the stumps of iron rails. Yags wrestled it, hugged it, and their fire corpi re-formed and enveloped the golem and began to bend its hard black metal with the intensity of their heat. It spilled into a pool, trying still to fight as its matter collapsed. It ran in rivulets, streams of molten golem.

The Councillors fought, but the elementals were racing through them with effortless carnage, scampering like dogs, like children. It was a terrible dangerous strategy to call the elementals, these animals, substances made predatory and playful flesh: they could not be domesticated. But the elementarii needed only to control them for this one quick attack. The yags and luftgeists were heading on, leaving footprints of fire and trails of ruined air, toward the perpetual train. The golems tried to face them—interventions, the manifestations of sentient control against the animalisation of raw forces. The elementals were winning.

But though the air elementals might blow apart the substance of earth golems in a spew of particles, they had to work harder against air golems. It was a strange, near-invisible fight. Almost the very last line of Judah's defences. Sudden gusts of unnatural wind came up and met the luftgeists, and there was a vague storm where they fought. The made and the wild, the intervention and the barely controlled, squabbled and tore each other apart.

Chunks of something dropped out of the sky and mussed the ground with impact. They were invisible, clots of air itself, Cutter realised, thrown down from the fight above, the torn-off meat of an air elemental discarded by an implacable air golem, the hands of a golem bitten through by a frantic luftgeist. The dead air-flesh lay and evanesced.

The yags were spitting flames. The proasmae were prowling, were sucking the last matter from corpses, grazing on the bodies of the dead. Cutter was very afraid.

From the sunken bed of a stream, way off on the militia's flanks, emerged horse-riding men. With them, in a powerful loping run, came Rahul the Remade man: and on his back, a bolas spinning in his hands, his hat pulled low, was Drogon, the ranchero, the whispersmith.

Gods, thought Cutter, *here come the uhlans, to save us.* He felt delirious.

The riflemen on their horses, some on Remade horses, having come up unseen through the gorges of the waterways, having run all the way from New Crobuzon or gods knew where, emerged and began with great expertise to fire. There were many seconds when the militia were too surprised or could not pin down their new enemies.

Though they were not many, the horesemen took up positions like hunters and fired on the militia from protected places. Their weapons shot puissant bullets that roared like splits in the aether, that muttered as they flew. The gunmen took two, three, four, a handful of the elementarii fast, dropping them, and the Councillors who could see it cheered.

Then, oh, fast, some of the militia spun their whips, and the gnoscourges flailed much too long like serpentine presences momentarily alive and playing with space, flicked the rumps of the yags that squealed in voices like burning and came back at a terrible rate, headed for the newcomers. The Iron Council's gunmen and bombardiers and thaumaturges attacked as they could, but the yags were coming fast.

"Control it. There, *there*," Cutter yelled, nodding toward the wedge of militia, and with Thick Shanks he tugged the mirrors against the resistant light golem. *Be,* Cutter thought. *Fucking be.*

He pulled against the drag of the half-born golem and watched the yags bear on the newcomers. *Who are they?* he thought. *Drogon's friends?* As they grew close, Drogon reared up on Rahul and put his hand to the side of his mouth, and must have whispered something. One of the elementarii flailed suddenly with his whip, sending the tip lashing across the gathering yags, and the scream they sent up was not playful but enraged.

Drogon whispered again and another militiaman did the same, scourged the oncoming elementals, and the yags reared and tumbled into each other, gobbed wads of burning sputum at their masters. Drogon whispered, whispered, sent commands to one and another elementarius, had them perform provocations, confusing the animals. The militia had to defend themselves with expert whip-play from the elementals' revenge.

The light golem was born. It existed. Suddenly. Cutter's mirror shook as the thing moved. It stood, out of the foetus of light it had been. It was a man, or a woman, a broad figure made of illumination that was impossible to look at yet did not shed light but seemed to *suck in* what light was there and gave a violent hard glow that impossibly did not spread beyond its own borders. It stood and stepped forward, and the mirrors were tugged with it. Cutter and Thick Shanks were half-following half-dictating its movements.

"There," Cutter shouted, and they twisted their mirrors so the golem strode forward with a construct's motion, past the outlying ranks of the Councillors who cried out, was this some seraph come to save them? They looked at each other with eyes momentarily occluded by its brightness, looked to its footsteps, which glowed with residue. The light golem strode into the yags. The golem stretched a little like some dough-thing, gripped the yags and began to shine.

Cutter felt weak. The golem wrestled them, and their fire did nothing against its solid light, and it grew brighter and brighter as it fought, became a humanoid star, shedding cold luminance that effaced the heat of the yags and grew much much too bright to see. And then the yags that had fought it were gone, washed out in its glow, and it was stronger. It moved with an unsound, a stillness.

Yags panicked. There were some that ran away in their animal motion across the landscape, and some who rallied and flew again at the light golem to be erased by its phosphorescence. There were elementarii whipping hard at the frightened fire elementals, but that enraged them and some in passing snapped petulant and pyrotic at their handlers and burnt them to death.

The militia were rallying. Little luftgeists like arrows hunted down the new gunmen, piercing them and drinking their blood. Drogon whispered his instructions, and the militia could not disobey him, and he made their whips flail destructively. They knew by then that he was their main enemy. They sent the proasmae toward him.

Cutter and Thick Shanks sent the golem for the militia, toward a group gathered around some kind of cannon. They were butchering animals. *What are they doing?*

They were siphoning something from the air, as their proasmae at last reached the newcomer gunmen and began to swim through them. The light golem came on. What were the militia calling?

A drizzle of luminance seemed to be pouring from the sky, very concentrate, a fine shaft just visible. It fell to the mechanism they surrounded. The light came out of the moon. The day-moon, just visible, very faint in sunlight. Out of its half-lustre came the moonlight into the machine, and at the end of the barrel a hole seemed to be opening.

In its deeps, something made of glow was moving. Cutter stared.

It took long moments to make sense of it—while he tried to march the light golem over the damage of still-exploding bombs, the wreckage left by the Councillors, who were advancing now that the yags had gone, now the proasmae were distracted by the newcomers, now the militia had lost control of their luftgeists that caused damage and death but only randomly as they gushed over the heavily protected train—but Cutter saw something in the opening. Its parameters changed, defied taxonomy. He tried to make sense of it.

Its shape altered with the seconds. A fish's skeleton, the ribs passing ripples along the length of a body like a rope of vertebrae or like some rubberised cord. And then there was something of the bear to it, and something of the rat, and it had horns, and a great weight, and it shone as if its guts and skin, its bones were phosphorus. As if it were all cold and bright rock. A firefly, a death mask, a wooden skull.

A fegkarion. A moon elemental.

Cutter had heard of them, of course, but could not believe that this onrushing skeletal insectile animal thing he saw only half a second in three and that was a suggestion or a fold of space was the moonthing about which there were so many stories. *Oh gods, oh Jabber.*

"Shanks . . . get the golem to that thing, now."

But the golem did not walk so fast. It went through the militia at a steady pace, laid out its hands as it came. It took time to touch each man it passed, to smother their heads with its hands and pour light into them, so each burst with light, beams exploding their helmets, shining hard and for yards from their ears, their anuses, their pricks, through their clothes, making them stars, before the golem let them fall.

The fegkarion was crawling out of the nothing. "Come *on,*" Cutter said.

The elementalists were withdrawing, gathering around the moon-callers to protect them. They slashed at the golem now and drew its substance with each whip-strike, sent gouts of light spraying. Each lash snapped back Cutter's and Thick Shanks' heads. They bled. They kept the thing moving.

The proasmae were neglected. The last of them roared through two more gunners then took its bone-and-innard body into the wilds, following its siblings, rolling away from Drogon and Rahul. Drogon kept whispering, but by some thaumaturgy the militia no longer obeyed him. They lashed at him; they lashed at the golem.

"Come on, come on."

Now the golem's light-stuff legs stamped through bodies of the men attacking it, and they burst with the shining. The moon elemental was close, was corkscrewing its chill and grey-glowing self through the hole that was opened, and it was *vast,* Cutter saw, it was monstrous, and he reached and the golem reached to block the lunic cannon, wedging itself into the hole, shoving through the stuff of the elemental itself and into the engine of the machine, and golem and elemental fought, and blistering light—cold, hot, grey and magnesium-white—came welling out of nothing like sweat.

The Councillors saw the proasmae were gone, sent in their heaviest squads, their cactacae and big Remade. "Take some alive!" someone was shouting, and the cactus hacked conscious and light-comaed militia, and there was a burst, a shattering, and the moon-engine combusted in harpoons of golem-light and moonlight.

The militia were broken. Stopped by Drogon and his men, and

by the light golem. The ground was scattered with dead elementarii and countless more dead from the Iron Council, with the burst residue of flesh elementals and their victims, with gobs of glow that trickled luminous into the earth. Those few militia still able rode into the wilds of Rohagi, following the slick tracks of the proasmae, which had become a wild herd: wet red blubber things prowling the dustland.

Those militia left were immobilised by bullets, by chakris or golem-light. Lying, spitting and raging at the Councillors as they came.

"Fuck you fuck you," one man said through the ruins of his reflective helmet. There was fear in his voice but mostly there was rage. "Fuck you, you send us through the fucking stain, you cowards, you think that'll stop us? We lost half our force but we're the fucking best, we can chase you wherever you go, and now we know the way through, we found our way, and maybe you got lucky with this bullshit, this bastard lightshow and fucking susurrator. We know the way." They shot him.

They shot all the militia left alive. They buried their own dead where they could, except for one, a Remade woman famous for mediating during The Idiocy, long before. They voted her a burial on the train's carried graveyard, in the flatcar cemetery of its greatest dead. They left the militia to rot, and some defiled the bodies.

When the sun rose again on the yag-scorched train, Cutter found Ann-Hari and the Council's leaders. They were exhausted. Drogon, Rahul and Thick Shanks were with them. Cutter stumbled with his own tiredness. He gripped Drogon and the Remade who had carried him.

"Last time we escaped the militia," Thick Shanks said. "This time we *beat* them. We *took them down.*" Something of his delight even entered Cutter himself, though he knew all the contingencies that had led to this victory.

"Yeah. You did."

"We did. You . . . the light . . . all of us did it."

"Yeah, we did, all right. We did."

"We got out, is all," said Rahul. Drogon whispered agreement. "We got lost. Came out of that tunnel, well, that alleyway, whatever, into the main part of the town. It took us a while to find where we were. But there was so much going on that night. We never saw nor heard a thing from you. Not from none of you. We didn't know if you'd fixed that Teshman or not. We'd no idea. You did, didn't you?

"It took us time to get back to the Collective, but honestly there were so many damn holes we could *walk* in. When we found out you'd gone—no, I don't blame you at all, sister, you couldn't have known we was coming—we had to get back.

"So we smuggled us out, and then old Drogon here goes off for two days and comes back with his brothers."

"*There ain't so many of us horse-wanderers,*" Drogon told Cutter. "*You can get word out. I know where to find them. And they owe me.*"

"Where are they now?"

"*Most are gone. Some ride tomorrow. These men are nomads, Cutter. Give them your thanks, any coin you can share, that's all they want.*"

"We knew the militia was coming," Rahul said. "We rode hard."

"You came out of nowhere."

"We came out of the trails. Drogon knows them. We came fast. I ain't never known horses like these men's. Where's the monk? Talking of secret trails. Qurabin. Oh no . . . Gods. And Ori? Did he . . . Ori? Gods, gods. And . . ."

"Elsie."

"Oh gods. No. Oh gods."

"I didn't think you could do it," Cutter said to the Councillors. "I admit that. I was wrong. I'm happy. But it ain't enough. I told you why Judah ain't here . . . he's working on something. In the Collective. But it's too fucking late. *It's too late.* He's trying to do what he can.

"Listen to me.

"The Collective's fallen. Shut your mouth, no, listen . . . The Collective was a . . . a dream, but it's over. It failed. If it ain't dead by now it'll be dead in days. You understand? *Days.*

"By the time the Council comes close to the city . . . the Collective'll be dead. New Crobuzon'll be under martial rule. And what then? Killed Stem-Fulcher, it didn't make a spit of difference: the system won't be beat—don't look at me like that, I don't like it any more'n you. And when you come rolling up saying *Hello, we're the* inspiration, *on cue,* you know what'll happen. You know what'll be waiting.

"Every militiaman and -woman in New Crobuzon. Every fucking war engine, every karcist, every thaumaturge, every construct, every spy and turncoat. They'll kill you in view of the city, and then the hope that you are—you still are—dies when you die.

"Listen. I'll give you Judah's message again.

"You have to turn. The Iron Council has to turn. Or leave the train. You come on to New Crobuzon, it's suicide. You'll die. They'll destroy you. And that can't be. That ain't acceptable. Iron Council has to turn."

CHAPTER THIRTY-TWO

"THEY'LL DESTROY YOU," HE SAID. "DO YOU WANT TO DIE?" HE SAID. "You owe yourself to the world, we *need* you."

Of course they would not be persuaded. They continued, pushed through the buckled land leaving the scabs of fight behind them. Cutter showed horror that they would not do as he said, but he had expected nothing else. He made his case and the Iron Councillors answered him in various ways.

Some gave the kind of idiot triumphalism that enraged him. "We beat New Crobuzon before, we'll do it again!" they might say. Cutter would stare uncomprehending because he saw that they *knew* what they said was untrue, that it would not be that way. They knew.

Others were more thought-through. They gave him pause.

"What would we be?" Thick Shanks said. The cactus-man etched a cicatrix into the skin of his inner arm, cutting a snake shape with an animal's tooth. "What would you have us be, bandits? We lived free in a republic we made. You want me to give that up, be a bloody wilderness hobo? I'd rather die fighting, Cutter."

"We have a responsibility," Ann-Hari said. Cutter never felt eased in her presence. The fervour in her unnerved him—it made him tired and uncertain of himself, as though she might win him over against his own will. He knew he was jealous—no one had had such an effect on Judah Low as Ann-Hari.

"We're a dream," she said. "The dream of the commons. Everything came to this, everything came here. We got to here. This is what we are. History's pushing us."

What does that mean? he thought. *What are you* saying?

"It's time for us to push through. Whatever happens. We have to come back now, you see?" That was all she would say.

The whispersmith's friends, his fellow cavalry, disappeared on their horses Remade and whole, becoming dustclouds as they headed east, south. Drogon stayed. Cutter was not sure why.

"What do you want this lot to do? You been in the city . . . you know we'll be killed if we go."

"*They'll be killed maybe.*" Drogon shrugged. "*They know what's happening. Who'm I to stop them? They can't stop now. You set yourself on a rail and it comes to be what you do. They have to keep going.*"

This ain't about argument, Cutter thought. He was horrified by what seemed to him quiescence. *If they tried to argue it, they'd lose . . . but even though they* know *that, they still go on . . . because in going against the facts, they change them.* It was a methodology of decision utterly unlike his own, unlike how he could ever think. Was it rational? He could not tell.

The Iron Council progressed through a landscape made of mist. The scarps and hillocks, the layers of trees seemed momentary thickenings of water in the air, seemed to curdle out of the vapour as the perpetual train came, and dissipate again in its aftermath.

They moved through scenery that was abruptly familiar, that

jogged old memories. This was New Crobuzon country. Siskins went between dripping haw-bushes. This was a New Crobuzon winter. They were a few weeks away.

"We had a man once, years and years ago," Ann-Hari said to Cutter. "When the Weaver came to us, before we was Council, and told us secrets. The man went mad, so he could only talk about the spider. He was like a prophet. But then he was boring, and then not even boring, just nothing. We didn't even hear him, you see? We heard nothing when he spoke.

"You're like that. 'Turn back, turn back.' " She smiled. "We don't hear you no more, man."

I've a mission, Cutter thought. *I've failed.* Knowing that his lover had expected it did nothing to stop his sadness.

He became a ghost. He was respected—one of the world-crossers, who had come to save Iron Council. His dissidence now, his insistence that the Council would die, was treated with polite uninterest. *I'm a ghost.*

Cutter could have left. He could have taken a horse from the township's stables and ridden. He would have found the foothills, the deserted tracks, Rudewood, he would have come to New Crobuzon. He could not. *I'm here now* was all he could think. He would run only when he had to.

He had seen the maps. The Council would go on east leaving spike-holes and the debris of track-pressed shale, recycling the iron road, and would at last hit the remains of the railway scores of miles south of New Crobuzon. And there they would couple to what remained of the old tracks, and steam on, and within hours would approach the city.

Cutter would run when he had to. But not now.

"We are a hope," Ann-Hari said.

Perhaps she's right. The train will come, the last of the Collective will rise, and the government will fall.

* * *

In these damp wilds they were not the only people. There were homesteads, little wood houses built on hills, one every few days. A few acres of sloped and stony ground raked beyond the dark under-hangs of hills. Orchards, root vegetables, paddocks of dirt-coloured sheep. The hill farmers and families of loners would come out as the Council took its hours to pass them. They stared, skin milky with inbreeding, in the deepest incomprehension at the great pres-ence. Sometimes they would bring goods to barter.

There must be some tradetowns but the Council did not pass any. The news of them—of the rogue train appearing from the west, escorted by an army of fReemade and their children, all of them proud—crossed the wet country by rumour's byways.

Word'll reach New Crobuzon. Maybe they'll come for us soon.

"Did you hear?" one toothless farmer woman asked them. She offered them applewood-cured ham, for what money they had (ar-cane westland doubloons) and a memento of the train (they gave her a greased cog that she took as reverential as if it were a holy book). "I heard of you. Did you hear?" She gave them proud passage through her paltry lands, insisting they carve their road through the middle of her field. "You'll be ploughing for me," she said. "Did you hear? They say that there's trouble in New Crobuzon."

Could mean the Collective's done. Could mean it's winning. Could mean anything.

There was more word of that trouble the farther east they went. "The war's over," a man told them. His shieling had become a sta-tion, his porch a platform. His nearest neighbours had travelled miles from their lowland holdings to be with him when the Iron Council came through. His fields were a sidings yard full of men and women. The farmers and the wilds people watched with stern pleasure.

"The war's done. They told me. They warred with Tesh, ain't it? Well it's over, and we won." *We? You never set foot in New Crobuzon, man. You never been a hundred miles from it.* "They did something and they beat them and now the Tesh want peace. Do I know what? The what? What's a Collective?"

New Crobuzon had done something. The story came back again. A secret mission, some said, an assassination. Something had been halted and life had changed, the Teshi had been restrained, forced into negotiation or surrender. *Something stopped Tesh's plans?* Cutter thought wryly. *Fancy.* And that triumph, it seemed, had bolstered Parliament and the mayor, had bled support from the Collective. That he could not be wry about. That he could not think about.

"The strikers? They're finished. The government sorted them out."

Through the rained-on downs came a spread of runaways from the city. They came and lived in the small towns by which the Iron Council was passing; they repopulated the deserted cow-towns they found, the residues of the old railway rush. The Council might come out of the low hills in an industrious multitude and lay down tracks along the preflattened paths, along the reclaimed main roads. New inhabitants would emerge from what had been the saloon, a church, a bawdyhouse, and stare as over hours (their progress faster daily) the crews put down the sleepers and rails on old horsetracks and passed where stagecoaches and drifters had been.

"Did you hear?" They heard the same stories scores of times. There must have been escapees from the Parliamentarian quarters too, but no one said so: everyone was a Collectivist, on the run from the militia. *Sure you're not some two-bit spiv?* Cutter thought cynically. *Sure you're really an organiser like you claim?*

"Did you hear?" *That the war's over, that we beat the Tesh, and that when we beat the Tesh the Mayor took control again, and everything was sorted, and the Collective went under?*

Yes, we heard. Though it was disputed.

They were entertained in these revenant towns, with sex and New Crobuzon cooking. "What have you come for? Did you not hear? Did you hear? There ain't no Collective no more. Only dregs, some terrorists in Dog Fenn, a few streets here or there." "That ain't what I heard, I heard it was there and still fighting." "You're coming to help, to fight for the Collective? I wouldn't go back. It's a damn *war* there." "I'd go back. Can I come? Can I come with you?"

Some of those who had left to be wanderers in the waste—some of the young—joined the perpetual train, to return to New Crobuzon, only weeks after their escape. "Tell us about the Iron Council!" they insisted, and their new compatriots told all their stories.

There were rumours of new kithless, unique powers. "Did you hear," Cutter heard, "about the golem-man Low?"

"What?" he said, crossing to where the refugee spoke.

"Golem-man Low, he's got an army of made men. He's making them of clay in his cellar, ready to take over the city. He's been seen, outside New Crobuzon, in the rail yards, on the sidings, by the tracks. He's got plans."

They came closer, and the escaped they met were more and more recent out of the city. "It's done," one said. "There ain't no Collective anymore. Wish to gods there was."

That night Cutter looked for Drogon and realised that the whispersmith had gone. He walked the length of the train, sent messages and queries, but there was nothing.

It was possible the susurrator was off riding, hunting, on a mission of his own, but Cutter was very suddenly certain that Drogon had gone. That they were close enough to New Crobuzon, that the horseman had had enough, and had ridden, his adventures with the Iron Council over.

Is that all? Such a slow deflation, such a lacklustre end. *Was that all you wanted, Drogon? Not tempted to say good-bye?*

Cutter prepared to leave. It could not be long. He felt a hollowness, a preemptive loss. He wondered how and where the militia would confront them and destroy the Council. The Remade and their families and comrades, the Councillors, all knew what was coming. Their track-laying songs became martial. They oiled their guns; the forges at trackside and in the carriages turned out weapons. The Iron Councillors carried made and stolen guns. The glass and brass foci of ordnance-shamanism. Racks of spears and west-coast weapons.

"We'll gather people with us, we'll be an army, we'll sweep in. We'll turn things around." Cutter winced to hear the dreams. "We're bringing history."

There was a drip of people across the land, on their way anywhere, without plans but away from the carnage of New Crobuzon.

Still empty land, only a few half-kept orchards, a few groves of temperate fruit-trees. There was a moment of transition. They were in the wilds, in unsafe lands, and then with a suddenness and a strange anticlimax they were in domesticated country. They knew they were close.

The graders and scouts returned. "Yonder. Just beyond." Over stone-flecked undulations. "The old rails. Down to Junctiontown, in the swamps. And up to New Crobuzon."

Two days away. Every moment they continued, Cutter expected a deployment of New Crobuzon troops to emerge from the tunnels and flint hides of that damp region, but they did not come. How long would he stay? He had tried to dissuade them. Would he handle the mirror one more time?

"Low the golemer's been seen, he's in the hills, he's watching over us. He's by the old rails."

Oh yes? Has he? Cutter was sour. He was very lonely. *Where are you, Judah?* He did not know what to do.

In small numbers, some Councillors—the older, mostly, the first generation, who remembered the punishment factories—left. Not many, but enough to be felt. They would go into the hills to scout for wood or food and would not come back. Their comrades, their sisters, shook their heads with scorn and care. Not everyone was unafraid, or willing or able to ignore their fear.

I'll decide the plan when I see the old rails, Cutter told himself, but then he walked with the track-layers as they bent the iron road through gaps between sediment and basalt stanchions and through the V the graders had cut in soft displaced earth and there, there, there wetly ashine, black but glowing, were the rails. More than twenty years old. Curving away, drawn together by perspective, slipped through geography. The metal path. The crossties were bucked by neglect but held the rails down.

The Councillors gave a cheer that was reedy in the cold wet air but that continued a long time. The track-layers waved their tools. The Remade gesticulated their unshaped limbs. The road to New Crobuzon. That old road. Left to moulder when the collapse of money and the stockpiles in warehouses had made an end to the TRT boom. They had been left to the shifting ground—Cutter could see where the banks of the cut had bowed and buried the metal. They were running grounds for wild things.

In some places the iron had been stolen by salvagers. The Council would have to lay down some from its own stock. The Iron Council had come this way before, unborn, when it was just a train. The wet of the stones, the dark and glistening way. Cutter stared. And what was it? What was happening in his city? Where the Collective was fighting? How should he run?

Judah, you bastard, where are you?

The hammermen laid down the rails, and with careful measured sideswipes of their mallets, they put in curves. They made bends, gently, so that their tracks came out of the west and skewed gradually through the banks of the train-gash up and onto the roadbed of the old rails.

* * *

This is all a postlude, Cutter thought. *This is all happening after the story.*

The Collective was falling or fallen and all there was was this unfolding of violence. *We'll swing it, change it,* Cutter thought with sad scorn, in the voice of a Councillor.

The greatest moment in the history of New Crobuzon. Laid low by war and by the end *of war, which was gods help me my doing, our doing. But what could we do? Could we let the city fall?* The Collective would have fallen anyway, he told himself, but he was not sure of that. He drew icons in the earth, making trains in outline, men and women running away or toward something. *Maybe the Collective's just hiding. Everyone in the city waiting. Maybe I should stay on the train.* He knew he would not.

There were guards around the sprawling train-town now for fear of militia and of the bandits. Mostly the brigands that came, fRee-made and whole, came to join the Council. They arrived daily, wondering if they had to audition, show their worth. The Councillors welcomed them, though some fretted about spies. There was too much chaos in those last days to worry. Cutter saw newcomers everywhere, with their tentative enthusiasm. Once with a start he thought he saw a man attached backward on a horse's neck.

Walking back through the cold at night, through a startled gust of rock pigeons, Cutter heard a voice. Deep in his ear.

"Come up here. I've something to tell you. Quiet. Please. Quietly."

"Drogon?" Nothing but the idiot fluting of the birds. "Drogon?" Only small stones skittering.

It was not a command but a request. The susurrator could have made him come, but had only asked.

Drogon was waiting in the dark hills overlooking the train.

"I thought you'd gone," Cutter said. "Where'd you go?"

Drogon stood with an old white-haired man. He held a gun, though it was not aimed.

"This one?" the old man said, and Drogon nodded.

"Who's this?" said Cutter. The old man held his arms behind his back. He wore an old-fashioned waistcoat. He was eighty or more, stood tall, looked at Cutter sternly, kindly.

"Who *is* this Drogon? Who the fuck *are* you?"

"Now, lad . . ."

"*Quiet*," said Drogon peremptorily in Cutter's ear. The old man was speaking.

"I'm here to tell you what's happening. This is holy work and I would not have you not know. I'll tell you the truth, son: I had and have no interest in you." He spoke with a singing cadence. "I was here to see the train. I've been wanting to see the train a long time, and I come by darkness. But your friend"—he indicated Drogon—"insisted we speak. Said you might want to hear this."

He inclined his head. Cutter looked at the gun in Drogon's hand.

"So here is what it is. I am Wrightby."

"Yes, I see you know me, you know who I am. I confess gratification, yes. I do." Cutter breathed hard. *Godsfuckingdamn.* Could it possibly be true? He eyed Drogon's gun.

"*Stand still.*" A whispered command. Cutter stood tall so fast his spine cracked. His limbs were rigid. "*Hold*," Drogon said.

Jabber . . . Cutter had forgotten what it was to be so ordered. He shook, tried to curl his fingers.

"I am Weather Wrightby and I am here to tell you thank you. For this thing you've done. Do you know? Do you know what it is you've done? You crossed the world. You crossed the world, something that's needed doing as long as I've lived, and that you did.

"More than once I tried, you know. With my men. We did what we could. Cut through the mountains, through creeping hills. Smokestone. All the landscapes. You know them. We tried, we died, we turned back. Eaten, killed. Taken by cold. Again and again, I tried. And then I was too old to try.

"All this"—he swept his arm up—"all this metal trail from New Crobuzon to the swamps, the split, to Cobsea, to Myrshock, it was something. But it wasn't what I worked for. Not really. Not my dream. You know that.

"No: that other thought, of iron stretched from sea to sea, that was mine. The continent cut open. From New Crobuzon west. That was mine. That's history. That's what I been fighting for, wanting. You know it, don't you, all of you? You know that.

"I won't pretend you didn't rile me. You did, of course you did, you riled me when you took my train. But then I saw what you were doing . . . Holy work. Much more than you'd been charged with. And while it weren't the easiest for me to see, I'd not stand in the way of that." Weather Wrightby shone; his eyes were passionate and wet. "I had to come see you. I had to tell you this. What you've done, what you did. I salute you."

Cutter shook like an animal in a trap, debased by the susurrator's techniques. He strived, moving and hearing again *"Be still"* deep in his ear. It seemed to resonate in the bone itself. *Gods, fucking, damn.* The air was utterly still. There was the snap of metal from below. It was cold.

"And then you were gone, off in the west and who knew where? It was over, but I knew I'd hear of you again and then, yes." Weather Wrightby smiled. "Even fallen and failed, I've my networks, I've my plans. I've my friends in Parliament who want me to succeed. I hear things. So when they *found* you—when one of their scouts or merchanteers went up through that sea, and heard of the train-town and sent word and sent scouts and found you—when that happened, I heard it. And when they sent their men to bring your heads, under cover of the war, I heard that too.

"What could I do? What could I do but come to you? *You know the route.* You know the way through the continent. Do you know? What that is? That's holy knowledge. I'd not let them bury that. You went as fast as you can, there's places I'd deviate, go souther near the Torque, but however it's finessed its *your way.* I needed to know.

"So I got word to your best defender in the city, one there when your Council was born. You think it isn't known?" He shook his head with gentle amusement. "Who's an idea where the Council might have gone? Of course we know. Known for a long time who their man is in the city. I've paid one of his friends, a long time, to keep a link to him. I got him word so he'd come find you. We knew he could. And we could come and help. To find the Council, to help it back. My whispersmith."

Drogon was an employee. He was security, an agent, for the TRT. Cutter's blood went from his stomach.

"He's somewhere near, you know, they say. Your defender, Low. He's been seen. He's like a lost thing now the Collective's near gone. He's been seen around the lines. Waiting for your end. We've what we needed.

"We came to help, and learn the way. We learnt it all. Drogon, my man. A good man. We'd not have them interrupt you. We had to stop them. So close, so nearly home. I couldn't let them interrupt you so near the city. We had to see you back again."

That's why Drogon came back. This mad bastard here, Wrightby's fucking mission. And those other cavalry, TRT all? Good gods. He needed us to come through. He had to know we'd made it all the way. Had to see our route. He fought the city. He killed the damn militia so he could see us get back.

"And now, you're here. Shhh, still now."

"*Still,*" said Drogon, and Cutter's slow struggling ended.

"Now you're *here*. You'll be on the rails tomorrow. And back to the city. You see, you've done what was needed. I've the route across the continent. By the cacotopic stain. The way you made out of your bodies and your need. We thank you for it."

Drogon, without sneer or show, inclined his head.

"You can be sure we'll use it. I'll build the iron way. This continent will be made again, Remade, it'll be made beautiful." Cutter stared at the visionary of money and iron. He stared and could not speak, could not move, could not tell Weather Wrightby he was mad. Now Wrightby could cross the continent, after so long trying and failing. He would plough a train-thin strip and siphon money to the west and suck it back again. He would change the world and New Crobuzon.

Can he? It's a long way. A damn long way.

But he knows *the way now.*

"Here's how it will be. They're waiting for you. The Collective's dead. You know that, yes? And the militia knows you're coming. They're waiting. They know where you'll arrive. To the sidings, the terminus we built. There'll be plenty of them."

There would be battalions. There would be whole brigades. Lined in rows, with their guns, with a patience of mass murder. They were waiting for their quarry to come, enter the fire and iron, the hotspit thaumaturgic carnage, at their own pace. No light golem, no moss-magic, no braveheart resistance of the fReemade and their kin, no cactus savagery, no shaman channelling, would defeat that massing.

"You'll die. I'm here to tell you that." He said it not like a warning, but as part of a conversation. *He'll not intercede again. This fucker helped for some religious craziness, some mercantile madness. Even against the government. But now we're back he's done with that. We're home, we've done what's needed, he has the way. He can do what he's always wanted. It's in Drogon's head, the bastard, in the tracks we left.*

"I want you to know you are magnificent. Such a brave thing, so strong. Like nothing I'd imagined. Well done, well done. You can end now.

"I tell you why I tell you this.

"It wouldn't be *seemly* for you not to know. You should know what you've become. When you turn those last curves, and see the trainyard, and the militia."

Cutter shook. Drogon watched him.

"Or you could go."

Cutter's heart beat faster as if it were only with the saying of it that Wrightby made it possible. As if he were giving him permission to escape. "You could go. Drogon wanted you to have that choice. That's why I'm here."

Drogon? Did you? Cutter had the strength, just, to move his eyes and look at his erstwhile companion. The ranch-hand hatted killer did not look up. Such attenuated camaraderie. What was this? Some last chance, granted to Cutter. *I always had a chance,* he thought, though he felt as if Drogon had given him a present.

"You've ridden history across the Rohagi steppes. You've made the TRT a truth though its name was always a lie before. It did—it crossed a continent. You can go now.

"Or. Or you could help us. You could help us cross back again. Once more. Leave the tracks behind us this time." Wrightby looked at him and Drogon did not. "Drogon's told me your facility, how you've learnt to travel, to grade, to scout. And you were always your own man. We know that. You could help us."

Gods, Jabber, Jabber and shit, godspit, godshit, you ain't saying that. You ain't. The true of it. A revelation. *So.* Even through Drogon's disabling hex, Cutter sneered.

That's it? He tried to talk but could not. The expression he dragged across his face said it. *You think what, you think what?*

What do you think I am? Think I'm so cut off from them as I've fought and travelled and fucked with that I'd go, leave them for you? For your money crusade? All your religiose dung comes to this? This was a recruitment speech? You want me on your team? Because I know the way? Because I've done this? You want me on your team? What do you think I am?

He was melted with disgust, standing in his whisper-hexed stillness, his hands by his side.

"What do you say?" Wrightby said.

Deep in Cutter's ear came Drogon's voice: *"Speak."*

"Fuck you," said Cutter instantly. Wrightby nodded, waited.

"Get away from my fucking train. You bastards, you *turncoat bastard*, Drogon, you'll never get away from us—" He breathed in to scream and Drogon silenced him again.

"We'll not get past you?" Wrightby said. He looked quizzical. "I'm not sure. Really, I think we will. We'll go now. I will be in the yard. When the train comes in. I'll be there, waiting. Come if you want to, if you change your opinions."

Drogon whispered again. Cutter was agonied by cramp. The whispersmith indicated a way through the hills, led Weather Wrightby away. He looked back and whispered to Cutter again.

"Just so you know," he said. *"I can't see as it'll make a spit of difference. But just in case. Because it has to finish now. Your mirrors are broken. Just to be sure."*

Weather Wrightby looked Cutter in the eyes. "You know where to find me."

And they were gone, and Cutter was straining. *Why didn't you kill me, you fuckers?*

His arm came up. It did not matter. He was no threat. What they had told him did not matter. *The militia are waiting*—he had said that for weeks. Everyone knew he thought that. However suddenly certain he was, it was what he had always said. Why would this change the Iron Council's messianic plans?

There was another reason Drogon and Wrightby had left him alive. They still thought he might turn. They thought he might get out, leave the Council as it steamed toward its carnage and its end, and join them. And he hated them for that but also thought, *What am I? What am I that they think that of me?*

He cried some. He did not know if it was the effort of breaking the hex, or something else. He saw himself as Drogon must have seen him: his sneers and loneliness making him seem a traitor in waiting.

*   *   *

The mirrors had been taken out of their careful wrapping in the armoury car. The glass was veined, the tain made dust. Cutter wanted to tell someone what had happened, but he was afraid of the bitterness in him, the miserable certainty of an expectation fulfilled—he was afraid that for all the real loss of it he would seem to crow. He hated it in him. He knew Drogon had sensed it. It was why they had approached him.

He took the broken mirrors to Ann-Hari, and told her.

The old rails shone back moonlight. At the edge of their vision, in the east, was a darker dark: Rudewood, closing. The lights of the train and its cooking fires shed tiny auras.

"Well?" Ann-Hari said.

"Well?"

"Yes."

"What will you do?"

"What would *you* do?"

"I'd turn *away,* for Jabber's sake. I'd turn and go south on the rails, not north."

"Into the swamp?"

"For a start. If that's what it takes to get away. To *live,* good gods, Ann-Hari. To live. They're *waiting.* Tomorrow, maybe the next day, they're *there.*"

"Are they? So?"

Cutter shouted. Right into the night. "'So?' Are you insane? Haven't you *listened* to me? And what do you mean 'Are they?'?" Abruptly he stopped. They watched each other. "You don't believe me."

"I don't know."

"You think I'm lying."

"Now now," she said. "Come. You're a good friend to the Council, Cutter, we know—"

"Oh my good gods, you think I'm *lying.* So what does that mean? You think, my gods, you think *I* broke the godsdamned mirrors?"

"Cutter, now."

"You *do*."

"*Cutter.* You didn't break the mirrors. I know that."

"So what, you think I'm lying about Drogon?"

"You never wanted us to come back, Cutter. You never wanted us here. And now you tell me the militia are waiting. How do you know Drogon or this man weren't lying? They know what you think; they know what to tell you. Maybe they want us to fear and fail."

Cutter stopped up short. Could Weather Wrightby be trying to frighten them away?

Perhaps the Collective had won. The refugees in the stony lands beyond the city were all wrong, and the Collective was establishing new democracy, had ended the suffrage lottery, had disarmed the militia and armed the populace. And there were statues to those fallen. Parliament was being rebuilt. And there were no militia pods, the clouds had no unmarked dirigibles in them, the air was full only of wyrmen, of balloons and bunting. Perhaps Weather Wrightby wanted them not to join that new New Crobuzon.

No. Cutter knew. He knew the truth. That was not how it was. He shook his head.

"You have to tell the Councillors," he said.

"What do you want me to tell?" Ann-Hari said. "You want me to tell them how someone we never knew or trusted brought another man we don't know here to tell us that the thing we always knew might be true *is* true, but gave no proof? You want that?"

Cutter felt a rise of something, some tremulous despair. "Oh my gods," he said. "You don't care."

She met his stare.

Even if, she was saying, even if you are right—even if that was Drogon, and that was Weather Wrightby, even if there are ten thousand militia ranged ready—this is where we are, this is what we are. This is where we have to be. Was this her madness?

"We are the Iron Council," she said. "We do not turn ever again."

Cutter thought of running into the night and shouting the truth at these dissidents he had come to care for—his comrades, his chaverim, his sisters—and having them turn, begging them to turn, telling them what was waiting, what he knew, what Ann-Hari knew. He said nothing. He did not shout. He was not sure it was not a failure in him—he was not sure it was not a weakness—but he could not announce the truth. Because he knew that it would make no difference, that none of them would turn away.

CHAPTER THIRTY-THREE

THE TRAIN WENT SLOW ON THE OLD RAILS, THE CREWS RUNNING ahead constantly to shore up a collapsing bank of stone, to sweep away detritus for a clear run. They welded split metal, rehammered spikes in bursts of rust. But it was not the ruin on the rails that kept them slow so much as disbelief, the theatre of where they were, what they were doing. At ten, fifteen miles an hour the perpetual train, Iron Council, went north, surrounded by cut, fangs of trap-rock, for New Crobuzon.

Every window was spiked with guns. The flatcars, the little grassed cemetery, the towers, the tent-towns on the rooftops were full of armed Councillors. They squatted, they sang war songs. "Tell us about New Crobuzon," the young ones said, those born to whores while the Council was still a work-train, or to free women in Bas-Lag's inner country, or to Iron Councillors.

Behind the train came the Councillors who could not fight. The children, the pregnant, those whose Remakings made them ill-suited. The old. They stretched a long way on the tracks, singing their own songs.

Wyrmen went overhead, went and came back screeching what they saw. Over the hours the roadbed rose, until the train was on a ridge ordering the granite-stubbled ground into this side and this side. Trees rose as they passed stumps of forest, and the things that lived in them shrieked in the canopies. Many miles west the miasma of trees became Rudewood.

The hours went fast with the mesmeric beat of train wheels that Cutter had forgotten, that the months had taken from his mind as the Iron Council crept too slowly to pick up any rhythm. The train moved just fast enough to make the noise come. The percussion of wheels, the beat of pistons. The *uh uh, uh uh,* like being tapped on the shoulder again and again, reminded of something, a nervous noise. Cutter rode the train's anxiety.

I'll know, in a moment I'll know, he said inside himself. *In a moment I'll decide.* And the perpetual train did not stop and it brought him miles and miles closer to New Crobuzon before, it seemed, he had a chance to think.

What will happen?

He had a weapon ready. He rode in the caboose with outsiders, refugees, who were excited and terribly afraid of what was ahead. It curved, it curved, as if trying to hide its terminus. *Miles yet,* Cutter thought, but the end of the line seemed to glow darkly just out of sight.

"I need to go home. They're waiting for me," someone said. *Something is,* Cutter thought. *Something's waiting for you.*

I won't stay. It was a certainty, suddenly. *I'll not go to that scum Drogon, but I'll not give him my death either.* What will you do? He gave the question a voice. *I'll run.* Where will you go? *Where I must.* And Judah Low? *If I can. If I can find him.* Judah Low.

Oh Judah oh Judah. Judah, Judah.

When the night came down as if darkness thickened the air, they did not stop. Light went from their windows across the grey plain and made the train a millipede on gaslight legs.

They must be a few tens of miles off now. Quite suddenly the tracks were clean and clear. Perhaps there had been some passage, Cutter thought; perhaps the city had had trains run the pointless distance this far and back, ferrying ghost passengers to ghost stations. Then in the bone light of such early morning he saw figures on the trackside darkness waving adzes and thick twig brooms, shouting for the train to *Go on, go on* and telling it *Welcome home.*

Fugitives from New Crobuzon's Collective. They were there in increasing numbers out of the black before the train, blinking pinned in its moony lights and waving. The day began to come. Deserters from the Collective's war who had come through Rudewood or the dangers of the alleys west of Dog Fenn, where the militia hunted and gave out revenge. They had come to be an unskilled work party clearing the lines.

The Crobuzoners waved their hats and scarves. *Run come home,* one shouted. Some were crying. They threw dried petals on the tracks. But there were some stood and waved their arms *No,* shouted, *No they'll kill you,* and others who wore a kind of sad pride.

They ran and leapt onto the Council. They threw winter flowers and food to the Councillors and their children, exchanged shouted words with them, dropped back. Those on the train had become stern and taciturn with history and mission, and it was their followers on foot who met the escapees and embraced them, merged.

People ran by the train, keeping pace with it, and shouted names. Bereft families.

"Nathaniel! Is he there? Nathaniel Besholm, Remade man, arms of wood. Went into the wilds with the lost train."

"Split Nose! My father. Never came back. Where is he?"

Names and snips of histories breathed out by those for whom the return of Iron Council was not only a myth come to be real but was a family hope redivivus. Letters addressed to those long-disappeared in exile now suddenly perhaps come back were thrown into the windows. Most were for the dead or those who had simply deserted: these were read and became messages to everyone.

It was day now—the day that the Iron Council would reach the end of the line. It was slowing, the drivers wanting every moment of the journey.

"Low the Golem-man!" one woman shouted in her old voice as they went past. "He's been prowling around, getting everything ready for you! Come faster!"

What? Cutter looked back. Up from inside him was a suspicion. *What?*

"Don't fear," someone shouted. "Listen, we're only hiding, us Collectivists, we're waiting, we're behind the militia lines waiting for you," but Cutter was looking for the woman who had spoken of Judah.

There isn't far. They would be there by noon perhaps, at the end of the line, to the ranks of military in the sidings. *Only a few miles left.* "I've a plan," Judah said. *Gods. Gods. He's here.*

Overhead the Iron Council wyrmen flew in both directions. Their outflyers would soon be at the city.

Cutter was on horseback, the easy long gallop he had learnt over the months he'd become a wilderness man. He could almost keep up with Ann-Hari, who rode Rahul the Remade.

Rahul's strides pounded, and he ran below the scree and pebble litter with the risen wall of the roadbed a windbreak beside him, dandelions and weeds in its slanted flank. Cutter rode where the wind was most resentful, throwing dust in his eyes. He ignored it. He pushed on under clouds that moved with sudden urgency and sowed rain nearby. He looked to the tracks, he looked ahead. He was beside the rail.

"Just come with me then if you want," he had said to Ann-Hari. "Prove me wrong. You can always come back. But if I'm right, I'm telling you . . . I'm telling you Judah has something planned." And

though Ann-Hari had been exasperated there was in his urgency
and the uncertain valence of his concern—was he excited, anxious,
angry?—something that struck her and had her ride with him.

He had failed Judah, and he had to see him, unsure as he was
what he sought to do—to persuade Judah to turn the Council if he
could, to explain himself, to have him accept Cutter's regret that he
had failed. When the horse-guards blocked him he demanded they
summon Ann-Hari. "You have to let me go," he said. "Give me a
fucking horse. Judah's ahead! I have to see him!"

She affected impatience but he saw her start. She said she would
come. "Whatever. Escort me if you don't trust me, I don't care, but
there's only a few hours left, and I have to fucking see him."

What's he doing?

Then. In the lands nearest New Crobuzon. Where rivers crossed
under the raised road, and the stones that gave cover were gnawed
by acid rain. Foothills stretched out their legs and rucked up the
land in untidy grass, where the piceous thick of Rudewood like a
black and black-green rash tided toward the train's path and even in
places stretched sparse little hands of forest to the edges of the
track. Cutter, Rahul and Ann-Hari passed through trees and tree-
shadow.

The perpetual train was quickly invisible behind them, the rails,
newly renewed, meandering. Cutter rode as if he were alone, beside
the metal raised like proud flesh, like slub in the land's weft. There
were some refugees still lining the iron who waved him on, but
most had run to be with the train itself. He ignored the halloos—
Where's the Council? Come to save us? They're ahead, boy, be careful.
He kept his stare to the tracks, the trackside. The train was no more
than an hour behind him.

He felt as if New Crobuzon sucked him in, as if its gravity—the
denseness of brick, cement, wood, iron, the vista of roofs, stippling
of smoke and chymical lights—as if its gravity took him. The
stoned land rose like floodtide toward the line, and Cutter's horse

descended past a place where the roadbed and the country were
level. Rahul was beside him. By a meadow of boulders Cutter saw a
barge passing. They were near the farmlands. He watched the trackside. The occasional mechanism where a signal might have stood,
some meter to read the speed or passage of trains. Here a clutch of
stones and metal debris in the train's path or by its side.

A flock of wyrmen tore back from New Crobuzon, scattered
below the fast clouds and screeched at them. "They waiting! Thousands and thousands and thousands! Rows of 'em! No!"

Cutter and Rahul were racing on the eastern side of the tracks,
eating the distance, so fast Cutter became hypnotised with it, until
after a last turn of rocks the tracks converged at the end of suddenly
bleak flatrock land, a stony pool and low marsh where there were
wading birds as grey as the environs. At the end of the perfect
perspective was a township of sidings, where the rails fanned.
The smoke of workshops, the winter-dulled corrugate iron of train
sheds, the sprawled terminus at the edge of New Crobuzon. Cutter
sounded and heard Rahul sound too, become a single mass in the
distance, one organism of pikes and cannon, clouded light reflected
from thousands of masks, were the militia.

"Oh my gods." *Judah, where are you?*

The troops waited.

"Where's Judah?" Ann-Hari said. She was staring at the waiting
men, miles off, and Cutter saw, good gods, he saw a challenge in her,
a fight-light in her eye. A smile.

"We must have missed him. Come on, I swear he's here . . ."

"You know nothing, don't you, you don't know nothing . . ."

"Godsdammit, Ann-Hari, we can find him." *Why are we looking? What will he do?*

The train would come from the sheltering stone gulley out into
that plateau with the New Crobuzon Militia waiting. Cutter saw the
train. Come and come through, and the faces of all the Councillors
pale when they saw what waited for them, but set with the knowl-

edge that there was nothing else to be done. By the time they slowed the engine the militia would be on them. Nothing was possible except a last bravery, a tough pugnacious death. The knowledge would come over them, and the sweating and terrored faces of all the hundreds of Councillors on the train would toughen again, and the train would speed up. It would accelerate toward the enemy.

Come on, *we taken the militia twice before, we can do it again,* would come the shouts, lies that everyone would gratefully pretend to believe. Some would whisper to their gods or dead ancestors or lovers, kiss charms that would not protect them. They would shout, *Iron Council!* and *For the Collective!* and *Remaking!*

The Iron Council, the perpetual train, would howl, smoke streaming, the whistles of its cabin shrill, the sounds of its guns a tempest of bullets. The train would come into the zone of the New Crobuzon guns, and in bucking fire and the stretch and split of metal, in the agony shouts of burning dissidents, of fReemade, as hot death took them, Iron Council would end.

Gods, gods.

The Councillors rode back toward the train a few hundred yards. Cutter forced a slower pace. He watched the metal. *Last chance.* A mile, no more, into the cosseting of the stone surrounds. Again wyrmen overhead, but these ones speaking with different accents, these were *city* wyrmen come to greet the newcomers. "Come, come," they shouted. "We're waiting. Behind militia. For you." They wheeled and went back toward some trackside machinery. Cutter rode.

"Ann-Hari." A call from the edge of the gulch, twenty feet above. Cutter looked up and it was Judah.

Cutter let out a sound. He stopped his horse as Rahul stopped and he and Ann-Hari looked up. Judah Low was standing. He moved in agitation, craving their attention.

"Ann, Ann-Hari," Judah shouted. "Cutter." He beckoned hugely.

"Judah," Cutter said.

"Come up, come up. What are you *doing* here? What are you doing? Gods, come up."

Rahul's great lizard weight could not take the incline, which slithered under him. He could only wait by the tracks as Cutter and Ann-Hari gripped handhold stubs of roots, ascended, stood, Cutter keeping his head down as long as he could so it was only at the very last that he raised his shale-grey face and looked at Judah Low.

Judah was looking at Ann-Hari with an opaque expression. He embraced her a long time, as Cutter watched. Cutter licked his lips. Cutter waited. Judah turned to him and with something at least half a smile gripped him too, and Cutter let Judah for a tiny moment take his weight. Cutter closed his eyes and rested his head, then made himself stand back again. They could see the tracks' exit from the raised land.

They watched, the three of them, watched each other. Here he was, the tall thin grey-haired man Judah Low. *What are you?* Cutter thought. Around Judah were signs that he had been waiting. A water bottle. The obscure debris of his golem craft. A telescope.

In this place there was no one around them. The last cut before the city. Wyrmen went overhead again and circled, and shouted hysterical warnings as they went.

"What you been doing?" Cutter said. "What are you *doing*? They wouldn't stop, Judah, they wouldn't turn. I tried . . ."

"I know. I knew they wouldn't. It doesn't matter."

"What happened? In the city?"

"Oh Cutter. Done, it's done." Judah was placid, cowish. He looked between Cutter and Ann-Hari's heads at the curve of the track, in the direction from which the perpetual train would come. Looked back at them, back at the tracks. His attention switched ceaselessly.

"What'll we do?" Cutter said.

"There's nothing to be done, now," Judah said. "It's not the same now. The city . . . it's changed again."

"Why are you here, Judah?" Ann-Hari said. "What are you here for, Judah Low?" She was complicitous. They were smiling at each other, just. A little play in their voices. Even with the carnage to come, even having seen the militia, there was something still playful in her. She reached and touched him again and again, and he her. The thing between them was like an animal coiling from him to her and back. He looked over her shoulder and back at her.

"Judah!" Cutter shouted, and Judah turned to him.

"Yes, yes, Cutter," he said. "Of course." He was calming. "Why did you come here?"

"What have you done, Judah?" Cutter said. But there was a noise, and Judah gave a happy gasp just like a little boy and jumped on his toes, again like a boy. There were tears in his eyes. A smile and crying.

A wraith of smoke emerged a half mile off. The perpetual train. It wriggled up, the discharge, like a soot grub from a burrow, faster, slewing a tight turn through blasted barriers and coming closer. A wind came up before the train and pushed at their faces, Cutter and Ann-Hari turning to watch the lamps that rounded and shone weakly through the daylight, washed out the stone and the tracks, and the Iron Council came into the last of the cut.

No. Cutter did not know if he spoke aloud. He did not believe there were revolutionists hidden behind the militia. He watched and shouted aloud or in his head, as the Iron Council came through cleft stone and rolled at speed toward death. *No.*

The flared guard made into teeth, the engine a fetish head, carved with stories, hung with animal spoils, crowded with the toughest warriors, the biggest Remade, the cactacae with scramasaxes ready, roaring, feted by New Crobuzon refugees who ran alongside, who cheered desperately and threw confetti. The second engine, all its follow-ons, the whole tracktop town become militant, become its weapons, the Iron Council become a fighting city. Its wheels beat the iron, smoke gouting from its chimneys, everyone poised to fight, with no plan but the imbecile bravery of *forward*.

Uh uh, uh uh. Cutter heard it, the wheels, the clatter of tracks. He ran to the edge of the gap and shouted though he could not be heard. He saw that Judah was crying but still smiling, and Ann-Hari was smiling only. The train, faster than it had ever gone, went past Rahul, who waved his human and his lizard hands.

Cutter stumbled, and behind him he heard Judah muttering, heard Judah repeat the two-part rhythm, the repeating beat of the train. He was singing along with the train, and there was something expectant in him. Cutter leaned over, looked down on the train and the Councillors preparing for war, their last war, for their city again. He saw ahead of them a strange pattern of obstructions between the ties, nothing heavy enough to derail or damage the engine, but a precise set of interruptions, looking from above like the points of a pictogram, over a few yards of track.

"Uh *uh* uh *uh,*" Judah said, and below in time sounded uh *uh,* and the front of the Iron Council passed over a mechanism Cutter had seen, that he had thought a signal relict or something half-finished; and as the wheels touched it and it clattered, it beat into motion, and Judah gasped and dropped to his knees. His skin stretched; the very meat of him seemed bled away. Cutter saw the force of his cathexis, the yank of energy.

He heard the syncopation of the train and of something else now, a complex interfering, percussion in antiphase. Iron Council tripped the switch that Judah had laid for it and the circuit he had left went live, siphoning force from him, and only Cutter could see. Cutter watched Judah blink and gasp.

The little blockade between the tracks, which Judah's first shout had stopped Cutter or Ann-Hari seeing, wedged in the shingle, propped on crossties—a blockage of pins, of metal rods, of blocks— was pushed over by the Iron Council. Each piece landed hard, onto the contacts Judah had laid, and their strange precise order, their materials, made each of them fall with its own sound. They com- bined into a careful and exact music of breaking, snaps and tolling iron that added to the flawless beat of the train; and for seconds, for a snatch of time, there was pulse-magic, a palimpsest tempo, and in that moment of complexity, each accented block of noise intervening in time, cutting time into shape so that as the huge hunter's head of the Iron Council emerged from the rock folds and synclines into open land the *moments themselves* were hacked by the noise, axed into shape, an intervention through the mechanism that sucked energy from Judah Low, the great self-taught somaturge of New Crobuzon, and crude, vigorous, ineluctable, the precision of that parcelled-up time *reshaped* time, was an argument *in* time,

reshaped the time itself, and made it

a golem

time golem

which stood into its ablife, a golem of sound and time, stood and did what it was instructed to do, its instruction become it, its instruction its existence, its command just *be,* and so it was. This animate figure carved out of time itself, the rough hew-marks of its making the unshaped seconds and crushed moments at its edges, the split instances where its timelimbs joined its timebody. It was. The shape of a figure in dimensions insensible even to its maker, unseen by any there; its contours, seen another way, enveloping the train.

The time golem stood and was, ignored the linearity around it, only was. It was a violence, a terrible intrusion in the succession of moments, a clot in diachrony, and with the dumb arrogance of its existence it paid the outrage of ontology no mind.

His face bloodied, making some beached fish-flapping motion as he crawled and smeared his gore on the earth, as he shambled like a drunk man to stand, broken by the effort of thaumaturgy, Judah Low looked into the cut and smiled. Cutter watched him.

There was an ugly noise. The tearing and crush of a weighty impact. Ann-Hari was screaming. She ran down the scree with a wake of dust. She fell and rolled and gathered herself, tearing her clothes. Rahul stood in his own shock, looked up at the Iron Council, scant feet from him. The Councillors and runaway citizens were standing, were waiting, quite uncertain. Everyone was looking at the train.

The perpetual train. The Iron Council itself. The renegade, returned, or returning and now waiting. Absolutely still. Absolutely unmoving in the body of the time golem. The train, its moment indurate.

It could not always clearly be seen. The crude rips in the temporal from which the golem was made gave it edges like facets, an opalescence of injured time. From some angles the train was hard to see, or hard to think of, or difficult to remember, instant to instant. But it was unmoving.

For yards over its chimneys the exhaust was fast as smokestone, motionless until the set billows reached the limits of the split in time, the golem's body, and above that random barrier gusted away in drifts, the last of the effluvia escaping into history. The Councillors were still poised, their weapons were still ready, the train was bursting into the plains beyond the city, and was without motion.

The last carriage, one of the two engines that pushed instead of pulling, had missed the protection of that cosseting unmoment, had stayed dynamic, and had been derailed and crushed against the sudden crisis of untimed matter. It had burst, scattering hot coal and debris and dying engineers. The last fringe of the car ahead of it was concertinaed and torn, and where it met the unending time golem, the edge of the wound was scored like a line.

Ann-Hari was screaming. The Council-followers were coming in more numbers out of the rock, telling each other what had happened, sending word back: *Iron Council has* . . . what?

No noise came from it. It was a huge silence shaped like women and men on a train. The Iron Council was made of quiet. Ann-Hari screamed and tried to grab it, to pull herself up onto it, and time slithered from her at the borders of the golem and sped her hand or deflected it or momentarily had the Council not there so she could not touch it, she could not touch it. She was in time. It was not, and it was beyond her. She could see it, and all the instant of her comrades, but she could not reach it. Others left behind in time were gathering around her. She was screaming.

At the head of the train, reaching with his brawny thorned arm, was Thick Shanks. He was staring at the massed militia in the distance. He was smiling, his mouth open. Beside him a laughing man whose string of spittle was stretched to the point of snapping. The train was occluded with suspended unmoving dust. Its headlights relucent, their shed light absolute and unwavering. Ann-Hari raged and tried and failed to rejoin Thick Shanks and the Iron Council.

Cutter looked on the impossibility. He jumped when Judah put his hands on him.

"Come," said the somaturge. His voice was not Judah's. A torn-up ruined thing that came up with blood and sputum, though he still smiled. "Come. I saved them. Come."

"How long? Will it last?" Cutter heard his quaver.

"Don't know. Perhaps till things are ready."

"They died." Cutter pointed at the train's rear. Judah turned his head away.

"It's what it is. I did all I could. Gods, I *saved* them. You saw." He rose. He held his stomach. He let out a gasp. He swayed and left a spatter pattern around him. The daylight seemed to strengthen him. He reached, and Cutter gave him his hand, and they began to descend, Judah lolling as if he were stitched from old cloth, down into the rocks, hidden from the tracks. In the very far off, noise said that the militia were coming. That they saw something was not as it should be, and were coming.

Cutter and Judah climbed down, away.

part ten

THE MONUMENT

CHAPTER THIRTY-FOUR

SCUFFING AND STUMBLING OVER LITTLE FOX-TRAILS, HOLDING JUDAH while he dry-retched and pulling Judah's hair back from his aging face, Cutter wanted the moments not to end. In a shallow brook he washed Judah's blood away. Judah Low did not pay him any notice, but breathed and spread out his fingers. While this time lasted Cutter could dissemble, could make himself believe that he thought it would end well.

By a sideling creep they went very slowly toward New Crobuzon. Cutter took them a long way from the route of the militia, whom they could see and hear approaching the frozen train. Cutter thought of the hundreds of Councillors who must be running, looking for hides in the rocks, heading swampward. The city refugees among them. The warren of stone forms must be full of the frightened.

"Judah," he said. He breathed the name. He did not know what emotion it was he spoke with. He thought of those killed by what Judah had done. "Judah."

They were hardly subtle or secretive; they left what must, Cutter thought, be blatant trails of footfalls and blood and broken branches. He hunkered under Judah, took the tall man's weight. Other Councillors must have climbed out of the cut and down into the outside land, but by some quirk of geography or timing Cutter and Judah seemed alone, hauling over gorse and through dry wintered brush. They were alone in the landscape. Spirits. When they came to open level land they would look and miles off see the advance of the militia. Once a vantage gave Cutter a look at the perpetual train. He saw it, slightly out of the world, as if reality bowed under its weight, as if it were at the bottom of a pit. He saw it quite unmoving.

With the slow move of the shadows, Cutter saw the winter day grow older. He knew that things must be changing, time creeping around the timeless. *I am here, under Judah's arm. I am taking him back to New Crobuzon.* The knowing in him that it would not last was a thorn.

I'll not ask you anything. I'll not ask you why you did what you did. Ain't got time. But even unbidden Judah began to speak.

"There was nothing that could be done, not really. Nothing to keep them from harm. History had gone on. It was the wrong time." He was very calm. He spoke not to Cutter but to the world. Like one delirious. He was still utterly weak, but he spoke strongly. "History'd gone and that was . . . I never knew! I never knew I could do it. It was so hard, all the planning, trying to work it out, such learning, and it was . . . so—" He shook his hands at his head. "—so draining . . ."

"All right, Judah, all right." Cutter patted him and did not take his hand away. Held Judah. He filled suddenly, closed his eyes, blinked it down. *What a pair we are,* he thought, and actually laughed, and Judah laughed too.

New Crobuzon's that way. Cutter directed their walk.

"Where shall we go, Judah?"

"Take me home," Judah said, and Cutter filled again.

"Yes," he said carefully. "Let me take you home."

Their little dissimulation, that they might make it. A long way around, up toward the rises behind the trainyard, where they might find a way north of the TRT sidings and eastward to New Crobuzon's slum suburbs. To Chimer, say, or on up through the foothills to the River Tar and the barge nomads and low merchants with whom they might take a ride and be pulled in past Raven's Gate, past Creekside and the remnants of the khepri ghetto, under the rails, to Smog Bend, into the innards of New Crobuzon. Cutter walked them north, as if that might be their plan.

What was that, Judah? What was that you did? Cutter remembered Judah's talk of the noncorporeal golems, the stiltspear and their arcane golemetry. *I didn't know you could do that, Judah.*

They saw people. "You're going the wrong way, mate," one caravanner said. Cutter and Judah pushed past them. The cart wheels scuffed and turned the earth and receded. Cutter looked up at birds. *More. A little more. A little longer.* He did not have any sense of to whom or to what he was pleading. Judah leant on him, and Cutter held him up.

"Look at you," he said. "Look at you." He wiped dirt off Judah's face, onto his own clothes. "Look at you."

A second tiny wave of runaways approached. This time all variegated. Humans with handcarts, a vodyanoi panting out of water. A fat she-cactus carrying a prodigious club. She hefted it at Cutter and Judah but set it down again when she saw them more closely. There were two khepri, their skinny women's bodies swaddled in shawls so they moved with tiny steps, conversing with their headscarabs, the iridescent beetles on their thin necks moving headlegs and mandibles in sign, emitting gusts of chymical meaning. Behind them, a kind of punctuation mark to this random Collective, was a construct.

Cutter stared at it. Even Judah looked, through the fug of his exhaustion. It waddled toward and past them on the ruts.

Limbs, a trunk and head in rough human configuration, its

body an iron tube, its head featured in pewter and glass. One arm was its own original, the other some later repair in a scrubbed, lighter steel. From a vent like a cluster of cigars it jetted breaths of smoke. It raised its cylinder legs and placed them down with inhuman precision. Wedged over what would be its shoulder it carried a bundle dangling on the end of a staff.

One of the city's rare legal constructs, the servant or plaything of someone rich? An underground machine, an illegal, hidden for years? *What are you?* Did it follow its owner into exile, was its meticulous stomping progress simple obedience to a mathematised rule in its analytical engine? Cutter watched it with the superstition of someone grown up after the Construct War.

It turned its head with a whinge of metal. It took them in with eyes that were milky and melancholy, and though it was absurd to think that some self-organised viral mind moved in the flywheels behind that glass, Cutter had a moment where he felt that, in the fall of the Collective, New Crobuzon had gone so grim that even the machines were running. The construct continued, and Cutter led Judah away.

They had some miles to go still. There was sound. The militia must, Cutter thought, have been by the paused Iron Council for hours. The sound came closer. Cutter tightened his eyes shut. The time was ending, as he had known it would.

In a little stone-cluttered clearance he and Judah came to face Rahul and, on his animal back, Ann-Hari. Her teeth were bared. She held a repeater pistol.

"Judah," she said. She dismounted. "Judah."

Cutter patted himself until he found his gun, tried unsteadily to raise it. Rahul crossed to him with spurt-quick lizard steps and held him in his saurian arms. He leant forward at the waist and took Cutter's weapon away. He tapped Cutter's face with brusque kindness. He moved, dragging Cutter as if he were his parent. Cutter protested, but so weakly it was as if he said nothing. He was almost sure his gun would not have fired. That it would have been clogged, or unloaded.

Judah swayed and watched Ann-Hari. He smiled at her with his vatic calm. Ann-Hari trembled. Cutter tried to say something, to stop this, but no one paid notice.

"Why?" Ann-Hari said, and came forward. She stood close to Judah Low. She was teary.

"They'd be dead," said Judah.

"You don't know. You don't *know*."

"Yes. You saw. You saw. You know what would have happened."

"You don't *know*, Judah, gods *damn you* ..."

Cutter had never seen Ann-Hari so raging, so uncontrolled. He wanted to speak but he could not because this was not his instant.

Judah looked at Ann-Hari and hid any fear, looked at her with an utterness of attention that snagged Cutter's insides. *Don't end now, like this.* Rahul's arms around him were protective.

"Ann-Hari," Judah said, his voice gentle though he must know. "Would you have had them *die*? Would you have died? I tried to turn you, we tried to ..." *You knew they wouldn't,* thought Cutter. "They're safe now. They're safe now. The Iron Council remains."

"You've *pickled* us, you bastard ..."

"You'd all have died ..."

"End it."

"I don't know how. I wouldn't, besides—you know that."

"*End* it."

"No. You'd all have died."

"You've no fucking right, Judah ..."

"You'd have died."

"*Maybe*." She spit the word. A long quiet followed. "Maybe we'd have died. But you don't know. You don't know there weren't Collectivists waiting behind them militia ready to take them, now all scared off because of what you done. You don't know that they weren't there, you don't know who wouldn't have been inspired when we come, too late or *not*. See? Too late or not, they might have been. See, Judah? You see? Whether we died or not."

"I had . . . it's the *Council*. I had to make them, you, safe . . ."

"It's not yours to choose, Judah. Not yours."

He moved his arms slightly out from his sides, stood square to her, looked down at her. The connection between them remained, a line of force. They seemed to draw in energy from the surrounds. Judah stared at her with patience, a readiness.

"It was not yours, Judah Low. You never understood that. You never knew." She raised her pistol and Cutter made a sound and moved in Rahul's grip. She pressed it against Judah's chest. He did not flinch. "The thing in you . . . You did not create the Iron Council, Judah Low. It was never yours." She stepped back and raised the pistol till he stared into its mouth. "And maybe you'll die not understanding, Judah. Judah Low. Iron Council was never yours. You don't get to choose. You don't decide when is the right time, when it fits your story. *This was the time we were here.* We knew. We decided. And you don't know, and now we don't either, we'll never know what would have happened. You stole all those people from themselves."

"I did it," Judah whispered, "for you, for the Iron Council. To save it."

"That I know," she said. She spoke quietly, but her voice still shook. "But we were never yours, Judah. We were something real, and we came in our time, and we made our decision, and it was *not yours*. Whether we were right or wrong, it was *our* history. You were never our augur Judah. Never our saviour.

"And you won't hear this, you can't, but this now isn't because you're a sacrifice to anything. This isn't how it needed to be. This is because you had no right."

* * *

Cutter heard the end in her voice and saw Ann-Hari's hand move. *Now,* he thought. *Now Judah, stop her.*

In the tiny splintered instant that she tightened her hand he thought: *Now.*

Call an earth golem. Judah could focus and drag from the hard earth before him a grey earth golem that would rise, levering itself out of the stuff of its own substance with weeds and weed-debris hanging still to it, the hillside itself become moving, and it could intervene. It could stand between Judah and Ann-Hari and take her bullet, stop it with the density of its matter, then reach and cuff the gun away and grip her close so that she could not fight and Judah would be safe from her, and could have the golem walk her away or keep her motionless while he turned with Cutter and they went on around the roots where trees had been torn up and past the powdering rocks to New Crobuzon.

An air golem. One hard gust of ab-live wind to close Ann-Hari's eyes and make her aim falter. An obedient figure made of air to stand before the Iron Councillor and throw her clothes into her face, to channel very hard and fast into the barrels of her pistol, to ruin any shots. And as the air around displaced by the dance of the new presence made whorls of dust rise and the gusting of dry leaf-matter where it still scabbed bushes, Judah and Cutter could leave.

Make her gun a golem. Turn the very pistol itself into a small and quick golem and have it close its mouth, have it eat the bullet before it spat it away, and then Judah might have the thing twist in Ann-Hari's hand and turn with what limited motion its shape allowed it, and point up into her face, a threat, and give Judah the time, while Ann-Hari was paralysed with that surprise and the menace of her own weapon, give him the time to get away, with Cutter, over the rise and the pathway.

Make the bullet a golem. And it could fall. *Make her clothes golems.* They might trip her. *Make a golem of those scattered lit-*

tle dead trees. Make a golem of clouds. Of the shadows, of her own shadow. Make another sound golem. Make a golem of sound and time to keep her unmoving. It was very cold. *Sing your rhythms again fast to make a golem of still time and stop her up and we'll go.*

But Judah did nothing and Ann-Hari pulled her trigger.

CHAPTER THIRTY-FIVE

IT WAS BY THE TAR THAT CUTTER REGAINED THE CITY. A NIGHT ENTRY. Slowly and under new laws, the New Crobuzon authorities were re-opening riverine trade. The barge-rangers were waiting to establish new runs. Cutter came back into New Crobuzon disguised in a coal-smeared overall, piloting a fat low-slung boat.

Around him the houses spread out from the wind of the river, tens then hundreds, and he heard their sounds and remembered them, the settling of architecture, and knew he was coming home. The bargeman he had bribed to crew him was eager for Cutter to leave. With the repeating cough of the engine they came past the tarry houses of Raven's Gate, the khepri warren of Creekside, the houses disguised by mucal addenda, and under the old brick bridges of New Crobuzon, while the boat left a rainbow discharge on the water.

Airships went. They stalked on searchlight legs. A fat glare pin-ioned the boat then blinked off, twice.

He walked through the warehouses of Smog Bend, the bleached

brick, the stained concrete. Past creosote, past bitumen and mouldered posters, past the dumps of building matter, powdered glass
and stone, into streets once held by the Collective. Cutter walked
past the lots where there had been meetings of residents voting
noisily on everything. Now they were as they had been, little wilder-
nesses of concrete-splitting bramble and cow-parsley, wildnesses
for the insects. There were spirals on the walls. Rain was washing
them away.

Days later and Cutter knew the new rules, knew how to avoid the
militia who patrolled the streets and locked down Creekside and
Murkside and above all Dog Fenn. They said there were still pockets of Collectivist treachery, and they were ruthless in their hunt.

Cutter said nothing when he saw the squads emerge from broken buildings with men and women screaming their innocence or
occasionally rebellion. He kept his eyes down. Numb as he was, he
negotiated the checkpoints, offering his forgeries without fear, because he did not care if he was challenged, and when he was not he
would walk on without triumph.

Uptown had its beauty. BilSantum Plaza, Perdido Street Station. It was as if there had been no war. The spirals were smears.
Perdido Street Station loomed like a god over the city. Cutter looked
up at its roofscape, at where he had been.

In the last days of the Collective there had been a desperate copy
of the skyrail attack. A train heavy with explosives had set out from
Saltpetre Station, accelerating toward Perdido Street Station with a
dream of immolating the vast edifice. It would never have happened. The Collectivist who drove it on his suicide mission, brave
with drink and the assuredness of death, had rammed the blockade
at Sly Station and powered on toward Spit Bazaar, but the militia
had detonated the train as it approached, tearing a hole in the
stitching of arches that went the length of New Crobuzon. The Sud
Line was severed and was being slowly rebuilt.

The posters on the kiosks, the newspapers, the wax proclamations that were free in the voxiterator booths told of the government's triumphs: Tesh's tribute payments, their war apologies, the rebirth of community. Hard, hopeful times, they said. There was word of new projects, expeditions across the continent. The promise of a new economy, of expansion. Cutter wandered. Creekside was a ruin. The khepri bodies left after the Quiller Massacre had been cleared, but there were stains still on some walls. In places the phlegm integuments exuded by home-grubs had been cracked and burnt, revealing the brick underneath.

Cutter wandered and watched the reconstruction. Throughout the centre of New Crobuzon were the holes torn by armaments, the thickets of concrete, mortar and broken marble, new raggedy passages linking alleys, paved with rubble. In Barrackham the militia tower's tip was swathed in scaffolding like cuckoo-spit. The drooping severed skyrail was gone. It would be restrung when the Barrackham Tower stood again.

In Mog Hill, near enough the Collective's old ground but just outside the militarised zone so not subject to martial law or curfew, Cutter found lodging. He gave his new name. Paid with the proceeds from his day-work, in areas he had not frequented in his life before.

New Crobuzon was wrecked. Its statues broken, districts stained and blistered by fire, whole streets become facades, the buildings eviscerated. Houses, churches, factories, foundries as hollow and brittle as old skulls. Wrecks floated in the rivers.

He knew how to become part of the whispering networks again, even broken as they were. Even now when no one spoke to anyone with trust, when citizens strove not to see each other's eyes as they passed, he knew how. Even now when a quickly clenched fist risked being interpreted as handslang and the militia might be called or there might be a quick vigilante killing to save the area from renegade insurgents and the death squads they would bring.

Cutter was careful and patient. Two weeks after his return he found Madeleina.

"It's better now," she said. "But in the first weeks, gods.

"Bodies by walls, every one of them 'resisting,' they said, while they were taken away. Resisting by tripping, or asking a moment's rest, or spitting, resisting by not coming fast enough when they were told.

"Up by the Arrowhead Pits, in the foothills," she said, "Camp Sutory. It's where they keep the Collectivists. Thousands. No one knows how many. There's an annex: go in, you don't come out, so they say. When they're done asking questions.

"Some of us escaped."

She listed those she had known, and what had happened to them. Cutter recognised some of the names. He could not tell if Madeleina trusted him, or was past care.

"We need to tell what happened," she said. "It's what we have to do. But if we tell the truth, those that weren't here will think we're lying. Exaggerating. So . . . do we make it less bad than it was, to be believed? Does that make sense?" She was very tired. He made her tell him all the story, everything about the fall of the Collective.

When he found out how long ago it had been it would have been easy for him to say to himself, *There was no one to fight for the Council,* but he did not. He did not because they could not know what might have happened, because it had not been allowed to. They could not know what Judah's intervention had done.

There were ten thousand rumours in New Crobuzon about the Iron Council.

Cutter went often to the slow-sculpture garden in Ludmead, to sit alone amid the art dedicated to the godling of patience. The gardens were ruined. The sculpted lawns and thickets were interrupted by huge sedimentary stones, each of them veined with layers and cracks, each carefully prepared: shafts drilled precisely, caustic agents dripped in, for a slight and so-slow dissolution of rock in exact planes, so that over years of weathering, slabs would fall in layers, coming off with the rain, and at very last taking their long-planned shapes. Slow-sculptors never disclosed what they had prepared, and their art revealed itself only long after their deaths.

He had always hated the sedateness of these gardens, but now that they were ruined he found them a comfort. Some Collectivist or sympathiser punks had climbed the wall weeks ago, before Dog Fenn had fallen, and taken chisels to several of the larger stones. With cheerful imprecision and disrespect they had made crude and quick and vulgar figures, lively and ugly, ground filthy and dissident slogans into their skins. They had ruined the meticulous boring and acid-work of the artists, preempting the erosion-sculptures with pornographic clowns. Cutter sat and leaned against a new stone figure stroking an oversized cock, carved out of what might have been intended as a swan or a boat or a flower or anything at all.

He did not remember much of that time in the hills. The grip of Rahul. Holding him while—did he flail? Did he cry? He suspected that yes he had cried and flailed. He had been held till exhaustion dropped him.

He remembered Ann-Hari walking, disappearing, not looking at him. He remembered her mounting Rahul and having him re-turn to the rocks. "Back," she had said. "The Council," and what that meant he had not known. He had not even heard her at the time. Only later when he was done mourning.

Was she at large? Had she looked for and found death? He had seen them disappear, Ann-Hari and Remade Rahul, toward the stones where the Iron Council waited. It was the last time he saw them.

When he had been able to, Cutter had strained to move Judah.

He had wanted to bury him. He had tried not to look Judah in his broken face. Finally he pulled him off the animal-track. Without looking, by touch, Cutter had closed Judah's eyes. He had held Judah's colding hand and had not been able to bring himself to touch the leather lips with his own though he so wanted to, so had kissed his own fingers instead and brought them a long time to Judah's breathless mouth. As if, if he waited long enough, Judah would have to move.

He had made a cairn over him. He could only think it in small moments.

The Council did not move. Cutter had not yet been to see it, though he knew he would, but everyone in New Crobuzon knew its state. Judah's death had not released it from its synchronic jail. The newspapers had outlandish theories for what had happened. Torque-residue was the most common suggestion, after its plunge through the cacotopic zone. Cutter was sure there were those in the government who knew the truth.

He would go to see it, when he could. He thought of Ann-Hari, walking the stone, riding Rahul.

Cutter tells Madeleina about Judah Low, and she listens with word-less sympathy for which he is broken with gratitude. One night she takes him with her to an abattoir in Ketch Heath. They go carefully, roundabout routes. There is a cat-howl as they come close. The animals are coming back, now they are not meat. Once there in the dark slaughterhouse, Cutter steps with di Farja over gutters of cloying blood, and in the hollow churchlike echoes, the ring of the now-empty meathooks against each other, in the smoulder from the fireboxes of the grinders, she shows him the hidden doors and the little printing press beyond.

They work together that night, turning the handles, making sure the ink does not clot. They turn out many hundreds of copies in the dark.

RUNAGATE RAMPANT.
LUNUARY 1806.

"Order reigns in New Crobuzon!" You stupid lackeys. Your order is built on sand. Tomorrow the Iron Council will move on again, and to your horror it will proclaim with its whistle blaring: *We say: We were, we are, we will be.*

Now through pathways in the strewn wires and razored wires that litter this open zone this flat land outside the city split by a seam of rail we come in numbers. Under the moon in grey or without it gathered in the dog drab of unlit night we will come.

There. There we will come to Iron Council. There we will come to the perpetual train, truly perpetual now perhaps poised always poised forever just about its wheels just about to finish turning. It waits. By its iron axles are devils of motion, waiting an eternal second.

Past guards patrolling a border. Where there are runnels beneath the wires we slip through, where there are none we cut or climb very careful, cushioned with rag. Through the selvage of history toward that moment become a place, that history instant a splinter in now, under now's skin.

We are incessant despite the penalties. Old women, young, men, human cactus khepri hotchi vodyanoi and Remade, even Remade. Here in the environs of the train those Remade who make the dangerous pilgrimage are given something, are for these yards around this moment equals. And scores of children. Rude little roughnecks, orphans living animal in New Crobuzon's streets self-organised in troupes to come to this strange playground. Through runoff and flyblown trains made of rust, the aggregate of industry in the TRT sidings, reaccreting power as its new projects begin, through beetle-tracked wasteland, through miles of greyed nothing and stones like the ghosts of stones the alley children come to the Iron Council.

There is a circuit. There are routes to be followed.

Climb the scree slopes to look down on the flash-frozen smoking from the chimneys. Stand on the very tongue of tracks between the iron to look into the face of the train. Slow circle widdershins the whole Council, a some-minutes' walk. No one can touch it. Everyone tries. Time slips around it. They are coming. Everyone can see it. The Iron Council is not stopped it is onrushing it is immanent and we see it only in this one moment. Circle it.

The engine smokestack towered and flared, a belch of black, keeping its shape, swept back fast by the wind embedded in that moment. We come in close scant hairs from the protuberance of animal-head horns and the blades of the warriors who wait, stand close up, stare at the Councillors preparing with shouts set on them.

That one is Thick Shanks. That big, age-discoloured cactus-man, him at the engine's window. He helped make Iron Council all the time ago. Here he is to bring it home.

There is a route from Councillor to Councillor, given names. Here is Spitter whose excited shout has left saliva spray in a parabolic fringe around his mouth; here is Leapfrog who has jumped from one carriage top toward another and hangs over the gap midway in her arc; here is the Gunner from whose rifle has emerged a bullet, ajut six inches from the barrel. The tradition is to stop, wave your hand between unmoving missile and gun.

Some of us knew these Councillors once. There is a woman who comes many times to speak to the same man, her father, come back to her, unmoving in history. She is not the only one who visits family.

The ivy-tower skirted with rust dust and smoke the cattletrucks made bunks and bedlam, panelled laboratory cars messhalls arsenals and church, here open-topped flatcars full of earth, gardens and a graveyard with its cenotaph, a cab whittled from driftwood and the bulbous triple-nucleated plasmic sac left where Torque warped those inside, the final engine with its snarl of metal teeth where the moment ended. These paused Council cars wait to salvage us.

We play around them; we come to them. Some come to pray. The ground around the Iron Council is a litter of written pleas.

The militia and their scientists and their thaumaturges try to send through violence, but the time golem only is, and is unhurt by their crude attacks. We come back again, again, again.

Years might pass and we will tell the story of the Iron Council and how it was made, how it made itself and went, and how it came back, and is coming, is still coming. Women and men cut a line across the dirtland and dragged history out and back across the world. They are still with shouts setting their mouths and we usher them in. They are coming out of the trenches of rock toward the brick shadows. They are always coming.

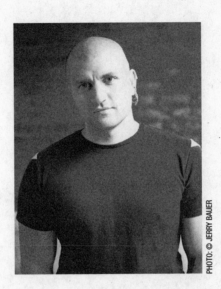

CHINA MIÉVILLE was born in 1972. He is the author of *King Rat,* which was nominated for an International Horror Guild Award and the Bram Stoker Prize; *Perdido Street Station,* which won the Arthur C. Clarke Award and the British Fantasy Award; and *The Scar,* which won the Locus Award and was a finalist for the Hugo Award, Philip K. Dick Award, World Fantasy Award, and the Arthur C. Clarke Award. He lives and works in London.